The Good Girl

The Good Girl

FIONA NEILL

PENGUIN BOOKS

PENGUIN BOOKS

UK | USA | Canada | Ireland | Australia
India | New Zealand | South Africa

Penguin Books is part of the Penguin Random House group of companies
whose addresses can be found at global.penguinrandomhouse.com.

First published by Michael Joseph 2015
Published in Penguin Books 2015
004

Copyright © Fiona Neill, 2015

The moral right of the author has been asserted

Typeset by Jouve (UK), Milton Keynes
Printed in Great Britain by Clays Ltd, St Ives plc

A CIP catalogue record for this book is available from the British Library

ISBN: 978-0-241-95256-6

www.greenpenguin.co.uk

MIX
Paper from
responsible sources
FSC
www.fsc.org   FSC® C018179

Penguin Random House is committed to a
sustainable future for our business, our readers
and our planet. This book is made from Forest
Stewardship Council® certified paper.

In memory of Hattie Longfield

The truth may be stretched thin, but it never breaks, and it always surfaces above lies, as oil floats on water.

Miguel de Cervantes Saavedra, *Don Quixote*

Prologue

It was Matt Harvey, the new head of Biology, who first drew her attention to the problem. Although now of course she wondered how many other people knew. Matt had knocked on her door, unannounced, in the middle of the first lesson after lunch, and asked if he could have a word. Ailsa was midway through an email to a local biotech company, requesting work experience for sixth-formers hoping to study science at university.

'Can it wait half an hour?' she asked apologetically, as he poked his head around the door. 'I really need to get this off.' She gently massaged a small circle between her eyebrows, hoping to ward off the frown line that was threatening to settle there.

'Sorry,' Matt said. 'It really can't.' He had such a panicked expression that Ailsa wondered whether he was about to resign. She glanced at his hand. He was holding something. To her relief, it wasn't an envelope but a mobile phone. This reprieve was immediately tempered by irritation that he needed to bring his phone with him at all. It was difficult enough to persuade students to sever the digital umbilical cord when they came into school, never mind if teachers failed to set an example.

Matt came in and shut the door abruptly so that the leaves of the cheese plant by her desk quivered. 'Sorry.' He opened his mouth and licked his lips a couple of times. Ailsa smiled in a way that she hoped was encouraging while retaining a professional distance. He looked away, unable to meet her eye.

'I'm not sure how to most effectively sort this one out,' he said, staring at his feet and drawing attention to the sort of casual footwear that sixth-formers were discouraged from wearing. *He must be in trouble*, thought Ailsa, trying to ignore the split infinitive. She ran through typical problems encountered by teachers in their first year at a new school: he had fallen foul of Mrs Arnold, her tricky deputy head pastoral (everyone did); he couldn't master the new internal communication network (no one could); he was worried he was going to miss his GCSE targets (she would agree with him that league tables were blunt instruments, but funding depended on results and she would suggest he organize some extra classes on Saturday to avoid any disasters).

She was good at getting these messages across in a way that was sympathetic but firm. All the psychometric tests she had completed during the interview process for this first headship came to the same conclusions: Ailsa was a natural born leader. Where she went, her staff generally followed.

'Sorry about the mess. I'm trying to do a million

things at once.' She spoke with a cultivated informality appropriate for a workforce which, for the most part, was younger than her. 'How can I help you?' she asked.

'Help me?' He squinted at her quizzically as if she were being deliberately obtuse, and his thick dark eyebrows caterpillared into a single line. She squinted back, vaguely remembering from a management course that the best way to make people feel comfortable was to mimic their body language. Perhaps it was a less orthodox issue: a pupil with a crush maybe. When Ailsa interviewed for a new head of Biology, the only point against Matt Harvey made by Mrs Arnold was that he was too good-looking. Ailsa had said, only half joking, that if that meant more girls did Biology A level, it was a risk worth taking, especially now that there was extra funding for students who studied science.

Ailsa abandoned the email mid-sentence and invited Matt to sit on the small sofa in the corner of the room by the radiator. The heating was about to go off as part of a new money-saving scheme that had been disguised as an example of the school's commitment to environ-mental issues, she explained.

'But don't tell anyone.'

'It might be more convenient to stay near the com-puter,' Matt suggested, walking purposefully towards her desk. 'I need to use it.'

Ailsa stood up to make way for him. There was an awkward moment as they repositioned themselves. He removed his jacket and sat down on her chair in front of the computer screen. She noticed shadows of sweat under his armpits. He undid his cuffs, carefully rolled up his sleeves and clicked each knuckle once, making Ailsa wince.

'Sorry. Forgot how you hate that,' he said, looking up at her with a smile so quick it had gone before it reached his eyes.

'It's like fingernails on a blackboard,' she said, and then instantly regretted betraying her age to someone who had only ever known whiteboards. Matt pulled the chair towards the computer screen and it screeched across the floor. Despite being someone who liked to melt into the background, everything he did was very loud.

His fingers moved deftly across the keyboard. So quickly that she couldn't see what he had typed into the Google bar. Ailsa watched the screen, intrigued to know what could be so important that he had to interrupt his lesson to show her. The afternoon was always the worst time to deal with a crisis. By then the optimism had been sucked out of the school day and she was filled with a wired energy fuelled by too much caffeine and too many unfinished to-do lists.

She impatiently smoothed down her skirt, trying to iron out the wrinkles and persuade it back towards her knees. You have to be careful what image you are projecting, she had told her seventeen-year-old daughter recently when she appeared in the sitting room wearing a minidress so short that when she bent over you could see her knickers. Ailsa understood the mysterious equation whereby teenagers responded to exhortations to be responsible with a similar urge towards independence, but was singularly unable to apply the science to her own children.

'It's a fancy-dress party. Dress code: Professor Green meets *A Midsummer Night's Dream*. I can't exactly wear a burka,' her daughter had laughed. 'The trouble with you, Mum, is you're obsessed with what people think of you.'

It was true, Ailsa thought. She often wondered how others might see her, especially her team of teachers, but also people whose opinion she didn't need to worry about, like the locum doctor who had missed her mother's heart problem or her New Age next-door neighbours.

'Someone in my A-level set gave the game away. I wasn't sure whether you already knew,' said Matt. He paused and held his head in his hands, staring down at the desk. He was behaving more like a drama teacher than a biology one. 'Christ, I feel like the messenger in *Julius Caesar*,' said Matt, his sweaty palm hovering near the screen.

'*Antony and Cleopatra*,' Ailsa corrected him, instantly regretting her fastidiousness. Once an English teacher, always an English teacher. She wondered how he really saw her. A hard-working and confident superior whose innovative schemes for incentivizing students had been adopted as policy by the Department of Education. A stickler for detail with an annoying radar for split infinitives in internal emails. Or a forty-two-year-old woman with a tendency to wear too much lipstick who didn't notice when flecks peeled from her lips and stuck to her teeth. Ailsa made a quick sweep of her front teeth with her tongue. Maybe someone past youth, but still worthy of sexual fantasy. A MILF perhaps. When her eldest son, Luke, had finally explained what the term meant last week she couldn't work out whether it had given middle-aged women a new lease of life or added a new layer of pressure.

It struck her that this was a good example of cognitive dissonance, the ability to hold contradictory thoughts about the same subject. She had covered this in that morning's assembly, using the example of smoking as something that gave pleasure but everyone knew was bad for them.

'Fuck,' he said. 'You've got filters. Give me a moment. I'll get round them.'

Ailsa was taken aback by his language. He was the teacher who had recently sent out a student for swearing in class.

'I'm in,' said Matt. His tone wasn't triumphant. He paused briefly, clicking his knuckles again. 'It's short. Shouldn't take more than two minutes.' He clicked play. 'I'll play it slow so you can absorb it properly, frame by frame.'

'Because of the resolution?' asked Ailsa, fumbling for the correct terminology.

'No. Because it's a sequence,' he said, furrow-browed as though puzzled that she still didn't grasp what was going on.

'Hadron Collider, string theory, meta data,' said Ailsa breezily. 'Technology is leaving me behind.' She was looking for words of reassurance. None came. But then she was unworthy of his sympathy. Later, when she couldn't remember how it felt not to be anxious, she realized that this was the last time she had felt truly light-hearted.

Ailsa focused on the screen. At first it was a little hazy; the person taking the video clearly wasn't a professional. There were half-head shots. Limbs at comical angles. And overuse of the zoom feature. Or maybe it was a faux hand-held technique to give authenticity to what followed? There were two figures. Judging by the length of her long fair hair, the one at the front was a girl, although it was difficult to tell any more. The camera zoomed out unexpectedly and Ailsa caught a glimpse of a low-ceilinged space with a light blub swaying in slow hypnotic circles. There were no windows and apart from what looked like a pile of rocks on the floor behind the boy the room was apparently empty. As more frames played, Ailsa could see a narrative forming.

'It's a lot to take on board,' Matt said apologetically.

'Why are you showing me this?' asked Ailsa, wondering if this was how twenty-something men hit on forty-something women. Except she knew how twenty-something men hit on forty-something women. Their eyes locked. He knew what she was thinking and just as quickly she knew that this time she was wrong.

'Look at the uniform,' said Matt, tapping the screen to get Ailsa's attention as the girl fumbled with the boy's zip. She leaned over his shoulder and he enlarged one of the frames until it filled the screen. How could she not have noticed? The girl's sweater had the distinctive green and yellow stripe of the Highfield Academy uniform around the neck and cuffs. Another of Ailsa's innovations. To give pupils high visibility. *Not so clever now*, she thought. He pressed play again and the girl inexpertly released the boy's penis from a pair of underpants. It was too much. Ailsa stepped back from the screen.

'How did you get hold of this?' she asked, casting around for something to say.

'I caught Stuart Tovey watching it just now.' He gave Ailsa the phone that he had been holding when he came in the door. 'Obviously I've confiscated it. To look for clues.'

Why did he talk in such short sentences? wondered Ailsa. Was he nervous or had his brain been atrophied by Twitter?

'Did you ask him how he got hold of it?'

'He said someone had forwarded it to him.'

'What do we know about the boy?'

'He's left-handed,' said Matt. 'That's about it.'

'How can you tell?'

'Look,' he said as the boy gripped his penis in his left hand.

'It's not Stuart Tovey, is it?' asked Ailsa, reluctantly turning her attention back to the screen, feeling like a grubby voyeur. 'You'd expect it to be but he's much shorter than this boy.'

'You don't get to see his face. Unfortunately. I can't work out if that was deliberate or down to poor technique.'

The girl was kissing the boy. He kissed her back. The passion was real or at least the acting was convincing. Just as Ailsa thought she was about to see the boy's face, the camera teasingly panned down for a mid-body shot. The girl got on her knees in front of the boy. Ailsa knew instinctively what she was about to do.

'What about her? Do you recognize her?' asked Ailsa, recoiling from the screen.

'Yes,' said Matt.

She wondered how she was going to deal with this. Cyber-bullying, contraception, chlamydia, chemical highs – even the drugs were high tech. But she had them all covered. It was the unknown unknowns that always got you in the end. She felt so bad for the girl. How would she tell her parents?

'Who filmed it? Do you think they did it themselves? Do you think the girl even knew?' She turned towards him, searching for answers. 'I think I've seen enough, Matt.'

'You need to watch to the end, Ailsa,' he insisted, using her name for the first time. 'I'm really sorry.' He got up from her chair. 'I think maybe you should sit down.'

When it was finished he leaned over her and dragged the file to the bottom right-hand corner of the screen.

The email she had been writing popped back up on screen. Ailsa glanced at the last word she had written, *aspiration*. It sounded like a medical procedure. She wished someone could perform it on her and wipe her memory of the images she had seen. But even if this were possible, she would be reminded of it in other people's faces. Because by now surely most of the school must know. People would tread on eggshells around her. It would be like when her mother died almost exactly a year ago. Already she knew this was different. Any sympathy this time would be tinged with judgement. How could you allow this to happen on your watch?

Matt explained to Ailsa that he was going to speak to the head of IT. 'We need to get the film taken down as quickly as possible,' he said gently.

He made the phone call without waiting for her response. Certain phrases from this conversation reverberated around her head. 'Inappropriate content . . . YouPorn . . . RedTube . . . Facebook . . . gone viral.'

She was relieved it was he who had approached her – his calm measured approach to helping nervous A-level students work out anything from revision timetables to genetic sequencing was exactly what she needed. The scale of the problem was beginning to dawn on Ailsa. Tsunami, earthquake, avalanche. The metaphors all involved natural disasters. But this was an unnatural disaster. It shouldn't have happened.

'No one will hold you responsible,' Matt said. His hand hovered by her shoulder but he didn't touch her.

'Of course they will,' Ailsa said. 'I am accountable.'

This was clear minutes later when the chairman of

the board of governors called to talk about the situation. In lieu of sympathy, he discussed strategy, for which Ailsa was grateful because she couldn't face any platitudes. He talked about crisis management and media blackouts. He pointed out that she was running a flagship academy and adverse publicity could be used to score political points. For legal reasons, he was overly concerned about whether 'the incident' had taken place on school property. He pointed out that a school scarf was visible in the background but agreed with himself that this wasn't conclusive evidence.

The only person who didn't seem to know anything was the girl. Ailsa had sent Mrs Arnold to call her out of class and positioned the venetian blinds so that she could see out of her office into the corridor outside but no one could see in. Romy was sitting on a narrow bench, leaning over so that her long hair covered her face like curtains. Ailsa could see her lips moving and at first wondered if she was rehearsing what to say but then realized that she was revising from a science textbook. Even though to her it was upside down, Ailsa could see she was looking at a cross section of a human heart. The girl had coloured each of the four chambers and blood vessels a different colour, transforming it into something beautiful. Right atrium, left atrium, inferior vena cava, superior vena cava. As she read each label, her finger drifted from one part of the diagram to the next, like a child learning to read for the first time.

It was such an innocent gesture. Ailsa felt her stomach heave and thought she might be sick. She swallowed a couple of times and took tiny sips from a glass of water. The girl wouldn't be revising anatomy if she knew. She would be nervously flicking through the pages of one of the magazines strategically placed on the table beside her. Or biting her nails. Or crying. Most likely crying.

It didn't surprise her that she was revising. In contrast to everything else that had happened, it was what she would have predicted. Ailsa skim-read the reports from staff for a second time to steady herself. Apart from a recent blip in a Biology exam, Romy was a straight-A student. She was taking four science A levels; she wanted to apply for medical school. 'Both parents are professionals,' the director of studies had noted, as though this gave her ambition credibility. Outside of class, there were no issues flagged. Her parents weren't divorced; there was no recent history of alcoholism, sexual abuse or drug addiction in the family. No involvement in gangs; no history of bullying or being bullied; no symptoms of depression. She was what Ailsa called a blank canvas.

The only hint that something might be wrong came from Matt, who said that over the past few months Romy had spoken back to him a couple of times in class and been sent out once. Ailsa put this to the back of her mind. There was nothing here that came close to offering an easy explanation.

Ailsa glanced out of the window again. She was discomposed to discover the girl was staring straight back at her, although of course she couldn't see through the venetian blind. Romy wasn't one of those girls coated in thick layers of foundation, lipstick and mascara. If Ailsa had been pressed to identify which girls might be vulnerable to this type of situation, Romy would have been close to the bottom of the list.

She was curious-looking. Pale-skinned and dark-eyed. Inherited from her father. Striking rather than beautiful. In her first term at the school a small group of children had mocked her for being albino. 'Why would I want to look like you?' Ailsa had heard her retort.

She looked nothing like her dark-haired older sibling, thought Ailsa. Ailsa's stomach clenched as she realized that perhaps Romy's older brother was already aware but didn't know how to deal with the situation. In which case she had failed him too. He sometimes hung out with Stuart, the boy who had the video on his phone. Perhaps he should see Mrs Arnold? Ailsa wrote this down in a new notebook specially dedicated to the scandal and underlined it several times.

Stuart swaggered along the corridor. Ailsa didn't know the name of every pupil in her school. She had decided early on that the effort of memorizing every student would be at the cost of something more strategically important. So she knew the names of the kids that came to her notice, either the clever ones or the naughty ones. Stuart fell into both categories.

He stopped beside Romy, which surprised Ailsa

because she couldn't imagine they were friends. Romy looked up. He had a striking profile. A long aquiline nose and big dark eyes. He had gone from boy to adult without the awkward transition through spotty adolescence. His body was ridiculously muscular; his school uniform barely contained his thick thighs and overworked shoulders. Steroid abuse was to boys what anorexia was to girls, thought Ailsa, remembering something she had read in the paper.

Stuart smiled at Romy. The smile turned into a lip curl and then suddenly he stuck his middle finger in his mouth and simulated the motions of oral sex. Romy looked taken aback. She frowned and shook her head. Stuart threw back his head, laughed and slouched off. When he passed her window, his lip turned into a half smile and he blew Ailsa a kiss as though he realized that she was watching.

Ailsa gripped the edge of her desk. Her hands were shaking. It was ten past three in the afternoon. She couldn't wait any longer for Romy's father to appear. It wasn't fair on the girl. Her anger towards Stuart transferred to him. Knowing what was at stake, how could he be late? She would have to be careful not to betray her feelings in front of the girl. One of the most important issues, Mrs Arnold had flagged, was to present a strategy that made Romy feel as though the adults around her were in control of the situation. They all had to present a united front.

She knew Romy would be feeling nervous about

being called from class. Since as far as she knew she wasn't in any trouble, she might be worried that something had happened to her family. Ailsa phoned her assistant to send Romy into the office.

'Everything is fine at home,' said Ailsa abruptly, as soon as the girl breezed through the door. She had spoken a little too quickly and Romy looked puzzled, as though unsettled at the possibility that something might be wrong. She left the door open. It was the best evidence yet that she had no idea what had happened.

Ailsa was overwhelmed with a desire to protect her. Perhaps Stuart was the only person in school who had seen the video clip? Perhaps she need never know? And then just as quickly she abandoned the idea because the file was like a forest fire. Matt had kept her updated through the afternoon on websites where it had appeared and what action had been taken to get it removed.

And besides, as Ailsa was fond of telling troubled students, everything that went wrong should be used as an experience to learn from. It was a way of encouraging children to believe in the possibility of renewal. People could evolve. Reputations could be rebuilt. Except in this case she wasn't sure she really believed her own rhetoric. She vaguely remembered the story of a girl in south London who threw herself off a building when a boy refused to delete sexual images of her from his phone. She felt a sudden venomous rage towards the boy in the video. He had obviously forced her to do this. She needed to confirm his identity as quickly as possible.

She would press the girl for details. After that she would have to speak to his parents. He would be expelled. The police would be called. He would be prosecuted. But none of this would make the girl feel any better. In fact it could make her feel worse.

Ailsa got up from her desk and slowly walked over to close the door. She wanted to delay the moment for as long as possible. She looked at the girl's face, knowing that in the next minute her world would tip on its axis.

'Is there something wrong?'

'How is your work going?'

'I was in a Biology exam.'

'Were you doing a practice paper?'

'Yes.'

'How was it?'

'Fine. I think. Now I'll never know, because I was only halfway through and it won't be a true result.'

'Medical school is very competitive.' Would this affect the girl's application? Ailsa wondered. A new worry rippled through her body. She had to accept that she had no control over the situation, Mrs Arnold had advised, barely able to disguise her excitement at this latest drama. Matt had said something similar, then he had contradicted himself by insisting that he would personally take charge of checking which websites were showing the film.

Even if they got to the bottom of how this had all started, there was no telling where it might end. She thought of the draft she had written for her next assembly. She wanted to warn the pupils about how in the digital age one badly thought-out decision could end up defining you for the rest of your life. She swallowed a couple of times.

'There's something you need to see, Romy,' said Ailsa.

'What are you talking about?' asked the girl.

Ailsa opened the file in the corner of her computer screen.

'I'll sit on the sofa while you watch. I've seen it already.'

'Is it something to help with my university application?' Romy asked as she pressed play.

Ailsa couldn't bear to watch again. She couldn't decide whether she was being cowardly or sensitive. She sat down on the yellow sofa. When Romy replayed this scene in her head, as surely she would, periodically, for the rest of her life, would it be worse for her to watch it alone or with someone else? Ailsa, usually so decisive, didn't know the right answer. She pressed her fingers into her temples until she could feel the blood vessel pulsing beneath. And then it was too late. Romy's face froze. Her usually pale complexion flushed until even the tips of her ears were red. Her lips turned down until she looked like the mask of the goddess of tragedy that hung above the door of the school theatre. It was as if her face was separating from her body. For a moment it was a perfect mask. Ailsa knew she was about to cry. Her life as she knew it had ended.

It was too late for anger, yet part of Ailsa wanted to shake Romy and demand why she had allowed this to happen. The other part wanted to hold her in her arms like a small child and protect her. She knew from experience that this was the moment when she had to ask the question. Children would always tell the truth when there was nothing left to lose.

'Who is the boy?'

There was a knock at the door. Her father came in before Romy could respond.

'Sorry,' Harry said without offering any explanation. Ailsa's anxiety spiked again at his bad timing. 'I got a call about giving a lecture in Cambridge.' He went over to his daughter and put his arms around her. Ailsa didn't say anything. The girl didn't need to ask how her mother would react. She knew already.

'Oh, Mum,' said Romy, getting up from the chair and looking at Ailsa for the first time. Ailsa walked over to her daughter, arms outstretched, like she did when her daughter first learned to walk. For a moment all three of them stood in a silent embrace. Ailsa looked up at Harry.

'How has this happened to us?'

I

Three months earlier

Ailsa woke up lying on her front, trying to piece together fragments of a dream that had already scattered. She allowed her hand to drift beneath the duvet until it reached the man in bed beside her. Good. He was still asleep. Keeping her eyes closed, she gently pressed a small circle of Harry's flesh with her fingertip and tried to guess which part of him she was touching, remembering a game they used to play when they first met.

Except it was instantly recognizable as the cleft above his left hip bone. Nineteen years together might have softened the angles but Ailsa was now more familiar with Harry's topography than her own. She could navigate his body like a blind person reading Braille. She wished for a moment that she could go back to the first time, to recapture that excitement of mutual discovery. Passion was commensurate with the amount of insecurity you could tolerate, Ailsa had recently read somewhere, probably in a magazine she had confiscated from a pupil at school. And after almost twenty years she and Harry should be very secure together.

His skin was hot to the touch. Its warmth made her

hesitate but if she curled herself around him to soak up his heat then he might wake up and misread the gesture as a desire for sex. The mechanics of early-morning arousal were as predictable as a metronome. The old post-coital euphoria had been replaced by the less glorious sensation of a job well done.

Outside it was snowing again. Ailsa could tell because the usual sounds of early morning were muffled as if someone had thrown a blanket over the house. It wasn't an illusion that snow created stillness and tranquillity, Romy had explained to her little brother, Ben, last night, during a family dinner characterized by a shortfall of both qualities. 'Snow is porous so it absorbs noise.' Nine-year-old Ben had stared at her in awe. 'Perfect conditions for a trainee spy who needs to pass on information, Grub,' she added. He nodded so vigorously that Harry outlined the results of a recent study showing that head-banging caused long-term brain damage.

'Granny once hit her head and came round speaking French,' said Ailsa's father wistfully. 'Do you remember, Ailsa?'

'Vaguely.'

The thought of her father strengthened her resolve. He was desperate to get back home to visit her mother's grave. It was six days since he had last been and he had started to fret that it might be covered with weeds; that the winter-flowering viburnum hastily hacked from a neighbour's shrub and left in a vase might have died; that the vase might have been stolen. Ailsa pointed out that all were most likely covered in a thick layer of snow but Adam was unconvinced.

'I need to see her,' he said firmly. 'Viburnum was one of her favourite flowers and I never bought her any when she was alive.' This became his excuse for opening another bottle of wine. And with the alcohol came the tears. 'I need to check that Georgia's all right. That she's not lonely.'

Romy had held his hand and tried to persuade him that Granny was fine. Ailsa's younger sister, Rachel, insisted viburnum was almost impossible to find in flower shops. Harry promised to plant a shrub in Adam's garden so that he had a ready supply throughout the season. Finally he was soothed.

If they left now, Ailsa would have time to drop him home and visit her mother's grave to check everything was all right before Adam went. She wanted to be there alone, to remember her mother without having to negotiate anyone else's grief. It was decided. If she didn't go now, the car would get stuck or it would be too icy to drive him home. She stealthily edged away from Harry, slowly relinquishing the duvet so that he wouldn't be woken up by a sudden blast of cold air.

She found last night's clothes in a pile and pulled on a jumper and pair of jeans, cursing Harry for his stinginess about switching the heating off at night. There was a time when they would have done anything for each other. No longer. Even the temperature of the house was up for negotiation. Ailsa zipped up the jeans. Underwear could wait until later.

She headed downstairs, deliberately ignoring the domestic rubble that she passed along the way, although unable to resist the temptation to apportion blame: chocolate reindeer wrapper. Ben. Empty Coke can. Ben. That was easy. Overturned glass on the landing table. Undoubtedly Adam. Teddy bear wearing new collar intended for Lucifer the cat. Possibly Luke. *The Real Spy's Guide to Becoming a Spy*. Ben. Box set of *True Detective*. Rachel. A book about growing your own vegetables. Harry. Did boys who read books about survival in the wilderness really grow into men who dreamed of allotments? Dustpan and brush. And beside it pieces of broken glass carefully wrapped in old Christmas paper. Also Harry. Only Romy hadn't left a trace.

Much later Ailsa remembered this detail. Or lack of detail. Because only then did its metaphorical significance resonate. In the sixteen years since her uncomplicated birth, Romy had been the least demanding member of the family.

The most placid of babies, even as a newborn Romy had only cried when she was hungry or tired and was unfussed when passed around from one person to the next. There was no separation anxiety. Luke had been completely different. The first time he played hide and seek, he had sobbed big fat tears when he put his hands over his eyes because he couldn't see his mother. Ben had issues around feeding. Rejected the breast. Cried for milk in the night. And refused solids until he was almost one.

But Ailsa should have known from growing up beside

the sea that a mirror-calm surface was often an illusion. Her mother had always warned that the most treacherous currents were invisible to the naked eye, a phrase that had always reduced her and Rachel to hopeless giggles. Ailsa smiled at the memory, already anticipating the sharp stab of loss that followed. The rapturous pain of memory, Rachel called it.

She didn't bother with the kitchen, shutting the door on Lucifer and last night's mess to avoid being sidetracked. One of the reasons she was determined her father should leave before lunch was that it would encourage Rachel to go at the same time. Seven nights with them both was enough. They hadn't spent time together so intensively since they were children. That's what a parent's death did to you. It sent you hurtling back through time.

Ailsa grabbed the car key from the hook by the back door, pulled on Romy's boots and a huge khaki jacket with fake fur around the hood that belonged to Luke. She zipped it up until only the top of her face was visible and headed outside. She breathed in deeply until the cold burned her lungs and squinted at the snow-bleached landscape. It was completely still. Every stem and leaf was covered in a glassy fleece of frozen snow. She stared up at the vast anaemic sky and felt a familiar surge of joy at the way it swallowed her up. Some instinct drew her gaze to the second-floor window of the house next door. She glanced over and saw a curtain move.

It wasn't until she had crunched her way down the

driveway to the road that Ailsa realized just how much snow had fallen in the night. Using the sleeve of Luke's coat, she wiped a circle of snow from the windscreen, climbed inside the car and slammed the door. It was like being inside an igloo. The only sign of the world outside was through the small porthole in the windscreen.

The car was a mess. The leather seats were peeling, the grille had come off the ventilation system so that you couldn't direct the jet of air, and the internal lights no longer worked. But the engine started as soon as Ailsa turned the key and the heating was immediately responsive. She jumped as the radio came on at full volume. The children had left it on Kiss FM. A rap song assaulted her senses, something about a girl sucking a man's dick and her sister being stabbed with an ice pick. Gruesome. Ailsa quickly switched to Radio 4, but the news was all about more changes to the exam system so she switched back. Perhaps if standards in English were raised, lyrics would improve. Although he could have gone for toothpick rather than ice pick. Rappers lacked irony.

Ailsa put the car into first gear and pressed the accelerator. When it didn't move, she pushed a little harder and heard the tyres spin. She should go and get a spade. But outside it had begun to snow again. She pressed her hand to the windscreen and watched as the tiny snowflakes melted. It occurred to her that the heat from the engine might do the same and then she could try again.

Leaving the engine running, she pulled out her mobile phone and dialled her mother's number. She had kept paying for her mother's phone just so she could listen to her message. No one else knew. Not even Rachel. 'It's Georgia here. Although obviously I'm not here at the moment because otherwise I would have answered this wretched phone, so please leave a message and I will get back to you.' For a couple of seconds her mother came back to life. Ailsa saw her in the kitchen of their family home, hair wet from swimming in the sea, excitedly describing how a seal had joined her in the water. Then just as quickly the memory dissolved.

Ailsa closed her eyes to trap the tears behind her lids, breathed in deeply and thought about their first Christmas without her. Her chest hurt. It was the hole left when Georgia had died. When she was sure she wouldn't cry she opened her eyes. On balance it had gone better than expected. They had survived. Ailsa jumped as the back door of the car suddenly opened.

'Thought you might want some company,' Rachel said, slamming the door behind her.

'Why didn't you get in the front?' asked Ailsa. It was typical of Rachel, who always complained that Ailsa treated her as a child, to behave like a child. Ailsa waited to see if she would put on her seatbelt without being told and then felt perversely irritated when Rachel clicked it into place.

'Because Dad will want to go in the front, won't he? Is he coming down?'

Ailsa ignored her questions and instead revved the car again.

'Careful or you'll flood it,' warned Rachel. 'You need to wait a minute and press the clutch up and down to get everything flowing.'

Ailsa glanced at Rachel in the mirror. She had a stripy scarf wrapped around her face and was wearing an over-sized bobble hat that belonged to Luke. Her unruly brown curly hair poked out wherever it could. Apart from a few crow's feet, as fine as lace, Rachel barely had a line on her face. And these just highlighted her startling grey-green eyes. Even her imperfections were beguiling: the tiny chip on her front tooth, the rabble of freckles on her slightly too wide nose and the gap across the outside edge of her right eyebrow, the legacy of stitches from a childhood accident. Her hands were deep in the pockets of the coat that Ailsa used for work. She winked at her older sister. Her eyes were their mother's.

'Are you wearing any of your own clothes?' asked Ailsa.

'I'm here. Isn't that enough?' asked Rachel. 'And I've just fed Lucifer.'

'I'm glad you've finally helped get a meal on the table,' Ailsa teased.

'You're a much better cook than me, Ails. Always was.'

Rachel always turned criticism of her into a compliment to Ailsa.

'Harry does all the cooking now.'

She put the car into gear again and tentatively pressed the accelerator. The wheels spun beneath her, digging even deeper trenches, sending a new spray of snow over the windows. She pressed harder and the wheels wheezed disapproval.

'You should have dug around the tyres,' suggested Rachel.

'That wouldn't work. I'm going to sit here with the engine running for a bit longer so the heat from the chassis melts the snow,' said Ailsa. She put Radio 4 on again. There was a severe weather warning for the south-east of England. Advice to stick to main roads. Essential journeys only. Freezing fog. Thundersnow. Not even the BBC spoke in proper sentences any more. *Stop noticing this shit*, Ailsa chided herself. It was so ageing.

'We'll be spending another week here if it goes on like this,' said Rachel, echoing Ailsa's worst fears. She felt guilty straight away. She loved her sister. And everyone said that grief was easier if you shared the different stages together. But they weren't synchronized. While Rachel had been poleaxed by their mother's death and had spent the funeral in a Valium haze, Ailsa had organized everything. By the time Ailsa gave in to the grief, Rachel had entered the angry phase.

'Did I tell you the last time I went to see Dad, just before Christmas, I couldn't find him when I went in the house?' said Ailsa over the noise of the engine and the radio.

'Who?'

'Dad. The front door was open. I went upstairs. His

bed was broken. It was at a thirty-degree angle. His head was hanging over the edge like he'd been decapitated.' Rachel didn't say anything. 'He could have had a stroke because of all the blood pooling in his head.'

'But he didn't.'

'Didn't what?' asked Ailsa.

'Didn't have a stroke.'

'He'd laid the table for lunch. There was a place set for Mum with those biscuits that she used to love. That's all he'd been eating. He could have starved. Or got scurvy.'

'KitKats?'

'No, the Scottish ones she used to have as a child.'

'Tunnock's.'

'Exactly.'

'But he didn't.'

'Didn't what?'

'Didn't starve.'

'What's your point, Rach?'

Rachel unwound the scarf from her face and leaned forward until she was jammed in the gap between the two front seats so that she could see her sister more closely. 'The trouble with you, Ailsa, is that you think you can control everything. You don't have superpowers. You're not omniscient. You can't prevent disasters. Shit happens. It just does. And we all have to get on with it. You can't inoculate us all against disaster.'

'We need to work out a routine. So that one of us

checks on him every four or five days,' Ailsa responded. 'I can't keep doing this on my own.'

'You're falling for his old tricks. Dad has always made everything about himself. That's probably why Mum ended up having a heart attack.'

I could say the same thing about you, thought Ailsa. 'He's one of those larger-than-life figures –'

'Which is shorthand for a recovered alcoholic with an overinflated sense of self,' Rachel interrupted.

'He's drinking again, Rach. It's been a really difficult time and it's worse when you see his grief close up. He's much more vulnerable than he used to be.' Still nothing. Ailsa turned towards her. 'The question is, what are we going to do, because doing nothing isn't an option, is it?'

Rachel's wild eyebrows furrowed. Ailsa was gratified to know that finally she had got through. The great thing about having a difficult conversation in a car was that you had a captive audience. It was a tactic she had learned soon after having children. Ailsa affectionately patted her sister on the shoulder. They had been through so much together. They would get through this. Rachel remained silent.

'Do you think I should be dating a man who is young enough to be my son?' she suddenly asked. 'I mean what are the real differences between my body and the body of a twenty-seven-year-old? Do you think people can tell if your internal organs are old?'

Ailsa gripped the steering wheel as hard as she could so she wouldn't say anything she regretted.

'I read somewhere that a woman in her early forties and a man in his twenties represent perfect sexual compatibility,' said Rachel dreamily. 'I'm in great shape for someone who is almost forty, don't you think? He's been so lovely to me about Mum. And he's not married. I know you have a problem with that. I'm not totally insensitive. So what's the verdict?'

'You'll probably get hurt,' said Ailsa, revving the engine again.

'Why?' asked Rachel.

'You'll meet his friends and they'll talk about things that you know nothing about.'

'Like what?'

'Music, apps you've never heard of. I don't know — that's the point.'

'Age doesn't exist any more. It's all about shared interests and experiences.'

'He'll want to have children,' warned Ailsa.

'We've already talked about freezing my eggs,' said Rachel. Ailsa pressed the accelerator. 'And he wants to get to know my family better.' This was why Rachel always ended up getting her own way. She just kept going until eventually the opposition capitulated. That's why she would be so good with their father, if only Ailsa could get her on board.

'Better?'

'You've met him already.'

'God, he's not one of your builders, is he?'

Ailsa put the car into reverse and pressed the acceler-ator to persuade the wheels to get purchase on the slippery snow. For a moment the wheels spun, churning up the snow as high as the windows. She pushed the accelerator as far down as it would go. The car burst into life and shot into the car parked behind. The bronchial alarm of the people carrier belonging to Ailsa's new next-door neighbours wheezed into action. Ailsa's head thumped back against the headrest.

'Shit,' she said.

'Shit indeed,' said Rachel. 'I've probably got whiplash. I might have the body of a thirty-year-old but I'll develop the posture of an old lady.'

In spite of herself, Ailsa couldn't help giggling. Rachel annoyed her more than anyone else she knew but she also made her laugh the most. Loveday came out of her front door straight away and Ailsa knew that it was she who had been looking out of the upstairs window. She berated herself for not making more effort with their new neighbours because it would have made everything easier now that she had crashed into the only car within a mile of the house.

She remembered how six weeks earlier, just after she had moved in, Loveday had come to the front door and Ailsa had ignored her and ducked down beneath the pic-ture window in the sitting room. Loveday wanted to invite them over for a drink. Ailsa knew this because she had told Harry over the garden fence. As the doorbell rang more and more insistently, Ailsa had imagined a future where their lives were seamlessly integrated like honeycomb. A hole would be cut in the fence between the two gardens and a gate erected so that the children could go in and out of each other's gardens as they pleased. The gate would never be shut. Crockery from one house would appear in the cupboard of the other. Books would be shared. Clothes would migrate. She instantly knew that this was not what she wanted. Eventually she would need new friends. But right now she didn't want the burden of absorbing anyone else's lives. They needed to rebuild their own. In the end Loveday had gone. But she had stayed long enough for Ailsa to know she was a woman who was used to getting her own way.

Loveday's arms were folded, probably against the cold, decided Ailsa as she opened the electric window to speak to her.

'I am so sorry,' said Ailsa. 'So sorry.' She wanted to get out of the car to assess the damage but Loveday's arms blocked her way.

'Are you all right?' asked Loveday. She smelled of patchouli oil and the musty aroma made Ailsa feel queasy.

'We're fine, aren't we, Rachel?'

Rachel nodded. Loveday leaned over and rested her forearms on the edge of the window so that Ailsa could see two sets of surprisingly long painted nails. She was wearing a big chunky necklace that banged against the car's paintwork. It was a silver eagle's skull, and the beak nestled between her breasts. Loveday noticed her looking.

'My talisman is an eagle,' she said.

'Sorry?'

'We all have an animal spirit that protects us. Mine is the eagle,' Loveday explained. She touched the necklace and lifted it towards Ailsa. 'The wings represent the balance between male and female. It denotes protection and survival.' Ailsa stumbled for a response. 'My husband is a bear,' said Loveday, filling in the silence.

'Polar or grizzly?' asked Rachel.

'How interesting,' said Ailsa, trying not to giggle.

'He's curious, secretive and fierce. All at the same time. It's a great combination. Bears and eagles are very compatible.'

'Unfortunately I don't have a talisman,' said Ailsa, stumbling over the unfamiliar concept in an effort to sound interested.

'Maybe if you did, this wouldn't have happened. Maybe that's what's been missing from our life,' said Rachel from the back of the car. 'Hi, I'm Ailsa's sister,' she explained to Loveday when it became apparent that Ailsa wasn't going to introduce her. 'Not the most auspicious way to meet, is it?'

'Really, it doesn't matter as long as both of you are fine,' said Loveday. 'It's your car that's taken the hit.'

'We were trying to get my father home. He's desperate to visit my mother's grave. She died earlier this year. But he'll just have to stay here until the snow clears. None of us will be going anywhere. The older children were meant to be going to a party. New Year's Eve is going to be a bit of a damp squib.' Ailsa listened to herself babble, trying to work out if she was in shock or trying to compensate for her previous indifference.

'It's settled,' said Loveday firmly as Ailsa stopped. 'You must come to us. Our friends can't get here and I've cooked enough food for a whole ashram. The children can hang out together.'

'What a lovely idea,' said Rachel before Ailsa could answer.

'It will be nice for everyone to meet properly,' said Ailsa, trying to regain control of the situation.

'There is always opportunity to be had in adversity,' said Loveday with a smile. 'That's one of my mantras.'

Another face appeared at the car window. Loveday introduced her son, Jay. He was wearing a hastily pulled-on T-shirt and pair of jeans. His eyes were half closed as he wearily offered to help.

'Jay?' questioned Rachel. 'Like the bird? Because your mother's an eagle?'

He looked perplexed. 'After my grandfather,' he then said with a smile. 'Shall we try giving it a push?'

Ailsa closed the window.

'Lock up your daughters,' Rachel laughed as Romy came out of the house to see what was going on. Jay looked across at her and their eyes met. Sometimes that was all it took.

'Actually, lock up your sister,' said Rachel. 'Did you see the definition in his arms? He's hot.'

'You're too old to call people hot,' says Ailsa. 'You're beginning to remind me of some old bottom pincher.'

Rachel leaned on Ailsa's shoulder and they clung to each other, laughing like they used to when they were children. Ailsa waited for Romy to come over and tell her to stop being embarrassing, but when she looked up at her Romy was smiling too.

2

We moved to Luckmore at the end of the summer of 2013 but all of us agree life there didn't really begin until the Fairports arrived next door a couple of months later. Until then we were just existing, hoping Mum's mantra that life was about getting on with it was true. 'If in doubt, create a routine,' was her personal philosophy. Sounded more like slow death to me, but stranded in the middle of the countryside with crap Wi-Fi, what else could you do but get up, eat, sleep, repeat?

At first we protested. Luke the loudest. We formed a united front, refusing to unpack our stuff, bring home new friends or leave the house, unless it was to go to school, until they promised we could go back to London. Ben wrote a petition. He told Mum and Dad that he would for ever look back on his childhood with sadness. Dad said he was absolutely right because traumatic experiences are stored in our long-term memory more than happy ones, and studies show 80 per cent of our earliest memories have negative associations. Mum and Dad were totally unmoved. Ben created a fantasy world where he was a British spy captured in Syria, because he had a theory that if something really bad happened, it helped to imagine an even worse scenario.

I couldn't imagine anything worse than leaving London. Things I missed: the cafés, the pavements, the smell of Indian food, and even things I could never imagine missing like street lights and dodging dog shit on the pavement. I longed for the smell of the Underground. I missed the noise of Shepherd's Bush Market. I was oppressed by the huge grey sky. Mum claimed it made her feel light and free, but I felt as if I was being buried alive, slowly suffocating beneath the weight of its constant scrutiny. She was from these parts. So she belonged to the landscape. I didn't.

I hated the attention-seeking wood pigeons and the gangs of deer that woke me up before it was light. Most of all I missed my friends. Mum suggested I invite them up for a weekend but I said they would die of boredom. Then she got angrier with me than she had with Luke, even though he had been a lot ruder. She told me not to be so selfish and reminded me that Granny had just died and we needed to move to Norfolk to look after Grandpa, which totally contradicted their cover story about having to move because of Mum's new job.

For the first month the only person we saw from our old life was Mum's sister, my Aunt Rachel, who was between writing jobs and came every weekend to help organize our new home. Rachel kept telling Mum that death and moving house were the most stressful life events apart from divorce. I wondered how useful it was to keep going on about this but now of course I realize there was a hidden warning in what she said.

I could have told her that going into the lower sixth of a new school where your mother is headmistress ranks pretty high on the stress gauge. Especially when Mum's first new policy involved introducing a school uniform with skirts so long that they made the Amish look slutty. But no one asked me how I felt. This isn't an excuse for what happened later, by the way. I'm only setting the scene.

At exactly five o'clock in the afternoon Rachel would start debating with Mum whether it was too early to open a bottle of wine.

'Just open it,' I wanted to tell them. 'What difference does an hour make?'

Because six o'clock seemed to be some magic cut-off point when adults were allowed to consume alcohol. Was this about control or self-control? I wondered. Or were the two linked? Did having control mean that you had self-control? There were so many unanswered questions.

Mum used to say that I had good self-control. But really I was just better than Luke at doing what she wanted. Revision timetables. Science Club. Texting her. Luke was always wilder than me. Shortly after we moved here I overheard Mum telling someone that really it was for Luke that we had left London. And for a couple of days Ben and I blamed him for the Miseries. But then Luke told me that he had heard Mum telling Aunt Rachel that it was really for me because girls in London grew up too quickly. If I had been consulted I would have told

Mum that Kim Kardashian, legal highs, Internet porn and all the other stuff she obsessed about had seeped everywhere, like oestrogen in the water table.

Finally Mum and Dad settled on a single version of events: we had moved here because of Mum's new job, and I think they grew to believe this. As Dad was so fond of saying, truth is subjective and the most important thing is to have a credible narrative. Then, just as we reached our lowest point, the Fairports came into our life and for a while everything made beautiful sense.

What can I tell you about Luckmore? You had to drive five miles to buy a pint of milk. Eight miles to find a cashpoint. There was no public transport. The average inhabitant was sixty-seven years old. It was a new village, built in the 1960s on either side of a quiet B road in the middle of nowhere by a local architect who saw himself as Norfolk's answer to Le Corbusier. At least this was what Mum told visitors. Apart from our house and its twin next door, the other houses in the village were all different. We were out on a limb on the other side of a piece of common ground. 'Less limb and more amputated leg,' Dad joked.

On the ground floor there was a double garage, a utility room and another room also accessible from the garden where Dad was supposedly writing his book. On the floor above were the kitchen and an open-plan sitting room. The acoustics meant that even if you were in the loo on the half landing upstairs, you could hear everything being said in the kitchen. We all slept on the second floor apart from Luke, who had been given the attic just because he was a year older than me. 'Older and wiser,' Luke said to me when this arrangement was revealed. Every morning I woke up to the thud, thud of him doing exercises. Mum didn't stop him because she thought his exercise routine demonstrated willpower. I could have told her that it had nothing to do with willpower and everything to do with getting girls but I was loyal to Luke.

A week after we moved in Dad insisted the television should be moved down into the garage when it became apparent that open-plan living meant listening to us overdosing on *Breaking Bad* while he cooked dinner. We told him it was a cookery programme but not that it was about cooking crystal meth. He couldn't concentrate on a recipe with another chef working in the background, he complained as we dragged furniture from the sitting room down into the garage. Cooking was a novelty to him. But then everything was new so we didn't take much notice of any of Dad's new habits. Besides, although I didn't know it at the time, it was one of his old ones that had triggered the Miseries.

Mum said that it was good to have a house without a history because then we could make our own. But she often says things that she doesn't really believe. Not because she's a bad or dishonest person. It's just she hopes that if you say something enough times it will become true. Dad says one of the most exciting discoveries of his lifetime is that the human brain is not fixed and that Mum's theory is therefore probably scientifically correct.

Hope is the most human of urges, it says in one of my A-level Biology textbooks. What Mum really meant was that we were at ground zero and that the narrative of family life had to be rewritten. But what is a family without history? I asked Luke. A boat without an engine, he said. What does that mean? I asked him. That we'll all drown in the end, he laughed. 'Stop overthinking stuff, Romeo. It's a bad habit.'

Luke is much better than me at laughing things off or laughing off things, as Mum would point out. I used to read his school reports in case there was something about him that I had missed. The conclusions were always the same. 'Luke's relaxed manner and even temperament make him popular among his peers but put a brake on his ambition.' Luke messed around in class, missed deadlines and lost essays. But unlike me he always had a party to go to and a girl to take with him.

It's easy to blame the Fairports for everything that happened. For a while Mum and Dad did just that. But the truth is we were already screwed before their removal van showed up as the leaves started falling that autumn and they began unloading. Although we didn't know it at the time, they had arrived just as our life was about to fall apart.

It must have been a warm day because they left their

boxes of books in the garden until all the furniture had been taken in. Ben looked through his binoculars and read out the titles. The only ones I recognized from our own house were a book of poetry by Allen Ginsberg and *The Hobbit*. The rest, Dad declared, was hippy shit. Then later denied he had ever said that. He was meant to be downstairs working on his book but even he was so bored in Norfolk that the arrival of the Fairports qualified as a major event. Poor Dad. He didn't say it but I knew that he didn't want to be here any more than the rest of us.

'*The Psychedelic Experience: A Manual Based on the Tibetan Book of the Dead, The Doors of Perception, We Are the People Our Parents Warned Us Against,*' Ben continued. There were two boxes of self-help. '*The Way of the Peaceful Warrior, The Seat of the Soul, Near Death Experiences and Spiritual Growth.*'

Dad groaned again. This kind of stuff was actually painful to him.

We were in our sitting room, standing by the huge window overlooking the garden of our new neighbours. We'd spent months complaining about this window because it was always dripping with condensation. Throughout that first winter at Luckmore we had to keep it open for at least a couple of hours a day. When we were really bored, like so bored that we thought we might die, we played a game where Luke, Ben and I would place bets on which drip would reach the bottom of the window first. Now the window came into its own. Suddenly it gave us access to the Fairports' world. This was part of their magic. Bad turned to good. Boredom to fun. I swear even the sky got smaller.

Dad stood to the side so that he could see without being seen. I knelt down by the window seat and used Lucifer as cover. Ben pulled up an armchair, put its back facing the window to steady his binoculars and knelt on the cushion.

'Freaks,' Luke shouted at us. But it was half-hearted. He was wearing a pair of headphones, playing Candy Crush on his iPad, pretending not to be interested. But he had moved the sofa so that his feet faced the window and he had his own sight line. The window was wide enough to give us all an unrestricted view. This didn't seem significant at the time but I now realize that rather than forming a unified view on the Fairports it meant we all formed our own separate impressions.

'What's in the other boxes, Romeo?' Luke asked me. He had called me Romeo for most of my teenage years because I was a late developer. Until last year, when my breasts magically grew, I had looked more like a boy than a girl. Also I wore braces. When we had to give an example of inverse correlation in a science lesson, I used the example of the upturn in braces and the downturn in teenage pregnancy. There was no bigger turn-off for boys. A girl at my old school nearly severed an artery in her boyfriend's penis while performing oral sex with a dodgy brace.

But before I could answer, a woman came into the

garden. She was wearing an ankle-length skirt and a jacket embroidered with Chinese dragons. Her hair, dyed a colour I recognized as poppy red, was pulled up into a shambolic bun held in place by pens. We knew this because she pulled one out of her hair to sign a piece of paper thrust into her hand by one of the removal men.

'That must be Loveday,' Luke exclaimed.

'How do you know her name?' asked Dad.

'Mum told us,' said Luke.

'What kind of name is that?' Ben asked.

'Cornish,' said Dad. 'Although she doesn't look Cornish.'

'How do Cornish people look?' I asked.

'More run-of-the-mill,' he said thoughtfully as Loveday sashayed down the garden path, occasionally stopping to stroke the leaf of a shrub or a piece of furniture.

'She's like a peacock,' said Ben.

Wolf was tall and lanky and wore his thick grey hair a little longer than was normal for someone over the age of fifty. He had an impressive beard. His face was tanned for the time of year and wrinkled in the right places. He wore baggy jeans, a white T-shirt several sizes too big that hung off his shoulders and a pair of flat leather boots with pointed toes. There was something light and delicate about him, as if he was made of balsa wood. What I remember most was the black waistcoat because this is what really made him stand out from my parents' friends. None of them would ever dream of wearing a waistcoat over a T-shirt.

'Exotic creatures,' said Ben, who had a habit of saying what everyone was thinking.

Wolf kneeled down on the ground beside a box and carefully started unloading musical instruments onto the front lawn.

'African,' said Luke coolly. Luke considered himself a music expert, but really his knowledge was limited to a genre that I called Fifty Shades of Nirvana. He knew for example that 'Teen Spirit' was named after a brand of deodorant but not that the larger bongo drum is called the female and the smaller one the male.

I waited for Loveday to go over to Wolf and squeeze his lower arm in the way that Mum did with Dad when she wanted him to stop doing something, but she didn't.

Their garden was already a chaos of half-open boxes and random objects that didn't fit into conventional packing schemes. Like, for example, a family of wooden giraffes, taller than Ben, which had been knocked over and now lay on their sides staring at us. Or the growing pile of woven carpets to the left of the back door. The packers already had to pick their way round these objects when they carried heavy bits of carved wooden furniture into the house. But Wolf continued to unpack instruments from the box until he found a set of bongos, which he placed in front of him and started playing. He sat cross-legged with his eyes closed.

'He's quite good,' said Ben.

'Anyone can play the bloody bongos,' said Dad. 'They're the African equivalent of the recorder.'

'That's a bit harsh,' I said.

'Four Fairports,' said Ben, pressing the binoculars so hard to his eyes that when he finally put them down it looked as though he was wearing red-rimmed glasses. He carefully wrote this down in one of his many notebooks.

I should probably say right now that Ben has some non-specific developmental issues that can't be parcelled up in a tidy title like dyslexia or dyspraxia. At least this is what I have heard my parents say to other adults. Basically he's a bit weird. Instead of labels I prefer descriptions. Ben keeps every bus, train and tube ticket that has ever been bought for him and sticks each one on his bedroom wall in a predetermined pattern. Once Luke removed a train ticket and replaced it with one of his own and Ben noticed immediately. He hoards food. Mum has found packets of crisps at the back of his wardrobe and we got mice at our old home because he had taken up a floorboard to hide biscuits. He also loves manuals and keeps box files of them in his bedroom: instructions for Lego, mobile phones, computers. He isn't choosy. He mostly beats us all at Cluedo, which is his current favourite obsession.

Sometimes I think that if Dad wasn't an expert in the adolescent brain Ben might just have been allowed to be the family eccentric instead of being sent off to specialists. Actually, this is what my grandfather said, but I tend to agree with him. Dad said Grandpa resisted labels because he used to be an alcoholic.

'I am a question with no answer,' Ben once declared over dinner after an autism expert decided that he didn't fit the criteria. But Dad is a scientist and believes there is an explanation for everything if you try hard enough to find it. I think that sometimes you just have to accept that there isn't. 'Shit happens, and you just have to deal with it,' as my Aunt Rachel is so fond of saying. Our family has a lot of sayings but they all tend to contradict each other.

I was so distracted by the drumming and Dad's reaction to it that I missed the moment when Jay walked into the garden for the first time.

'Two boys,' declared Ben, squinting through his binoculars again. 'Bish, bash, bosh.'

Later I asked Ben why he said that. Was it because he once had a Bish Bash Bosh train as part of his Thomas the Tank Engine set? Was it something recorded in his notebook on the page reserved for favourite phrases? Or did he see Jay and Marley shove each other? Did they jostle to see who could get through the gate first? Ben couldn't remember. He consulted his notebook for clues. But on the page dedicated to the first day the Fairports moved in next door there was nothing but a rough pencil drawing of a huge fire. A vital clue had been lost.

The four of them came together to stand in an arc, looking up at their new home. Just as they were still, the sun came out from behind a cloud, bathing them in a blinding arc of light. A ray bounced off our window and the Fairports all turned towards us at the same time, shielding their eyes from the glare. Jay pointed directly at me. His hair was thick and curly and hid his eyes so I couldn't see where he was looking. We all ducked down, even Dad, and giggled manically.

'What on earth are you all doing?' asked Mum. We were so involved in what was going on in the Fairports' garden that we hadn't heard her coming in through the front door. She noisily piled bags of shopping on the table to make us feel guilty and came over to the window.

'Good day?' asked Dad, tickling Ben until he pleaded for mercy.

'The deputy head pastoral, as she insists on being called, needs managing,' said Mum. 'Someone with a deep sense of irony put her in that post. But the head of Biology is a great appointment. Even if I say so myself. What are you hiding from? A family of wooden giraffes?'

We looked out of the window. The Fairports had disappeared into their new home. But one of them had righted the giraffes so that they now stared at us. In part it was nervous laughter because we had been caught doing something faintly illicit. We all laughed longer than the joke deserved. But mainly because over the past year Mum had stopped making jokes, and even though it wasn't that funny it seemed that my parents' hopes of the dawning of a great new era weren't so misplaced after all. Dad stepped out from behind the curtain and hugged her from behind. And for once she didn't pull away. Had they always been like this? I wondered. Or was it that I had just started to notice? In my head I thought it had something to do with my grandmother's death. Mum tried not to cry in front of us but the sunglasses were a giveaway.

The day after this Marley and Jay started school. They had the wrong uniform but didn't seem to care. Marley lit up in the playground during break and negotiated his way out of detention by arguing that his old school in Ibiza had a more relaxed policy. Very cool. Jay kept himself to himself, hiding beneath his fringe. I don't think I spoke a word to him until New Year's Eve. That's when everything kicked off.

3

'Just explain why we are doing this,' said Harry after locking the front door behind him. 'I thought the forecast said to avoid unnecessary journeys.'

He put his arm around Ailsa to emphasize this was a joke rather than a challenge and tried to kiss her on the cheek, but at the last minute she moved and he ended up kissing thin air. For a moment they stood together at the top of the stairs locked in a slightly reluctant embrace.

There had been no recriminations over the car. Harry wanted her to acknowledge his tolerance in the same way that he wanted her to respond each time he texted her at school to say that he had put on a wash or renewed the car licence. He had never worked from home before and neither of them had foreseen how their domestic dealings would have to be recalibrated.

Relationships were like amoebas. Constantly changing shape. *Sensitive to tiny environmental changes*, thought Ailsa, staring down at the shiny cream surface of the trifle she was holding. It was their contribution to the Fairports' New Year's Eve party. Harry hadn't waited for the custard to cool and it was leaching into the cream topping like tiny trails of snot. It had been made for her father, in memory of her mother, by her husband, a sequence of events that was unimaginable less than a year ago. Ailsa wondered what would happen if she plunged her fingers in the cream and shoved a handful into her mouth. She knew her orderly habits irritated those around her. It would be nice to confound expectations and see how that played out.

'It is a necessary journey,' called out Rachel from the garden below. 'Ailsa has to do penance for crashing into them.' No mention of her role in the drama. Ailsa struggled to conjure up irritation towards Rachel for her latest entanglement but she couldn't. She never managed to stay angry with her sister for long. Besides, it was no more likely to fail or succeed than any other of her relationships and she didn't want the burden of disapproval.

'I was ambushed in a moment of weakness,' said Ailsa as she carefully negotiated her way down the icy steps into the garden, trifle cradled under one arm, and joined everyone else at the bottom to debate the best route through the thick snow to the house next door. 'They've asked before and I've turned them down. I couldn't say no again.'

'We need some new friends,' said Harry.

'I suppose it's marginally better than staying at home like a bunch of sad fucks . . .'

'Luke,' warned Ailsa, nudging him in the small of the back with the crystal bowl, but he didn't feel anything through the layers of thick clothes.

'I think I'd rather be a sad fuck,' muttered Romy.

The snow had stopped and the moon was visible for the first time in days. Everything was white and even usually murky corners of the garden gave off a strange luminous glow. It had snowed so much again that the bumper dislocated from the car earlier that day was already buried.

'It's radioactive,' shouted Ben. 'Like a nuclear winter.'

'God, you can see for miles,' said Adam, looking across the street to the fields beyond. His anxiety about getting back home to visit the grave had dissipated as soon as the prospect of a party presented itself.

'It's to do with the luminosity of snow,' explained Romy. 'The snow albedo is really high. I learned it in Physics.'

'You are so knowledgeable,' said Harry. It was the wrong thing to say. Romy was immune to flattery, and his increasing desperation to maintain the closeness they had once enjoyed only pushed her further away. She had never been a people pleaser.

'Millions of Physics students know that,' said Romy with a shrug. 'It's in all the textbooks.'

The recently cleared path to the front gate was covered in a thick layer of fresh snow and beneath it was as slippery as glass. Ben gingerly stepped out to test the ground and fell over. He lay on his back, rolling around like a seal and giggling. A half-eaten chocolate reindeer slipped out of his pocket. Romy pulled him up.

'Let's go through their back garden,' said Ben. 'It'll be easier for Grandpa.'

'How do we do that?' questioned Ailsa, suspicious of Ben's sudden attack of empathy.

'There's nothing wrong with my legs,' protested Adam. 'The doctor said I've got the flexibility of a thirty-five-year-old.'

'I've created an opening,' Ben announced. 'It's a really good route. But you mustn't tell anyone.'

'What do you mean?' asked Harry.

'I took down some of the fence so that I could come and go into the woods,' explained Ben. He had timed his revelation well.

'Wreck head,' said Romy. It was probably an insult but since Ailsa didn't know what it meant she could hardly pull her up. Instead Ailsa's attention was drawn to Romy's long bare legs. She was wearing a denim mini-skirt and fur-lined Ugg boots. Don't say anything, she warned herself.

'You'll freeze,' Ailsa said seconds after this thought.

'I've thought about the message I'm sending out,' said Romy. 'I'm telling people that I have really healthy circulation because I don't feel the cold, which means I have a good supply of oxygen in my bloodstream.'

'The message you think you are sending might not be the message that other people receive,' Ailsa pointed out.

'They all wear the same thing,' Luke intervened. 'Marnie and Becca look exactly the same.'

Ailsa tried a new tack. 'Have you ever considered why female singers perform in their underwear while the men get to keep their clothes on?' she asked, remembering something she had read in a book she had bought for the library at her old school.

'Because they make more money,' replied Romy. 'There's an inverse correlation between the amount of clothes they wear and the money they earn. Look, I'm not exactly going out in my underwear, Mum.'

'I can practically see your knickers.'

'If Luke was wearing this outfit would you have the same reaction? Because I think there's a double standard operating here.'

'Girls are becoming conditioned to the idea that they have to look sexually available all the time by showing more flesh than boys,' said Ailsa. 'You don't see Harry Styles dancing in his pants.'

'Unfortunately,' said Rachel.

'Girls have nicer bodies,' said Luke.

'Not helpful, Luke,' said Ailsa. 'Or Rachel.'

'It's because we live in a country where we aren't required to hide our sexuality behind a veil,' said Romy. 'What is it you're scared of, Mum? Do you think I look slutty? That I might get the wrong attention from the wrong man? Because if I do, I think that is his problem not mine. Or is it that I don't reflect well on you? Because I thought that feminism was about being free to wear what you like.' She sounded genuinely confused. And so was Ailsa. There was a lot of cognitive dissonance involved in being the parent of a girl. She told Romy frequently that she could do anything with her life but not that she would still have to work harder than any man to prove herself. She said that any job was within her reach but not that she might want to choose a career that was compatible with family life. She told her that she regretted hating so many parts of her own body when she was a teenager then berated Romy when she had the confidence in hers to wear short skirts.

'You look great, Romy,' said Ailsa finally.

'Thanks,' said Romy deadpan.

Badly done, Ailsa, Ailsa told herself.

Away from the path, the snow was deeper but less slippery. Ben led the way, making deep footprints with his snow boots so that everyone else could follow in his tracks. Adam shuffled along in his trail, wearing wellington boots two sizes too big. Rachel walked behind her father, ostentatiously holding her arms out to catch him, to demonstrate that at least for tonight she was there for him. Harry opted for the virgin snow beside Ailsa and offered to carry the trifle. Ben stopped beside a deep flower bed by the fence separating the two properties. He narrowed his eyes to examine a snow-covered willow, shaking a branch to create a mini flurry that fell onto everyone's heads.

'It's this one,' he said triumphantly.

'How can you tell?' asked Luke, peering into the flower bed.

'The branches look like a corkscrew,' said Ben. He stepped four paces forward and turned left into the undergrowth. Moments later he emerged holding four slats of wood, which he stacked beneath the willow in a well-practised routine.

'Follow me,' he instructed. They obediently walked

behind him in single file, heads bowed, like an army in retreat, and guiltily regrouped in the Fairports' back garden. 'Don't break any branches. According to Ray Mears, it's a dead giveaway.'

'What exactly do you do here, Ben?' asked Rachel.

'Observe,' said Ben, gratified by the attention. 'Mum wanted to know what they were building in the woods. And I can tell you even though it's got shelves, it definitely isn't a pizza oven. It's way too big. Unless they're going to cook human beings.'

'Don't use me as an excuse for your nosiness,' retorted Ailsa. She paused. 'So what does it look like inside?'

'I can stand but my head almost touches the roof. It's really long and there's a big pit in the middle,' explained Ben. 'In one corner there's lots of really big stones and a shelf with candles. It's really dark. And there aren't any windows.'

'Spooky,' teased Harry.

'What have you learned about them?' asked Luke. 'Because people are generally way more interesting than buildings.'

'The youngest boy smokes in his room and has a poster of Nicki Minaj on the wall. His room is painted blood red, even the ceiling.'

'I can see that from my room,' scoffed Luke.

'Who's Nicki Minaj?' asked Harry.

'She's a singer. Looks like porno Barbie,' said Luke. 'Breast implants, buttock implants, lip implants, toe implants. The works.'

'Luke,' warned Ailsa.

'What does porno mean?' asked Ben.

'Pawnee,' said Luke quickly, 'as in the native Indian tribe from Nebraska.'

Luke stopped for a moment. Ailsa noticed his shoulders were already straining against a jacket bought only one month earlier. For the past three years Romy had looked down on her brother from a position of willowy grace. In less than six months Luke had overtaken first her, then Ailsa and finally his own father. Ailsa often caught herself staring at him in the kitchen, observing how the box of breakfast cereal looked tiny in his enormous hand or how dark hair had suddenly sprouted on his calves. His school trousers were already too short and even his hands were hairy. She couldn't remember such sudden changes since he was a baby. Back then every new development had been faithfully recorded with a camera. Now she had to steal a glimpse. Everything about him was extreme. He was either immobile, sprawled on the sofa listening to music through headphones, or in loud, clumsy motion. He was ravenously hungry or completely full. Very angry or very happy. The polarity took her breath away.

He had fallen in with a new crowd almost as soon as he'd started at school. Not quite the right crowd but better than the crew he hung out with in London. He'd been suspended from Ailsa's old school for stealing a rotary evaporator from the chemistry lab in a botched attempt to concoct his own version of the legal high mephedrone from bath salts. Except it transpired that he couldn't even get this right because Romy told Ailsa that the lab equipment he had taken turned liquids into solids. At Highfield the worst he'd done so far was get caught smoking by the head of Biology and he had got off with a verbal warning.

After the smoking incident Ailsa and Harry had sat down with Luke and explained that his behaviour reflected badly on his parents and undermined his mother. Luke professed to understand and was apologetic rather than defensive. Then last week Ailsa had found a packet of cigarette papers in his school blazer. She had mentioned this to Harry, who had told Luke that if he smoked too much marijuana his hippocampus would shrink and his short-term memory would fail. 'I'll bear that in mind, Dad,' said Luke. 'If I remember.'

'I went there once with your mother,' said Adam as they walked across the Fairports' garden. 'Ailsa, are you listening?'

Ailsa pulled herself out of her thoughts.

'What are you talking about, Dad?' asked Rachel.

'Nebraska. We went up into the mountains to go fishing in Big Elk Park. I caught a huge salmon but your mother wanted me to put it back in the water. I refused. I tried to find my club to kill it but it was at the bottom of the bag.'

Adam stopped and stared straight ahead as if describing a scene unfolding in front of him.

'The fish flapped around our feet, trying to slide back into the water. The more it struggled the wider its eyes got. It was pleading for a second chance but I didn't let it have one. It choked to death. I regret that decision now. It wasn't the worst one I ever made. But it was close. Georgia never forgave me. Refused to eat fish ever again. Probably why she ended up having a heart attack. Omega oil deficiency.'

'Come on, Dad,' said Ailsa gently, taking his arm.

'Don't worry, Grandpa, a fish's brain isn't developed enough to feel pain,' said Romy. 'We learned about it in Biology Club.'

'I remember Mum eating fish,' said Rachel. *Let it go*, thought Ailsa. *Don't pick a fight.*

'She ate it all the time,' Rachel continued.

'She never ate trout again,' said Adam.

'You said it was a salmon,' said Rachel.

'What else do you learn in Biology Club?' Ailsa asked.

'We're about to do a big project on blood groups as part of genetics. Mr Harvey is big into extension topics –'

'Wolf is really good at making things. He did the tiling in the kitchen on his own. And he's been building the oven at the end of the garden,' interrupted Ben, sensing he was losing their attention. He unzipped his coat, pulled out a notebook from his inside pocket and switched on his torch.

'The parents lock themselves in their bedroom the same time every weekend. At exactly two o'clock Wolf comes to the window. He opens it, even if it's snowing, and breathes in and out really fast for fifteen counts. Then he holds his breath for around five seconds and puts his hands in the air and chants.'

'What does he say?' asked Harry.

Ben had regained their attention.

'I can't hear. I can only lip-read. And I think he says, "Messi is a god."'

Everyone laughed. Ben snapped shut his notebook in irritation. No one ever took him seriously.

'Messi?' questioned Adam. 'As in the Barcelona foot-baller?'

'Yes, Grandpa.'

'Why would he know about Messi? Isn't he American?' questioned Adam.

'Messi is Argentinian,' said Luke.

'I mean the neighbour,' said Adam. 'Isn't the neighbour American?'

'I would say from somewhere in the south, like Texas,' said Harry. 'But I only met him for five minutes.'

'He would say it because it's true,' said Ben, starting to get frustrated. 'Messi is a god. He's one of the greatest footballers ever to have lived.' He paused for a moment for maximum impact to deliver his killer piece of information. 'And when he says it, he's completely naked. Out of respect. I think.'

'Then what?' questioned Romy.

'He gets down on all fours and sometimes Loveday joins him.'

'Oh my God,' said Ailsa.

'What are they doing?' persisted Luke.

'I don't know, I can't see any more,' said Ben.

'They do downward dog,' said Romy triumphantly. 'He's saying downward dog, not Messi is a god. They're doing yoga together. Simples.'

'Aren't you going to get angry with him, Mum?' asked Luke, who was the most disappointed by this explanation. 'You're always going on about how the Facebook generation doesn't value privacy. Ben's been spying on our new neighbours. That's worse than anything Mark Zuckerberg has done.'

'It's harmless,' said Ailsa. 'He's bored.' She ruffled Ben's hair and pulled him towards her even though his jacket was soaking wet. 'It's good to have someone watching over us, making sure that everyone is safe.'

'Did you see Mark Zuckerberg has bought all the houses surrounding his own to prevent anyone from taking pictures of him?' said Harry. 'I sense a double standard when it comes to his own privacy.'

'I've only been a couple of times,' said Ben, realizing he was losing their attention again. Ailsa looked at the trail between the two gardens. Unlike the rest of the flower bed there were no weeds or plucky daffodil stems poking up through the snow. This was a well-trodden route.

'Let's go to the front of the house so we don't need to tell them about the fence,' suggested Ailsa. They walked in silence. Ben rang the bell.

'The most interesting thing about Wolf is that he

wears his wedding ring on his penis,' he said suddenly. 'Why would he do that?'

'Because it's less likely to get stolen?' suggested Ailsa just as Loveday opened the front door. Everyone giggled helplessly. And so Loveday's first impression of the Fields was that they were the perfect nuclear family.

The house was the mirror image of their own. *The floor plan must be identical down to the last square foot*, thought Ailsa as she stared from the huge window of Wolf and Loveday's sitting room into her own. She had left a light on in the kitchen and could see that Lucifer was taking advantage of their absence to finish off a mug of milk that Ben had left on the table. Beside the mug was her Christmas present from Harry, a new iPhone, still in its packaging.

Whereas Ailsa had embraced the simple lines and stark 1960s design because it was so different from the unruly chaos of their Victorian London terrace, the Fairports had softened the hard-edged modernism with throws in geometric prints, brightly painted wooden furniture and ethnic rugs.

It looked as though they'd lived there for several generations. It was a good quality, decided Ailsa as she turned her back on the window to scrutinize the rest of the room while Wolf went to fetch drinks and Loveday installed Adam in a wooden rocking chair with a cosy sheepskin cushion.

A wooden floor-to-ceiling shelving system now created a wall between the open-plan hallway and the sitting room. Hundreds of books were organized according to the colour of their covers. One shelf contained dozens of tiny glass eggs that Wolf said were hand-painted in the Ukraine. There was a collection of what looked like carved wooden magic wands, apparently used by Latin American shamans during ayahuasca ceremonies. An entire shelf was devoted to semi-precious stones gathered during their travels. A few minutes were spent discussing this collection, and it soon became clear that there was hardly a country in the world that the Fairports hadn't visited. Lapiz lazuli from Afghanistan. Amethyst from Brazil. Blue topaz from Mexico.

'Topaz is the symbol of love and fidelity,' said Wolf as he offered Ailsa a margarita from a tray that he was carrying around the room. 'I gave it to Loveday on our tenth anniversary.' Ailsa hated tequila. But it seemed rude to refuse and instead of grappling for an adequate response to his topaz comment, she took the glass and admired the way he had successfully encrusted salt around the rim.

It would take longer to empty this one room than to pack up the entire contents of next door. Ailsa thought about Harry's basement office, still full of sealed boxes piled as high as the ceiling, containing their entire family history: photo albums, Luke's football medals, envelopes with locks of hair from first haircuts, Romy's collection of Roman mystery books, Luke's first paintings. The further you got from the past, the more it was diluted. At least that was Rachel's advice. The key was to keep moving forward and not look backwards. Rachel was good at moving forward, although the fact that she always went out with inappropriate men would suggest she hadn't entirely left her past behind.

'What's that smell?' Adam interrupted her thoughts. He spoke a little too forcefully so that the skin under his chin wobbled like a turkey's wattle.

'Incense,' whispered Ailsa. She paused for a moment. 'Try and take it easy, Dad.' Since Georgia had died, Adam had resumed drinking red wine for the first time in years. Adam understood and saluted. She was assuming the role of enforcer.

'Don't honour Mum's memory by turning into her,' Rachel whispered and left the room before Ailsa could explain that if her sister shared the burden a bit more she might not feel so responsible.

Ailsa left Adam in the chair, walked across a huge faded Moroccan kilim that covered the whole floor, and stood at the fireplace in between the wooden giraffes, who haughtily eyed the guests as though protecting ancient territory.

Harry was talking to Loveday. She was as tall as him and stood erect, like a dancer. She must be younger than her husband. She had a feline face with slightly slanting eyes and wore her breasts like a woman who had received a compliment about them many years earlier and had never forgotten. A display cabinet couldn't have shown them off any better. *Well-engineered bra or cosmetic surgery?* wondered Ailsa as Loveday threw back her head and

laughed at something Harry had said, her breasts pointing straight in the air. Harry carefully maintained eye
contact. She wasn't his type. You knew that kind of thing
straight away.

'Communication in a relationship is everything,' said
Loveday.

'Marriages wouldn't last more than a week if you
always said how you felt,' countered Harry. Loveday
laughed. It was a version of what Ailsa thought but it
still rankled.

She took a deep breath and braced herself for the
evening ahead, holding on to the mantelpiece for ballast.
A tiny clay figure fell on its side. She picked it up and
held it between her fingers. She looked at it more closely:
it was a seal playing a bassoon, part of a miniature
orchestra of animals, each holding a tiny instrument.
Her mother would have loved it.

She closed her eyes and pressed the onyx stone of her
engagement ring hard into her right knuckle to put off
the tears pricking at her eyelids. Death threw you off
course. Each day something happened that she wanted
to share with her mother. And every time Ailsa remembered that she couldn't, she tumbled back into the black
hole of grief. At least now, almost six months on, the
route out was familiar.

'I hope you're not worrying about the car,' said a voice
beside her, removing the bassoon-playing seal from
between her fingers and putting it back on the mantelpiece. 'It's really not important.' Wolf saw the red mark

on her knuckles but didn't say anything. He urged Ailsa towards the sofa next to the fireplace. It was an L-shaped modular unit on which you could find yourself stranded in a corner with your knees touching the person cramped up on the short end. Ailsa opted for the middle of the long side of the sofa. Wolf sat down in the space next to her.

'More haste, less speed. I spend my life trying to get my children to think of the repercussions of their actions and then I ignore my own advice,' said Ailsa, putting the red-knuckled hand firmly in a pocket. He was being kind, and she should respond with something more than platitudes.

To her relief, Rachel came back into the sitting room. Ailsa smiled until she saw her sister was holding a large glass of whisky and water without ice for Adam.

'Go and take a look at the kitchen,' said Rachel enthusiastically. 'It's gorgeous. There's an amazing old sink that they found in a skip and the tiles are from Mexico. It's rare to meet a man these days who can grout, Wolf.'

'How do you know I can grout?' asked Wolf.

'I know a grouter when I see one,' said Rachel, realizing she had almost given Ben away.

Ailsa forced a half smile. *Please don't flirt with him, Rach.* And yet she admired the way her sister could establish intimacy with men so quickly.

'Did you always think about the repercussions of

your actions when you were younger?' Wolf asked, turning back to Ailsa.

'Sorry?' said Ailsa.

'You were talking about responsibility,' Wolf reminded her.

'Probably not,' said Ailsa, trying to focus.

'So what was the worst thing that you did and was it really so disastrous?' he asked. He stared at her longer than was comfortable through his watery blue eyes, and she wondered what he would think if she really told him.

'Ailsa didn't do anything bad,' interjected Rachel. 'I was the one who caused all the trouble. Still do actually.' She slumped down in the sofa and Wolf sat between them in the middle, closer to Rachel than was necessary. Ailsa was relieved to be the object of his attention no longer. He shifted position until he was sitting cross-legged, his knee touching Rachel's thigh.

They were probably swingers. Ailsa looked around the room, searching for evidence, before concluding that swinging probably didn't require accessories. Then she almost laughed out loud at her ridiculousness. She would tell Harry later. It would make him laugh. She used to be good at making him laugh.

She checked her watch. It was after six o'clock.

'It's safe . . .' said Romy.

For a moment Ailsa worried that she had said something out loud.

'To drink,' Romy said with a frown. 'It's after six.' She was trying to make a joke, Ailsa realized too late. She had missed the beat. Another opportunity for closeness that she had failed to exploit. Perhaps if she hadn't worked so hard through Romy's childhood she would feel closer to her now. If she had taken her shopping more then she might have had more influence over what she wore. Even as the thought crossed her mind she smiled at its absurdity. Of course Luke was right. They all dressed the same way. If you couldn't wear a skirt like that at her age when could you?

She watched Romy take her phone out of her pocket and scroll down through her messages. She had no idea whether she was on Facebook, Snapchat, Instagram or some new service that Ailsa had never heard of. Teenagers were so digitally promiscuous, restlessly moving from one technology to another the moment their parents knew how to use it.

The Fairports' younger son, Jay, who was the same age as Romy, came in the room, mumbled hello and then did the same thing with his phone. They stood beside each other, heads bowed, tapping keyboards, and then miraculously stopped at exactly the same time as though it were part of an elaborate introduction ritual dating back centuries.

Jay's dark hair was so long and wild that you couldn't see his eyes, and when he finally looked up to suggest they all go outside for a snowball fight, Ailsa had to stop herself from commenting on their blueness. It would have betrayed the fact that even though Jay was a pupil at her school, she hadn't addressed a word to him.

Ailsa resolved to tell his parents at an appropriate point in the evening how well he had settled. She had no evidence for this beyond the fact that none of his teachers had brought him to her attention. His older brother, Marley, was a different matter.

'Let's go,' said Marley.

'Sure.' Luke shrugged. Romy followed them.

'Did you know that the average teenager messages a hundred and fifty times a day?' said Harry as they left the room. 'It's probably causing structural change to their brain.'

'How so?' asked Wolf.

'The thumb area in their cerebral cortex gets bigger,' he explained. 'It's like violinists. The part of the brain that directs the fingers of the left hand is five times bigger than in people who don't play an instrument.'

'That is so interesting,' said Loveday.

'Mum, I'm going outside with them. Mum, can you hear me?' Ben was standing in front of Ailsa.

He had taken a can of Coke and put another full one in his pocket. She could see it bulging out of a trouser pocket. He smiled, confident that she wouldn't make a scene in front of people she didn't know, and backed out of the door.

'Coat!' shouted Ailsa into thin air.

'They learn that for themselves pretty quickly, don't you think?' said Loveday, stepping towards her with a plate of hot pitta bread and a brown sludge that she identified as aubergine dip. 'I'm a great believer in children learning from experience. Without experiences, what is life?'

'I guess it depends on the experience,' said Ailsa quickly, biting into the pitta bread so that she couldn't say what she really thought. Years as a teacher meant she was expert at summing up parents. She took in the whitened teeth and perfectly nail-varnished hands. Manicured hippy. Lots of effort in looking effortless. She would have spent at least half an hour smudging those kohl-smeared eyes and finding the right shade of lipstick. Their children would be allowed to run wild and when they got into trouble the parents would tell Ailsa that they believed in encouraging creativity and freedom of spirit. 'You don't want to learn the hard way that you need to look left and right before you cross the road.'

It was meant to be a joke but it came out slant.

'If you don't suffer, you don't grow,' said Loveday, who asked questions without waiting for the answers. As she spoke, Loveday swayed from side to side to the music, making Ailsa feel vaguely seasick.

'Stress can stunt growth,' said Ailsa.

'I mean grow as a human being, spiritual growth,' said Loveday. 'You're very literal. Are you a Virgo?'

'I am,' said Ailsa, irritated that she had guessed correctly.

'I can plot your astrological chart if you like,' Loveday offered.

'Er, thanks,' said Ailsa, unsure how else to respond.

'What beautiful material,' said Rachel, leaning forward from the sofa to touch the heavily embroidered fabric of Lovejoy's skirt. 'How daring to put all these colours together.'

'It's a Seminole Indian skirt from the 1940s,' explained Loveday. 'Wolf and I spent six months living on a Lakota reservation years ago to study tribal medicine, and it was a leaving present.'

'Gosh, that must have been really fascinating,' said Rachel.

'So, after all your travels how have you ended up moving to this neck of the woods?' Harry addressed Wolf.

'We'd been living in Ibiza for a while, then sold our business and decided to have an adventure. We did some research and discovered that Luckmore was an ancient medieval site with special spiritual significance.'

'There's a very auspicious ley line running through the village,' said Loveday when no one spoke.

'You mean the south-east railway route,' said Harry, who clearly thought they were joking. 'The village is littered with the corpses of people who have died waiting for that train to come.'

Everyone laughed apart from Wolf and Loveday.

'It's very important for Wolf and me to have a spiritual connection with the place where we live for our work,' she explained. 'Especially in this new phase of our life. Luckmore has magical qualities.'

'It's not exactly bloody Stonehenge though, is it?' interrupted Adam.

'Physically, mentally, emotionally and spiritually, we feel close to Mother Earth here,' said Loveday seriously. 'This is a place where we can give, share, cleanse and nurture in peace and harmony.'

'So what line of business are you in?' asked Adam.

'We're in the healing business,' said Loveday, resting her hand on Adam's forearm.

'Doctors?'

'Therapists,' said Wolf.

'Do you have any particular area of expertise?' asked Adam.

'We do,' said Loveday. 'Sexual healing. Are you aware that human beings are the only species on earth who have sex primarily for pleasure rather than procreation?'

'I hadn't really thought about it,' said Adam.

'So what exactly is it that you do?' asked Rachel.

'Wolf and I try and help couples achieve prolonged multiple intercourse with the same partner,' explained Loveday. 'We believe in mutual respect between men and women and reverence for the sexual act. We try and help distinguish between healthy and unhealthy habits.'

'What kind of unhealthy habits?' asked Rachel when no one else spoke.

'Lack of foreplay, the destructive nature of pornography, the dangers of over-ejaculation for men,' replied Loveday.

'And will you be continuing that same line of work

now you've moved here?' asked Harry as if they had just told them they were accountants.

'We will continue to see our regular clients,' said Wolf. 'And we're hoping to set up a healing centre.'

'Well, that's great,' said Rachel. 'Really lovely. It's not easy making a living somewhere like this.'

'We fell for the house too,' said Wolf quickly. 'All the early-morning light flooding through those huge glass windows. I can't imagine ever living anywhere else now.'

'I think everyone has a dream house in their head,' said Rachel. 'When I wake up at four o'clock in the morning and can't get back to sleep I imagine where I would really like to live and build it in my imagination. I see myself sitting in a really big apartment somewhere in southern France. It's got a huge sitting room with two sets of long double doors that open out onto a balcony with black wrought-iron railings that runs the whole way along the front of the house. It overlooks a lake and I have a small rowing boat moored by a jetty. When I get back to sleep I always have the same dream. There's a small table with a white lace tablecloth beside one of the open windows and a meal for two waiting on the table and someone waiting for me to sit down.'

'Who is it?' asked Ailsa, grateful for Rachel's efforts to get the conversation back on track.

'I don't know, I never see his face,' said Rachel. 'Only the back of him.'

'So what brought you folks here?' asked Wolf.

'Ailsa's job really. I'm stepping back for a while to

write a book based on my research and do the domestic stuff until she gets on top of it all,' said Harry. He walked behind the sofa and put a hand on Ailsa's shoulder. Ailsa stayed still.

'How generous to put your wife's career before your own,' said Loveday. It had been said many times before but Harry never tired of the mostly female adulation. 'It requires real confidence for a man to do that.'

'Women do it all the time,' said Ailsa, instantly regretting the comment because it made her sound ungrateful and faintly defensive.

'Also Ailsa's parents live close by,' Harry continued. 'Lived, I should say. Adam still does. Her mother died shortly before we arrived in the summer. Completely unexpected. Sealed the decision to move. We're hoping it was the storm before the calm.'

'I'm sorry to hear about your loss,' said Wolf to Ailsa and Adam. His straightforward approach to death marked him out as an American more than his accent, which lurched between English vowel sounds and diphthongs from the Deep South.

'Thank you,' said Ailsa. 'It's been a tough year.' Her voice faltered. 'We were living in central London and we thought Luckmore would be a safer environment for our teenagers to push the boundaries.'

'We were beginning to have a few problems with Luke,' added Harry. 'And it's a better school. Especially with such a safe pair of hands at the helm.'

'So what do you do, Harry?' asked Loveday.

'I'm a cognitive neuroscientist,' he replied.

'What does that involve?'

'I study how the brain affects behaviour.'

'Wow. I'm impressed,' said Loveday. 'That must be very interesting.'

'Mostly it involves spending hours in airless basements with no natural daylight repeating the same experiment over and over again,' joked Harry.

'So what's the upside?' asked Wolf.

'It gives you a fascinating insight into the neural mechanisms underlying cognition. The way the mind and the brain work. Helps us all understand each other a little bit more or at least understand why we do the things we do.'

'What's the book about?' asked Loveday.

'I've spent the past decade researching the development of the teenage brain. I'm trying to make the science real for a wider audience so that it helps us understand what kids are going through during puberty.'

'And what have you discovered?' asked Loveday, arching one of her eyebrows. Somehow she made even the most innocuous question sound flirtatious.

'We used to think that the teenage brain was simply a version of the adult brain. But we've discovered that the frontal lobes that control impulsive behaviour and inhibit inappropriate behaviour get pruned through adolescence while the thrill-seeking part goes into overdrive. This has a big effect on behaviour. Teenagers basically have Ferrari engines and Fiat brakes because the rational pre-frontal cortex ends up playing second fiddle to the risk-taking ventral striatum. The front of your brain isn't fully developed until your late twenties.'

'It's a book based on science but hopefully with wide appeal to parents up and down the land,' Ailsa explained.

'Most mental health problems start in adolescence, and the neural pathways laid down then run very deep,' Harry added.

'So what you're saying is that parents have to function as a temporary pre-frontal cortex to their teenage children?' said Wolf.

'I couldn't have put it any better myself,' said Harry.

'Harry is very big on impulse control,' said Rachel, a hint of alcohol-fuelled menace in her tone. 'But there's a big difference between theory and practice, isn't there, Harry?'

'So why are teenagers so impulsive?' asked Loveday.

'In a nutshell,' Harry began, 'during adolescence there's an increase in the activity of neural circuits using dopamine, a neurotransmitter central in creating our drive for reward. Increased dopamine means adolescents are drawn to thrilling and exhilarating sensations. Their baseline level of dopamine is low but its release in response to experience is higher, which is why they say they are bored a lot and very impulsive. They are focused on the positive rewards from experiences but can't value the risks and downside. All addictive behaviours and substances involve the release of dopamine. Addictive pathways get laid down and so it's more difficult for teenagers to change addictive habits.'

'You blow my mind, Harry,' said Loveday. 'That's wild.'

'It's just science,' said Harry enthusiastically.

The front door banged and the children returned. Luke and Marley came back into the sitting room and leaned against the bookshelf, feigning nonchalance, but Ailsa could see from the red glow of their cheeks and the easy banter that the sullen teenage posturing was just that. Luke was taller than anyone else in the room, Ailsa noted, as his shoulder nudged the bookshelf and one of the Ukrainian eggs rolled alarmingly close to the edge. Ben shuffled in last. His fringe was frozen with snow like an Exmoor pony's. His teeth were chattering and his bare feet had turned a gentle shade of blue.

'Why does the hair on your arm stand up when you're cold, Dad?' Ben asked.

'It's a reflex inherited from our much hairier ancestors to try and keep warm,' Harry explained.

'Come, stand by the fire, Ben,' said Loveday, dragging a beanbag seat over to the hearth. 'We'll thaw you out.'

The conversation stalled and atomized. Ailsa listened to fragments of other people's talk like a dog chasing different scents. Deodorant. Could be a killer. Reading Festival. Luke had come back to find someone had done a shit inside his tent. Rapeseed oil. The new wonder food. Could also be used as fuel. The price of fuel. Fracking. Rachel confessed to Loveday that she was dating someone much younger. Loveday approved of the match by pointing out that their sex drives would be perfectly matched. Ailsa heard Rachel whisper that they hadn't had sex yet. That surprised her. Rachel questioned Loveday about depilation. How much was enough? What would the average twenty-seven-year-old man expect?

'It depends how he's been conditioned,' said Loveday.

'What do you mean?' asked Rachel.

'If he's twenty-seven that means he was fourteen when the Internet hit the mainstream so I would say less is definitely more. There's a chance he might never have seen a fully grown muff. They're practically endangered.'

'That's so true,' agreed Rachel. 'A teacher at Ailsa's school told me that when he showed a film on childbirth several of the boys asked what the women had between their legs because they had never seen pubic hair. One of them who's doing Shakespeare for A-level English thought it was a merkin.'

It suddenly occurred to Ailsa that this was something Matt Harvey, her recently recruited head of Biology, must have told her sister. Rachel and Matt had met for five minutes in her office three months earlier when Rachel had come to meet Ailsa for lunch. She had left them alone for all of thirty seconds while she had a brief discussion with her assistant about the agenda for a governors' meeting. When she came back he was asking Rachel about where she had spent her summer holiday. They couldn't have talked about his Sex Ed class then.

They must have seen each other again. Ailsa frowned as an idea took shape.

'What's a merkin?' questioned Loveday.

'A pubic wig,' Rachel elaborated. 'The teacher blamed Internet porn. That's where they learn about sex, and all the women are completely bald.'

Loveday agreed.

'What do you think, Harry?' Rachel asked drunkenly. 'What would the expectation be?'

'How would I know?' he replied.

'You must come across lots of young students,' she said.

'Enough, Rachel,' said Harry. Rachel stopped but only because she had cleaved another groove. 'Even the ancient Egyptians liked to wax.'

Ailsa checked Ben. To her relief he was playing cards with Luke and Marley. They were playing for money. Letting Ben win.

'Landing strip. You can't go wrong with a landing strip,' recommended Loveday.

'But it's the commitment. A Brazilian isn't for Christmas. It's for life. You have to go back every four weeks,' said Rachel.

'Let's eat,' said Wolf. He stood up and herded everyone into the kitchen. Ailsa obediently followed. She stared at the feast prepared by the Fairports, grateful for the distraction. At the centre of the table was a chicken cooked in a lemon and honey sauce, rice with onion, lentils and pistachio nuts, aubergine with pomegranate seeds and a saffron-infused yogurt sauce, Loveday explained. There was roast pork belly with a pink relish identified as plum and rhubarb, and a salad and chickpeas and sweet potatoes. As she picked up a plate, it dawned on Ailsa with absolute clarity: Matt must be Rachel's younger man.

Ailsa felt a sudden rage towards Rachel. Could she not see that starting a relationship with one of Ailsa's teachers might be awkward for her? Matt hadn't even finished his probation period. If other members of staff found out it would look completely unprofessional. They would watch her to see if she treated him more leniently or more harshly. Either way her authority would be undermined, especially after only one term on the job.

She unthinkingly spooned plum and rhubarb relish onto her plate until a sizeable mound had formed. Ailsa liked to compartmentalize her life. To keep her different worlds separate. Rachel knew this. She even teased her that she would make a good man. Rachel knew how much was riding on this clean break from the past. And yet she had come sniffing around Ailsa's territory like a dog on heat and pissed all over her new beginning.

She put her plate on the table and began unloading the plum and rhubarb relish back onto the dish. Matt had betrayed nothing. His deceit bothered her too. She tried to remember her last encounter with him. They had discussed the possibility of additional funding for the after-school Biology Club to buy sixty finger pinprick tests. His enthusiasm and energy had reminded her of when she first started out in the classroom and she had quickly agreed to all his requests. There was nothing to indicate that he was sleeping with her sister. Or about to sleep with her. Or that he even knew Rachel.

Ailsa was generally disapproving of relationships at work but now she wished he could have got involved with the art teacher. At least she was the same age. Because of course the absurd age gap was another source of embarrassment. The question wasn't what Rachel was doing with him, it was what he was doing with her. Why would a twenty-seven-year-old man go out with a thirty-nine-year-old woman? Although of course Rachel looked good for her age. Not just good. Great, as Harry had recently observed after Rachel had spent a three-month fallow period between jobs going to the gym every day. Using her free time for self-improvement rather than helping out with Adam. Ailsa glanced down at her plate and realized that she had now transplanted all of the relish back onto it.

'Are you OK?' she saw Harry mouth from the other side of the table.

'Fine,' she said abruptly. She needed to separate the strands. Keep how she felt about Rachel away from how she felt about Harry. She forced herself to focus on Harry's trifle, which Wolf was now holding aloft as though examining an ancient relic. Beside the feast prepared by the Fairports, it looked absurd. An inadequate afterthought transported through time from the darkest period in British cuisine. It would have been better to have arrived empty-handed or made an ironic Angel Delight. She felt a sudden urge to laugh hysterically. The Fairports, however, professed delight. Wolf said he'd never seen a trifle before and examined the layers of pear, sponge and custard through the crystal bowl.

'Beautiful,' said Wolf. 'I love the marbling effect and the way different layers of sediment have formed.'

'It was the least I could do,' said Harry, whose foray into family cooking was so recent that he considered an omelette a fantastic achievement.

'Where are Jay and Romy?' asked Loveday. 'They need to come and eat.'

'Upstairs. They never came outside with us,' said Marley.

'I'll go and get them,' said Ailsa, putting down her now-empty plate, relieved to have an excuse to leave the room.

Ailsa knew exactly where to find the toilet. She even knew how many stairs there were to the little half landing halfway up between the ground and first floor. She locked the door, leaned straight-armed over the tiny sink and stared at herself in the mirror. Why is it that people's mouths turn down as they get older? Is it gravitational pull or because they smile less? Eventually would her mouth turn into an upside-down smile? She pulled the sides of her lips up because Harry had told her that even if you pulled a fake smile, it still released endorphins. It was the same conversation where he explained that children laugh on average three hundred times a day and people over the age of forty just four. Harry liked facts. They gave him certainty.

She ran the tap. The water was ice-cold. She splashed her face until it stung and then checked herself in the mirror again. Her usually pale cheeks were comically rosy, as though Ben had daubed blusher on them. Ailsa traced a line across a cheekbone. Her face was thinner than it had been at any point since her early twenties. It was the stress of changing job and moving house.

There was a joss stick burning on a wicker shelf beside the sink. It had a sweet sickly smell that made Ailsa feel nauseous so she held it under the tap until it had gone out. Then she pulled down the loo seat and sat down to collect her thoughts.

The toilet wall reminded Ailsa of an attention-seeking toddler, a jumble of apparently random objects all clamouring to be noticed. She was grateful for the distraction. There was a small carved wooden Swiss chalet for predicting the weather, except it was all wrong because the woman in the sun bonnet was outside rather than the man dressed for the cold. Beside it hung a framed poster of a Nirvana concert signed by Kurt Cobain and the original artwork for a Talking Heads album. Ailsa remembered Wolf mentioning downstairs that his father had been a record producer. To the left was a series of what looked like original prints from Chinese pillow books demonstrating different sexual positions. 'Mule in the springtime'. 'Posture of the bee stirring the honey'.

Her gaze lingered on a photograph of Wolf and Loveday that must have been taken in their twenties. They were standing on a beach. Had they got the future they had imagined for themselves back then? she wondered. She moved quickly on to a map showing the reduction in Native American land in the southern states of America. *Good subject for a school project*, she thought.

To her right was another wicker shelf with small piles of books and magazines. There was the *I Ching*, *The Tibetan Book of the Dead* and a well-thumbed copy of *The Prophet* by Khahil Gibran. She picked up a magazine and started to read a piece about Transcendental Meditation. She couldn't get beyond the first two paragraphs about the importance of the out breath. It dawned on Ailsa as she breathed in through her mouth and out through her nose that she had stopped buying magazines and hadn't finished reading a novel for almost a year. She carefully slid the magazine back in exactly the same place and pulled out another one. It opened on a dog-eared page in the middle. There was a double-page spread of Wolf and Loveday and their children sitting in a jeep outside their home in Ibiza. Ailsa flicked to the next page. Loveday was sitting at a bar beside a swimming pool. Wolf was standing beside her. He was wearing a pair of shorts. Loveday was in a bikini top and denim miniskirt. His arm was casually draped around her shoulder, his fingers entwined in her bikini strap. There was a cheeky hint of dark aureole through the white bikini top. Both were barefoot and yet they still managed to exude a glamour that made Ailsa simultaneously envious and fearful. There were pictures of a vivid pink shower room with his and hers showers beside each other, a wall covered with vintage skateboards and teal-coloured lacquered furniture.

She quickly decided that the magazine had been strategically placed precisely so that people would find it. She turned the page. It was a question-and-answer format. She began skim-reading. All thoughts of yogic breathing disappeared. The first question was about how long Wolf and Loveday had been running sexual healing workshops. Twenty years. Probably since the photo on the wall was taken, decided Ailsa. The second was about the most important lesson couples should learn. Wolf gave a one-word answer: the clitoris. He talked about it with the kind of precision that another man might describe the engine of a BMW. It was ten centimetres long. It stretched deep into the vagina. It could swell up to three times its original size. He recommended their DVD as the best method of learning about deep vaginal massage. Loveday was asked about celebrity clients. She said she couldn't possibly comment but didn't deny any of the names put to her. Wolf said that violent pornography was the biggest threat to human sexuality because it undermined the concept of female pleasure. There was a website address at the bottom of the page.

At the end the magazine asked them lifestyle questions. What's your favourite holiday drink? Caipirinha. What music do you wake up to in the morning? Miles Davis. Ailsa snapped shut the magazine and carefully placed it back in the pile, carefully repositioning the dog-ear. Two thoughts struck her almost simultaneously: one, their intentions were honourable, and two, she really didn't want to spend any more time with Wolf and Loveday than strictly necessary. Another good example of cognitive dissonance.

Ailsa came out of the toilet and heard noises coming from the floor above. She remembered the purpose of her foray upstairs and followed a trail of laughter that led her directly to a room with a bright red door and a poster of London Grammar Blu-tacked to the surface. It was closed. She listened outside and recognized Romy. It was the kind of hilarity that made your stomach ache and squeezed fat tears from your eyes. A belly laugh, as Ben would say. She hadn't heard Romy laugh like this since they moved to Luckmore. It was such a good sound it made her smile. She knocked on the door three times and thought she heard someone yell back. She noisily turned the handle before opening the door.

But of course they didn't hear. They were too wrapped up in each other. Later, Ailsa thought many times about what she saw when she came into Jay's bedroom. The image was frozen in her mind like one of those Dutch paintings where every object contained hidden symbolism. She tried different interpretations of the same scene.

She viewed it from the perspective of other people who were in the house at the same time, wondering if they would have got it so wrong. She envisaged how she might have seen it if she had come at it from a different angle, say from the window overlooking the garden. She considered how she might have reacted had she bothered to imagine in advance what she might encounter. But she had been both overly distracted and influenced by her discovery about Rachel and what she had just read in the magazine.

The room was as Ben had described. Blood red. The poster of the ridiculous pop star on her hands and knees, bum in the air, breasts pouring out of her crop top. A side lamp draped with a purple scarf so the bed was cast in a half shadow. The duvet crumpled at the foot of the bed. A pair of underpants lying on the floor. On the bed parallel to the door there were two figures. Jay was straddling Romy, pinning her arms above her head. Her T-shirt had ridden up so that Ailsa could see her belly button. The top button of her skirt was undone, revealing her knickers. His zip was down. Beside them was a laptop.

'What the hell is going on here?' said Ailsa. 'Downstairs now.'

4

Mum calls Ben the Punctilio because he pays such close attention to detail and routines. Takes one to know one, I say. So it was no surprise that he was the first one to notice there was something wrong with her. Some time early last year, when we were still living in London and had no idea of what lay ahead, Ben came into my room way after his bedtime to show me one of his notebooks.

This in itself wasn't strange. Ben was Mum and Dad's beautiful mistake, born after they had been told they wouldn't be able to have any more children. Back then we all probably indulged him more than we should, especially Mum. We'd pretend to take great interest in his secret life as an international spy and his accounts of survival techniques.

I was usually patient with him. Still am really. But it was the weekend before my mock GCSEs and I needed to get on top of variation and classification to hit the targets on the Biology revision timetable hanging on the wall above my desk. It was the only topic without a neat red line sliced through the middle. I was trying to focus on genetic variation in blood groups. Mum, who had almost exploded with pleasure when I told her I was thinking about studying medicine, had recently told me that she was B negative and Dad was AB negative. This meant our family belonged to one of the rarest blood groups in the world. At the time this seemed a wondrous revelation. Finally, something that made us a little more interesting. Everyone wants a life less ordinary, don't they?

'Not now, Ben, I'm revising,' I said as he came into the bedroom and sat down on the bed right beside my desk. 'Show me tomorrow.'

I tapped the revision timetable with my finger because he got schedules and I noticed that at the bottom, written in the same red pen in small letters so Mum wouldn't notice, were the words FUCKING NERD, a contribution from Luke, who had what Mum called a free-range approach to exams that basically involved drinking four cans of Red Bull the evening before they started and pulling an all-nighter. Revision definitely isn't genetic.

Ben pulled out one of his small notebooks from the pocket of his favourite Dalek pyjamas. 'You're not working, you're looking at Instagram,' he said, peering over my shoulder at my mobile.

'I'm taking a break,' I replied more sharply than I intended.

'If you don't let me tell you this now then I'll tell Mum,' he said.

'She won't mind,' I said. 'Mum trusts me.'

'This is more important than exams,' he said. There was a hint of desperation in his voice. 'Please, Romy.'

I turned towards him. His eyes were saucer wide. I held his chin in my hand. His hamster cheeks glowed red.

'Have you done something you shouldn't have done, Grub?' I asked, using my pet name for him.

'It's nothing I've done.'

'Then can't it wait until tomorrow?'

'But it does affect me.'

He gripped my upper arm tightly and leaned forward so close to me that I could feel hot little breaths of recently brushed teeth on my face.

'There's something wrong with Mum.'

'What do you mean?'

He opened up the notebook somewhere in the middle and I saw several pages of his strange sloping handwriting. This was going to be a long one.

'She's doing things differently,' he said.

'Are you worried she's ill?' I asked.

'Mum's changed,' he said simply. 'She's stopped doing stuff.'

'What do you mean, stuff?'

'It's all here.'

I can't remember the exact details. But some time after the beginning of the year Mum's habits changed. It was the small things Ben noticed first. She stopped coming into his room every night to check whether his light was out at eight thirty. Some nights she didn't even say goodnight. Others she lay on the bed beside him with the light on until she fell asleep. She forgot to water the plants in the containers in the back garden and didn't seem to care when they wilted and died. Even the rare African lily Dad had given her for her birthday.

Everything was half finished. Novels were started and abandoned by the side of her bed. Spine down, which Mum usually said was a crime against books. Meals were barely touched. She left half-finished mugs of tea lying around until mould grew on the dregs in rooms where she spent hours in hushed phone conversations with 'persons unknown'. Ben had underlined this phrase because it was something that needed following up. His attention to detail made me smile. I pulled him onto my knee and rested my chin on top of his head.

Considered individually, none of these would have been significant. But I agreed with Ben, when added together a pattern formed. A memory bubbled to the surface. A couple of weeks into February on the bus on the way back from school, I had seen Mum's car stopped by the side of the road a few streets away from our old house. She was staring out of the windscreen, hands gripping the steering wheel, even though the car was parked. This was the first time that I noticed she had lost weight. Her face had a constant taut expression as though the skin was pulled too tightly over her skull. Beside her on the front seat sat a pile of papers that I guessed were from her A-level English class. The bus stopped in traffic right beside the car, so close that I could see a copy of *A Midsummer Night's Dream* on top of the essays.

I was with my friends and generally tried to ignore Mum at school, so I didn't wave or knock to catch her attention. Instead I turned away and pressed my back against the window to block their view to avoid any embarrassment. When the bus pulled away I turned back and saw Mum in exactly the same position. She looked as though she was in a trance. I called her phone. She didn't answer. Unless she was teaching she always took my calls. I didn't tell Ben any of this.

'What do you think it means, Romy?' asked Ben, getting into my bed and pulling the duvet up to his chin. 'She's here but she's not here.'

'She's probably feeling stressed,' I said. This was the simplest explanation for any irrational behaviour with parents. 'Exams are coming up, so she's got lots of essays to mark and she's probably worried about Grandpa.'

'Why Grandpa?'

'Because he's worrying about Granny feeling tired all the time,' I said, one eye on the revision timetable as I tried to calculate whether I could afford to delay blood groups until the following morning.

'Why is she worrying about Grandpa when Granny is the one who is tired?'

'Because Grandpa is more high maintenance,' I said, repeating a phrase I had heard Aunt Rachel use to describe him.

'Is Dad worrying about Mum?' asked Ben. 'Because he should be.' It was a good question.

'I have no idea.'

A couple of months later Mum had applied for a new job, Dad had resigned from his university post and they were both trying to convince us all that leaving London, our friends and the home we'd grown up in was the best thing that had ever happened. Then my grandmother died and suddenly they were telling everyone who cared to ask that they needed to move to be close to my grandfather. None of it made any sense.

'What do you think?' I asked Jay. He had listened to me without interrupting once. We were sitting on his desk by the bedroom window, sharing a cigarette. When we moved to Luckmore, Mum and Dad had emphasized the importance of trying new things so I took up smoking the same week that Mum introduced the school uniform policy. Blazers were good for hiding the paraphernalia of cigarettes and I had sewn a pocket into the lining to keep mine hidden. But my heart wasn't really in it.

The storm outside had entered a different phase. The wind had picked up and changed direction. Its low moan overwhelmed Justin Chancellor's bass guitar riff, which Jay had announced was the top in his best bass riff list. I had argued in favour of 'Good Times' by Chic, but although he had a poster of Nile Rodgers on the wall, he stuck with Justin Chancellor.

The light in the centre of the room kept flickering. We sat with the hoods of our coats pulled up before the open window and I noticed how the tree where Ben had created his opening was now doubled over as if exhausted by this new weather event. My calves were still burning from the snow during the walk here and my boots were soaked. But I didn't move away from the window in case Jay suggested we go back downstairs.

'Has your mum ever behaved like that before?' Jay asked, staring at me as he took a deep toke on the cigarette before passing it back. 'It's always useful to spot patterns.'

I thought about Jay's question for a moment. His curly fringe bobbed up and down when he talked. When I caught a glimpse of his blue eyes beneath the fringe, they were so pale that I had to blink to stop my own from watering.

'Like what?' I said, flicking ash out of the window.

'If my dad takes even a sip of alcohol, Mum stops having sex with him.'

'How do you know that?'

'They're hippies. They talk about everything with everyone. And he gets really fucking grumpy.'

'And you don't talk about everything?'

'I think a lot of shit is best unsaid. There's too much information out there. And I'm choosy about who I tell stuff too.'

Actually, although it seems incredible now, my biggest criticism of Mum used to be how boring her life was. Living by lists, timetables, planning ahead all the time. Totally oppressive. I used to think that endlessly doing things was a way for her to avoid actually thinking about things. But when she stopped doing things our life fell apart. Routine is only comforting when you don't have it any more.

'She's never done anything like this before,' I said, leaning forward to blow the smoke out of the window. 'She used to be a very steady person.'

'Elaborate.' This, I quickly learned, was one of Jay's favourite words.

'When she painted the sitting room in our old house she tested twenty-three samples until she had found the exact shade of blue she wanted. She did the Christmas shopping in October. Booked dentist's appointments six months ahead.'

Jay had begun eating a chocolate reindeer that Ben had given him in exchange for another can of Coke. He ate it as though it was an ice cream, with slow licks. And I tried to stay focused on the cigarette because I didn't want him to catch me watching how his tongue curled around the reindeer and wondering how it might feel if he did the same to me.

'Did it definitely start before your grandmother died?' he asked. I nodded, appreciating his forensic approach to the problem. 'If you think too much about the past you don't focus on the present,' which, I was soon to learn, was his stock answer when anything went wrong. 'And she never mentioned that she was unhappy with her old job?' Jay continued.

'She loved it. She was deputy head of a really good school.'

'You know, people who say they are moving to make a new life are generally trying to escape something they don't like about their old one,' he said.

'So what do you think she was trying to escape?'

'I think that you need to think about whether you really want to know the answer to that question,' he said. 'Sometimes it's better not to know stuff. But in my experience if you really want to know what's going on in someone's life, you should look in their bathroom cabinet.'

I laughed because after all his analysis this seemed so unscientific. He smiled back. Unoffended.

'What do you mean?'

'Mum and Dad eat organic and refuse to use antibiotics but there's a big stash of Viagra hidden in a tin of Bach Rescue Remedy at the back of theirs. Not very tantric.'

I looked at the clock on his bedside table. It was ten minutes to ten on New Year's Eve and I already knew that Jay Fairport was one of the best things that had ever happened to me. We had already covered a lot of ground: why Stuart Tovey took his brother's Ritalin to help him revise for science tests; how dogs and wolves share almost 99 per cent of the same genes; why waves in the Pacific were better for surfing than those in the Atlantic; how my recently acquired best friend at school, Marnie Hall, fancied his brother, Marley; whether it was better to be a good person who has done a bad thing or a bad person who has done a good thing.

I had been in his bedroom for one hour and forty-seven minutes but it seemed like five minutes, and yet it felt as though we had known each other for years. I understood why physicists argue that time doesn't exist. I thought about how we might have missed this moment if I hadn't been freezing in my skirt and boots because Luke had thrown snowballs at me on the way through their garden. If I had gone outside with the others for a snowball fight instead of accepting Jay's offer to go and watch series two of *Breaking Bad* we might never have got to know each other.

'Life is really random,' he said, and I wondered if he could actually read my mind.

Even a couple of weeks later, I could almost make myself cry thinking about the possibility that our paths might never have crossed. I regretted the six weeks that we had been living next door to each other, travelling on the same bus to school and getting on and off at the same stop without talking to each other. I tried to calculate the lost hours. I wondered why we had never spoken before when the pull towards each other was so irresistible.

We finished the cigarette. Jay slammed the window shut and carried his laptop over to the bed. He kicked a pair of crumpled underpants under his bed and I knew that this was all unplanned. He settled down cross-legged on a pillow and the springs of the mattress shrieked. There was a wooden box beside the bed that acted as a table, and I recognized the paraphernalia of teenage boy, the spot cream, the crumpled tissues, the overlapping circular stains from coffee mugs like the potato prints that Ben used to do. He smoothed the duvet and plumped the pillows beside him and indicated that I should come and sit next to him. Apart from my brothers', I had never sat on a boy's bed before. This was his kingdom and I was being asked to enter it. I must have hesitated.

'You can keep your boots on,' he said, in case this was my dilemma. Then he added, 'The sheets are clean,' as if I might be worried about sitting on a tiny damp patch of sperm, which I was actually, because girls don't make as much mess. I remembered Mum saying something about how if you feel uncomfortable with someone you should mimic their body language so I sat down cross-legged on the throne of pillows beside him.

'Will you listen to something?' he asked.

'Sure,' I said.

'I mean really listen and tell me what you think. You can close your eyes if you like.'

I nodded. A piece of music started playing. I didn't recognize it. The first part was instrumental. A guitar, some drums in the background and sad strings, possibly cellos. I closed my eyes, glad to have something to focus on so I didn't think about our proximity. A man began singing. I could hear the lyrics clearly. It started slowly. The first verse was about a man walking blindly through a wood. He was lost but unsure if he wanted anyone to find him. He wondered if he should give love a chance to drive out his darkness. The singer had a mournful, gravelly voice. The bass guitar and drums built up in layers to the chorus, angry and passionate, but catchy, like something Deaf Havana might do.

You are the best of times. You are the worst of times.
And I know if you show me my better self then you
   will leave me.

There was a second verse. He had found love. The light had extinguished the darkness. They danced as though there was no one watching. Then the chorus again; this time it sounded more hopeful, like the coda to a romcom. The final verse was desperate. She had left him. He was alone again, hated for what he was rather than loved for what he wasn't.

'What do you think?'

'It's beautiful, angry and sad, all at the same time. What's the name of the band? Maybe we could go and check them out in Norwich?'

'It's me,' he said. 'I've never played it to anyone before. If you didn't like it I would have destroyed it.'

'It's amazing,' I said. 'Is it about something that happened to you?'

'Perhaps but not necessarily,' he said. If I hadn't been so distracted by the way his eyes were consuming me and wondering what this meant I might have saved myself a lot of heartache later. He looked away.

'Shall we watch *Breaking Bad*?'

We settled on our fronts beside each other. He put on

the DVD and pressed pause at the bit where the charred pink and white bear floats in the pool. Jay rolled onto his side and leaned on his arm.

'You know you have the blondest hair and darkest eyes I have ever seen,' he said.

'And you have the darkest hair and bluest eyes that I have ever seen,' I replied, turning towards him. We were facing each other. Outside the wind howled. And at that moment it felt as if we were the last people on earth.

'We're like photographic negatives.'

'My Armenian ancestry,' he said. 'My grandfather survived the 1915 massacre and migrated to the USA. He was the only male in his family to survive.'

'That combination of black hair and blue eyes is a really rare genetic mutation.'

'How so?'

'You really want to know?' I asked, because one thing I had learned about boys you liked was that being clever could count against you. He put out his hand and it drifted towards my face, lingering by the side of my cheek so that I could feel its heat. I tried not to think about what might happen next because from my limited experience of clumsy fumblings I knew that anticipation mostly beat the event. But he didn't try to touch me and instead put his hand back on his hip.

'I want to know everything about you,' he said.

'The genes for dark hair and blue eyes don't usually travel together. They're further apart on Chromosome 15.'

'How do you know this shit?'

'I just do,' I said. 'My dad's a scientist. He has an explanation for everything.'

'Why don't you ask him about your mum then?'

We were back where we started. And that's how it usually worked with boys. You talked and thought you were getting somewhere, and then they retreated because they thought they'd invested enough time on the pre-amble. From previous experience I knew this was the point he might suggest half jokingly that I might want to blow him. The Internet had reduced oral sex to a form of extreme kissing, and even though most girls refused, enough said yes to make it worth a punt. But Jay didn't follow the script.

'You know our bedrooms face each other?' he said, suddenly biting off the head of the reindeer.

'I didn't until today.'

'Why do you close your curtains during the day and open them at night?'

'It's much darker here at night than in London. I get scared.'

'I really like the way you dance and pretend your hairbrush is a microphone,' he said. 'I like the way you move. So fluid. Like you're made of liquid.'

'You've been watching me!'

'It made me feel less lonely.'

'I don't mind.'

'I feel like I've got to know you without the pressure of getting to know you, if you know what I mean.'

'I think so.' Actually that part I didn't understand. And by the time I did, I was in too deep. But according to my dad, when you meet someone for the first time and you really like them there's a part of your brain which switches off your response to anything that might make you feel uncomfortable.

'Why don't you have anything hanging on your walls?' he asked. 'It looks like you could pack up your room and disappear without a trace in less than ten minutes. We were wondering if your family was in some kind of witness protection programme. Are you living in a safe house under an assumed identity? Might you just disappear one day without telling us?'

'It's because none of us really wants to accept that we've moved here,' I explained. 'It's the same with Mum and Dad's room. Only Ben has made everything exactly the same as it was in London. Luke hasn't even bothered to put his clothes in drawers. He keeps everything in boxes and bags on the floor.'

'Luke sleeps with a lot of girls,' said Jay.

'You think that's why his room is a shit hole?'

'My room is a shit hole and I haven't got lucky.'

I laughed to give myself time to analyse his response. Were we both equally inexperienced? Because boys do Sex Ed on the Internet, which makes them long on knowledge and short on experience. In which case sex could be reminiscent of the Biology class when we had to put the condom on a banana and Mr Harvey messed it up by peeling it first and then apologized 'for the cock-up' with no sense of irony.

Or did he mean he had slept with other girls but just not as many as Luke? It was a more intimidating thought but might prove a better outcome. I hadn't seen him hanging out with any girls at school, so maybe he was talking about girlfriends at his old school in Ibiza.

'That's not enough of a sample group to draw any conclusions or do you have more empirical evidence?' I asked, doing a pretty good imitation of Mr Harvey.

'Judging by his disastrous condom technique, I would say Mr Harvey's bedroom is pretty tidy,' said Jay, lobbing a pillow at me. I caught it and tried to throw it back but Jay was too quick for me. We tussled over the pillow for a moment and then suddenly he was on top of me, straddling my hips and pinning down my arms with his hands. 'What do you think? Can you elaborate?'

'I would say the empirical evidence suggests that was his first relationship with a tropical fruit,' I responded. We laughed. Really laughed. Jay let go of my arms and I could feel the weight of him on top of me, his thighs squeezing my hips.

'If you want to start *Breaking Bad* some time this year, you better start soon,' said Jay, staring down at me. He leaned towards me and kissed me on the lips. And then suddenly Mum was in his bedroom. I still can't work out how she actually got there and why we didn't hear her come in. Afterwards Jay joked about her being a shape-shifter but I didn't laugh. She stared at us for a moment, her eyes darting from me to Jay.

'What the hell is going on here? Downstairs now.' Her face was bright red. Even the tip of her nose and her earlobes. I focused on the earlobes because she was wearing the pair of yin and yang earrings that I had given her for Christmas and I thought that if she remembered them she might pull back from the brink. They were meant to bring harmony but she looked angrier than when Luke told her that he'd done an essay on how magic mushroom omelette was his favourite meal in his GCSE English, angrier than when Grandpa got drunk at Granny's funeral and asked the caterer if she would come and live with him, angrier than when Dad told her a few weeks ago that he had been offered a part-time teaching post at his old university, which meant he'd have to go to London once a month.

Jay threw himself off me and sat straight-backed on the edge of the bed. After all Mum was his headmistress.

'We're just watching *Breaking Bad*, Mrs Field,' said Jay politely. 'Romy said she'd watched the first series so I figured you wouldn't mind. It's an American series. Won loads of Emmys.'

'I thought you were outside with the others,' Mum said.

'I was cold so I came back in. Please, can you stop acting so weird?'

Then Loveday was in the room, asking if everything

was fine. We all agreed that it was even though it wasn't, and Jay and I fled downstairs. Mum looked shocked but I think it was with herself rather than me.

Back in the kitchen Ben was taking photos of the meal with Mum's old iPod Touch. Dad had given her a new iPhone for Christmas that she hadn't even bothered to take out of its packaging. Everyone was circling the table with plates and cutlery, piling up food, completely unaware of what had just occurred upstairs. I didn't feel like eating any more. I followed Jay around the table, taking whatever he took, and then sat down beside him opposite Marley and Luke.

'What's up?' asked Luke.

'Mum's gone mad,' I said, trying to muster a smile.

'Old news.' Luke shrugged.

'This is amazing,' said Rachel, who was now more than slightly drunk. A pomegranate seed was stuck to her cheek.

'Wolf cooked it all,' said Loveday.

'It's good for a man to know how to cook,' said my grandfather. 'I wish I had learned.'

'Three and a half whiskies,' I heard Dad whisper to Rachel. He gestured to my aunt to pour water into my grandfather's glass but she ignored him. Then Dad tried to pull off the pomegranate seed but she swatted his hand away.

'I've existed off Weetabix and baked beans since Georgia died,' said my grandfather. 'Plus the odd raw carrot that I've pulled out of the garden. It's played havoc with my lower intestine.'

'At least it's low fat,' I said, hoping to distract him from talking about his bowel movements.

'There's a chicken pie in the freezer that Georgia made, but I can't bear to eat it. Otherwise I'll never eat anything cooked by her again. The day before she died I threw away half an apple pie that she had made just because the crust was a little stale and I knew she'd make another one. I regret that now. Just as I regret that our last conversation was an argument. Her last words to me were that I was a cantankerous old fart.'

'She was right of course,' said Rachel. Everyone laughed.

Mum came into the kitchen. Her face was flushed and her eyes looked a little puffy. She didn't look at me. Dad piled food on a plate for her and she sat down beside Wolf.

'Are you all right?' Dad asked her. And that's when I knew she wasn't because parents only ask each other if everything is all right when it isn't.

'We would have been married fifty years in October,' said my grandfather.

'That's an amazing achievement,' said Wolf.

'None of us thought that Mum would go before Dad,' said Rachel. 'There was no forewarning. Just a little tiredness. We didn't factor in the stress of living with Dad for half a century.'

'Rachel,' warned Mum.

'Would you boys like some beers?' Wolf asked Marley and Luke. They waved half-empty bottles in response. 'Romy?'

'No, thanks,' I said.

'Romy's not a big drinker,' said Mum.

'It's so annoying when parents think they know you better than you know yourself, isn't it, Romy?' said Loveday, smiling at me. At that moment I felt she knew me better than Mum. Or that at least her version of me was closer to who I was than Mum's version.

Then Loveday got up and put on the radio. Big Ben rang out midnight. I realized I no longer missed London. We all stood up and cheered, champagne was opened, and even though I didn't like the taste, I had a glass to prove Mum wrong. Loveday and Rachel shrieked and embraced and then pulled apart, uncertain what to do next. Ben fired a party popper in Luke's face and burned his cheek. Jay expertly slit open the leaf of an aloe vera plant that was sitting on the windowsill and rubbed the juice on the burn. Dad headed towards Mum, but she put up her arm and he ended up awkwardly shaking her hand as though they had come to the end of a business meeting. Grandpa wiped away a tear and made a weak joke about a man called Wolf giving him a bear hug. Jay and I turned towards each other. I waited for a gesture, a quick hug, his hand on my hand or even a high five. We stared at each other and then he looked away.

'It's time for a game,' announced Loveday, clapping her hands to get everyone's attention.

'I think perhaps we should be getting back,' said Mum apologetically. 'I need to get up early to try and get Dad home and Ben is way past his sell-by date. So is Dad.' She looked at my grandfather, waiting for him to agree.

'Don't use me as an excuse, I haven't had so much fun in ages,' said Grandpa, who looked happier than I'd seen him since Granny died.

'We play it every New Year's Eve,' pleaded Loveday. 'Please. It's a family ritual.'

'Ben takes after his grandfather,' said Dad. 'He's a night owl. He'll be fine. And if he gets bored he can watch TV.'

'I'm a night owl that has drunk three cans of Coke,' said Ben. 'Can I play too?'

'Open to all comers,' said Loveday, sensing victory.

'What's it called?' asked Ben.

'Resolutions,' said Loveday. 'It's very easy. All of you need to write down four New Year resolutions, put them in a hat and then we go round the table, trying to guess who has made each one.'

'How do you win?' asked Ben.

'It's not really about winning, it's more about what you learn along the way,' said Loveday. 'But you get a point every time you guess right first time.'

'What's the point of playing a game if you can't win it?' insisted Ben.

'It's a psychological game. Should appeal to the neuroscientist in you, Harry,' explained Loveday.

Someone turned up the music. Wolf handed round pens and paper and poured more champagne.

'It's a game about renewal. Makes you think about what you want from life over the next twelve months,' he said encouragingly. 'And what you don't want. Gives you a road map anyway. You can be as silly as you like as long as you mean what you say. Be true to yourself.'

'Sounds fun,' said Mum, but I knew she was counting the minutes until she could escape.

'Do you get it?' Jay asked me. It was the first thing he had said to me since we came downstairs.

'Sure,' I said.

'Don't forget to disguise your handwriting,' he warned.

Everyone fell quiet as they wrote down their resolutions, folded up the tiny bits of paper and threw them into a hat in the middle of the table. Ben demanded to go first. The hat was passed to him and he pulled out the first piece of paper.

'Grow a beard,' he shouted gleefully. 'I guess Luke because Wolf has already got a bit of a goatee going, Grandpa doesn't trust anyone with a beard and Jay looks as though he's shaved off even his chest hair.'

'Got it in one,' said Luke, who had got so hairy over the past six months that I wondered if he was taking a testosterone supplement.

'Very good, Ben,' said Loveday appreciatively. 'You're a natural.'

Ben unfurled another piece of paper. 'Learn to use a

ride-on lawnmower.' This one required more careful thought. He stared at the piece of paper, looking serious.

'It's not Wolf or Loveday,' he said, 'because you can't sit on their lawnmower.'

'How do you know what our lawnmower looks like? We've never used it here,' asked Wolf, looking genuinely puzzled.

'We saw it the day you moved in,' I said quickly. Ben looked relieved.

He made a few guesses. Adam. Harry. Luke. All were wrong. Finally when everyone began to wonder whether it was a bluff, Mum confessed that it was her.

'I want to get back into gardening,' she said, pleased by everyone's surprised faces. This was significant. Dad effusively welcomed the idea, rashly offering to buy Mum a second-hand one as an early birthday present.

'That's great, Mum,' said Ben. 'I'll buy you some daffodils. You used to love them in our old garden. Do you remember, Mum?' Luckily everyone was too drunk to notice the insistence in Ben's tone.

The next round was mostly very guessable. After a couple of stumbles Dad correctly concluded that 'Eat meat' belonged to Loveday, who for the first time in twenty years had woken up craving rare steak. 'Make a film' wasn't Marley or Luke but in fact Ben, who proudly held up Mum's old iPod Touch to announce he wanted to be a director. There was a pause while Mum explained to Wolf and Loveday that Aunt Rachel was a script editor who had worked on at least a couple of films they had seen. Wolf sweetly asked Ben if he would make a film of the building he was constructing in the woods at the bottom of their garden. Ben agreed.

I remember Jay's resolutions best of all. They were quirky and funny. 'Stop eating my toenails' caused collective disgust. 'Run a mile for every hour of computer each day' followed nicely from his resolution to get a six-pack.

'Typically egocentric,' said Marley, whose aspirations centred on a surprising desire to please his girlfriend. 'Get a Brazilian' was clearly Aunt Rachel.

'Why not an Argentinian?' questioned Ben. 'Like Messi. I'd really like him to be my uncle.'

My grandfather's first resolution was to show more gratitude to his children. He raised his glass to Mum and Rachel. His second was to drink less. That was slightly ruined when he celebrated by finishing off his glass of whisky and decided to switch to champagne for the rest of the night. His third fooled everyone.

'Take a holiday alone.' It was Dad's turn to guess. I could tell he was worried it was Mum because he made a weak joke about it and tried to catch her eye. When she didn't respond, he asked her directly, except it sounded more like an accusation than a question.

'Why on earth would Ailsa want to go away without you?' Loveday asked, leaning in towards him to rest her head on his shoulder. 'If she abandons you, Harry, you can always come to Ibiza with us.'

'I might want to get away from me,' said Dad.

'It's not me,' said Mum a little too quickly.

'It's me,' confessed my grandfather, delighted by all the attention. There was a break to discuss where he might go and whether he should join one of those guided trips advertised in the newspaper or find a nice hotel somewhere in Europe. I heard Rachel ask Dad how a tour company might cope with an unpredictable binge drinker and Mum telling Rachel that of course he would never go but it was good he was thinking about the future. I willed them not to start an argument.

Luke pulled another clue from the hat. 'Learn to drive.'

'That belongs to you, Luke,' said Ben. 'Put it back.'

'It's not me,' said Luke. 'I've already learned to drive.'

'Not sure about your use of the past tense,' said Dad, who had been giving him lessons for the past month.

Luke looked at Mum, shook his mane of long thick hair and smiled. His intuition was correct.

'Very funny, Mum,' he said. Everyone laughed as Mum confirmed his hunch.

'Mum and Luke are almost telepathic,' I explained. 'Sometimes it's quite spooky.'

I think it was at this point that I realized Dad hadn't joined in the game. I felt guilty for not noticing and annoyed with Mum, who must have realized much earlier and said nothing. I looked over at Dad and thought how sad he seemed. He was pouring wine in Loveday's glass, and when she put her hand on his to tell him to stop I swear I saw him wince. He gave one of his quick smiles that disappeared so fast you questioned whether you had really seen it in the first place. The diagonal frown line between his eyebrows that used to appear when he was tired was now there all the time.

And I blamed Mum because his happiness was her responsibility. She was the one who had forced him to come here. I thought about his lonely desk in the base-ment surrounded by walls of boxes and I blamed her for that too. Because they followed the rules in the good parenting handbook, they had presented the move here as a joint decision. But of course this was never the case. He had actually given up his job, his friends, his poker nights and his place on the football team at the univer-sity where he used to work, all for Mum's sake. And still it wasn't enough. She was still unhappy. I wish I had written 'Look after Dad' on one of the pieces of paper.

Luke took the last resolution out of the hat, looked at it and then screwed it up into a tiny ball and put his beer bottle on top of it.

'I'm not going there,' he said. 'It's just not right.' He looked slightly panicked.

'That's unlike you to know when to stop,' joked my grandfather, grabbing it from beneath the beer bottle. 'It must be one that you put in.'

'Leave it, Grandpa,' said Luke. But it was too late. He was carefully ironing out the tiny piece of paper with his hand. He held it up to his nose and read it out: 'Get laid.'

Loveday drunkenly started to list the people round the table who it couldn't apply to.

'Mum,' warned Marley. 'We've only just met these people.'

'I think perhaps we should stop here,' said Dad. 'It's a family game.'

'I know what it means,' interrupted Ben, assuming that everyone wanted the game stopped for his sake. 'I'm old enough to play.'

Wolf stood up and carefully put all the resolutions into the hat.

'Let's go outside and burn them,' he said. 'That's the last part of the game. Otherwise they don't come true.'

He left the one that Luke had pulled out last on the table. I saw Mum waiting until everyone else had left the room and then examining the handwriting, convinced that it must be me. But it wasn't. Which meant it must be Jay.

My phone buzzed.

Keep your curtains open.

5

'Get in the car, Romy. Grandpa isn't answering the phone. We need to go right away. Please.' Ailsa rehearsed the sentence out loud a couple of times, experimenting with word order and tone, using Lucifer, who was sitting on the kitchen table, as a substitute for Romy, who had been avoiding her for the best part of a week.

If anyone asked what was wrong with Romy after New Year's Eve, Ailsa said that she was about to get her period. Talk of menstruation closed down most unwanted lines of questioning among other members of the family, even Ben, who was the most interested in bodily functions. Ailsa didn't need to interpret Romy's icy silence. She knew her daughter was furious with her.

'I messed up, Lucifer,' she told the cat, this time doing a poor imitation of Wolf's Texan accent. Lucifer gave a languid yawn.

She hadn't told Harry what had happened that night, even though he would have rescued the comedy in the situation. She didn't want to be reminded of the toxic mix of anger and embarrassment on Romy's face when she had burst into Jay's room. Or relive the moment when she had sobbed on Loveday's shoulder, one hot cheek resting on a lace bra strap as tears slid down that dark cleft between her next-door neighbour's breasts. 'You need to tune into the earth's frequency and release those emotions,' Loveday had said, holding her hands, palms down and fingers splayed, just above Ailsa's head to draw out negativity. Mostly she didn't want to think about the way she had lost her self-control. She blamed the cocktail. Hadn't Kenny Chesney written a song about tequila sending you crazy?

She cut herself a slice of bread and put it in the toaster. It could have been worse, she told herself, adopting Ben's favourite tactic when he messed up. Romy and Jay could have witnessed the scene with Loveday; Ailsa could have done something unhinged like kiss her on those full lips; or the stale sickly smell of Loveday's patchouli oil could have made her vomit all over the irreplaceable antique Seminole Indian skirt.

Instead the worst thing that had happened was that when her mobile rang the next day and Loveday's number flashed up on the screen Ailsa knew she had to take the call and invite her round for a cup of tea. There was always a price to be paid for intimacy with strangers and Ailsa implicitly understood that this was the quid pro quo for Loveday's discretion. Loveday wanted to talk about what had happened, so Ailsa pre-empted the conversation by quickly explaining before she had even sat down at the kitchen table that it was her first Christmas without her mother and that if she talked about how she felt she would cry again.

'Is this, like, an elaborate ploy to force me into a road trip with you, Mum?' Romy asked, trying to suppress a smile as she sloped into the kitchen, shoulders hunched and headed towards the fridge. She had obviously over-heard Ailsa's exchange with the cat.

'Good use of *ploy*. Bad use of *like*,' Ailsa responded, recognizing this was a rapprochement of sorts. She tried not to sound too pleased about the exchange.

'*Like* is a verbal filler. Even the Anglo-Saxons used them. I'm surprised you don't appreciate that.' Romy opened the fridge door as wide as it could go. She took out a carton of milk and swallowed the contents in great gulps and then left the carton dripping on its side on the kitchen counter.

'Why is there never anything to eat in this house?' Romy asked, ignoring the loaf of bread that was now soaking up the pool of spilt milk. She said the same thing every morning. Even when the fridge was full.

'I can't get hold of Grandpa again.' Ailsa had lost count of how many times this had happened over the past six months. 'I've been trying since seven o'clock in the morn-ing.' She dialled the landline again and let it ring and ring.

'Try the cleaning lady,' Romy suggested.

'I did. She told me he'd fired her before Christmas. I had no idea. She was so upset she could hardly speak.'

'Did she say why?'

'Because she kept touching things that belonged to Granny. She tried to tidy her dressing table and threw away a vase of flowers Granny had picked from the garden.'

'They must have been there for months.'

'Nothing left of them but a few shrivelled petals and dead stalks. He's not himself.'

'I'll come with you,' said Romy finally. 'But I'm doing it for Grandpa not you.'

'Where are you both going?'

They both jumped as Ben popped up from behind the sofa in the sitting room, clutching one of his notebooks. He brought it over to the table and showed them intricate drawings of the building Wolf was constructing in the woods and announced that he was going to spend the day helping to put on the roof.

'Wolf asked me to film the whole process,' he said proudly.

'How fantastic,' said Ailsa. Her enthusiasm was less for the film than for the fact that if Ben was next door Harry wouldn't be able to complain about not being able to work.

'Can you go and tell Dad what's happening, please, Romy?'

'Where is he?'

'In his office in the basement. Working.'

'You mean the storeroom?'

'It's his office, actually.'

'How can anyone work in that mess? Why don't you make it nice? Why don't you make an effort for him?'

'Dad can look after himself.'

'Don't you find the lyrics to this song completely dubious and banal?' asked Ailsa as they hit the road that snaked along the coast later that morning. As part of her appeasement she had put on Radio 1 as soon as they got in the car. But for the first twenty minutes of the journey Romy had barely looked up from her phone. Her elegant fingers had fluttered across the screen as she sent messages and scrolled up and down.

Ailsa remembered her as a tiny baby tracing intricate patterns in the air with her fingers like a semaphore as she slept and how Harry had pretended he could decipher their secret meaning. 'Our spiritual leader says we should open another bottle of Chablis,' he would say so that Ailsa couldn't protest. Unlike Rachel, she had never developed much of a taste for alcohol.

Seeing her father drunk as a child had been the best aversion therapy, she had joked to Harry shortly after they met, entertaining him with amusing anecdotes about his drunken mishaps (Adam mistakenly getting into bed with the wife of one of his friends during a family holiday in Spain; Adam turning up drunk for a school open day and having a row with the History teacher over American involvement in the Second World War; Adam stopping off at a pub on his way to deliver a George III dresser to a client in London and coming back at closing time to find it stolen).

'Addiction is a disease of the brain,' Harry had replied with utter conviction and without any sense of judgement. It seemed incredible now that Harry's certainty had been one of his main attractions.

'If they're dubious, which they are, they can't really be banal,' said Romy suddenly, just as Ailsa had abandoned the idea of conversation.

'What does he mean when he says you know you want it?' Ailsa waved her hand for emphasis and accidentally hit the windscreen wipers.

'I think you know what he means. I think you have a radar for it,' said Romy in a bored tone. 'It's been controversial.'

'Like he doesn't think no means no,' Ailsa continued.

'That's why it's called "Blurred Lines",' said Romy. 'Lots of people find it kind of rapey.'

'Do you?'

'Mum, if you are trying to get into a conversation about New Year's Eve and how my body is my temple and the importance of having sex within the context of a loving relationship, then I've heard it all before. But relationships take up a lot of time and energy that I could be using for revision. They hold you back. I need to be really focused if I want to get into medical school.'

'Aren't the lyrics repetitive?' said Ailsa, trying to regain equilibrium.

'You know, Mum, sometimes it's good to be brain dead. To think about nothing. Stops your imagination running wild. You should try it some time. Stop analysing everything and see if you loosen up a little.'

Romy always expressed her frustration with her hands, and Ailsa could tell from her wild gesticulations that she had annoyed her again. Romy pulled headphones from her bag and indicated that she was going to listen to her own music.

Ailsa glanced at Romy's long delicate fingers as

they unravelled the headphones. Harry had excitedly announced when Romy was around ten years old that she had surgeon's hands after watching her painting a picture of wild flowers in a jam jar in the kitchen at her grandparents' house. Ailsa suddenly remembered how Romy had once spent hours painting sprigs of heather picked from the marshes and then held up the painting, tilted her head left and then right and knotted her brow. Before anyone realized what she was thinking she had torn it up into tiny pieces because it wasn't perfect. Harry's excitement about her steady hands had eclipsed the more significant revelation about her uncompromising nature.

'I don't like this song either, Mum. You should have more faith in my judgement. In everything.'

Romy was completely right. Ailsa felt guilty. It was the first time that her daughter had failed to match her expectations. Over the past year Romy had remained steadfast. She had accepted moving out of London with relative equanimity, especially compared to her brothers. She had worked like a dog for her GCSEs, even as her familiar world crumbled around her, and scored some of the highest results in her year. She had changed school and apparently fairly seamlessly fallen in with a new group of friends. Romy was entitled to have sex with whoever she wanted to. After all hadn't Ailsa at almost exactly the same age? Maybe that was the problem.

Another niggling thought weevilled its way into Ailsa's head. This was less palatable. Maybe she required

Romy to be predictable to counterbalance Luke. She could talk to people about Romy's aspirations and achievements and in the next breath joke about Luke's recent rocky patch and total lack of ambition. Romy made her feel like a good mother. Luke didn't.

'I'm really sorry, Romy. I shouldn't have reacted like that. I was being overprotective. I mean, you haven't even had a proper boyfriend and suddenly I find you straddled beneath some boy you hardly know with your skirt halfway up your hips. What am I meant to think?'

'I do know Jay. We're at school together and I like him, but he's not my type, and even if he was, I wouldn't stand a chance after your psycho-mum episode. You should trust me more.'

'I realize that now. Actually, I realized it almost immediately. And I do trust you, but can you see how I might have misinterpreted the scene?'

'Even if there was something going on, you still had no right to barge in like that.'

'First love can be very powerful,' said Ailsa. 'Even overwhelming. All subsequent relationships are cast in its shadow. Like a chimera.'

'Is that so, Obi-Wan Kenobi?' said Romy, looking down at her phone again.

'So significant that Dad has dedicated an entire chapter of his book to it,' Ailsa gamely continued. She precised the chapter explaining how love flooded the brain with dopamine. 'Like a tsunami, Romy. Heart rate and blood pressure go up. Serotonin levels go down, which takes away your appetite and affects your mood. Activity in the amygdala slows down, judgement is impaired and fear is suppressed. Lust makes people do irrational things, Romy.'

'You make it sound like an illness.'

'Actually it is. "There is always some madness in love. But there is always some reason in madness."'

'Who said that?' asked Romy.

'Nietzsche. I found it for the beginning of Dad's chapter.'

'I thought Nietzsche was meant to be a complete kill-joy,' said Romy.

'He fell in love with the wrong person,' said Ailsa.

Romy groaned. 'Know when to stop, Mum. That's what you're always telling us.'

'This is a big year for you.'

'Don't you think I know that?'

'And sex is great as part of a long-term loving relationship . . . but you have to choose the right person.'

Even as she said it Ailsa wasn't sure she believed it herself. Sex was sometimes even better when you knew you wouldn't see the person ever again.

'Mum, please, you're beginning to sound like one of those banal songs you hate so much.'

'You don't want to get distracted by a load of messy link-ups —'

'Hook-up not link-up, Mum. Have you considered that you might be having the right conversation with the wrong child? Luke is the king of the hook-up, not me.'

It was true. A couple of weeks after he started school last term Luke had asked if he could invite someone home for the night. Gratified that at last they might get to meet a potential girlfriend, Ailsa and Harry had enthusiastically agreed. But Luke and the girl got home so late and she left so early that they never got to meet her. The following night he brought a different girl home. On Monday morning Ailsa had found a thong, coiled like a spring, under his bed. The next weekend, a different girl had made so much noise at 3 a.m. that she had woken them up.

When Harry casually mentioned to Luke the next day that they could hear everything, 'and I mean everything', Luke joked they should feel proud that he was such an unselfish lay. Harry said it was unfortunate that he didn't pay the same kind of close attention to his schoolwork. Shortly after this they decided to tell Luke their recently implemented policy of allowing girls to stay the night was over. They explained that when they rashly agreed to his request, they hadn't realized he would bring home a different girl every night. Luke argued the experiment hadn't lasted long enough to draw any conclusions. Harry remained resolute and bravely tried to have a conversation about sexually transmitted diseases, even going as far as to point out that there was a link between throat cancer and oral sex with reference to Michael Douglas. 'Please. I get it, Dad,' said Luke, putting up his hand. Their brief foray into liberal parenting was over.

'We spoke to Luke. He's reined himself in.'

'Don't be ridiculous. He just takes them back to other shag pads. Now, please. Let me listen to my music.'

Ailsa took a hand off the steering wheel and fumbled for the headphones and pinned them down in Romy's lap.

'Look, it's been a tough Christmas, Romy. We're all trying to find our way without Granny. It's new territory for everyone. And Grandpa isn't coping very well without her. We all miss her. I'm sorry I overstepped the mark.'

'You can't blame everything on Granny dying.'

'I don't.'

'I even heard Dad tell the Fairports we moved here because she died. It's not true. You had already sold the house in London. Why do you and Dad keep rewriting history to suit your own version of events?'

Romy put on the headphones. She turned up the volume until it was so loud Ailsa could hear she was listening to Tim Hardin. 'Reason to Believe'. It was a track written before Ailsa was born.

Their conversation was over but progress had been made. Romy turned away from Ailsa to stare out of the window at the slate-grey sky. Ailsa switched off the radio. She had reached a long flat stretch of coast where an estuary meandered out to the sea across boggy fields. A few sheep were standing under trees blown into strange arthritic contortions by the wind. The sea was raging.

She drove faster, anxious about her father. The road snaked closer to the coast and marshland where she had grown up. A land with no foreground, her father called it. It was true there were no trees, no gates or railings. It was a land without limits.

Ailsa caught the flash of a rock pool glimmering under the hoary grey sky and knew that beneath its inky surface it would be bubbling with molluscs, crabs and sand shrimps. She passed the turn to a beach where a dead sperm whale had been washed up one summer when they were teenagers. They had gone to see it with their mother and Rachel. She frowned with the effort of recalling all the details. They had walked all the way there. Why hadn't they gone by car? Then she remembered Georgia couldn't drive because her arm was in plaster and she couldn't change gear. Her mother had wiped away discreet tears. Was she crying for herself or for the whale? Rachel had wondered.

When the golden ridge of shingle bank appeared in the distance Ailsa knew she was almost home. Behind lay the beach where she had bunked off school to go swimming on hot summer afternoons. A bird flew over the road. It was a spoonbill. The way he carried his neck drawn back between his shoulders was a dead giveaway.

The presence of her mother was so overwhelming that for a moment Ailsa forgot that she had come to the house to check on her father. Or that Romy was waiting in the car outside. A pile of unopened envelopes addressed to Mrs Georgia Peploe caught her eye on the hall table. Beside it lay one of her mother's notebooks with floral covers. Ailsa picked it up and turned to the last entry. There was a carefully handwritten list of guests to be invited to their fiftieth wedding anniversary party. A few names had been struck off, not because they had fallen out of favour but because they had died before the invitations were sent out. 'The curse of Peploe,' Adam had joked. Less than a week later Georgia was dead and the list was being used to let the same friends know about funeral plans. Totally unexpected. No flowers. Donations to be made to the British Heart Foundation.

This room was the last place she had seen her mother alive. Ailsa now wished the content of her last conversation with her had been more significant. If she had known she would never see Georgia again, what would she have asked her? She might have asked why she had stuck with their father through the lost years. If there was a point in her life where she felt she could relax and know that everything was sorted. Whether Georgia had any inkling about what had happened the night before Ailsa got married. And if she did, why she had never said anything.

Instead they had a slightly cross conversation about why it was correct in a mobile phone conversation to say a call was breaking up but not that it was breaking down. Since Georgia hardly ever used her mobile phone and rarely switched it on because she was afraid of wasting the battery, it was a particularly futile exchange. But Ailsa knew it was a displacement argument to avoid discussing the end of Rachel's most recent relationship.

'Let's hope Rachel's break-up doesn't lead to a

breakdown,' her mother had said finally, trying to introduce levity back into the conversation.

'Marriage isn't the only construct available to forty-something women nowadays, Mum,' said Ailsa. 'Rach has a great job, great friends and some pretty exciting relationships. A quarter of women her age don't have children any more.'

'What will she do when she's sixty?' asked Georgia. 'She could be living alone for the next third of her life.'

'She can move in with one of her gay friends.'

Her mother had gone over to the bookshelf that dominated the right side of the room and pulled out a pocket guide to the birds of Britain. She had opened it on a page dedicated to the Arctic tern and excitedly explained that for only the second time in her life she had seen one on the marshes the previous day.

'It travels over 44,000 miles a year so that it can have two summers. One here and one in the Arctic,' Georgia marvelled as she showed Ailsa a picture of a bird that was indistinguishable from a seagull apart from its blood-red bill. 'So it makes the most of everything. That's how we should all live. And it mates for life. Amazing.'

She went on to say that she was alone when she spotted it and that Adam doubted that she had really seen it at all because only two had been sighted in the past decade.

'If you knew how to work your phone you could have taken a photo to prove him wrong,' Ailsa had chided her.

'I know what I saw,' said Georgia. 'And that's all that matters. As long as you know the truth, it doesn't matter what anyone else thinks.'

The cardigan her mother had been wearing that day was still hanging over the back of the armchair from where Georgia used to watch the sun set over the marshes in the evening through the hall window. Ailsa couldn't help herself: she closed her eyes and lifted the cardigan to her nose and inhaled the scent of her mother. It was a blend of the Anais Anais perfume she had worn for the best part of half a century, the heathery musk of the marshes and smoke from the fire she was tending in the garden when her heart failed her. When Ailsa dropped the cardigan back onto the chair, she felt light-headed with loss.

'Dad,' she called out as she went from the hall into the small kitchen at the back of the house. No one answered. The floor was like a hamster cage. There were porridge oats, grains of instant coffee and scabs of burned rice underfoot. Ailsa crunched her way over to the sink. It was full of dirty crockery. On the windowsill she found his pills untouched.

She opened the dishwasher but shut it immediately because the smell of decaying food and rancid milk was overwhelming. Apart from a half-bottle of tonic water and an open tin of baked beans, the fridge was almost empty. The freezer, however, was filled with all the food that Ailsa had made. There were portions of shepherd's pie, chicken casserole, meatballs, neatly marked with labels and suggestions about which vegetables might be compatible. None had been used. Ailsa could tell from the empty packets of Weetabix and the bottles lined up by the back door that Adam was probably existing on a diet of breakfast cereal washed down with milk and whisky.

'Dad,' she called out again. She went into the sitting room, half prepared to find him slumped in a chair. An old bar heater that had lost its grille glowed red hot in the corner and steam emanated from a pair of underpants that he was drying on an upturned bucket just inches away from the bars. Ailsa tried to remove them from the bucket but they had fused to the melted plastic. A cup of tea was stuck to the surface of the table. Ailsa dipped a finger into the mug. It was stone cold. Feeling anxious, she headed towards the staircase. She ignored the banks of photographs on the wall as she went up, taking the stairs two at a time.

'Adam,' she shouted, thinking he might respond to his name. Since Georgia had died he had started taking a nap in the afternoon. He hated getting into bed on his own, he had confessed to Ailsa over Christmas. It took him hours to get to sleep and he woke up as soon as it got light in the morning. Not wanting to frighten him, Ailsa tentatively opened his bedroom door. The bed covers were so crumpled that it took a moment for Ailsa to realize there wasn't a body beneath.

The back legs of the bed were still broken, and it now sloped at an even steeper angle. Ailsa could see that her father had tried to prop up the base with a makeshift pile of bricks that had collapsed, leaving a fine coating of red dust over the furniture. The sheets were filthy. He might have been sleeping in his shoes. On the bedside table on the side where her mother used to sleep, nothing had been moved. A book lay face down in the same position as her mother had left it. *Slipstream* by Elizabeth Jane Howard. There was a half-drunk glass of water. Ailsa held it up to the light and could see the faint imprint of her mother's lipstick around the rim. Georgia's nightdress was still under the pillow.

He wasn't here. The bedroom window was open. It was so cold that Ailsa could see her own quickening breath. She looked outside and saw Romy in the car below. She tried to attract her attention, shouting and knocking on the glass, but Romy was wired up to the headphones, oblivious. She looked out towards the marshes, wondering if Adam had gone for a walk. He had slowed down over the past six months, and when the tide was in it was a struggle for him to get beyond the first few small wooden bridges across the mudflats. She couldn't see him.

Ailsa went back downstairs and out into the back garden and stood for a moment in the exact place where Georgia's heart had stopped beating, trying to collect her thoughts. Her father was the one who took a cocktail of pills for blood-pressure problems, high cholesterol and palpitations, and it had been an unspoken assumption that he would go first. So there had been no dress rehearsal for the moment when Adam had phoned to say their mother had gone outside to light a fire in the garden and never come back in.

Most likely sudden cardiac arrest, the paramedics explained to Adam. A loud label for such a silent death, Adam told Ailsa and Rachel when they arrived. He was sitting at the kitchen table in shock. His hands shook so much that the cup of sugary tea made for him by a paramedic slopped onto his trousers. She told him over and over again that there was nothing he could have done. The electrical pulse in Georgia's heart had catastrophically short-circuited. The blood supply to her lungs and brain had been immediately cut off.

'We were having an argument,' Adam said, wiping huge tears from his face with a tea towel. 'I thought she was ignoring me but she was suffocating like the fish I killed in Canada. She died, gasping for air, while I sat at the kitchen table arguing about how many people to invite to our party.'

'If arguments killed, Mum would have been dead long ago, Dad,' said Rachel, trying to be comforting. She was crying too, Ailsa remembered.

'I can't believe she's gone,' he sobbed.

The first couple of months after she died Ailsa kept seeing Georgia everywhere. Through the window of a train pulling out from Shepherd's Bush station; walking through the Department of Neuroscience to meet Harry for lunch; and in the sushi restaurant at the

Westfield shopping centre. It was strange, she explained to Rachel, because she thought she saw her in places where Georgia had never gone, and yet when she went up to Norfolk she never had the same sensation. 'That's because you can feel her presence there. You don't need to look for her,' Rachel had said. It was true. In this house and on the marshes her mother was everywhere.

Now her father had disappeared. Ailsa had read a statistic about how 20 per cent of married couples died within six months of their spouse dying, and Adam was doing his best to conform to this pattern. She headed back to the car, opened the door and removed the headphones from Romy's ears.

'He's not in the house. And I can't see anyone out on the marshes. Will you come and help look for him?'

Romy wordlessly climbed out. It had started sleeting, and the only coat in the car belonged to Ben. Romy allowed Ailsa to drape it around her shoulders like a cape and they headed onto the road in silence.

'He'll be in the graveyard,' said Romy in a flat, matter-of-fact tone as they walked past a couple of vacant second homes.

'How do you know?' asked Ailsa.

'He told me he goes there to have tea with Granny every afternoon.'

'I didn't know that.'

'He told me not to tell anyone.'

'It's not normal behaviour.'

'What's normal when someone dies? I thought it was

sweet. On the Day of the Dead in Mexico people go to eat on the graves of their relatives.'

'It's a lot warmer in Mexico.'

Ailsa could see the church from the road. It was built with its back to the sea, up on a hill, protected from the great flood of 1953, ridiculously large even by comparison with other churches built on the spoils of the wool trade. It also faced back to front so that the graveyard overlooked the marshes. They could see Adam sitting on the ground beside the earthy mound where Ailsa's mother was buried. He was hunched as though the bitter east wind that blew in straight from the Urals had blown him over.

'Do you think he's all right?' asked Romy.

There was a tablecloth spread over the grave and two plates with rain-soaked sandwiches on top. Adam was seated on the edge of the tablecloth, drinking from a hip flask. As they came through the gate into the churchyard, they could hear him talking loudly. Every so often he would pause. At first Ailsa thought he was catching his breath, but as they got closer she realized that he was leaving time for responses.

'I'm scared, Mum,' said Romy, slipping her hand into Ailsa's for the first time in many years. 'Do you think he's lost it?'

'He's sad and lonely and he can't cope without Granny,' said Ailsa. They reached Adam. He looked terrible. He had attempted to shave but there were small irregular islands of unkempt beard and a series of ugly gashes where he had cut himself with the razor.

'You'll tell me not to be such a foolish old bastard,' Adam was saying. 'Of course you won't say *bastard*, because you hardly ever swear, but I can't get the fucking washing machine to work. So I've been trying to wash a few things in the bathroom sink. And the cooker won't start so it's either sandwiches or cereal.'

He paused for a moment and nodded several times as if agreeing with someone.

'Regrets, of course I've got regrets, Georgia. And one of the biggest is that I didn't get you to write a manual of how all these bloody things work. And I'm sorry for the lost years. Bloody sorry.'

Every time he swore he fumbled in his pocket for a coin, which he tossed into a jam jar at the foot of the grave.

'What does he mean, *the lost years*?' asked Romy.

'He's confused,' said Ailsa gently. Dad!' She shook his shoulder. He turned round and squinted at Ailsa and Romy.

'Who are you? Have you come to mend the washing machine?' he asked through chattering teeth.

'It's me. Ailsa. And Romy.'

'The fucking Arctic tern flew over earlier. Can you believe it? Taunting me. She was always right about everything.'

'His hands are blue, Mummy,' said Romy, slipping her

own out of her mother's and reaching out for her grandfather. 'He's freezing.'

'It was probably a seagull. It's the wrong time of year for terns,' said Ailsa.

'That's what I told your mother. Why didn't I just agree with her?'

'We need to go, Dad,' said Ailsa firmly.

'Someone stole the flowers,' he said. 'I think it was that cleaning lady. The viburnum had disappeared. And it was Georgia's favourite flower and I never bought her any when she was alive.'

'Even the tip of his nose is blue,' whispered Romy, putting Ben's tiny jacket around her grandfather. 'He could have the beginnings of hypothermia. What should we do?'

'We need to get him home as quickly as possible,' said Ailsa.

Back at the car Romy found Ben's SAS survival handbook under the front seat. She brought it into the house and read the section on frostbite out loud. The words soothed Adam and he didn't protest when Ailsa pulled a bobble hat on his head. She could remember her mother knitting it and being affronted when Adam refused to wear it because it was emasculating. He argued that the enormous pompom made the top of the hat droop to one side like a limp penis.

Romy pushed the armchair with Adam sitting in it towards the bar heater and layered him with blankets until finally the pom-pom stopped quivering. Ailsa made him hot tea and held the mug to his lips, urging him to drink. He didn't try to take the cup from her. In between small sips he opened his mouth and allowed her to feed him bits of chocolate biscuit. She felt like a priest dishing out Holy Communion. It was the first time she had ever fed one of her parents and she was acutely aware of the symbolism. For a split second she wished it were her mother rather than her father. Familiar doubts swirled. She hadn't taken enough care of her mother during the lost years. If she had, maybe she would still be around. She heard Rachel's voice in her head reassuring her that it was beyond Ailsa's control.

'It says we mustn't thaw him too quickly, Mum,' Romy said. 'He needs to be slowly warmed up.'

'I'm not a shepherd's pie,' said Adam impatiently. They laughed with relief.

Ailsa reached for her phone and called Rachel. Just as she was convinced that Rachel wasn't going to pick up, she answered. Ailsa could imagine her sister frowning at the screen, trying to gauge whether taking a call from Ailsa on a Saturday afternoon might jeopardize the rest of her weekend.

'Hi, Rachel.' There was a voice in the background. Ailsa could hear Matt Harvey asking when she was coming back to bed.

'Give me one minute,' she heard Rachel tell him.

'It's Dad, Rach,' said Ailsa. Her voice caught.

'Is he OK?' asked Rachel, sounding worried.

Ailsa described in careful detail the way they had found

him almost freezing to death in a state of confusion in the graveyard, the uneaten food in the freezer, the filthy kitchen and the half-drunk bottle of whisky in his bed-room. At the end she pointed out that had they been a couple of hours later, he might have died.

'But he didn't, Ailsa.'

'He can't live on his own any more, Rach. He can't cope. His clothes are filthy. God knows when he last took a shower. He looks like a tramp.'

'Can you stop talking about me as though I'm invis-ible,' shouted Adam.

'He doesn't sound in such bad form,' said Rachel. 'Could we talk about this tomorrow? I'm on a deadline with this script.'

'I heard him.'

'What do you mean?'

'I heard my head of Biology asking you to come back to bed. He has a very distinctive voice.'

'You don't own him.'

'Is Aunt Rachel going out with Mr Harvey?' asked Romy incredulously. 'Gross.'

'I was wondering if you would come up here and spend the rest of the weekend with Dad and maybe a couple of days early next week, until we've worked out what to do?'

'I'm perfectly all right,' shouted Adam. 'Don't listen to your sister. She's overreacting. I don't need any help.'

Ailsa went over to the window out of earshot.

'I can't do it,' said Rachel. 'I've got a big meeting about

a new script next week and I need Sunday to prepare. It could be really good for me.'

'Come on, Rach. Please. We're all in this together. The new term starts for me on Monday. I have to be there.'

'Why is your career more important than mine?'

'We need to share the load, Rachel; I can't do this on my own.'

'You've got to remember Dad is a classic attention-seeker, Ailsa. He had Mum running around him for fifty years and now she's not around, he's transferring his demands to you.'

'If you were here and could see him you'd understand that he can't be left alone.'

'Well leave him with Harry then.' She paused for a moment. 'He owes you. Sorry but I've got to go. I'll call you later.'

'Don't move that,' barked Adam as Romy picked up a copy of the *Radio Times* to add to a pile of newspapers for recycling. 'Give it to me.'

'It's months out of date, Grandpa,' said Romy, looking startled.

'It's the one from the week she died,' he said, running his finger backwards and forwards over a page where episodes of *Midsomer Murders* were highlighted with fluorescent pen. 'I want to bring it with me.'

Ailsa went upstairs and bundled up her father's dirty clothes into plastic bags.

She would come back and clean up another time.

6

In our first Biology practical of the new term Mr Harvey announced that instead of dissecting a frog, he was giving us a surprise test on control, genomes and the environment to see how much we could remember. I was sitting in the middle of the back row beside Becca and she was so agitated by this that she didn't notice when Jay blew apart last term's seating arrangement by sitting down on the other side of me. He manoeuvred his stool close enough that I could feel the heat from his thigh without him actually touching me.

I took deep breaths until the comforting smell of formaldehyde and bleach hit my lungs. Then I turned over the paper and tried to concentrate on the first question. There were two pictures of cats, one a Scottish wildcat and the other a colourpoint Persian. I knew even before I looked that there would be questions on their possible genotypes, phenotypic differences and the physiological problems of domesticated cats and that I would be able to answer them all correctly. I would never tell anyone how easy this was for me.

'Have you heard? Marley Fairport's having a party,' Becca whispered.

'Luke told me,' I said under my breath.

'Think he'll invite us?' Becca asked. 'Can't cope with Marnie if he doesn't.'

'Maybe,' I said.

'Couldn't you get us invited, Roms? You spent New Year's Eve with them, didn't you?'

'I'll give it a go,' I mumbled. 'Promise.'

'Romy, get your head down,' said Mr Harvey. I felt myself blush. Mr Harvey didn't get the innuendo and blamed me when everyone giggled. Stuart Tovey turned around from the bench in front of me.

'Come on, brainiac, suck my dick,' he whispered.

'Sexist pig,' hissed Becca.

'You wouldn't say no, would you?' retorted Stuart.

From beneath his shaggy fringe Jay was watching me watching them. I stared back at him and he arched one dark eyebrow and smiled for at least a couple of beats too long. My guts twisted and I felt myself go even redder until even the tips of my ears were burning. I thought about states of matter and wondered if I was changing from solid into liquid.

'If you find it difficult to resist the temptation to chat to your friends, Romy, then I can move you to the front of the class,' warned Mr Harvey. 'Will that be necessary?'

'No,' I mumbled, trying to focus on the Persian cat.

I checked to see if Becca had noticed anything, but she was too busy glaring at the first page of questions. I thought for the first time in ages that Mum was right about something. Jay was seriously distracting.

Dad would have some logical scientific explanation for what I was experiencing. He would find it interesting and want to attach electrodes to my scalp to see which bits of my brain lit up, and run all the data through a computer program. He would then make a pronouncement about how the brain's reward system works in the same way for desire as it does for drugs. But being able to explain things doesn't mean that you can control them. I couldn't believe the King of Impulse Control would understand that.

'Imagine, one day he might be your uncle,' whispered Becca. She giggled again. It took me a while to get what she was talking about, then I remembered that I had confided in her and Marnie about Mr Harvey and my aunt. 'Maybe they'll have baby cougars.'

I groaned, grateful for the distraction. Telling Becca and Marnie was part of a deal that I had struck with myself after New Year's Eve. I reasoned that if I let them in on that, I could keep what had happened with Jay secret. Somehow even then I knew that we could wilt under too much scrutiny.

Besides I was trying to create some history with these new girlfriends and I realized Jay would only get in the way. So when I described the evening at the Fairports, I mentioned Marley, and Marnie instantly took the bait. She wanted to know what he had talked about (clubbing in Ibiza, how tattoos done with the wrong ink can cause cancer, whether you could get an electric shock from playing bass guitar with your teeth) and whether he had mentioned her (he'd asked if I'd noticed that the freckles on Marnie's nose looked like a star constellation, possibly the Big Dipper), and I told her how he said he couldn't stand bitchy girls, which was good because Marnie wasn't. She pushed me for details on what kind of girls I thought he might like and I told her that she should be herself, even though I knew that boys found Marnie too emotionally demanding. To be honest, sometimes I did too.

'Uncle Matt and Aunt Rachel,' I whispered to Becca. 'Sounds good.'

'Is there something you want to share with the class, Romy?' asked Mr Harvey, staring straight at me.

'Yes. Actually there is,' I said. I stared him down until he looked away to scan the exam paper on his desk.

Jay edged away and I felt bereft. I forced myself to tackle the first six questions without thinking about him, to prove to myself I could, and dealt with an easy one about the increased concentration of hydrogen ions and reduction in force in a contracting muscle. *Textbook*, I thought to myself as I checked back through my answers, adding a bit more detail on why athletes might take cold baths after running. I couldn't ever remember working with such clarity and wondered if this was how Stuart felt when he took his brother's ADHD medicine.

Then I rewarded myself with a lingering inspection of Jay. He was left-handed. An inherited characteristic. He bent his arm awkwardly around the paper to write, and I could see his pen was chewed down as far as the cartridge so it leaked blue ink onto his index finger. The pen looked too small in his clumsy wide hand. I examined his face and noticed how his tongue stuck out the side of his mouth and his eyes narrowed when he was concentrating hard. He had taken off his blazer and rolled up his shirtsleeves. His forearm was covered in a thin layer of fine dark hair. Just above his wrist bone was a small mole. I carefully logged all these details so I could play them back to myself later. I saved the best for last, allowed myself to glance down at his leg, and just the outline of his thigh in his black school trousers sent shock waves of pleasure through my body. This was a new experience for me, the way looking at him stirred me. I crossed and uncrossed my legs. Desire was definitely a central nervous system issue.

I checked out what Mr Harvey was up to, and when I saw he was gazing out of the window I pushed over the section I had answered on chromosomes to give Becca an unrestricted view because I knew she found this tricky. She mouthed a grateful thank you and I looked up again at Mr Harvey. He was lost in his own world. His hands were in his pockets and he was slowly rocking back and forth from his heels onto his toes. Probably lusting over my aunt. Marnie claimed she would, and we trusted her judgement because she was the only one of the three of us who had had sex, even though it was over so quickly she wasn't sure it really qualified. I couldn't see it, in the same way I couldn't really see why

Mum was freaked out by the age gap between them. They were both ancient.

I followed his gaze out of the window, across the central courtyard, where Mum's car was parked, and down to the ground floor on the opposite side of the D-shaped complex, where the canteen was located next to a series of rooms with big glass windows at the quietest end of the school. It took me a moment to realize that he was staring straight down into Mum's office. I could see her at her desk, squinting at her computer screen without typing, no doubt worrying about Grandpa, who had come to stay for two nights and almost a week later showed no symptoms of wanting to go home.

I'd heard Mum and Dad arguing about him last night. They were down in the storeroom, also known as Dad's office. The door from the storeroom into the garden was half open. I was in their bathroom, having decided to follow Jay's advice and check out the cabinet. Grandpa was in his usual position, in Dad's armchair in the sitting room next to the kitchen, reading Dad's copy of the *Guardian* and complaining about it being left wing. This was the reason for the row. But, like most arguments between parents, it wasn't about that at all. It was about everything that lurked beneath and then periodically erupted onto the surface like an outbreak of acne.

I had instructed Ben to stand outside the bedroom door in the corridor and was glad because not only would he take his duties as lookout seriously, he wouldn't hear the row taking place two floors below. I stared in the mirror of the bathroom cabinet before I opened it, turning my head from side to side, worrying that the reason Jay hadn't suggested meeting up after New Year was because my nostrils were too flared, my forehead too prominent and my mouth too pale. Luke once stopped going out with a girl because her earlobes were too big.

All this was eclipsed by what Mum said next. 'Remember, Harry, how the marriage guidance counsellor told us how important it is to identify what is annoying you and say you hate that, rather than, "I hate you."'

Good advice, I thought to myself, until it hit me that Mum was talking about her and Dad. This was serious: their marriage was in such trouble that they had recruited someone else to unravel the knots. I waited for Mum to deliver one of her favourite lines, 'Hate is a very strong word.' But she didn't. My reflection in the mirror looked worried at this unexpected revelation. Yet part of me was almost gratified. There was something wrong and I had intuited it despite what Dad called 'the fog of teenage narcissism'. The other part of me sneered at myself for not considering this possibility before. How could I not have realized? I knew the differences between a bacterial and viral infection; I knew how atoms were ionized in a mass spectrometer; and how domestic inbreeding meant Persian cats were more likely to die prematurely than wild cats. But I hadn't recognized the symptoms of my parents' marriage decaying. And yet now it was obvious what had happened. Mum had been miserable living in London. Dad had agreed to leave his job so she could take this promotion but still it wasn't enough. No matter how hard Dad tried to please her, it would never be enough.

I imagined a new reality where my parents split up, moved into different houses, and we spent every other weekend with Dad. I thought how upsetting this would be for Ben, who didn't like change, and Lucifer, who adored Dad. I imagined Luke arguing that he was old enough to decide which bed he wanted to sleep in and never visiting Dad because, although no one said it, he was closer to Mum. I tried to think of the advantages: more holidays; guilt-fuelled high-tech gifts, possibly a new iPhone; an excuse if I didn't get the grades to do medicine; finally a proper drama to share with Becca and Marnie, who wouldn't be impressed unless there was a really compelling backstory, because both their sets of parents divorced years ago.

I opened the bathroom cabinet slowly, convinced I was about to uncover conclusive evidence. Jay had briefed me what to look for. Xanax. Prozac. Seroxat. Wolf and Loveday were expert in the dark arts of self-medication, he told me. But there was nothing inside. No trace of my parents. None of Mum's Tampax nestling against Dad's razors. No spare toothpaste or antacids. No half-used suntan cream or dental floss. No strip wax. Just an unopened packet of tissues. I felt a sense of overwhelming anticlimax and turned my attention back to what was happening downstairs.

'OK,' shouted Dad. 'Have it your way.' For a moment I thought that was it. Then he continued. He had that icy staccato tone that he used when he was really angry. 'I don't hate your dad. I just hate him being here. Under this roof. I hate the way you jump every time he clicks his fingers. I hate the way he sits in my chair and scratches his nails on the arms when we're watching the news. I hate the way that when he eats toast the butter dribbles down the side of his chin. Most of all I hate the way he drinks whisky and water with his lunch and tries to pretend it's ginger beer. Is that enough to be going on with?'

I hadn't noticed Ben come into the bathroom. He was standing beside me, holding Mum's old iPod Touch, filming everything, including the empty bathroom cabinet. I should have told him to stop, to go back downstairs, that it isn't good to spy on people in case you misinterpret what's going on, but I didn't want to miss Mum's response. So I put an arm round him as he leaned towards the open window beside me.

'What can I do? He can't live on his own. We don't have enough money to pay for someone to look after him.' Mum sounded calm. Reasonable even, which was annoying because I had her playing the role of Dementor. 'I can't keep driving over to his house every couple of days after work to go and see him. Even if I only spend an hour it's a ninety-minute round trip.'

'Take him to a home,' shouted Dad.

'He's not a stray dog, Harry. It would be easier to

rehome him if he was. There isn't somewhere that we can dump him,' she said. 'We have to take responsibility.'

'Haven't we got enough on our plates?' shouted Dad. 'Luke's got A levels that he's probably going to fail. Ben is spending more time next door than with us. Why do you want to pile even more pressure on us? I don't see Rachel taking any responsibility. I see her leaving you to deal with all the shit while she fucks around with someone young enough to be her son.'

At this point I put my fingers in Ben's ears. He pulled away.

'Only if she'd had an underage pregnancy,' Mum pointed out.

'She's right,' whispered Ben. 'Aunt Rachel would have had to have given birth to Mr Harvey when she was twelve for him to be her son.'

'You know what I mean. It's absurd,' said Dad. 'She's pissing on your parade. And when it all goes tits up she'll be here too, wanting you to look after her.'

'I don't think you're really in a position to judge Rachel's behaviour, Harry,' said Mum in an ominously even tone. This was news to me because historically Dad was always judging Aunt Rachel's behaviour and finding it lacking. But before I could analyse any further Dad started shouting again. I had never heard my parents talk to each other like this. It was both shocking and mesmerizing, like the first time you learn how people really have sex.

'You're at work all day. I'm the one who has to get him lunch and make sure he hasn't wandered off somewhere.

Last week when I saw him heading down the road I just let him go. It was pouring with rain and he wasn't wearing a coat, and when he came back looking like a drowned rat I felt depressed that he hadn't fallen in a ditch and drowned. He takes bottles of wine without asking. He puts the television on full volume. I can't hear myself think let alone work properly.'

'He's only got half his hearing,' said Mum. 'Try and be more humane, Harry.'

'It's easy to be humane when you're out of the house ten hours a day and I'm at home trying to write a book, cook dinner, get Ben to do his homework, keep an eye on Luke and remind myself not to ignore Romy because she is the only member of our family who has got her shit together. Compassion fatigue sets in pretty quickly.'

'You seem to forget that the reason we're here is because of you,' said Mum coolly. That really was news to me. I waited for Dad to lob back a hand grenade of his own but he didn't. 'You're starting to believe your own propaganda, Harry.'

'You've brought him to live with us to punish me,' said Dad. His voice was quieter now. He sounded defeated. And then it stopped. Or they closed the door. *Unsatisfactorily inconclusive*, I thought to myself. It was the kind of comment that Mr Harvey would write at the bottom of my Biology homework.

I realized that I must have been staring at Mr Harvey all the time I was thinking about this row, my eyes following him even as he moved to his desk. He looked up, caught my eye, checked the clock and told us we had fifteen minutes left to finish the paper. At the end of the lesson he asked me to stay behind.

'Is everything all right, Romy?' he asked. 'You seem a little distracted.'

'Sure,' I said, wanting to get this over and done with as quickly as possible. I focused on my feet so I didn't have to look him in the eye. Even though I'm not religious I prayed that he wouldn't mention Aunt Rachel.

'I rely on you to set the tone in the classroom,' he said, piling up textbooks on his desk. 'Don't squander your talent.'

'Why don't you mark my test first and then decide if I'm squandering my talent,' I replied. He smiled. It was a good response.

'OK. Point taken. Now I was wondering whether you've thought about which medical schools you might want to apply to next year. Part of my role here is to help students who want to study science at university. Any areas you're particularly interested in? Research or surgery? Head or heart?'

'Something to do with the brain,' I mumbled, embarrassed by my certainty. 'Maybe Neurology.'

'It would be good to get some work experience. Do you think your dad could help organize something? Your mum said that you didn't do any after your GCSEs because of all the upheaval when your grandmother died.'

'Before she died,' I corrected him. 'The upheaval came before.'

'Right,' he said, clearly uninterested in the chronology. 'Let me know if I can help with anything.'

Unlike Luke, I had never been any good at working a situation to my advantage. But suddenly I saw how my Biology teacher could help me stay in Luckmore. I liked Mr Harvey, we all did, because he really cared about our results and was genuinely interested in what we wanted to do with our lives. He was solid.

'You can actually,' I blurted out. 'My aunt is so distracted by you that she's not helping my mum to take care of my grandfather, and I think it's putting a strain on my parents' marriage,' I told him. His eyes opened really wide and his forehead concertinaed. He looked so alarmed that I almost felt sorry for him. 'My parents have had to deal with a lot of stuff the past year. Maybe you could persuade Rachel to do her share? I really don't want to have to move house again.'

'I'm really sorry about all this, Romy, but I think you're blurring the lines between my professional and personal capacities. I don't have as much power as you think.'

Teachers are so bloody moist.

I was almost certain that Jay would be waiting for me outside the Biology room. I checked up and down the corridor, hoping to see a woolly thatch of black curly hair emerge from a doorway. I looked at my phone to see if he'd called. Nothing. It was now ten days since

New Year's Eve, and although we'd messaged and he was friendly at school he hadn't shown any interest in seeing me alone again. Back then there was a lot of ambiguity with Jay, and if I'd known the complications of what was coming next I might have tried to enjoy that ride a bit more.

'Radio silence. The kindest cut,' Luke always said when he was trying to let a girl down gently. I would have liked to ask Luke what might be going on in Jay's head but I knew he would take the piss and probably tell Marley. I even wondered if I had misread the signals. I had gone over that evening in my head so many times that it now ran on a loop like a well-edited short film. I remembered the weight of him as he sat on top of me, the dark hair under his arms and how he smelled of something sweet and musty, like coconut and yeast or oranges and ash. I weighed up the empirical evidence. I remembered something Mr Harvey had said about not looking for evidence to prove a hypothesis but allowing the evidence to point to the hypothesis, and finally understood what he meant. I blamed Mum for putting him off, for interfering with our energy.

In the canteen I caught up with Becca and Marnie. Every day I was grateful for the miracle of their friendship. They had adopted me on my first day at school, and forgiven me for being the daughter of the woman who had introduced a proper uniform to the school for the first time in almost quarter of a century and even worse made a rule about skirt length. Becca had come up to me in our first Biology class and asked if I would be her dissecting partner. 'Love your hair,' she said as she sliced through a pig's heart with her scalpel. Still holding the bloody scalpel she ran the fingers of her other hand through my side fringe. 'So cool. So white. Like metal.' It was as simple as that. The fact that I had lived in London sealed the deal. Luke and I were accepted simply because we'd come from Shepherd's Bush.

Becca was straightforward without being straight, which I instantly appreciated. Her features were neat and in proportion, even her nose seemed certain. She wore her brown hair in a loose ponytail, with just the right amount of stray hair poking out the side. She forced us to go and see bands we had never heard of in Norwich and join the school kickboxing club.

She introduced me to Marnie later that first day. Marnie was sitting beneath a tree at the end of the playing fields. She was in crisis. The boy in her Art class who she had fancied the entire previous year had confided in her on the last day of the summer holidays that he was gay. He loved her. They had tried to have sex. He couldn't. Marnie had draped her long hair around her face so that people couldn't see her crying. She wondered if you could have a relationship without having sex. Whether he might become straight. She cried because it was a waste that such a perfect specimen of the male species (her words not mine) didn't love women in the way she wanted to be loved.

'You can pretend to be a lot of things in life, but not

a boy, so I guess that's that,' I had said, taking a cigarette from the packet Becca was offering me. It wasn't meant to be funny, but Marnie and Becca found it hilarious.

'Oh my actual God,' laughed Marnie, using one of her favourite phrases. She stood up, so pale and thin that I wondered whether, if I blew too hard, she would topple over. Mum had this theory that everyone had a soundtrack that described their personality better than any words. After I introduced her to Marnie for the first time she played the music to *Death in Venice* and I understood completely.

'She's Mahleresque,' Dad said to Mum, who immediately questioned whether such an adjective existed.

The next day when they got on the bus they came and sat down next to me.

It took a few weeks to absorb how lucky I was to have these new friends. At Highfield there were the same cliques as back in London: the geeks, the wreck heads, the goths, the cool gang. There were kids with anger issues, a girl my age who had taken a year out to have a baby, and another who was self-harming. But everything was a little less extreme than in London. Mum said London kids looked sophisticated but were more brittle inside. I agreed with this although not with her wacky theory about how the landscape made Norfolk kids strong. But they had all known each other for years, sometimes generations, and if you didn't make friends at school there was nowhere else to go.

So as I headed towards Becca and Marnie with a tray

that was empty apart from a neat pile of salad I said a quick thanks to Philotes, the Greek goddess of friendship. I did a quick sweep of the canteen for Jay but I couldn't see him. Unlike his brother he was good at melting into the background.

'We were here first,' whispered Marnie, sounding elated. I noticed she had undone an extra button of her shirt and had taken the tie out of her sleek chestnut hair so that the ends formed upside-down question marks over each breast, but I didn't understand the significance of what she was saying until Becca's eyes darted to the opposite end of the table, where Marley, Stuart and Luke were sitting.

'What's he doing now?' Marnie asked as she fiddled with her phone.

'He's scratching his hair with a plastic fork,' said Becca.

'God, I wish I was that fork,' said Marnie.

'It's a disposable fork,' I pointed out.

'Is he still doing it?'

'Significant development. He's putting the fork back down on the table,' said Becca.

'What do you think it means?' asked Marnie, taking tiny sips from a carton of orange juice because she couldn't eat when Marley was around. She swallowed the juice delicately like a little bird.

'He's got an itchy scalp,' I said. 'It's a sign of something.'

'Of what?' asked Marnie hopefully because she wanted to keep the conversation focused on Marley.

I leaned across the table towards her. 'Of nits,' I said.

We all giggled, which attracted their attention. Luke looked up and nodded at me as though I was a business acquaintance. Then they stood up together and headed over, holding their trays. I looked for traces of Jay in Marley, noting the same wide shoulders and slouchy gait. But his face was more angular, less flat, and his eyes slanted up like his mother's.

'I can't believe this is happening,' whispered Marnie. 'I have waited so long for this moment.'

'Fags, Romeo,' said Luke, putting out one hand and holding up the tray in his other like a French waiter. 'Three, please.'

I undid my blazer and pulled out the packet hidden in the lining and gave Luke three cigarettes.

'I always get my little sister to do my dirty work,' he told Marley. 'Nothing sticks with her.'

'I'd like your sister to do my dirty work,' said Stuart.

'Shut the fuck up,' said Luke.

Why did he want to hang out with such a loser?

'I'm having a party, Romy. Come if you like,' said Marley, in passing, as they were about to walk away. 'You can keep Jay company.'

Becca kicked me under the table.

'Can I bring a couple of girlfriends?' I asked a little too quickly.

He paused for a moment, looking Marnie and Becca up and down as though he'd just noticed them for the first time.

'Sure.'

They slouched away. I expected Marnie to be elated. But as she did up the button of her shirt ready for her next class I saw her big lower lip tremble in the way that it did when she was on the verge of tears. All Marnie's emotions went to her mouth.

'Result,' said Becca, slapping Marnie on the back. 'Let's talk outfits.'

'He didn't ask me. Romy asked if we could come. It's not the same.'

'Five minutes ago, all you wanted was to be asked to Marley Fairport's party. Now you've got the invite you're even unhappier than you were before. Sometimes I don't get you,' said Becca.

'He didn't have to say yes,' I pointed out. 'That's a good sign. He could have said no.'

'Do you really think so?' Marnie persisted.

'You're on his radar now,' said Becca, looking at me for back-up. 'You might even get to speak to him at his party.'

'He asked about you at New Year,' I said, remembering the comment about the freckles.

'What exactly did he say?'

'He said you reminded him of the night sky,' I said.

Becca frowned at me disbelievingly. Marley Fairport had good ball skills. He could mend broken computers and talk to girls without being weird. But he wasn't poetic.

'Luke says he's broken up with his girlfriend. So you've

got as good a chance as any,' I said. Luckily the bell rang and we had to go back to class.

Sometimes after school I walk home from the bus stop in the dark. It usually takes less than twenty minutes but Mum generally doesn't like me going alone because there are hardly any street lights and the houses either side of the main road are set back behind rows of trees and super-size hedges. After the clocks changed in October it became non-negotiable. Either I had to walk with Luke, or Dad had to pick me up. Mum had found a story on the Internet about a twenty-year-old woman who had gone missing a few years earlier.

'It was 2 a.m., she was a prostitute in the city centre and she was killed by a serial killer who was given a life sentence,' said Dad in exasperation when she showed him the piece from the *Eastern Daily Press*.

'She was still a real person,' said Mum.

'That's not what I meant and you know it,' said Dad. He put up his hands in defeat. 'I accept it is my fate to be the family chauffeur. I'll collect Romy.'

Mum calmed down. The following week Dad and I made an agreement that I could walk alone but we wouldn't tell Mum.

'Mum's a bit overprotective at the moment,' said Dad. 'She's had a lot to deal with. She needs to feel in control of things.'

'She's a control freak,' I said, and he didn't contradict me.

I thought it was nice of him, the way he wanted to shield her from worry. Over a cup of tea at our house on New Year's Day, Loveday had teased Mum for having irrational fears about me walking home and jokingly asked if she was scared of the dark. She made the kind of noises kids make when they are trying to scare each other at Halloween and pointed out that no one had ever been mugged in Luckmore. Then she poked fun at Mum for locking the car and her habit of returning to the house three times to check whether the front door was closed properly. I wondered how she knew this and might have defended Mum had she not been such a psychopath the previous evening. I was convinced this was why Jay hadn't come over with Loveday.

Instead of laughing it off, Mum had rounded on Loveday and said in her most haughty headmistress tone that parents of girls used a different equation to measure risk. I think it was a message aimed at me to try and explain her mad behaviour. Dad had quickly intervened with one of his theories about the reckless teenage brain, and Loveday was efficiently diverted, but I could see that Mum was riled and that Loveday either didn't notice or didn't care.

I assumed I could walk home with Luke but he had unexpectedly got off the bus with Marley and Stuart at the previous stop. Becca reluctantly trailed after them with Marnie. I called Mum to see if she could collect me but she had to stay at school for a teachers' meeting. So I texted Dad and told him I was setting off on my own.

Unlike London, with its rows of identical terraces, the houses in our new village are all unique. Dad had given them names the first week to try and stem Ben's tears when they walked together to his new primary school. There was Blue Jasmine, with its lapis-coloured tiles, turquoise shutters and creepers; Simon Cowell, a squat mock-Tudor pile with an overly neat lawn; Three Lions, with its moss-covered statues at the front gate. Before he even met the Fairports, he had christened their house the Trippy Hippy.

As I walked past these houses now, I thought about Dad and tried to work out what Mum might have meant when she said it was his fault that we had moved here. It was obvious now that I had been focusing on the wrong parent. I tried to remember the sequence of events last year when Dad first announced that he had resigned from work.

It was the end of the Easter term. Mum was sitting at the kitchen table, marking essays. Ben was reading a code-breaking book. Luke was making toast; Mum's cooking by that time was too erratic to satisfy his enormous appetite. Luke had taken to buying his own loaf of white bread and pot of Nutella, which he kept in his room and refused to share with anyone. Dad came in and instead of his usual irritating greeting ('What's up, folks,' said rhetorically in an American accent) he put his arms around Mum's shoulders and told her that it was over. I remember noticing that from behind Mum's shoulders were so bony that they resembled a coat hanger with oversized clothes draped on it. Maybe she had anorexia, I wondered, considering how embarrassing it would be to have a mother with an eating disorder. Mum didn't move and I don't think she said anything. Dad announced that he had resigned from his job. At the time his choice of words didn't seem odd. He was weirdly matter-of-fact and seemed quite calm. He said it in a way that suggested Mum should be pleased, but she didn't react. It didn't occur to me that he might have been fired.

Luke's toast popped up. 'Well done, Dad,' I said when no one else spoke. I didn't know if it was the right thing to say. I felt sorry for him. He loved his job. But he didn't seem upset. By this time I was definitely fed up with Mum's retreat from the world. Mealtimes had become torture. I couldn't bear the way she pushed food around her plate without really eating it. We had steak that night and she cut it into so many tiny pieces and left it for so long that it reminded me of the wood shavings at the bottom of the hamster cage. Ben anxiously asked if she wanted to test him on his eight times table; she agreed and then didn't notice when he said that four times eight was thirty-six.

Now, as I walked past the house with the blue tiles and the turquoise shutters, I realized with certainty that at that point none of us had any idea they were thinking about leaving London or that Mum was going to apply for the job in Luckmore. Ben had asked if we would have less money. Dad said he had been given a small advance to write a book about the teenage brain from a neuroscience perspective. None of us pressed him for details. Luke said he hoped that the fact Dad would be around more didn't mean that he would try and get more involved in his life. Dad promised not to. I asked if I could still go on holiday with my friend's parents and Mum and Dad said I could. But they must have known because a few days later I found the estate agent's details for the house where we now live beneath a pile of English essays that Mum was marking.

I was in a dark stretch of the path between Simon Cowell and Blue Jasmine. I put my school bag across my back so that my hands were free and walked light-footed like a cat, getting faster as the pavement ran out and turned into a dirt track. I began to run, lowering my head and closing my fingers to make myself more aerodynamic, feeling the shape of the ground beneath my feet. As I picked up speed and headed through the gate into our front garden I thought about how Usain Bolt reached a terminal velocity of 12.2 metres per second when he broke the world 100 metres record in 2009 and how much force he must have used to overcome the wind resistance. And in my mind Dad was Usain Bolt and Mum was the wind resistance holding him back and dragging him down.

The front door was unlocked and the lights downstairs were ablaze. Apart from Lucifer there was no one at home. The cat threaded himself in and out of my legs as

I did an inventory of the fridge. There was nothing to eat apart from a jar of olives stuffed with garlic and the remains of yesterday's pesto sauce. The kitchen counter looked promising but delivered a big *nada*: sumac, nutmeg, pine nuts, cumin, molasses. Why couldn't Dad make a recipe with ordinary ingredients?

There was nothing that qualified as a simple snack.

Beside the recipe book was a paper on brain neurotransmitters that he was due to deliver in London to a group of postgrad students at UCL the following week. I skim-read the introduction. 'The brain has the consistency of firm jelly and is therefore protected by the thick, bony skull. It floats in 150 millilitres of cerebrospinal fluid.' I imagined my own brain peacefully bobbing around inside my skull and considered how noisy my thoughts were when it must be so quiet inside my head. I thought about Jay's comment about me being liquid and how in fact it was true. I wondered about the consistency of the cerebrospinal fluid, whether it was watery or thick like gravy and how it might taste.

A cross section of the skull followed. Dad loved his visuals. Images were recorded in a different part of the brain from words and were easier to remember, he said. I flicked through a few more pages with different headings highlighted in fluorescent pen (general comments about neurotransmitters, sympathetic and parasympathetic nervous systems, why Alzheimer's patients have a severe reduction in nucleus neurons).

A paragraph caught my attention. It was about a brain

amino acid called PEA that was apparently responsible for the 'love-excitement' of sexual attraction and emotional infatuation. 'Levels are highest in the reward centre of the brain and spike during orgasm and ovulation,' Dad had written. 'An American study at the University of San Francisco has shown that lap dancers earn higher tips when they are ovulating.' I oscillated between shock that my dad would talk about this in front of a group of students and intrigue over how it might be relevant to me. According to Dad, its chemical structure and the way it released endorphins meant PEA acted like a drug. There was also a quote from Pablo Neruda: 'Love is so short and forgetting so long.' This was another of his quirks, finding the science in poetry, he said. Although it was Mum who supplied him with ideas. But I didn't want to focus on that because in the current domestic narrative running in my head Mum always played the role of the bad guy.

I went through into the sitting room to switch on some music. Nick Cave, 'The Boat Song', came on, and because Luke wasn't home to question my taste and Mum wasn't there to use this as part of her psychological profiling of me, I left it on. I went over to the huge sitting-room window where I had first seen Jay in the garden next door and was taken aback to see Dad, Ben and my grandfather all sitting round the Fairports' kitchen table. Not for the first time, but never before on a school night. Ben was playing Uno with Wolf. Loveday was stirring a pot on the cooker. Dad was leaning against the sink beside her. My grandfather was halfway through a glass of red wine. They were all becoming friends.

There were also some adults I didn't recognize. Jay grumbled that there were always different people turning up unannounced to stay with them. His dad had been brought up on a commune in California and couldn't stand being alone, Jay said. He was always getting at him for spending so much time alone in his room.

I debated whether I should head over. Wolf and Loveday wouldn't mind and their fridge would be full of food. I looked up and saw a familiar red glow through the window of Jay's bedroom. He was probably doing homework and there was no guarantee that he would make an appearance downstairs. I suddenly remembered Mr Harvey's hastily shouted instructions at the end of class to put together a ten-minute tutorial on the human heart ready for the following day. Becca had tried to negotiate a longer deadline but he insisted the pressure was good preparation for the real world and ignored her attempts to sidetrack him with a debate about the subjective nature of reality by reminding us to watch a *Harvard Business Review* online tutorial on how to do killer presentations. He was a good teacher. I'll give him that. But only that. Because he played his role in all this.

I dropped pasta piece by piece into a saucepan and enjoyed dodging the boiling water that splashed back over my fingers. I planned the homework, how I would label the photographs taken during our dissection class, describe each section of the heart and draw the path that blood takes through the circulatory system. My palette would be shades of orange and red, and I would make the arrows move to demonstrate the flow of blood. It would look beautiful.

My phone buzzed. Marnie's number flashed up. I couldn't face another conversation about Marley so I let it drift to voicemail and then felt guilty. Dad called to see if I had got home and I went over to the sitting-room window and told him to turn round. He waved at me to join them. I was tempted to go purely because it would annoy Mum. Instead I waved my Biology textbook at him. But he had already turned back to Loveday.

I headed up to my room, switched on the light and tipped the contents of my school bag onto the unmade bed. The picture of the two cats floated onto my pillow. A small speech bubble came from the mouth of the feral cat: 'Take a walk on the wild side.' I went over to my window and saw Jay standing at the window opposite. We each stood centre frame, face on. We stared at each other as though we were children playing a game of chicken and the first one to look away would lose. He nervously ran his hand through his hair a couple of times. I wished I were with him so that I could wrap my fingers around those wild curls and pull him towards me.

He smiled slowly, more tentative than I had seen him before, and for a moment remained completely still, as if poised on the edge of something, like a surfer about to stand on his board. Then suddenly he took off his T-shirt. Backlit by the orange light above, his upper body seemed to glow. He swallowed a couple of times as he gave me time to trace a line from one shoulder to the other, taking in the contours of his arms, the breadth of his chest and finally the shadow of soft black hair that trailed from his belly button into the waistband of his black trousers.

I pulled out my white shirt from my black skirt and circled the smooth edges of the bottom button between my fingers for a moment without looking away. He smiled encouragingly. Random thoughts collided in my head. Some people have a phobia of buttons. The Amish aren't allowed them because they are too worldly. My grandmother had a jar of them. I undid the first one. Jay didn't blink. The next button was missing, and my shirt billowed open so that I could feel the cold from the window lick my stomach. I shivered and ran a hand across from one hip bone to the other.

Jay stepped forward. No ambiguity now. He was so close to the window that his breath clouded the glass. He rubbed the cloudy patch slowly with his finger until it cleared. *He is in thrall to me*, I thought, understanding for the first time what this really meant. I fumbled with the buttons at the top of the shirt until it was completely undone and waited for a moment before taking it off and letting it fall to the floor. My hand drifted to the zip at the side of my skirt. He gently shook his head and his eyes moved back to my breasts. He nodded at me, a slight tilt of the head, and I understood.

I wished I was wearing a different bra, one that you

could pull over the top of your head; instead I awk-wardly stretched my arms behind my back, leaning forward slightly as I fumbled for the clasp. Jay watched unblinkingly, and when finally I undid it and pulled the straps off my shoulders, he moved even closer to the window. I pressed myself against the pane so that my breasts were compressed against the glass without worrying whether they were too fat or my nipples too pink. The cold was a relief. I heard a noise, a soft animal moan, wondered where it came from and realized it was me.

Jay moved. He put a hand up on the window, fingers splayed, and I wondered for a moment if I had got this wrong and he was telling me to stop or if he was trying to signal a desire for more proximity, like when Ben used to make Mum kiss him goodbye through the window at nursery. Then I realized that he was using the window to steady himself as he unzipped his trousers and pulled out his dick. It slapped inelegantly against his stomach and he clasped it in his thick fist as if to try and tame it. His hand began moving slowly up and down. I stepped back.

There was a flicker of something in his eye and I knew he didn't want me to look away. He smiled at me again, looking for reassurance, and I smiled back. The moon came out from behind a cloud and shone its approval upon us. His rhythm quickened.

I touched my breasts and pushed them together. Then I put my hand inside my skirt to touch myself. 'Yes,'

I saw him mouth. He leaned forward until his forehead touched the glass and I could see his face was taut with desire. The tendon in his arm bulged with tension. His hand moved faster and faster until suddenly his eyes orbited, his mouth hung open and it was over. There was a moment of grace. He looked at me reverently. I went away from the window and lay on the bed and finished what he had started. My phone buzzed and I knew it would be him. *u slay me*, the message read.

There are events in life that come to define all others, and although I didn't realize it at the time this was one of them. When we met again years later Jay told me it was the same for him. Everything was measured against this moment.

7

As Romy slumped back on her bed trying to work out what exactly had just taken place between her and Jay, Ailsa sat in her office reviewing the record list of candidates planning to sit Chemistry A level that summer. There still weren't enough girls, but even the notoriously difficult-to-please new head of governors had been impressed by the figures. Matt Harvey was right. *Breaking Bad* had probably inspired more children to study science than any policy the government could dream up. It brought chemistry to life.

The head of Chemistry, Paul Taylor, had bristled at his comment, saying that even a monkey could make crystal meth and that the trend might have more to do with the inspired teaching in his department. A heated debate about the accuracy of chemistry in *Breaking Bad* threatened to derail the entire meeting. Paul said it was impossible to make blue crystal meth; Matt pointed out that there was a Chemistry professor consulting on the series. Paul, possibly the most thin-skinned member of staff, said he might not be a university professor but what he lacked in expertise he made up for with experience. Or maybe it was the other way round. Ailsa firmly told them they were going off on a tangent. Sometimes she felt like the ringmaster of a shambolic circus trying to find its rhythm with a truculent set of new performers vying for her attention.

In a diplomatic intervention that seemed to placate Paul she commended his inspired teaching and the improvement in results since he had taken up the post, but privately she thought that Matt's theory made more sense. Especially when they turned to the next point on the agenda – whether to bring a drug expert into the school to talk to students about legal highs. There were now more than 250 recognized by the European Drug Commission, Mrs Arnold had explained.

Forget the pupils, it was the teachers who needed educating first, suggested Matt, explaining that he had heard a couple of boys talking about something called M-Cat and asked whether it was something to do with pet food. Everyone had laughed, including Ailsa. He knew how to lighten an atmosphere without undermining his authority or distracting colleagues from the serious point he was trying to make. Ailsa reluctantly acknowledged that he was a positive presence in the school, popular with staff and teachers. If the school managed to be the first in Norfolk to become a business and enterprise specialist, it would in good part be down to him. As Romy might say, he had good energy. Which reminded Ailsa how she had to shut down a conversation with Rachel the other night when she tried to embark on a discussion about their sex life. 'Not appropriate,

Rach,' she said, citing the need for professional distance but secretly wondering if she was jealous.

Ailsa checked her phone. It was almost eight o'clock. She messaged Luke and Romy to check whether they had got home and called Harry but he didn't pick up. He was probably putting Ben to bed. There was no point dialling the landline because Adam couldn't hear the phone. Her phone buzzed. *Yes*, it read. Ailsa felt a guilty stab of gratitude towards Romy for being the only reliable member of the family and marshalled the last pile of papers on her desk.

She confirmed her attendance at a conference for head teachers at the Institute of Education the following week. 'Seizing Success' it said at the top of the paper. Who came up with these titles? Almost certainly not someone who had become head of a school where so many girls wanted to become hairdressers that there was a teaching salon on the premises. She skim-read a document on how the Pupil Premium had been spent on each child eligible for a free school lunch, put it in her bag to edit at home and checked through a twelve-page application for the school to be granted the Investors in Families Award. Someone in Whitehall needed to be told that all this bureaucracy stifled initiative rather than encouraged it.

After that she reluctantly flicked through a couple of brochures for old people's homes with optimistic names that belied the fact that they were places where people went to die. Ocean Heights. The Pastures. Sunshine Dreams. With all their talk of staff ratios, singing groups and puréed food, they sounded like the nursery schools she had scouted for Ben in London. She chose one to take home and leave on the bedside table to appease Harry. There was no way she was sending her father to one of these places. Since Adam had moved in with them and started eating and sleeping properly, he had begun to recover some of his old bluster. It would kill him to go into a home.

Rachel had announced she was coming this weekend to review options for their father. *Review Matt Harvey more like*, thought Ailsa, but she was pleased about her sister's attack of conscience. She hid the brochure for Sunshine Dreams at the bottom of her bag beneath a pile of prospectuses from English departments at universities that Luke would never get into, resolving to leave them at strategic points around the house in case he picked one up. Finally she jammed a thick government report on children and the Internet into her bag.

Reading this was a priority. Before the *Breaking Bad* debate, much of the meeting had been spent discussing the issue of a boy in Romy's year who had had a fake Facebook page set up in his name where vile comments, presumably but not necessarily from anonymous classmates, had been posted. His head had been superimposed on a photograph of a naked man with a deformed penis. The parents insisted the school should take the lead on pursuing those responsible and try to get Facebook to take it down. Ailsa had agreed, even though she didn't know where to start. The Internet had totally blurred the line between school and parental responsibility.

Satisfied her desk was in reasonable shape for the following morning, she headed towards her car. It was parked in the space reserved for the head of school, the only one delineated with a border of pot plants. Even after a term in the job it still gave her a burst of pleasure to know this space belonged to her. She had been working for this from the moment she had taken up her place at the Institute of Education after leaving university almost two decades earlier. Although she had always envisaged running a school in London because she had never taught anywhere else, now she was back in Norfolk she realized she could be more useful. It was all about creating aspirations, building bridges with local businesses, making sure every member of staff shared her vision and that every student had a plan. Schools in London were way ahead of the curve. Here there was an opportunity to make a real change.

As she walked she deconstructed the staff meeting, summarizing priorities and gauging how the different personalities around the table worked together. The head of Physics was dead wood. Closed to innovation. Cynical about her students. Unwilling to introduce a syllabus with more challenging practical work. She would have to go. The head of Drama, Lucy Drummond, was like every head of Drama Ailsa had ever come across: hugely enthusiastic but in constant need of hyperbolic praise, which Ailsa had duly given when Lucy announced that she was going to direct *Love and Information* as this year's school play. If she pulled it off Ailsa would reward her with promotion to head of Year 7, a position currently vacant. What is your best quality? she had been asked by the head of governors during her final interview for the position of head teacher. Decisiveness, she had responded so quickly that the interview panel had burst out laughing.

The rain had turned to hail that blew sideways across the car park into her face. She opened her mouth to catch a few nuggets. Winter empowered her. She didn't feel the cold like other people and it made her feel superhuman. Rachel said it was because they had grown up swimming in the North Sea. As she rummaged in her handbag for the car keys a radical thought crossed her mind: if she could hold out for another hour or so she would miss Harry's chicken cacciatore.

His meals were announced in advance amidst great fanfare, and his need for immediate affirmation as she picked up her knife and fork at the end of another production exhausted her. The way he watched and waited as she ate the first mouthful, alert for her response, reminded Ailsa of a sheepdog.

In almost two decades of marriage I have cooked chicken cacciatore a thousand times and not once have I demanded anyone reflect on the tenderness of the meat, the superiority of the field mushroom over the button mushroom or the way the rosemary infuses the stock with a flavour reminiscent of freshly mown hay, Ailsa reflected wryly.

If she got home at ten she could also miss the predictable drama of a school night. She could avoid arguing with Ben over when to switch off his light, and trying to ascertain if Luke really was revising for his A levels up in his bedroom. She could have a break from the low-level hostility that emanated from Romy and the competition for her attention waged between Harry and Adam.

It was decided. She would play truant from her family. She would go to the pub at the end of the road, read all the papers she was now piling into the boot of the car and because there would be no interruptions it would take half the time. It was a gastropub, one of the biggest gifts to women since the development of the washer-dryer. A place where she could eat a home-cooked meal without making it herself, where no one would stare at her for being alone or make lewd remarks about the size of her breasts, which, unlike Loveday's, weren't attention-seeking in any way. She slammed the boot shut and the car quivered. The bumper was still in the garage at home, where it would remain for the next year.

'Poor old thing,' she said, patting the vehicle on the bottom in the same way that she did with Ben when he hurt himself. 'Most faithful friend.' They had been through a lot together.

'Ailsa,' a muffled voice shouted.

Ailsa jumped.

'Sorry. I didn't mean to startle you.'

'Who is it?' she asked, squinting through the hail.

'It's Matt. Matt Harvey.' He came closer until she could see him. He was wearing a raincoat with the hood done up so tightly that only the upper part of his face was visible. 'I know. I look like Kenny from *South Park*.'

'I don't watch *South Park*.'

'I was in the Biology lab and saw you out of the window.'

'Right,' said Ailsa.

'I wanted to have a word. I couldn't find the right time after the meeting. Too many people milling around. Do you have a moment?'

'I need to get going. Homework crisis.' She patted her bag and forced a laugh.

'It'll take ten minutes. Max.'

'Any more than that and we'll freeze,' she said.

'Sorry about the *Breaking Bad* diversion. That was one for the staffroom. We got carried away.' He paused for a moment and tried to unravel the toggles on his hood.

'It didn't matter. It was entertaining after all the Facebook nastiness, and I think you're probably right.' Ailsa opened the car door.

'That's not why I wanted to speak to you.' He pulled at the toggles again, making the knots ever tighter. 'It's something more personal. But I think it has to be said.' Ailsa sighed. She understood what this was about now.

'Look. I really don't have a problem with you and

Rachel. But I don't have anything to say about it.' She should have put a comma rather than a full stop between each statement. The space in between sounded too defensive. She looked at the top half of his face. His brow crumpled. Even before he spoke she knew that she had totally misread his intent.

'That's not what I wanted to talk to you about either,' he said finally.

'Right,' said Ailsa, trying to sound more composed than she felt.

She headed round to the driver's side to avoid his gaze and opened the door. Matt followed her and leaned his forearm on top of the window so that she couldn't close the door without appearing rude. She put one hand across her face to shield it from the hail and the other on top of the car door, a few inches away from his, to underline her desire to get home. They now faced each other.

'And why would you have a problem?' he asked, sounding almost hurt.

'I realize that scientists aren't big on empathy,' Ailsa said drily, 'or imagination. But surely you can see this from my point of view.'

'What do you mean?'

'If you've been feeling lonely because you've moved somewhere new and you need some female company to get you through your first winter out in the sticks, why don't you go and pick someone up at the pub down the road? Or use one of those apps where you can meet strangers for sex.' She was about to add, 'like Rachel', but loyalty prevailed.

'I thought that pub was where people go to eat organic beef with beetroot mousse and locally sourced seasonal vegetables. I wasn't aware it was a hotbed of steamy sexual liaisons. Otherwise of course I would have gone there as soon as I arrived at Highfield.'

Not bad use of alliteration, thought Ailsa. She struggled to wrap her anger around her.

'Don't you think some people might think it's a bit strange, arriving at a new school and hitting on the head-mistress's sister after meeting her for less than sixty seconds? Some people might think that the fact she is almost forty and you are twenty-seven is a little embarrassing, if not inappropriate. Some people might think that the right thing to do would have been to let me know what was going on so that I didn't have to discover it for myself at a New Year's Eve party.'

'Some people might think you're behaving like the bloody Taliban. Why don't you dig a hole on the sports pitch and bury me in it up to my neck and get some people to throw stones at me?'

'Because the ground's too hard, and health and safety regs don't allow boulders in the school grounds. Otherwise I would.'

Matt looked down at the ground and swept a few hailstones away with the side of his foot. His shoulders shook with anger. Ailsa began to construct further barbs in her head, wondering where this would end. He was a great teacher and her first recruit. She recognized enough of herself in him to know that he was in the job for all the right reasons. He loved his subject, cared about his students and took pleasure in their achievements. She was lucky to have persuaded him away from London. It wouldn't look good if he left after a term. Her judgement would be questioned. She waited for him to fire off another volley. Instead he laughed.

'You're so funny. You don't mean to be. But you are,' he said. 'Like the way you talk to your car as if it was a friend.'

This was not what Ailsa expected. She was relieved that somehow they had managed to pull back from the brink, but his reaction wrong-footed her. At least now he might reconsider before offering his resignation. Good Biology teachers were an endangered species and here was one who had not only offered to initiate an after-school David Attenborough club but also promised to shoot his own rabbits for students to get experience with dissection.

'I'm sorry,' she said. 'I didn't mean to be harsh. I love my sister. But I wish she wouldn't shit on my doorstep.'

'My intentions are honourable,' he said, doing a small bow. 'Rach is great. She's a right swipe come good.'

'I don't understand.'

'Right swipe. Tinder. I met her through Tinder. She came to your office when I was there so that we didn't have to explain how we met.'

He stood upright and finally liberated himself from his hood. The top of his thick dark hair had been flattened. He shook his head and a few hailstones tumbled around his face.

'That wasn't what I wanted to talk to you about. But I'm glad we've cleared the air.'

'There's more?' asked Ailsa.

'Something came up with one of your kids. I was in two minds whether to say anything but I think you should know.'

'How long will it take?' Ailsa asked, knowing that everything to do with Luke took time.

'We could freeze to death out here or I could tell you over a beer in the local lap-dancing club,' he suggested, going round to open the passenger door before she could respond. His confidence was both reassuring and unsettling.

The pub was practically empty. This was a place for out-of-towners. Not enough people in Luckmore had twenty pounds to spend on dinner during the week. The barman was sitting on a stool engrossed in a book. Ailsa smiled as he dragged himself back to reality. She recognized that feeling.

'Think we need to warm up. Both literally and metaphorically,' said Matt, heading towards a table beside the huge open fire. A couple with a toddler sat the other side of the hearth. The father was aimlessly scrolling up and down messages on his BlackBerry, trying to ignore his daughter's grizzling.

Ailsa sat down with her back to the window on a

bench that was so deep that if she leaned back her legs wouldn't reach the ground. So she perched on the edge. Matt volunteered to buy drinks. He put his bag abruptly on the table. The salt and pepper toppled over. Ailsa righted them and requested a half of cider.

'Whatever they've got. Organic preferably. Or French. Or the weakest one they have. If there's an organic French pear cider I'll take it over an inorganic English one made from apples. The French use fewer sulphates.'

He held up his hand. 'Remember, the male brain finds it difficult to hold on to more than one instruction at a time,' he said, mimicking something she had said about teenage boys in the meeting. She grimaced at his teasing tone and then felt irritated that he made her want to pull rank. His informality was unnerving. She focused on the couple with the child on the other side of the fireplace.

'We need to get on with it,' said the mother. 'Otherwise the gap will be too big.'

'We should have gone away on our own,' said the man without looking up. Ailsa recognized the symptoms. A row was brewing.

Her thoughts turned to Luke. Whatever Matt wanted to tell her, it wouldn't be good, because it never was. She closed her eyes for a moment. Two terms. Luke had roughly five months to turn things round, to conjure up some reasonable exam grades and fix on a university course. Hopefully find a nice girlfriend to steady him.

The first two problems might be resolved by the third. Though his high rate of preliminary success with girls didn't seem to translate into anything more enduring than one-night stands.

Luke had always been like tumbleweed, blowing back and forth wherever the wind took him. She smiled as she remembered the way he used to tear off his nappy at baby massage. As a small child, he made a friend who loved football. For a couple of months he played non-stop. Ailsa bought all the kit for him to play for a local team. Then he fell into a different crowd who hated football but loved World of Warcraft. He gave up football and took up gaming. Soon afterwards he met a girl who played the guitar and he insisted he wanted lessons. For eight months he thought he was Bob Dylan. Then he got into electronic music.

Luke was a chameleon. He could adapt to any environment. He always had a revolving door of friends. Ailsa had tried to convince Harry this could be a virtue, but where she saw freedom of spirit and curiosity, he saw lack of direction. The truth was that Luke had always been more her child than Romy and Ben. She imagined him in his forties, seeing a therapist, trying to unpick his relationship with his parents and the therapist finding fault with her overindulgence. Would he realize that Ailsa had to love him more because Harry loved him less?

She remembered something Luke had said last year, just before she had finally decided to accept the job in Norfolk, when she was at her lowest ebb. He was sitting at the kitchen table, allowing Romy to style his shoulder length hair. They were talking but Ailsa could hear nothing except the voice in her head on a loop. Stick or twist. Stay or go. She would have liked to present all the information to a statistician, who could have worked out the probability of where they would be least unhappy. Because now it was all about damage limitation. Harry would do whatever she wanted. He always said this with an affectionate arm around her shoulder but it just added to the weight of her decision. He would give up his job for her. He would take time out to write his book and take care of the children.

'Mum's having a gap year from parenting,' she heard Luke say to Romy. It was meant to be a joke but the truth stung. 'She's trying to find herself.'

'It must be challenging teaching at a school where your children are students,' said Matt, interrupting her thoughts. He was holding drinks and carrying a packet of crisps under each arm. *When did pupils become students?* Ailsa wondered. How long was it before she turned into a service provider? He tore open the crisps, apologized for spilling them, and used the side of his hand to corral them into a neat pile in the centre of the table. Grateful for something to do with her hands, Ailsa picked at them.

'I want no more to do with them than they want to do with me.' She took a couple of gulps of cider and enjoyed the way it warmed her stomach. 'It's a good incentive to stay away from trouble.'

rue. But not reflective of the last year in London, en Luke had become a chronic problem. The head teacher had only kept him on because she couldn't afford to lose her deputy.

'My mum used to teach at my school,' Matt explained. 'She was an English teacher.'

'And how was that?'

'Fine, until she left my dad for the History teacher.' He licked a finger and used it to soak up stray fragments of crisps. 'That's why I ended up doing science A levels. They offered the possibility of a more rational exist-ence.' Her eyes must have narrowed.

'I know what you're thinking.'

'I wasn't going to say anything.'

'No, but you were thinking it,' he said. 'Your face is very expressive.'

'Is it?' asked Ailsa, trying not to arch her eyebrows in surprise.

'But in response to your thought, I've never gone out with anyone older than me before. The relationship between my mum and the History teacher lasted less than a year and then she moved back in with us as if nothing had happened.' His eye line moved from the crisps she was holding in the palm of her hand, up her arm to her shoulder and finally to her face.

'How was that?' asked Ailsa.

'The house became tidy again.' He shrugged, his mouth full of crisps. 'They were nicer to each other. Because they'd almost lost each other, I guess. Mum's knowledge of history had improved but they never watched any war movies together again. My younger sisters took longer than me to forgive her. Order was restored.' He leaned towards her and rested his arms on the table, palms flat on the surface, fingers splayed. She was surprised by the dark hair on his forearms, even though it perfectly matched his thick head of hair. His left leg was now anchored to the inside of Ailsa's right knee. He gulped down his beer.

'Everything leaves a trace though, doesn't it? Even though you can't ever measure the imprint with absolute accuracy,' she said.

'End of therapy session, Ailsa.' He leaned back but his leg stayed in the same position. 'I'm over it.'

She shifted position. She was talking about her childhood not his, but he didn't realize.

'Sorry,' said Ailsa. 'I'm trying to delay talking about Luke.'

'Luke?'

'Legal highs. I presume it was him.'

'I don't teach Luke. That was Stuart Tovey. He was going on about his brother taking Ritalin and how he'd been using it to stay awake longer to revise for exams. He was telling Marnie that it had a similar chemical structure to cocaine. I looked it up on the Internet. He's right. It's a stimulant. Like Adderall. We should probably all be taking it.'

It was a joke but Ailsa didn't react so he continued. 'I had a word with him. Talked about delayed gratification.

Told him that if he wanted to screw up his life he should at least put it off until he'd done his A levels.'

'Sounds as good advice as any. Nothing else has worked with him.' She picked up the cider again and took a few more sips.

'Stuart is trouble. Not in a malicious way. In a risk-taking adolescent kind of way. Teenagers can be reckless.'

'So can adults,' Ailsa said.

'Really?' he said. 'What's the most reckless thing you've done? Apart from coming to the pub with me.'

His mobile phone rang. He looked at the screen. Years in a classroom meant Ailsa was expert at reading upside down and she could see it was Rachel calling. He quickly answered and leaned back in his chair.

'I'm in the middle of something,' he said. 'Can I call you later?'

Seconds later Ailsa's phone rang. She knew without looking that it would be Rachel. She caught his eye and let the call go to voicemail.

'It was Romy I wanted to talk about.'

This was unexpected. No one ever complained about Romy.

'She seemed a bit unsettled in class so I kept her back at the end of the lesson. After a bit of meandering she told me that my relationship with your sister means that Rachel isn't pulling her weight with your father. Thinks it's causing you a lot of stress. She asked me to get Rach to help out more.'

'Well, that's not what I was anticipating,' said Ailsa in

the even tone that she had perfected over the years when she was uncertain how to react to a situation.

'I'm telling you this as a friend, rather than a colleague,' he quickly added. 'That's why I didn't want to talk about it on school grounds. Didn't want to muddy the waters. But I thought you should know. And I also wanted to say that I won't add to your problems. I'll encourage Rachel to help out.'

'Thank you,' she replied, because what else could she say?

Later she would stew over the detail. But Ailsa grasped that in a matter of seconds the balance of power in their relationship had subtly shifted so that somehow she was now beholden to Matt. He had crossed the boundary into her personal life. She couldn't dismiss Romy's worries because the essence of what she was saying rang true and the content wasn't particularly contentious.

She stared into her cider so that he couldn't read her expression. What puzzled her was why Romy had confided in him. Of course she argued with Harry about Adam. It didn't require huge amounts of insight to imagine her father's presence generating pressure. But this was the regular *Sturm und Drang* of family life. It wasn't sufficiently calamitous for Romy to need to share it with one of her teachers.

'She seemed worried that you might move from Luckmore if this isn't resolved,' said Matt.

'Why would she worry about that? She hates living here,' said Ailsa.

He shrugged. 'That's not the impression she gave me. Another round?'

Ailsa looked at her watch. It was ten o'clock. Ben would already be in bed.

'Sure. But make it a half, please.'

Ailsa parked the car just beyond the house so she could slip inside unnoticed. She had given Matt a lift back to school to collect his bike and it was almost eleven o'clock by the time she got home. She shut the door behind her and leaned against it for a moment, pleased to be back, noting that this was the first time she had thought of Luckmore as home. She was growing to like this house. She liked the futuristic-looking toilets with their hidden cisterns and toilet bowls that appeared to float against the wall; she liked the way the wooden floor didn't reveal any history, the brand-new oil tank and the hatch where you could pass food from the larder to the kitchen. She was glad to be living far from her friends with their anxious questions about how things were going. It was a good house to keep secrets. She didn't turn on the light, and found herself drawn to the big window that overlooked the Fairports. There was a crowd of people sitting around their kitchen table. It was littered with empty wine bottles. They were in the midst of yet another party. Where did they find the stamina?

She observed the man sitting beside Loveday talking animatedly. And how she took him by the hand and turned it towards the ceiling. She was probably going to read his palm. Ailsa heard herself snort. Given that Loveday had come round to ask where and when she was born so that she could start plotting Ailsa's astrological chart, it wouldn't be surprising. Instead Loveday slowly traced a line across his wrist. This was more unexpected. *Careful how you react*, Ailsa thought; the biggest problems start with the tiniest gestures. The man obviously knew this because his hand balled into a tight fist and he pulled it away as though he had been stung.

She could now see his face and was taken aback to realize it was Harry. Wolf was watching and shook his finger at Loveday, laughing as you might at a child who had done something naughtily endearing. Harry's gaze nervously flicked from Wolf to Loveday. Everyone suddenly turned to stare at the other end of the table. Ailsa saw her father get up, his trousers stained red from a glass of wine he must have just spilt. She could tell from his slow, somnambulant movements that he was drunk. Harry got up, presumably to help Adam, but instead he headed towards the sofa, where a child was stirring beneath a blanket. Harry bent down beside him and Ben sat up and rubbed his eyes. What was Harry thinking, keeping him out so late on a school night? For the second time that evening she tried to summon anger that she didn't feel. *Let Harry sort out Ben and her father*, thought Ailsa. She went upstairs and checked on Romy. She was asleep on her side, her fingers curled around the edge of the duvet. Her curtains were open. Ailsa went over and shut them.

8

It was Aunt Rachel who gave the game away about Mum and Dad. She didn't mean to. But Rachel likes a drink and can be very mouthy after a few glasses of wine. Mum always says she is the perfect example of how the same qualities that make you good can also make you bad.

Since Rachel has what my parents describe as 'a very chequered history' with men, I was surprised Mum had ever confided in her at all about her problems with Dad. Still am really. Perhaps Mum decided it was payback time for all the hours she had spent at the kitchen table with Rachel excitedly describing a new relationship or sobbing over the end of an old one. If Mum had asked me I would have told her that the same quality that made Rachel such awesome company might make her a flaky confidante. It didn't make her a bad person. That's just how she rolled.

'Rach's life is like one long Abba song,' Dad used to say whenever she turned up at our old home wearing sunglasses and clutching a bottle of wine. She would head off downstairs with barely a glance at him. Sometimes he'd whistle the tune to 'Mamma Mia' as she and Mum talked in the kitchen oblivious to the rest of us. It was more a tease than criticism. Dad was quite fond of Rachel.

I remembered that as Mum sympathized and gave advice she would always be doing something else, like ironing, or cooking a week's supply of chilli con carne, or doing an Internet shop, because she couldn't afford to stop. BTM – before the Miseries – Mum obeyed all the laws of physics. She was constantly in motion although I wasn't convinced her forces were in balance.

Rachel would always sit in my seat at the kitchen table. As she spoke, she would run her nails up and down its oak surface, leaving tiny hieroglyphics that Luke and I named after the boyfriend that had caused the latest upset. Because even when she ended a relationship, there was still a drama. When Granny was alive she used to say that Rachel felt things more than anyone else, as though her heightened sensitivity was a superhuman quality that elevated her above the rest of us. Dad said she lacked self-control, and although I wasn't sure what he meant I agreed with him. But back then I knew nothing about the complications of love.

The deepest grooves, a series of stubby lines close to where I still sit, we called Steve after a man who broke her heart because he chose a life of abstinence as a Buddhist monk and was sent to live in Mexico. Mum's theory was that Steve was a good man, but because Rachel lost him to religion rather than another woman she couldn't generate the anger necessary to truly purge him from her system. After Steve, boyfriends tended to have one or two of Steve's ingredients but never enough to replicate the exact recipe. I wasn't sure that Mum's cooking metaphor worked but we all understood what she meant.

Last year Steve came back from Mexico for a visit. I overheard Rachel tell Mum he wanted to have sex with her one last time but she turned him down because she didn't want the responsibility of holding back a man trying to reach nirvana.

Then there was a small series of concentric circles by Ben's seat for Budgie, an enormous motorbike courier Rachel met after he delivered a package containing a script to her home. It was a horror movie, the first one my aunt had ever worked on. Apparently she had been brought in to try and give the central character emotional depth.

Rachel's relationship with him was completely physical, Mum explained to Dad. 'Sounds good to me,' Dad had teased. They used to banter like that, as if they had some private language that the rest of us couldn't speak as fluently.

Rachel spent quite a lot of time trying to work out why she found Budgie's blend of leather and motorbike fumes quite so intoxicating. Finally, Mum, who was usually really patient, told her that all she was doing was trying to inject the relationship with a mythology it didn't deserve. 'Never forget, sex is a chemical addiction, Rach.'

I tried to imagine Dad being an addictive substance and felt slightly sick.

I also overheard Rachel telling Mum that she preferred having sex with Budgie when he wore his leather trousers, even though the leather chafed her thighs so badly that it looked as though someone had had a go at her with a cheese grater. Even more interestingly, Budgie could only have sex to the sound of a motorbike revving in the background. Mum had laughed so much when Rachel told her this and even more when she revealed that it had to be a 990cc Harley-Davidson engine. Rachel had finally managed a smile. She knew it was time to tell Budgie the relationship was over. 'You can't compete with a motorbike,' were Mum's last words on the subject.

And of course now there was Mr Harvey, my Biology teacher. I had overheard Mum on the phone earlier in the week explaining to Rachel that she couldn't, for professional reasons, listen to her talk about their sex life. But because Mr Harvey was a new teacher who was very hot on pastoral care and mistakenly thought that age made you wise, he asked Rachel's opinion about issues at school and she in turn told Mum what was going on. Which was something Mum described as a virtuous circle.

So this is how I learned the reason Stuart Tovey was such a freak was that his stepdad knocked his mother around. Mr Harvey thought this accounted for his outbursts of anger and poisonous attitude towards women, especially female teachers. I didn't understand why watching your mother getting beaten up by your stepdad would make you angry with her rather than him or how this might make you offer a tenner to a girl in the year below to give you a blow job in the lunch break, but apparently Mr Harvey did. He firmly believed that deviancy was created, not inherited. And like Mum he went on and on about context all the time.

I was less sure. I was born on 22 June, the same day that, in 2003, a DNA sequence of the human genome was finally unravelled. So maybe my view was coloured. But Dad told me researchers have discovered a gene that is linked to antisocial and aggressive behaviour and that murderers and psychopaths have a smaller and less active pre-frontal cortex. We now know that anything from baldness to eczema is genetic. So maybe Stuart was born plain bad rather than made bad. And, as Ben said, the only fact you needed to know about Stuart Tovey was that it was best to stay away.

Mum also told Dad that apart from the fact that when Rachel went out on their first date people wondered if Mr Harvey was her son, he came 'without any obvious complicating issues', so perhaps there would be no grooves on the table. I wondered if Jay came without complicating issues and knew instinctively that he didn't.

Grandpa had been staying with us for around ten days when Rachel came to visit. Apparently she couldn't come earlier because of work commitments, Mum explained as we sat around the kitchen table waiting for her to arrive. Apparently all the actors in her zombie film were getting together for a script read-through. There were always lots of apparentlys with my aunt.

Since the film would be less than two hours long Mum couldn't understand why it had taken ten days to get from beginning to end. It was a fair point. Dad didn't react because he knew that while Mum could say what she liked about Rachel, nobody else was allowed to criticize her.

'That's the thing about zombies, Mum,' said Ben seriously, after listening to Mum complaining. 'They're very unpredictable. That can be a big problem. Especially if there's a horde.'

We all laughed apart from Ben, who always suspected he wasn't being taken seriously. He was sitting at the kitchen table fiddling with Mum's old iPhone.

'I know a lot about this kind of stuff,' he said without looking up.

'Thank God there's only one of you and not a horde,' said Dad, tickling him until he begged for mercy and the iPod Touch tumbled to the floor.

'Don't!' Ben shrieked. 'I'm editing my film to show Aunt Rachel.'

'Can we have a look?' asked Mum.

'Sorry. I promised she would see the premiere,' said Ben apologetically.

'How did you do that?' asked Mum.

'On Skype,' said Ben.

'You have a Skype account?' Mum turned to Dad and gave him one of her questioning looks. Dad shrugged.

'What's your film about?' he asked Ben.

'The sauna Wolf is building at the end of their garden.'

'Sounds like it's got massive popular appeal,' commented Luke from the sofa. 'Who plays the sauna?' I looked away so that Ben couldn't see me smile.

'What are you talking about?' asked Mum. Ben knew this had grabbed her attention.

'I've filmed it at the same time every week so you can see Wolf's progress. He's paying me to do it.' He said this with a mixture of pride and bluster.

'That huge building is going to be a sauna?' Mum asked.

'A sweat lodge is the correct term,' said my grandfather.

'You knew about this?' Mum asked.

'Can someone explain to me in God's name what a sweat lodge is?' asked Dad. Now they both sounded exasperated but at least they were in agreement.

'Your mother and I once saw one on a Navajo reservation,' said Grandpa dreamily.

'Wolf and Loveday aren't Navajo,' Mum interrupted.

'He was very interested in my experience,' continued Grandpa. 'We were on a fishing trip in Nebraska. Have I ever told you about it? We went up into the mountains to go fishing in Big Elk Park. I caught a huge salmon but your mother wanted me to put it back in the water and –'

'We've heard it all before, Adam,' said Dad sharply.

'Please, Harry,' warned Mum.

'What's a sweat lodge, Grub?' I asked Ben, hoping to derail yet another argument about my grandfather, who was blissfully unaware of the tension he caused between my parents.

'It's like a sauna,' explained Ben. 'You light the fire in the middle and it gets really, really hot. Wolf chants and plays the bongos in total darkness. Then you sweat out all your toxins for hours and come out reborn because you are reconnected with the universe and your problems have gone. Wolf's can fit sixty people inside. They're going to charge thousands of pounds.'

'What a load of bollocks,' Dad laughed. 'Sweating is the way the body regulates temperature. Sweat glands don't get rid of toxins.'

'Surely you need planning permission to build something like that, Harry?' Mum asked Dad.

'Who's going to notice out here?' said Dad. 'Or care.'

'My film is going on their website,' said Ben defensively. 'Jay is helping me load it.'

At the mention of Jay's name a jolt of electric pleasure shot through my body. I got up from the table and went over to the big window that looked out onto the side of the Fairports' house, to see if he was waiting for me. His curtains were open and his lamp bathed his room in an orange glow.

It was exactly two weeks since our first encounter. And one day since our last.

I hadn't told Becca or Marnie what was going on

because the excitement was slightly dampened by my lack of vocabulary to describe it and the sense that it wasn't quite normal. The experience didn't resemble anything my friends had ever discussed. I looked for answers on the Internet, willing what had happened to fit the definition of mutual masturbation, which sounded very Zen, and at least fitted with my expectations of sexual possibilities as outlined by Marnie. But since Jay and I hadn't touched, it didn't. We weren't going out with each other. We hadn't hooked up. We weren't having sex. I knew what the relationship wasn't but I wasn't sure what it was.

'Are you looking for Juliet, Romeo?' asked Luke, making me jump. For someone totally wrapped up in his own world, Luke had a spooky way of accidentally stumbling upon essential truths.

'God, you're pathetic,' I said, rolling up a newspaper and hitting him on the head as hard as I could.

Ben filmed the fight.

'Hit a nerve, have I, Romeo?' teased Luke. I hit him again.

'Hey!' shouted Dad. 'Cut it out, you two.'

'She's killing hundreds of neurons with every blow,' said Luke, holding his head in his hands.

'Don't be ridiculous,' I said, throwing the newspaper on the floor so that it scattered into a patchwork of loose pages. Dad cleared his throat as he always did when he was about to go into scientific mode.

'Actually,' Dad started, 'even a mild blow can cause a protein called tau to fall off the microtubules inside the neurons. In fact a series of mild blows can be as serious as a couple of bad bumps.'

He looked at his watch and began carping on about Rachel being late again.

'Maybe she's doing a trilogy,' suggested Luke. He had picked up one of my A-level Chemistry books just to be annoying. I grabbed it from his hand. Dad asked why he was suddenly interested in Chemistry when he'd done so little work for his GCSE that he'd given it up a couple of weeks before the exam. I could tell by the way Luke's eyes narrowed that this had hurt him. I felt bad for Luke and then irritated that I felt bad when he had started the argument.

'That's what they do nowadays with action movies. They work out all the sequels before they even release the first film.' He began listing examples. Luke was impressive like that. 'Maybe Ben should plan *Sweat Lodge II*,' he suggested.

'Good idea,' said Ben. He thought for a moment. 'But what would it be about?'

'You could do a romance,' suggested Luke. 'Why don't you consult Rachel? She's big on romance.'

'Rachel is always in big demand,' said my grandfather, who often irritated Mum by insisting Rachel was busier than her. 'She's probably been held up at work. Marvellous how much she takes on.' Mum bristled.

We all now knew, apart from Grandpa, that Rachel was coming for a summit meeting to discuss what to do with him. Mum and Dad had had another big row after he used Dad's chainsaw to scalp the hedge that marked the boundary between our house and the Fairports'. After this they had finally agreed that he was well enough to go home but not well enough to live on his own. But I should have known from previous experience with Mum and Aunt Rachel that the motion up for debate was rarely the one they ended up wrangling over.

In the end Rachel arrived so late that evening that tempers had already frayed. Dad's butterflied lamb was overcooked and he wanted Mum to concede that Rachel was 'selfish, narcissistic and probably at Mr Harvey's house having a preprandial shag'. Dad thought we were out of earshot.

'What's a preprandial shag?' Ben had asked.

'It's something people do to work up a good appetite,' said Rachel, suddenly appearing in the kitchen. She looked amazing. She was actually glowing. I wondered if this was how people looked after they had sex. Dad didn't flinch. I knew he felt bad because later when we had eaten pudding he asked her how everything was going with Mr Harvey.

'It's brilliant,' said Rachel. 'Even better than your almond and orange polenta cake.'

'Must be very good then,' said Dad.

'It's early days though, Rach,' Mum advised. 'Take it slowly.'

Which completely contradicted her favourite piece of advice about seizing the moment. 'Like you did with me?' teased Dad, putting his arm around Mum. It was part of family mythology the way Mum had met Dad, got married and given birth to Luke exactly nine months later, all because of Johnny Cash. A *coup de foudre*, as Dad called it. Although now I knew it was more likely lust at first sight.

'Time for bed, Ben,' said Mum, evil-eyeing Dad for encouraging Rachel's reckless streak.

'Show me your film tomorrow, Ben,' said Rachel.

'Sure.'

Ben grabbed the last slice of cake without asking and ran upstairs before Mum could stop him.

'He's going to hide it in his bedroom,' Mum told Rachel.

'He's still doing that?'

'Old habits die hard,' said Mum.

'Let him be,' said my grandfather. 'He's a good lad. Did you know he's teaching me how to use the Internet to book my holiday?'

'You're going away?' asked Rachel incredulously.

'I'm planning a tour of eastern Europe,' said my grandfather joyously. That was news to all of us.

'You can't possibly go away on your own,' said Rachel, who was always far more direct with my grandfather than Mum.

'Are you planning to travel independently or go with a tour operator?' asked Mum, trying to humour him without really agreeing to anything. It was a strategy she employed with us.

'Stop treating me like a child, Ailsa,' he said abruptly.

Grandpa started outlining possible itineraries. It all sounded so convincing that I began to wonder whether it really was a bad idea. Then I remembered the day Mum and I found him by Granny's grave and imagined what would happen if he got confused and wandered off.

'Dad, you've got to face up to reality,' said Rachel angrily. 'We need to talk about your future.'

'Calm down, Rach,' Mum urged. 'That isn't the way to handle him.'

'I don't need handling,' shouted my grandfather.

'I'm off out,' announced Luke, getting up from the table and throwing on his jacket. He was always the first to leave at the first sniff of trouble.

'Really?' said Mum. 'It's after ten thirty.'

'Friday night,' said Luke with a shrug. His shoulders strained against his coat. 'I might stay over at Stuart's.'

'You've got mocks in less than a week. And you won't see Rachel.'

'I'm staying at Matt's . . . so I won't be here until lunchtime,' said Rachel, trying to sound apologetic but unable to hide her joy at the prospect. Mum opened her mouth but said nothing.

'Of course,' said Dad quickly. 'That makes complete sense.'

'I'll be back by lunch and I'll revise in the afternoon,' said Luke.

'How are you planning to get to Stuart's?' asked Mum.

'Loveday's giving Marley and I a lift,' he said, as he closed the door behind him.

'Marley and me,' said Mum, muttering, 'Bloody woman,' under her breath. I couldn't face listening to her moan about Loveday so I went into the sitting room and took advantage of Luke's departure to lie on the sofa. I picked up my Chemistry book and was furious to see that he'd drawn smiley faces on all the atoms in the chapter on nuclear fission.

'She's fine, Ailsa,' said Dad. 'Different. But fine.'

'I'll say just one word: denim miniskirt.'

'That's two,' said Dad.

'Legs like a thoroughbred,' said my grandfather, using one of his favourite phrases. 'Nothing more boring than growing old gracefully.'

'At least that's one affliction you've spared us from, Dad,' said Rachel. They all giggled, even Mum.

'They're good neighbours,' said Dad. 'And we need some new friends.'

'What's wrong with our old ones?' asked Mum.

'They're not here.'

'She has no parameters,' said Mum. 'Who lets their teenage children go out at eleven o'clock at night the week before exams?'

'Quite right. I used a bike to get everywhere,' said my grandfather, as if it was the mode of transport that was the problem. 'Georgia and I used to cycle all the way along the coast to go to dances in Cromer. I remember one night a harvest moon came up from behind the marshes. We stopped to watch. It was so heavy and voluptuous. Georgia bet me a pound it wouldn't be able to rise. I won. I kept the one-pound note.' He stopped. I didn't turn round. I imagined his eyes filling with tears. Instead he continued cheerily, 'Did I tell you that Wolf let me have a go on his exercise bike this afternoon? It's hooked up to a screen, and I cycled through Prague so I get to know the layout of the city before my trip.'

'I hope they don't mind you spending so much time at their house,' said Mum. It was a good example of her doublespeak. What she really meant was that she'd rather he didn't go there at all. 'Maybe you should think about going on a cruise?' she suggested. 'There are plenty of people to help you out in case something goes wrong. They even have defibrillators on board.'

'Don't indulge him,' warned Rachel.

'Why do you always assume something will go wrong, Ailsa?' said my grandfather. '*Chicken Licken* was always her favourite story as a child. The sky is falling! The sky is falling!'

I could hear more wine being poured. 'Don't open another one,' Mum warned.

Rachel ignored her, arguing that she wasn't leaving without opening the wine she had bought in Châteauneuf-du-Pape the previous weekend.

'I thought you said you were working,' said Mum.

'I can work anywhere,' said Rachel, realizing her mistake.

'Why would I want to be stuck on a boat with a bunch of old-age pensioners?' asked Grandpa. 'Going on a cruise is like being in an open-plan prison except the company is more boring.'

'The food is better though,' said Mum.

'People are forever getting food poisoning on those big boats,' said Grandpa. 'You're always reading stories about cruise ships full of sick people with E. coli which aren't allowed to dock at any port in case they infect the local population. Toilets overflowing, people wiping their arses with their hand. They won't let them on dry land, even in Mogadishu. They're part of a conspiracy to kill old people. It's part of your plan to get rid of me.'

'If we wanted to get rid of you, we'd let you cut the hedge with the chainsaw,' said Mum. I stifled a giggle.

'I don't believe this,' said Rachel, gulping down her newly poured glass of wine.

'If you're on a cruise down the Danube I fail to see how you can end up in Somalia,' said Mum, not unreasonably. 'In fact I'm not sure that it's even geographically possible.'

'What can't you believe, Rachel?' asked my grandfather. They were both argumentative drunks.

'Well, given that I'd come here to discuss whether you should move into a care home, this wasn't exactly the row that I'd been anticipating.'

A terrible silence fell. I looked around the corner of the sofa. My grandfather's face had gone limp so that it looked as if it was melting. His mouth hung open and his tongue stuck to one side of his lower lip like some-one who had had a stroke. Mum, who was sitting next to him, put her hand on his shoulder. He shrugged her off. Then he stood up, pulled his shoulders back and puffed out his chest like an angry turkey and walked to the door.

'If you want to get hold of me I'll be in Bratislava,' were his parting words.

'It was a joke, Dad,' Rachel called out behind him. 'Come back.'

'The definition of a joke is that it's funny,' shouted my grandfather as he headed upstairs, his shoes drumming a slow beat on the stairs like a dirge.

'Well, that went well,' said Rachel.

I wanted to go after him, but my desire to hear what was going to happen next was stronger than my urge to com-fort him. It occurred to me that this lack of humanity made me spiritually more of a journalist than a doctor and perhaps I should reconsider my university application.

'That was very unhelpful, Rachel,' said Mum in the even tone that she used when she was about to send someone out of the classroom. She had moved to the sink and was noisily scouring a saucepan. I waited for Dad to say that she would scratch the metal, a particular obsession of his since he had gone domestic. He remained silent. 'A flat has come up in some sheltered accommodation in Cromer. Dad could have his own space but there's someone on hand to keep an eye on him. It would have been good to talk about that in a measured way.' The scouring noises got faster and louder.

'I thought it might be a good way to open up the discussion,' said Rachel finally. I knew from previous experience that she found it very difficult ever to admit that she had done anything wrong and that this was as close as Mum would get to an apology. 'It's getting late and someone needed to get to the point. Otherwise this trip's a complete waste of my time.'

'Don't even try and make excuses,' warned Dad.

'Harry,' Mum said. 'Don't get involved. It's nothing to do with you.'

'Ailsa's right. This is something we need to resolve together,' said Rachel, sensing an opportunity for a rapprochement with Mum.

'I am involved,' said Dad. 'In fact I'm fuck of a lot more involved with your dad than you are, Rachel. I cook lunch for him almost every day. I drive him into town to stock up on Johnnie Walker. I wash his underwear and hang it out in the garden to dry. I listen to him when he tells the same story about the fish dying in front of your mother and the harvest moon. I take him to the doctor when he gets breathless and I make sure that he's taken his medicine. What have you done?'

'I phone him almost every day,' said Rachel. Dad said nothing. 'I'm grateful, Harry, really I am. I know I haven't been pulling my weight and that's why I'm here now.'

'You wanted to hurt his feelings and you did,' said

Mum to Rachel. 'And you've totally undermined our efforts to talk about what happens next in a practical, non-emotive way.'

'I'm still angry with him,' said Rachel. 'For how he treated Mum. It's better to express those feelings than keep them inside.'

'Better for who?' Dad questioned her. 'Perhaps for you but not for those of us at the coalface trying to do the right thing by him.'

'Dad needs to acknowledge how I feel,' Rachel insisted.

'He'll have forgotten ten minutes later,' said Dad. 'His short-term memory is appalling. He's an old man with a thin grasp on reality who can't really cope on his own any more.'

'You need to let go of the past, Rach. It's not helpful,' said Mum. 'You can't hold him to account for things he can't remember happening nearly half a century ago.'

'I know you don't like talking about it,' said Rachel, 'but that was a big part of the problem, everyone ignoring what was going on and sweeping everything under the carpet until the next time.'

'We've talked about it before. He was a dysfunctional alcoholic; it was shit for a while and he managed to put it behind him. There's nothing more to say,' said Mum. 'We need to deal with the current problem.'

'I still remember the bad times, Ailsa,' said Rachel. 'Has she told you what happened, Harry?'

'Of course she has,' said Dad. 'But your dad pulled

back from all that years ago. You have to give him credit for evolving, for overcoming his addiction.'

There was a loud crash as a bottle tipped over.

'Shit,' said Dad, his chair screeching backwards across the stone floor.

'Sorry,' said Rachel. 'Did she tell you how we had to help Mum haul him upstairs and get him undressed, Harry? How sometimes he shat himself? Do you know about the knife that Mum kept in the drawer to scrape the vomit off his clothes the next day? Or how we couldn't bring home friends because we never knew what state he'd be in?'

'Stop raking over ancient history, Rachel. You need to move on,' shouted Mum.

'We didn't have a childhood because of him,' said Rachel.

'Bits of it were good and bits of it were bad,' said Mum. 'Like the rest of life.'

I lay back rigid on the sofa, making myself as flat and still as possible in case they noticed me. I tried to process what they were saying. We all knew that Grandpa occasionally enjoyed a drink but not that he had ever been a complete drunk. I couldn't believe that he had ever behaved like this. It was as though Rachel was describing a totally different childhood from the one that Mum had recounted to us. It had gone from *Famous Five* to *Shameless* in less than five minutes. I buried myself deeper in the sofa, alert to what was coming next.

'You believed all his excuses and false promises, just like Mum. It takes courage to face up to our history,' continued Rachel. She sounded breathless but it could have been because she was wiping up the spilt wine. 'That's why Mum had a heart attack, because she tried too hard for too long.'

'And what's wrong with trying?' asked Mum. 'She was trying to protect us. You only faced up to what was going on when it was all over. I was the one struggling to keep the show on the road.'

'You should know better than anyone that glossing over a problem makes it worse in the long run. You've done the same thing with Harry. You've ended up dragging your entire family here so that you can repaint your marriage in pastel colours. And why did you bring them back to the scene of all that childhood misery? God, a therapist would have a field day with you, Ailsa.'

'Sometimes it takes more courage to forgive someone and move on,' volunteered Dad when Mum didn't say anything. 'It's the grown-up thing to do.'

'Well, you would say that, wouldn't you, Harry?'

'What do you mean?'

'Because it suits you if Ailsa forgives and forgets.'

'Well, of course it does,' said Dad, sounding exasperated.

'Do you think that just because you've moved here he's stopped communicating with her?' said Rachel. 'You're such an ostrich, Ailsa.' She got up and stormed out of the room. Open-plan houses don't have many doors so there was only one to slam.

'Well, that's her gone,' said Dad flatly.

A jolt surged through my body and my stomach listed so violently that I thought I might be sick. Sensing bad karma, Lucifer jumped onto me with his claws out and speared my stomach. I pushed him roughly away.

'I'd forgotten about the knife,' said Mum, her voice so quiet that I could hardly hear what she said.

'She's trying to exaggerate historical events to justify her current negligence and find an excuse not to help look after your father.'

'Why do we remember everything so differently?'

'Memories are ephemeral,' said Dad. I could tell by the way his voice slowed and deepened that he was going into lecture mode. 'Your mind isn't a video camera recording and storing events to review. The act of repeating a narrative corrupts its content, and the fact that Rachel can recall all these details doesn't mean her account of events is any more accurate than yours. You've simply re-transcribed the memory differently.'

'Have you been in touch with her?' Mum asked.

There were sounds of washing-up. I was good at interpreting the secret language of low-grade domestic conflict and waited for the stormy clash of plates being stacked and the tap violently spewing too much water into the sink. But it didn't happen.

'Do you really think I would have made all these changes to my life and blow it all by communicating with her?' said Dad. 'I want to make this work, Ailsa. Moving away from her is part of my commitment to you. You have open access to my phone, my emails. Take a look if you don't believe me.'

'It's difficult to believe you after so many lies.'

They left the room and went upstairs to bed. I thought about Jay's comment about it being better not to know about things and realized that the main reason for this was that uncovering the truth almost always posed more questions than it answered.

I went upstairs to my room and stood by the window, waiting for Jay to appear. When he didn't, I messaged him and tried to call. Eventually I gave up and lay down on top of the duvet fully dressed. It was cold but the physical discomfort helped to cool down the thoughts boiling in my brain. Dad had betrayed Mum with another woman. I had to try and reorder the paradigm in my head whereby Dad had been the victim. But both of them had betrayed us with their lies, and it was this thought that proved most corrosive.

I tried to think about things that were much bigger than me: the fact that there are a hundred billion galaxies in the cosmos; that all the matter that makes up the human race could be reduced to the size of a sugar cube; and that the number of possible histories is finite because there has been a finite number of events with a finite number of outcomes. In the back of my mind lay the certainty that the reason we had moved here was because Dad had cheated on Mum. I drew little comfort from the fact that this history had been played out a million times before.

The next day was Saturday. I had to see Jay. I waited in my room until eleven o'clock and then slipped out the back door and headed through the now permanent hole in the fence to the Fairports' house. On the right was the muddy track that led to the sweat lodge in the woods. I turned left towards the house and let myself in through the back door, carrying a pile of Biology books to add credibility to my excuse that we were doing homework together.

Jay was alone in the kitchen, cracking eggs into a mixing bowl, his back to me. The only scenario I hadn't anticipated was the one now before me, and I hadn't rehearsed what to say to him. He began to whisk the eggs with a fork and from behind the motion reminded me of the way his hand went up and down his dick.

'Hi,' I said, feeling shy, which was ridiculous given the complete lack of inhibition of the previous weeks. I held the books close to my chest and stared at the wooden floor. He turned round.

'Hello, you,' he said warmly. 'Do you fancy some frittata?' He didn't seem fazed to see me. Actually he seemed quite pleased.

'What's frittata?' I asked, staring at the beaten eggs and chopped bacon sliding into the frying pan so that I didn't have to look at him.

'A cross between an omelette and a tortilla,' he explained. It smelled really good.

He stirred the mixture and urged me to sit down at the head of the table.

'There's no one else here,' he explained. 'We can pretend that we're a normal couple sitting down to breakfast. What do you think we'd talk about after twenty years together? Do you think we'd be one of those couples who still talk?'

He fashioned a ring from a piece of tin foil, brought it over and placed it on my finger. Then strolled back to the cooker as though what he had done had no more significance than cracking an egg.

'I don't know. I guess it depends on what we're doing, where we're living, whether we've had kids,' I said. 'There are an infinite number of variables.' I always sounded geekier when I was nervous.

'We're in London. We've got two children, a boy and a girl. I'm a record producer and you're a neurosurgeon. It's all mapped out.'

'There is no certainty but uncertainty,' I said, trying and failing to sum up my feelings. 'What do your parents talk about over breakfast?'

'Dad talks about how his holistic healing centre will help pay off the mortgage on this house, the advantages of living in a country where hip replacements are free and the ruinous marriages of their friends in Ibiza. Mum wonders if we've done the right thing moving back to England. She misses her friends' ruinous marriages. She thinks you learn more from the university of life than you do at school and that people here are too conventional and conservative.'

'You mean us?' I asked, because really who else was there?

'Probably,' said Jay vaguely.

'Not any longer. I've just discovered the reason we moved here was because Dad was having an affair with another woman. So maybe your mum will feel more at home with us now.'

'Shit. Did you find clues in the bathroom cabinet?' he asked, putting a plate of frittata in front of me.

I cut off a small slice and put it in my mouth. 'Delicious,' I said, even though I couldn't taste anything. 'I overheard an argument. My aunt gave it away. She accused Mum of being an ostrich for thinking that she can reinvent their marriage by running away from the woman who came between her and Dad. I know they've been to marriage guidance so I guess Rachel got that partly wrong. She accused Dad of still being in touch with the woman.'

'Who is she?'

'I think she might be someone he worked with and that's why he had to leave his job. It makes sense. All this time I've blamed Mum for moving here when it was Dad's fault. I don't get why anyone would fancy him.'

'My mum thinks he's an attractive guy,' said Jay. It wasn't what I wanted to hear right that moment. 'At least it sounds as though they want to make things work,' he added. I was taken aback by the logic of this comment.

I wasn't ready to see the good in anything. Or adopt a measured view. For months I had seen Dad as the victim of Mum's whimsy and I was now furious with him for going along with this deceit and with Mum for allowing it.

'Do you like the ring?' he asked.

I held out my hand and his fingers curled around mine. He squeezed my hand and ran his finger around each knuckle and up my arm.

'This is the first time since New Year that we've touched,' I told him. 'Or is touching too conventional and conservative for you?'

He leaned towards me and I could feel his breath on my face. He stroked the side of my cheek and tilted my chin towards his face. My heart was pumping so fast, I wondered if Jay could hear it. I tried to calm myself down by telling myself that it was simply responding to a signal from my brain.

'You're so gorgeous, Romy. I love everything about you.'

'I waited for you last night. I needed to see you. But you never came.' My voice sounded higher than usual as though I was about to cry. He put his hand on my shoulder and I leaned towards it.

'We've got to stop. It's not right. You deserve better.' He said them slowly but I could tell he had practised these lines.

'That's the kind of thing Luke says when he wants to let a girl down gently.'

'It's way more complicated than that.'

'How so?'

His fingers ran across my lips to silence me and he moved towards me. I closed my eyes. We kissed, his tongue deep in my mouth. I pushed back against him, tasting the inside of his cheek and feeling the grooves on the roof of his mouth. *I kiss, you kiss, he, she or it kisses,* I thought, trying to slow my breathing through my nose so that I wouldn't have to come up for air.

He pulled me onto his lap and we kept kissing. He tugged at my top, pulling it out from my jeans, and I could feel the cold air from the back door against my skin. I curled my body into him and we fitted perfectly together as I knew we would. His hand filled the space beneath my top and skin and I shivered as he explored my back and pulled down a bra strap to cup a breast in his hand. Every part of my body was poised for pleasure. Even my scalp shivered. This was the real thing, I thought to myself. But suddenly Jay pushed me away and stood up, sending the chair flying. I thought maybe someone was watching from our house, but when I looked across to our sitting room, there was no one there.

'I'm sorry, Romy. I can't do this.' His voice was heavy with regret. He walked towards the cooker and turned his back towards me, staring at the floor.

'What's wrong?' I asked him breathlessly, putting my arms around him from behind. He was taller than me and my head rested against his shoulder blade. His body was taut with tension. 'Don't you want to?'

'I want to but I can't.' I stroked his head in the same way that Mum used to stroke Ben's when he was upset, relishing the way his hair slipped through my fingers. He didn't try and disentangle himself from me.

'I'm really sorry.' He leaned back into me.

'What do you mean?'

'It's complicated.'

'Try me.'

'Properly complicated. You'll hate me if I tell you.'

I tried to think of something profound and philosophical to say. I experimented with a sentence along the lines of, 'The web we are weaving around ourselves is too fragile for words,' but it sounded too much like a Coldplay lyric.

'Is it because you've never slept with a girl before?' I asked hopefully, because that we could overcome.

'I haven't, but that's not the problem. I like you more than any girl I have ever met, Romy. I think about you all of the time. When something happens, you're the first person that I want to tell. Like this morning, when I woke up I looked out the window and there was a deer at the end of the garden. Or when Marley accidentally drove the lawnmower through the side of Dad's sweat lodge yesterday. When I play music I hear you in the notes.'

'Are you trying to say that you just want to be friends?'

'God, no. You really turn me on. I love your body. I love the shape of you. I draw it in my head before I go to sleep. I think about your breasts a lot too. They're so perfect. They're really the best tits that I have ever seen.'

I considered my breasts, recently escaped from my bra, slightly disbelieving that they could be the object of so much adulation. I mean I liked them, or at least I didn't feel hostile to them in the way that I did to some other parts of my body.

'Do you have many points of comparison?' I asked. He turned round.

'Thousands,' he said. I laughed but his expression was deadly serious.

'Maybe we could sleep with each other once and then go back to being friends. I wouldn't mind. But I'd like my first time to be with someone like you,' I said, the words tumbling out.

'No, you wouldn't,' he said. His eyes burned into mine. 'I'm messed up. Properly messed up.'

'Are you gay?' I asked, remembering Marnie's experience.

'That would be straightforward,' he said. He paused. 'Do you believe in the possibility of change? Or do you think we're born one way and we're stuck with who we are, like the way a walnut grows into its shell?'

'Dad says that the human brain never stops evolving, which means in theory it's being rewired all the time.'

'Really?'

'But 95 per cent of what it does is subconscious, which means that if you want to change a bad habit only

5 per cent of your brain is available to do it. He says this to Luke a lot.'

'So if I wanted to change something about myself I could?' He sounded hopeful.

'Yes, but the odds are stacked against you.'

'I'm going to tell you,' he said abruptly. 'I've never discussed this with anyone else. You've got to promise two things: one, you won't say anything, and two, that you won't hate me.'

'Promise,' I said. The melodrama was worthy of Marnie. But I wasn't expecting what came next.

'I can't have sex with real women.'

'What do you mean?'

'I've tried a couple of times but I can't do it, so I'd sort of given up. Then I met you and I thought you might be the cure for my problem but now I'm not sure.'

I started to feel anxious. Did this mean that he fancied me when he first met me but didn't any more? Mum always says that if you don't understand something you should ask questions until you do, so I tried a different tactic.

'Do you find girls attractive?'

'Yes.'

'Do you find me attractive?'

'Yes.'

'Do you want to touch me?'

'Yes.'

'You're not making this easy. Can you give me a bit more, please?'

He turned to face me and put his hands on my shoulders and dropped down until his head was level with mine and our foreheads were touching.

'I've got this problem, Romy.' His left leg jiggled nervously up and down and he chewed the side of his lower lip so hard that when he stopped it was slightly swollen. 'I can only get off watching stuff on the Internet.'

'What kind of stuff?'

'Porn. Basically. Basically porn.'

This was new territory for me. Of course I knew what porn was and some girls in my year were into watching it, mainly to expand their repertoire, but it held no interest for me. I pulled away from him.

'I think quite a lot of boys do that,' I said, remembering a conversation I'd overheard between Dad and Luke last year where Dad warned my brother that watching too much porn could distort his view of sex and Luke suggested he interview his previous girlfriends before drawing the wrong conclusions.

'You're not hearing me,' he said, taking my hand and stroking it tenderly as though he was telling me that someone had just died. 'That's the only way I can have sex.'

He held my gaze. I didn't flinch, but he must have seen the fear in my eyes.

'I knew I'd freak you out.'

'It's just not what I was expecting.' I stopped speaking because I didn't know what to say. Then Jay began talking and the words spewed out.

'It started when we were living in Ibiza. For research

purposes. I'd met a girl and I was looking to improve my range. But the girl disappeared and the porn habit didn't. After a while I couldn't stop thinking about it. I'd go to the beach in Ibiza and I'd see a woman and catch the curve of her arse against her bikini or that cleft between a woman's breasts and have to go straight back home to have a bash. Which would have been fine if it was once a day but it wasn't. And isn't. It's more like six or seven.'

'You're addicted to Internet porn?' I said the words slowly, trying to get my head round what he was telling me.

'I guess so,' he said, 'although I've never thought of it like that.'

'I'm not sure what to say.' I must have recoiled from him. He stepped towards me, looking desperate. He put out a hand but I didn't want him to touch me.

'I don't have any really bad kinks,' he said hastily. 'No furries, BDSM ... There's a lot of deviant shit out there.'

'I don't even know what any of that means,' I said, feeling totally out of my depth.

'I get off on different stuff but my main area of interest is oral. I always come back to that. It's my specialist subject.' He almost sounded like he was writing his personal statement for university. His voice went really quiet. 'No girl in real life has ever been as good as watching it on the Internet.'

This was as bad as it gets. Stratospherically beyond my experience. I could see my reactions reflected in his as I fast-forwarded from fear to contempt, panic and pity and back to fear again. Surely it was good that he had confided in me? For a moment a small part of me even felt flattered. But almost as quickly I understood that it would have been better never to know because this knowledge was corrosive. And I knew from the reactivity series that corrosion is an irreversible reaction.

'That's so messed up.'

He didn't disagree. 'It's like junk food. You crave it and a couple of hours later you want the same thing all over again. I've never got as far with a real girl as I have with you and believe me, Romy, it is progress that I can think about you in this way. But I'm stuck in something I can't get out of. It controls me. I can't control it.'

I couldn't find the right words and he mistook my silence for disapproval.

'I told you you'd hate me.'

'I don't hate you,' I said, feeling totally out of my depth. 'But I'm not sure where to go from here.' So I went home.

9

As soon as she sat down in the restaurant opposite Harry's old office, Ailsa realized it was a bad idea. But midway through the final speaker of the Seizing Success conference at the Institute of Education she found herself ignoring the conclusions on what makes a good head outstanding and began plotting the quickest route to the ramshackle sprawl of Victorian buildings that Harry affectionately used to call the Warren.

Harry always said that life was a competition between impulse and self-control.

And when Ailsa described to Rachel what she did next, her only explanation was that her self-regulatory system had momentarily short-circuited. When she left Norfolk for London she was not intending to go back to the Italian restaurant opposite the Department of Neuroscience where she had occasionally met Harry for lunch before they had children. The idea only occurred to her as the speaker summed up her conclusions on how to get parents more involved in their children's education. And there was no obvious connection between the two.

Whispering hurried goodbyes to colleagues sitting either side of her, Ailsa explained she had a train to catch and left the auditorium two stairs at a time. 'Like a woman possessed,' she later told Rachel.

As she stared down at the mozzarella salad that the waiter had put down in front of her, it occurred to Ailsa that the last time she had eaten here with Harry she had been heavily pregnant with Luke. She could remember the sensation of her half-undone zip pressing into her stomach and the tiny track marks it left on her skin when she leaned over the table to spoon pasta into her mouth: her fault for refusing to wear those ugly maternity trousers until the last possible moment. She had endured the discomfort like a Christian wearing sackcloth, telling herself the pain was atonement for the lie she had just told Harry, her husband of less than a year.

The restaurant had barely changed since then. The same black and white photos of Palermo hung on the wall. The menu of typical Sicilian dishes was identical. The owner, originally from East Grinstead, now spoke English with an Italian accent. *Just goes to show if you pretend something for long enough, it can become the truth*, thought Ailsa.

'Is everything all right, madam?' he said with a discreet bow.

'Could I have a glass of house white, please?' Ailsa asked, unconsciously mimicking the upward lilt at the end of his sentence.

She got out a pen and notebook from her bag to review her conference notes. 'How to emulate the success of the Finnish school system,' she had written.

'Ditch competition, standardization, test-based account-ability and choice. Focus on collaboration, personalized learning and ending standardized tests. The reverse of current government policy.' The implications made her feel dizzy. Someone in the Department of Education would see this and another slew of reforms would rain down into her in-box. Change was sexier than consolidation. God, one bad report from the school inspectors and a head teacher could be out on her ear. She was done with change.

'Long day?' asked the owner of the restaurant, returning with her drink.

'It's not over yet,' said Ailsa. She took tiny delicate sips of the wine, like a bee sucking nectar.

From her window seat in the restaurant she had an unrestricted view across to the steps that led up to the main door of the Department of Neuroscience. Since Harry's departure a glass box had been constructed around the ornate Victorian entrance to give the building the illusion of modernity. A group of students tumbled down the steps and waited inside for the rain to stop. Ailsa hadn't been back to London since the move to Luckmore and she had forgotten how it never really got dark. Everywhere was aglow. There were street lamps, well-lit shops, offices with strip lighting. Visibility was way better than she could have hoped. She glanced from face to face. Was the girl among them? Would she recognize her? Because of course this was why she had come. The Neuroscience students always came here after evening lectures. She could admit it to herself now. She needed to know if Harry was telling the truth.

Harry had complained bitterly about the introduction of evening sessions for postgrads when the university had floated the idea fourteen months earlier. It was a small tutorial group, he had explained, but nevertheless would take time away from his work. All lecturers were required to do it, even those who were involved in research. He couldn't let his students down. He had sounded totally beleaguered.

Ailsa had been broadly sympathetic. Harry had always given the best part of himself to his students. His lectures were legendary. He'd even done a TED Talk on adolescent brain development. Or rather lack of development. Because only in the past decade had technology allowed neuroscientists to discover that the rational, decision-making part of the brain didn't finish developing until your late twenties. After a decade in airless basements scanning the pre-frontal cortices of teenage volunteers Harry was finally making a name for himself. She offered to pick up the slack at weekends so he could claw back time to work on his projects. He had been grateful. He hugged her and she noticed through his thick winter coat that he had lost his paunch.

'So exploitative the way you now have to teach so many evenings,' Ailsa had mentioned to Kath Mason, one of Harry's colleagues, over dinner at her house a couple of weeks later. Harry had wanted to cancel at the last minute but Ailsa had insisted they should go. 'Especially with the pay freeze. Harry is exhausted. You'll all end up in an early grave.' It was a throwaway comment at the end of a long conversation with Kath about how average life expectancy had increased by fifteen years since Harry and Kath had graduated from medical school.

It was the way that Kath had paused and put down her pudding spoon that caught Ailsa's attention. Her eyes told a different story from the carefully composed sentence that came out of her mouth. It was a duality Ailsa recognized from dealing with kids who were in trouble at school.

'We're all on different schedules,' Kath had said firmly. Later Ailsa wondered if she meant to tell her something. Or if it had occurred to Kath that Harry was lying at exactly the same moment that it occurred to her. Perhaps for that five-second interval when neither of them spoke they were both weighing up the evidence and coming to the same conclusion. Because how many reasons were there for a husband to lie to his wife about why he wasn't coming home in the evening?

They had outstayed their welcome that night. Ailsa could tell by the way Kath curled towards her husband on the sofa and rested her head on his shoulder after they finished coffee. She sat as far from Ailsa and Harry as possible, as if marital problems might be contagious. Having wanted to cancel the dinner earlier that day, Harry would not stop talking about the new scanner at work. Perhaps he knew he was living on borrowed time. He explained to Kath's husband how it was a powerful giant magnet that measured the hydrogen atoms in blood vessels. 'Blood flow means busy neurons,' he kept repeating. 'The region of the brain where most is going on is the region where there is most blood flow.' When they left, Kath hugged Ailsa a little too tightly.

Ailsa didn't confront Harry on the way home. If he came up with a credible excuse it would be too tempting to believe him to avoid the upheaval that surely lay ahead. He was drunkenly affectionate and insisted on holding hands as they weaved along the pavement when the night bus didn't arrive. When they got home he couldn't find his keys. Harry never lost anything. As he turned out his pockets Ailsa tried not to reflect on what Kath had said. But when old receipts, coins and business cards fell to the ground she picked them up and found herself looking for clues, resentful of the way that he had so swiftly turned her into a suspicious snooper. In the end they had to wake up Romy to let them in. Romy noticed her mood. Harry didn't.

Ailsa never managed to pin down the exact chronology of events that followed that evening. The details remained for ever elusive. As far as she could recall, some time the following week she instructed Romy to collect Ben from after-school club so that she could go and see Rachel at her flat in Kensal Rise. She couldn't remember if this was before or after she had found a restaurant bill for two from this same Italian restaurant on an evening Harry was meant to be teaching.

She arrived unannounced, worried that Rachel would hear the unease in her voice and elaborate melodramatic scenarios to explain the unscheduled visit or, even worse, phone their mother for clues. She feared Rachel's overactive imagination and the way she could say things without any thought of their consequences, yet she was the person Ailsa trusted most to help her work out what was going on and what to do. Fearless honesty, their mother had called it. Lack of filter, Harry said.

As Ailsa waited on the pavement for Rachel to throw down the keys to her flat from the first-floor window she had a sudden image of herself as a child sitting on Rachel's stomach, trying to force her sister's fingers from her ears so that she had to listen to the argument going on downstairs. They needed to do something, Ailsa insisted, pinning Rachel's arms by her side. Someone could die. Rachel had responded by flinging her head from side to side, singing 'Ring of Fire' as loudly as possible. Ailsa had hugged Rachel until she stopped.

Rachel's sitting-room floor was covered in pages from the script she was working on. Some had Post-it notes attached with tiny handwritten instructions. Ailsa picked up a couple of pages to open up a trail to her sister. She read a couple of lines of dialogue marked with pink highlighter. 'I didn't choose to be born this way. I can't help who I am. I have to kill the thing I love most.

And that person is you. Then we can be together for eternity.'

'Ignore the cliché. Does he sound like a zombie with a soul?' Rachel had asked as she gave Ailsa a hug. She pulled out a pencil that was holding her hair up in a bun.

'Completely,' Ailsa said. 'Although it might be difficult to distinguish him from a vampire.'

'Traditionally vampires have been more romantic and articulate,' said Rachel. 'We're trying to redefine a genre. Create a more intellectual kind of zombie.' She turned her back on Ailsa and put the page back on the floor. 'I know why you're here by the way. I just wanted to have sex with him one last time. But I couldn't tell Mum that.'

Ailsa smiled. Not for the first time she was grateful for her sister's self-absorption. It was a good escape from her own problems. Rachel assumed Ailsa had come because less than a week after promising to end her relationship with Budgie she had taken him to Norfolk to stay with their parents. Budgie had chopped enough wood to see Adam and Georgia through the rest of the winter. He had drained the radiators and mended a broken tile, said Rachel, trying to justify her volte-face.

He had even taken Adam for a ride on his motorbike along the coast road. They had dressed up Adam in Budgie's leathers. Rachel showed Ailsa the photos on her phone. There was a close-up of Adam wearing a helmet with the visor up. His face was florid. Ailsa was fascinated by the network of tiny broken blood capillaries on his nose. Was it all the red wine that had turned them so purple? She wondered why there were no pictures of their mother. Georgia was too tired to stay up, Rachel explained.

'Budgie got on really well with Dad,' said Rachel almost reproachfully.

'That's not a reason to stay with him,' said Ailsa firmly.

'Dad needs a playmate,' Rachel laughed.

'True,' said Ailsa.

'I told him it was over. It was all very civilized. But we agreed we could keep seeing each other casually. Best of both worlds, don't you think?'

There was a lull in the conversation. Ailsa braced herself. 'Harry's been lying to me.' She hadn't articulated the thought out loud before. She was sitting on the sofa. The one where Rachel had had sex with Budgie for the first time, Ailsa remembered, abruptly removing her arm from the back. Johnny Cash was playing in the background. *I Walk the Line*. The soundtrack to their childhood. 'I'm not sure exactly what's going on.'

'Spit it out,' said Rachel, sitting cross-legged on the floor in front of her. She poured another large glass of wine for each of them. Ailsa tried to stick to the facts, sketchy as they were, and avoid interpretation. Apart from the fact Harry was coming home late more nights than he wasn't, there had been other changes. He had developed insomnia, which he put down to work stress. He was more impatient with the children, especially Luke, but then with less than a week before his mock

GCSEs Luke had decided to drop Physics and Chemistry, and Harry had taken it personally. He was more sexually adventurous than he had been for a while. In fact in terms of frequency and quality it was better than it had been for years.

Rachel put up a hand. 'Spare me the details, please.'

Ailsa didn't point out the hypocrisy of this comment. 'So what do you think?' she asked.

'You need to explore all avenues. From the least obvious to the most obvious.'

'That's why I came to you,' said Ailsa. Rachel ran her finger round and round the wine glass until it made a low hum.

'Maybe he's got addicted to online poker and is spending hours gambling. Budgie was doing that when he met me.'

'He could do that at home.'

'You'd notice,' said Rachel. 'Secrecy is a big part of the attraction.'

'Harry's not an addict. Don't you remember his head was scanned for a medical textbook as an example of a normal brain?'

'Or he could be preparing a surprise for you. Isn't your birthday coming up?'

'What kind of surprise?'

Rachel frowned into the middle distance. 'He could be learning a new skill to impress you. A South American dance, like the salsa or capoeira. Or the tango.'

Ailsa laughed at the absurdity of this idea. She wished

it were true that she could inspire such a romantic gesture in her husband. 'It takes two to tango. As Louis Armstrong once said. And Harry is completely uncoordinated. But I like your thinking.'

'Maybe he's making something for you. I read a script once where an artist devoted herself to sculpting her boyfriend's erect penis in secret as a present for his birthday, but he killed himself because he thought the reason that she stopped visiting him was because she'd taken a lover. Totally tragic.'

Ailsa started giggling uncontrollably. She hadn't eaten all day and the wine had made her light-headed. It was a release from the dark thoughts swirling around her head.

'It wasn't meant to be a comedy,' said Rachel.

'How could she sculpt her boyfriend's erect penis?'

'Easy. Take a wax mould.'

'But then he would have known and it wouldn't be a secret.'

'God, why do you always have to be so literal?'

'I think Harry would notice if I suddenly poured boiling wax over his cock. And wouldn't it set hard?'

'If you dip the mould in cold water it comes off like a glove. Then you can cast it in bronze.'

'How do you know all this, Rach? Because of research for the script?'

'Don't tell anyone. Budgie tried it. It worked fine apart from the fact he dripped the wax all over his balls and ended up losing a lot of pubic hair.'

'Please, have mercy,' said Ailsa. She was laughing so much that tears dripped down her cheeks.

'If you really want to know what's going on, you need to get hold of his bank statements or look at his mobile phone,' Rachel said, finishing the bottle of wine.

'Maybe I shouldn't find out. Sometimes knowing the truth causes even more uncertainty than the uncertainty of not knowing,' said Ailsa. 'Maybe if he's having an affair I should let it run its course.'

'I'm the one who avoids responsibility. Not you, Ailsa,' said Rachel gently. 'You always try to sort things out. I've always admired you for that. Ever since we were children.'

They hugged.

Rachel continued: 'If you do nothing he'll get in deeper and deeper with another woman and end up leaving you. Whatever the outcome, you need to be one step ahead. Take a look at his phone.'

'I don't know the password.'

'Go to one of those shops in Camden Market. I'll come with you if you like.'

'I can't imagine Harry getting into anything that would distract him from his work,' said Ailsa. 'He's not the type.'

'I'm not very wise when it comes to choosing boy-friends, Ailsa, but one thing I know from the married men I've slept with in my time is that there isn't a type. Gather the evidence. If you find something suspect take a few days to get your head together. And tackle him when you're ready. You need to be one step ahead. Men always try to lie their way out of these situations. It's not in Harry's interests to be honest.'

Ailsa bided her time. Rachel got impatient. A few weeks later Harry came home from work early. 'I'm in trouble.' This was it, thought Ailsa, her shoulders tensing. She was organizing the fridge. Why did everyone start a new carton of milk before the old one was finished? His voice was higher than usual and taut with emotion. *Could you clench your vocal cords?* she wondered as she turned to face him. It was 5 February. That date was etched in her memory.

'What kind of trouble?' She wasn't going to make this easy for him. 'Did you kick up a fuss about the new time-table? Kath said it was having a big impact on family life.'

Harry swallowed a couple of times, his Adam's apple bobbing up and down pathetically. He headed towards the kitchen sink and began washing a dirty mug, squeezing far too much washing-up liquid into the bottom so that when he turned on the tap, bubbles spewed onto his jumper sleeve. He literally couldn't face her. *Right use of literally*, thought Ailsa. It was one of those words that were rarely used correctly any more.

'I love you, Ailsa. And I love our children.' He spoke slowly as though every word were coated with something viscous. He didn't sound like Harry. But he had stopped sounding like Harry months ago. 'I love our life together. But I've done something really stupid. I don't really understand how it's happened or why it's happened but I do know that I've never done anything that I regret more. I've lost my way. I'm so sorry.'

Ailsa sat down at the end of the kitchen table so that she could observe him from behind. She suddenly found everything about him ridiculous: his shoulder blades poking through the back of his shirt, the hair growing on the nape of his neck, the incipient bald patch, the worn heels of his shoes. Anger was a mask for pain, Rachel had told her during their most recent conversation. She longed to pick up the jug of daffodils that he had bought for her yesterday and throw it at him. She looked down at her hands. They were gently shaking. He offered to make tea but forgot to switch on the kettle.

Welcome to my world, Ailsa wanted to tell him, because since the dinner at Kath's she had found herself frequently distracted from basic tasks. Ben had sweetly taken to making her a cup of tea when they got home after school. The way her eight-year-old son noticed something was wrong and could complete this simple task and her forty-five-year-old husband couldn't made her feel furious all over again.

Harry sat down and took her hand, stroking her fingers like Ben stroked the ear of his teddy. She held his gaze until he couldn't bear it any more. He was wallowing in self-pity.

'It's complicated.'

'There's no mystery, Harry. You're just another middle-aged cliché.'

There was no originality in her situation. She knew the script: the marriage wasn't right, it hadn't been for ages; he had tried to talk to her but she was unresponsive, remote and too wrapped up in the children. He had finally met someone who understood him.

'It's not what you think.'

'What do you think I think?'

He looked up at her. His dark eyes were so watery that she blinked. He rubbed them and his shoulders slumped from the effort required simply to speak.

'I'm so sorry.'

'Have you fallen in love with someone else?'

'It's not that straightforward.'

'I wouldn't describe infidelity as straightforward.'

'That's not what I meant.'

'What did you mean then?'

'I got involved with a student.' It was the most direct answer he had given to a question so far.

'Another cliché,' said Ailsa, anger making her dangerously clear-headed.

'Don't worry, she's a postgrad,' he said quickly.

'How old exactly?'

'Almost twenty-six.'

'So she's twenty-five,' said Ailsa. She thought the weeks of indecision had allowed her to dissect every possible scenario, but a new wave of anxiety crashed over her as she absorbed this unexpected fact.

'I guess if you're going to have a midlife crisis you might as well do it properly.'

'She's an old soul,' said Harry. He regretted saying this and opened and closed his mouth as though trying to recapture the words.

'With a young body,' said Ailsa. Harry winced, putting his hand up in front of his face to try and block her anger.

'I told you, it's more complicated than that.'

He explained that she was doing a PhD on the decrease of dopamine in the adolescent brain. When Ailsa didn't say anything he wrongly assumed that she wanted him to continue. It was interesting research because drugs and alcohol activate the pleasure-producing chemistry of the brain, especially dopamine, and an overstimulation of the pleasure-producing pathways could perhaps eventually adversely affect normal experience of joy and affect decision-making. Especially among teenagers.

'Are you trying to tell me you fell in love with her mind? Or that you were doing method science?' asked Ailsa, enraged by the way he could soothe himself by talking about work when she couldn't. She didn't like the dry, sarcastic tone she had adopted, but in the face of his shame and her pain it was impossible to disguise her contempt. It occurred to her that what she wanted to feel was nothing.

'I'm trying to explain why we started spending time together,' he said.

'Please, spare me your pathetic excuses.'

'Things haven't been easy between us, Ailsa.'

'What do you mean?'

'You've been spending a lot of time with your parents. You just spent the whole weekend away looking after your mother.'

'She had a doctor's appointment. Who else was going to take her?'

'Your dad. Or Rachel. We hardly ever see each other. We both work long hours. We have three children. There are a lot of extenuating circumstances.'

'This sounds like a well-rehearsed self-justification. Couldn't you at least have had the decency to let me know what was going on in your head before you got so involved?'

'I didn't want to burden you with more worries. You were dealing with all of Luke's problems.'

'What has Luke got to do with any of this?'

'He's put us under a lot of pressure. Caused a lot of arguments.'

'So you thought the best way to deal with this was to have sex with a student?' asked Ailsa. 'Teenagers mess up. It's a neuro-programming issue. That's what you normally say. But you never apply your great theories to Luke.' Harry was always harder on him than on Romy and Ben. She pushed this thought away.

'You always try to find excuses for him. That's part of the problem,' said Harry.

'You always find excuses for everyone apart from him,' Ailsa retorted. 'Your expectations are so low that he's lost any incentive to please you. You have no idea how bad he feels about himself.'

'Is that what you really think?'

'I admit that Luke can be difficult but I think you've stopped trying.'

'Please, will you just listen to me for a moment and stop being so defensive.'

Ailsa fell quiet. Harry spoke about Luke and how difficult he found it being his father. He felt he didn't know him and they had nothing in common. He described how he felt like an intruder on Luke's relationship with Ailsa. He remembered how he had spent hours persuading Luke to build a Lego castle with him when he was Ben's age and how, just as they had completed it, Luke had held it in the air and dropped it on the floor on purpose.

Ailsa remembered this too. It was an accident, she pleaded. Harry put up his hand to stop her. He continued. Even when he was little, Luke never wanted Harry to read him a story or help with his homework. If he had a problem he always sought out Ailsa. Until Romy was born Harry thought he was doing it all wrong. She was so different. A noise that sounded like the sea echoed in Ailsa's head. She couldn't hear. She thought of all the tiny networks of capillaries, veins and arteries and realized the sound she could hear was the blood flowing through her head. She pressed her temples as hard as she could. Harry put his hand on her cheek and asked something. She pulled away. His touch was too painful.

'Girls are always closer to their dads,' she said as the noise faded. What about Ben? he asked. He couldn't be closer to Ben. For the second time that evening Harry's eyes filled with tears. Now Luke was a teenager his connection with his eldest son was even more tenuous, and soon it would be too late because Luke would be gone. He wiped his nose with his sleeve.

'You can't hold Luke responsible for your entanglement with this girl,' said Ailsa.

'I'm not. I take full responsibility for my actions. I'm just trying to contextualize. I'm trying to work out why after all these years she was the one who got to me. It's not the first time that a student has been interested in me.'

'I had no idea you were so irresistible,' said Ailsa sarcastically. 'How long have you been sleeping with her?'

'It's not that simple.'

Harry started speaking again. She had started a postgrad course in September. He was her tutor. They had fallen for each other almost immediately but nothing had happened for a couple of months. They started going out together a couple of nights a week. He thought he was in love. He had fantasized about leaving Ailsa and the children and moving abroad with her to a university in the US or Australia. He had even checked out jobs in Sydney. It was this that really got to Ailsa. He had always dismissed her efforts to persuade him out of London. Harry didn't notice her anger. She realized he had stopped taking her into account months ago.

He wouldn't stop talking. He was looking for a way out of his old life, but as the fantasy took shape he realized their entanglement was about escape. He was flattered by the way the girl desired and idolized him, and they had done some great work together. But unlike his life with Ailsa, it wasn't real. He wasn't in love with her. So he had decided to end the relationship.

'Well, congratulations, Harry,' said Ailsa.

'I realized that in the greater scheme of things she doesn't mean anything to me.' He gave Ailsa a nervous smile. She didn't smile back. 'But that's not all,' he said. He was beginning to resemble one of those Dr Seuss books she used to read the children when they were little. Which one was it? She tried to remember. Either *The Cat in the Hat* or *The Cat in the Hat Comes Back*. Ailsa tried to focus.

'Why would you risk your marriage and your entire family life for someone who didn't mean anything to you?' she asked.

Harry couldn't answer. His eyes shifted uncomfortably around the kitchen, resting first on the coffee maker, then on Lucifer, and finally on the daffodils.

'And if it's over why are you telling me about it now?'

'Because it's important to be honest,' he said.

'That's the most dishonest thing you've said so far.'

His eyes were again fixed on the coffee maker.

'People found out. Colleagues. Her friends. It doesn't seem fair that you don't know and they do. Today I was called to see the vice chancellor. Obviously I have to hand her over to another tutor to supervise. All very awkward.'

This was not what Ailsa was expecting. Now she was afraid. This was no longer simply about the threat to her happiness. Already she knew that although it would be a heavy price to pay, it was a cost she could bear. If this got out he might struggle to get another job. His children would hate him. It could blow apart the life they had built together. Damn him for turning it into a situation where she wasn't allowed to fall apart. She tried to compose herself.

'How did they find out?' She already knew the answer to the question before Harry spoke. 'She told them?'

Harry nodded slowly as if his head was unbearably heavy. His whole body drooped.

'I tried to end the relationship. She thought we were moving to Australia. There was a big gulf in expectations. She was devastated.'

'How could you let yourself get in so deep?'

'It wasn't a normal affair.'

'What do you mean?'

'We didn't have sex much, at least in the conventional sense.'

'I don't understand.'

'We texted each other a lot. It got out of hand.'

He finally looked up at her. His eyes were panicked, like Ben's after he had woken up from a nightmare.

He started explaining how the modern world held

many temptations. Drugs, alcohol. Risky sexual behaviour. Sugar. He spoke fast. His pupils were dilated.

'There are so many stimuli in our environment that can activate cravings,' Harry said in a tone that sounded almost pleading. 'My self-regulatory capacity has been seriously compromised.' He started to explain how he had suppressed his pre-frontal cortex. 'There are two pathways that mediate frontal regulation of emotion and I have moved from a frontal-striatal pathway associated with successful regulation to a frontal-amygdala pathway.'

'What are you talking about?' said Ailsa.

Harry's head bowed until it was almost touching his knees. She again noticed his hairline had receded. It made him look so vulnerable.

'The texts were sexual. Once it started I couldn't stop.'

Ailsa opened her mouth to speak but the words stuck in her throat. She swallowed. He offered to get her water. She shook her head. She didn't want to accept anything from him. Their rules of engagement were already being redrawn. She resolved never again to allow herself to be in a position where Harry could cause her pain. It was, to quote Romy's favourite phrase of the week, an inviolable truth.

'What did they say?'

'She'd describe what she wanted to do to me. I'd say what I wanted to do to her. You know, the usual kind of thing.'

'I don't actually.'

'She sent them to the vice chancellor. There was a disciplinary panel. Five people, including Kath, sat in a row examining the evidence and decided that I hadn't broken any rules. They couldn't look me in the eye. They can't fire me. The vice chancellor said he hoped I would stay, but I could tell he didn't mean it. Obviously the girl is really sorry, now she's seen all the trouble she's caused. She's begging me not to go. I'm under such pressure, Ailsa, I don't see how I can keep working at the department. It's untenable. I don't know what to do.'

Ailsa knew instantly. She didn't want to get divorced. Rachel would argue that she had no pride, but it wasn't that simple when you had children and hadn't she done an assembly on how pride was a sin in almost every religion from Christianity to Islam? She thought of all the hard work that lay ahead just to get back to where they were forty minutes ago. Her stomach cramped as though her lower intestine was slowly being squeezed tighter and tighter. Sometimes staying in a marriage required more courage than leaving it. Who had said that? Then she remembered: it was her mother.

She must have made a noise because someone was at her side and a hand was on her wrist. It wasn't the waiter's because he was fluttering around with a dustpan and brush, sweeping up mozzarella salad and bits of broken plate from the floor. Harry was right: it was always a mistake to look back. Dissecting their relationship had been like picking up shards of broken glass. Piecing it back together had been even bloodier.

Harry had endured marriage guidance therapy as part of his punishment but loathed its idiom. *How does naming all these feelings help get over them?* Ailsa had sobbed at the end of another searing session. The therapist wanted Ailsa to read the text messages from Harry to the student. 'You have to know what it is that you are forgiving,' she advised. Harry had reared from his seat to protest.

'Don't you realize that the release of cortisol under stress means that the amygdala imprints memories that have a strong emotional charge?' The therapist shook her head. Ailsa intervened. She explained that if she read them she might never have sex with him again. And one of the few things they had going for them was the fact that even at the peak of his infatuation they had still managed to find each other attractive. Harry confessed that he had kept this from the student, a fact that Ailsa felt was significant.

The past had to be analysed in order to let it go, the counsellor insisted, otherwise they couldn't build a new future together. Bollocks, Harry had said. Was she aware of research after 9/11 that showed that retelling a story in a detailed way was like re-experiencing the original trauma over and over again? Ultimately it deepened the distress. After five sessions they decided not to go back. It was the first time they had agreed on anything in ages. They would make it work. They owed it to their children.

Ailsa applied for a job in Norfolk. The timing wasn't

great but the location quelled any doubts. She suddenly realized that more than anything she wanted to go home. Harry readily agreed. Then just as Ailsa couldn't imagine going through anything more painful, her mother died.

Ailsa felt the hand stroke the inside of her wrist. *I have spent a lifetime imposing order on chaos and I am tired of it.* She wondered if she had said it out loud.

'Excuse me, can you hear me?'

Ailsa glanced at the hand, taking in the chipped nail varnish and torn skin around the nails. Someone was searching for her pulse. She noticed her fork on the floor and a slice of tomato stuck on the end. Everything seemed very red.

'Are you all right?' a worried voice asked. 'Because you look very grey. I was worried you might be having a stroke or something. Do you have any loss of sensation? Can you speak?'

Ailsa looked up and knew instinctively it was her. She had imagined this moment many times, but now that she stood before her Ailsa could think of nothing to say. She looked ridiculously young. Prey rather than predator. Her red lipstick and gamine haircut reminded her of when Romy used to dress up in Ailsa's clothes and makeup. She would have no understanding of the carnage she had left in her wake. Ailsa was reminded of herself at the same age. Hadn't she been equally irresponsible? And hadn't she got away with it? Ailsa realized with absolute clarity that she felt no bitterness towards the young woman standing beside her.

'Migraine,' said Ailsa, rubbing her temples.

A young man came over and put a protective arm around the shoulder of his girlfriend. He was worried about her getting involved in a drama that had nothing to do with them. He picked up the fork from the floor and put it back on the table.

The woman pulled away from him. Her kohl-rimmed eyes narrowed. 'Do I know you from somewhere?' she asked Ailsa. 'Have we met before?'

'I don't think so,' said Ailsa. 'A previous life perhaps.'

'I'm a scientist, I don't believe in that kind of thing.' She smiled.

'What are you studying?' asked Ailsa.

'Postgrad in Neuroscience.' She pointed at the building opposite.

'Any particular area?'

'Adolescent brain development.'

'I have two of those. Adolescents, I mean. Any tips?'

She looked at Ailsa thoughtfully. 'Actions have consequences,' she said.

'I'll pass that on,' said Ailsa, getting up to go and pay the bill. The couple sat down again, arms wrapped around each other. Ailsa left the restaurant without looking back. Harry was telling the truth. His relationship with the girl was over.

Love at first sight is pure biology, Harry had told Ailsa the night after their first encounter. It was Glastonbury 1994, and they had met at a Johnny Cash concert the previous afternoon. Romy always joked that this was the first and last time that her parents had ever been cool. 'Except it was Johnny Cash when it could have been Pulp,' Luke always pointed out because Jarvis Cocker was playing at the same time.

Serendipity played its part. They were both alone because none of their friends wanted to see Johnny Cash. And it was daylight, which meant that Harry noticed that Ailsa was one of the few people standing close to him who knew all the words to 'Folsom Prison Blues'. He could describe to the children exactly what she was wearing: a pair of trousers with a strawberry motif and a white T-shirt knotted around her stomach. Definitely not thinking about how much flesh she was revealing.

When Johnny Cash started playing 'If I Were a Carpenter' Harry noticed that Ailsa had intervened in an argument between a couple over who wrote the original version. Tim Hardin, Ailsa said with absolute conviction, adding that he had played it at Woodstock in 1969.

By the time he played 'Ghost Riders in the Sky' they were standing together. *You need to feel really comfortable with someone to be able to sing 'yippee ay aye' at the top of your voice,* Ailsa remembered thinking as she shot a glance at the blond curly-haired man standing beside her. His hair was so big that it moved with its own mysterious rhythms to the music. He was such a terrible dancer that it was almost endearing. Anyway, some time in the middle of 'Ring of Fire' she had put her hand out to touch his hair.

She grasped a tangle of curls in her hand but they slipped through her fingers. After a few moments Harry had grabbed her wrist and pulled her towards him. They kissed for the first time during 'Delia'. Harry always teased Ailsa that she had made the first move. Ailsa insisted that it depended on your definition of first move. The couple beside them asked how long they had been seeing each other and Harry said without hesitating, 'Six months.' He was so sure of himself.

When the children pressed them for details of their first date Ailsa had to confess they'd never had one. She spent that night in his tent. They both agreed on that version of events. She was meant to be with a couple of university friends and Harry was meant to be sharing his tent with a girlfriend who had called off sick at the last minute, although he didn't reveal this detail to Ailsa until they met again in London the following week.

'We make beautiful science together,' he said to her the next morning after they had sex for the third time. Ailsa giggled because it was such an offbeat comment. They were both euphoric.

'I would love, love, love,' Harry said, whispering into her ear, 'to scan our brains to see what's going on in our pleasure centres right now.'

'What are you on?' Ailsa asked, disappointed that this was going to be one of those drug-fuelled episodes that were quickly forgotten.

He looked confused. 'Nothing. I'm a scientist.' He explained that he was doing a postgrad neuroscience degree at university in London. It turned out his faculty was five minutes' walk from the Institute of Education.

'I'm not meant to fall for a scientist,' Ailsa groaned.

'So you've fallen for me, have you?' Harry teased as he kissed her.

They were lying naked on top of his sleeping bag. When the sun rose, everything in the tent glowed orange.

He started to tell her about his favourite experiment. A scientist in the 1950s had discovered the brain's pleasure centres by implanting an electrode into the septal region of the limbic system.

'When he turned it on, the patients experienced a euphoria so powerful that when he switched it off they begged him not to stop. The same region fires when you have an orgasm. And get this, Ailsa, because this could help you: animals learn more easily when their pleasure centres are activated.'

'I'm not sure how I'm meant to apply that theory to my pupils,' Ailsa giggled.

When they met up the following week Harry asked Ailsa why she had gone to see Johnny Cash in concert instead of Jarvis Cocker.

'I had a Johnny Cash childhood,' Ailsa explained.

'Did your fifteen-year-old brother die after his neck got stuck in a circular saw at the mill where he worked?' Harry asked.

'Not that part. Although my sister does have a bald patch in her eyebrow because when she was five she fell on a limpet bed on the marshes where we grew up. I put mud on it to stop it bleeding.'

'You were alone?'

'My mum was at home looking after my dad.'

'What was wrong with your dad?'

'He drank. Too much. This was the Johnny Cash bit. Mum used to try and calm him down by playing his music. He once put his fist through our piano during "Riders in the Sky". He even accidentally set fire to the rubbish bin during "Ring of Fire".'

Rachel used to accuse her of using humour to deflect from the seriousness of their father's problem. Ailsa tried to explain that it was better to make people laugh than make them feel sorry for you. But she told Harry everything. He didn't flinch from the details and nor did he patronize her with pity.

Her father had defied the pathways in his brain by giving up alcohol. There was no judgement. Harry told Ailsa that Johnny Cash's dogs were called Sin and Redemption. He wasn't fazed by anything. And this was an important quality.

'By the way. Did you know that limpets go back to the exact spot on the same rock for years?' asked Ailsa. 'That's how I'll be. I'll always be trying to head home.'

'Then I'll follow you.'

And he had.

There was a long period after the affair when she couldn't remember who Harry was or how their relationship used to be. Then gradually memories of the good times seeped back. She remembered going to stay with her parents after her last set of exams at the Institute of Education and opening the front door late one Saturday night to find Harry standing there, blown almost sideways by a vicious east wind.

'What are you doing here?' Ailsa shouted.

'I was on my way to Russia,' he had joked. Because she lived on the edge of the world. There was nowhere else to go once you reached Salthouse. Harry explained he couldn't stand to be without her. He presented her with a book about the history of the marshes with pages of particular interest marked with Post-it notes. The next day she had told him that her old boyfriend swam in the sea all year round, and Harry valiantly stripped off and plunged beneath the slate-grey surface. His legs were blue when he came out, and when she told him she was joking about the ex-boyfriend, he lifted her across his shoulder and threw her into the sea fully clothed.

She thought about all this on the way home on the train. It was almost midnight by the time she got back from the station. She parked the car outside the front gate so that she wouldn't wake up Adam, who was sleeping in Ben's room at the front of the house. Then she almost sabotaged her plan by slamming the passenger door. 'Sorry, car,' she whispered. When no bedroom light came on, Ailsa took a moment to stare up at the night sky. Unlike London, it was alive with stars. She searched for Polaris and found it straight away. Somehow, since

Georgia's death the North Star and her mother had become entwined. *Most dependable guide*, thought Ailsa.

She looked up at the star and explained to her mother that she had thought she wanted to meet Harry's student to tell her about the pain she had inflicted on all of them. She had imagined shouting at her about how Harry had had to leave his job and uproot his entire family to Norfolk. She reluctantly confessed that perhaps she wanted to frighten her a little. But as soon as she saw the girl with her boyfriend she realized that her new life was the one she wanted to be living and that the past no longer had a hold over her.

She spotted twinkling Sirius and looked for lights moving across the sky because Ben had announced earlier that week that the International Space Station would pass over Norfolk this month. 'How do you know this stuff?' Harry had asked him. 'Nasa website,' he replied coolly. She would go up to Ben's bedroom and plant a kiss on his hot little cheek. The idea filled her with joy. She had managed to keep her family together and it was beginning to feel like an achievement.

Her neck ached. She rotated it a couple of times and breathed in deeply. She was pleased to be home. There was an unfamiliar smell in the air, not the sweet rot of damp leaves but something more medicinal. Ailsa sniffed the air like a dog, reminded of hunting games that she used to play with Rachel when they were children. She remembered an Indian headdress that Adam had found at an auction and how they used to fight over who was going to wear it. Rachel nearly always won. She was the free-spirited Indian; Ailsa was inevitably the law-enforcing cowboy. Rachel was wrong. Their childhood wasn't all Heartbreak Hotel.

She walked past the house, past the huge sitting-room window – inside, Lucifer was eating leftovers from plates that hadn't made it to the dishwasher – and past the washing line. She glanced up at Romy's bedroom and saw the curtains were open and the light was on.

Ailsa continued deep into the back garden, ignoring the fact that water from the sodden lawn was soaking through her shoes. A trail of smoke led towards the wood at the end of the Fairports' garden. Ailsa climbed through the hole in the fence and the smell finally came to her: it was eucalyptus. She followed the newly laid path into the wood from the garden until she reached the sweat lodge. Smoke billowed out of a chimney in the middle of the construction. The white plastic dome glowed orange like a spaceship. Although she didn't want to admit it, the lodge looked quite inviting. There was music coming from inside. Nothing recognizable. Hippy shit, Harry would call it. Chanting rather than singing. Dolphins blowing pan pipes. She wished Harry were with her so that they could laugh together. That was something they used to be good at.

She reached the outside of the sweat lodge, tentatively lifted the plastic flap and went inside. It was so warm that it hurt her lungs to breathe. Apart from candles placed in a semicircle on a ledge around the edge there was no light, and it took a moment for her eyes to adjust. The ceiling by the door was so low that she had to stoop to stop her head from rubbing against the plastic. Ailsa continued forward. Antlers and buffalo hides hung on the wall. At the centre was a brick-lined hearth dug into the ground where red-hot stones burned. Three figures lay on their backs on a wooden platform circling the stones. Their eyes were closed against the heat. They were all holding bottles of beer. One of them was Harry, wearing nothing more than boxer shorts. He lay next to Wolf and Loveday. The eucalyptus smell was now so strong that Ailsa's eyes were watering. It was unbelievably hot.

A platoon of empty bottles stood on a makeshift table behind them. They were in the midst of one of those aimless conversations fuelled by too much wine and too little sleep in which no one can remember what the last person said.

'You can recover from the truth . . . Change is a great pain in the arse . . . If you don't mind, it doesn't matter . . . If we are our brains, where does that leave free will?' It reminded Ailsa of the kind of stoned conversation that she used to have when she was a student.

'Hi,' she said, feeling like an intruder.

The three of them lazily lifted their heads and squinted at Ailsa. Harry made no attempt to get up.

'Hey,' he said. Harry never said *hey*.

'Hey,' said Ailsa pointedly.

'Hey, hey,' said Harry. He giggled, which made Wolf

and Loveday giggle. He was stoned, realized Ailsa. They all were. It was so unlikely that it almost made sense. As far as she knew Harry hadn't even inhaled at university.

'Weren't you meant to stay with Rachel?' Harry asked, which made it sound as though he had been caught out.

'I decided to come home. I wanted to be here more than I wanted to be in London.'

'Cool,' said Loveday. 'We're christening the sweat lodge. So far so good. You might want to take off your jacket.'

'I'm being healed and cleansed,' said Harry, attempting to placate her with irony. 'Can you tell?'

'How was work?' Ailsa asked him. It sounded more pointed than she intended. He sat up. Now she was closer, Ailsa could see his face was bright red. There was a small pool of sweat in the pouch beneath each eye and in the creases in his stomach. His body was so shiny it looked as though he had been wrapped in cling film. She touched her face. It was already coated in a fine film of sweat.

'I've finished a draft on the chapter about how teenagers process reward stimuli differently,' he explained.

'You're going to have to sex that up if you want the book to be a best-seller, Harry,' said Loveday in a throaty whisper. She was wearing a bikini top and a pair of patched denim shorts. Wolf was stroking the inside of her arm. A rivulet of sweat snaked down between her breasts, highlighting puckered skin that had been prematurely aged by years in the sun.

'Adolescent brains have a more intense reaction to new experiences that makes them want more of the same thing,' said Harry, speaking so slowly that Ailsa found herself mouthing the words.

'Better,' said Loveday. 'But still not convincing. Come and sit down, Ailsa.'

Wolf offered her a beer. Ailsa moved towards them and sat down, her back leaning uncomfortably against the table.

'But what can you do about it, Harry? How can you stop teenagers fucking up?' asked Loveday.

What about adults? thought Ailsa. But she could no longer summon any anger. Something had shifted inside her. She felt a loosening of the constraints that had bound her over the past twelve months since Harry's fall from grace, and a sense of tranquillity that no amount of yoga stretches, self-help books and the occasional diazepam had managed to induce. She tried to view the feeling with suspicion, in case it proved ephemeral. But somehow seeing the girl had made Ailsa realize that Harry's infidelity had everything to do with him and very little to do with her, no matter how awful it had made her feel. She felt a sense of elation at her liberation.

'I only pose questions; I don't have answers,' said Harry, bowing his head slightly as though he were some kind of guru. 'It's not a self-help book.'

'We should get Harry to speak at one of our retreats,' said Loveday, moving onto her side so her back was to Wolf. 'What do you think, Harry?'

'I'd like that,' said Harry.

No, you wouldn't, thought Ailsa; *it would drive you crazy. All those repetitive old dope smokers with their messed-up neurons backfiring.*

'What retreats?' asked Ailsa.

'We're going to be running week-long intensive live-in programmes. Offer a wraparound service – yoga, meditation, couples therapy – all culminating in a four-hour session in the sweat lodge at the end.'

'You have got to be kidding,' said Ailsa.

'It's ambitious, I know,' said Loveday. 'But we have a lot of experience in this area.'

The conversation shifted again. They began discussing future job prospects for their children.

'There's big potential in depilation,' said Loveday. 'All these chemicals that mimic hormones will make us way hairier.'

'Not if they imitate oestrogen,' pointed out Harry.

Wolf ran through current trends. Payday lending, obesity, diabetes, nail bars. There was no point in going to university, he said. The Western spirit was sick and needed healing. That was where the money was. He was wondering if he should retrain as a shaman.

'Actually things were far worse in the early twentieth century,' pointed out Ailsa. 'People forget a third of children didn't make it to adolescence in the pre-antibiotic era. There were millions of men with post-traumatic stress from the wars. What about the Holocaust? And Stalin? And rickets?'

'By the way, I've completed your natal report,' said Loveday, putting her hand on Ailsa's knee, who gave Loveday a look of utter incomprehension.

She pointed at a bunch of papers on the table. On the front was a large circle with three smaller circles inside. Ailsa vaguely recognized the symbols of the zodiac on the outer edge of the biggest circle.

'Your astrological chart. Remember you gave me all the details about what date and time you were born a couple of weeks ago.'

'Oh yes,' said Ailsa vaguely.

'It must have taken ages to compile,' said Harry, gently nudging Ailsa's calf with the tip of his toe.

'Thanks very much,' said Ailsa.

'Shall I go through it with you now? Just the headlines? It's one of the most interesting readings I've done in ages.'

'I've had a really long day,' said Ailsa. 'My head is about to explode. Maybe over the weekend?'

Loveday looked disappointed.

'We're dying to hear what it says,' said Harry. Ailsa looked at Harry and was gratified to see that he winked at her. She glanced at the contents list: chart patterns, important features, angular planets, sun, moon rising, other aspects.

'Looks very comprehensive,' said Ailsa, putting it down beside her. Loveday picked it up again.

'You have the planetary pattern type called the funnel shape. It's the first time I've come across it,' said Loveday. Ailsa didn't respond.

'What does that mean?' asked Harry politely.

'Ailsa has a serious and conscientious personality and is very practical with a talent for working with the public. She's a good manager and has a strong drive to achieve success. She can be fearful of taking risks and her achievements come from hard work.'

'I'd agree with that,' said Harry. Loveday took this as licence to continue. 'Sun in Libra, that's interesting. The sun is the second house, ruler of the rising sign. You seek harmony, you support both sides in a dispute and you may have a hard time making a decision, but Pluto in Leo means there is potential for sudden bursts of anger due to repressed emotions exploding.'

'Also very true,' said Harry. He showed Loveday a scar on his calf. 'She's like an animal when she's pushed.'

'That's all very interesting, Loveday, but I think I might absorb it better after a good night's sleep,' said Ailsa.

'That's the sun in Libra speaking,' said Loveday. 'Let me read you the part on the sun in square with Chiron.'

'I'm quite tired too,' said Harry, pulling himself upright. 'I need to be back at my desk by nine o'clock tomorrow morning.'

'Chiron is the wounded healer; it represents loss which leads to empathy. It's a powerful connection with your sun. You have experienced pain and frustration, perhaps through your relationship with your father.'

'It's the same for me,' said Wolf as if to demonstrate

his empathy. 'I longed to be close to my father, but the more I tried, the more he pushed me away. He feared intimacy.' He put his hand on Ailsa's shoulder.

'Well, that's not a problem with my father, because he's sleeping like a baby in Ben's bedroom, less than a hundred metres away,' said Ailsa.

Harry stumbled towards the door. Ailsa put her arm out to steady him.

'I know exactly what's going on,' he slurred. 'My brain is producing anandamide.'

'*Ananda* is Sanskrit for bliss,' said Loveday. 'Isn't that a beautiful coincidence?'

'It's the science that's beautiful,' said Harry. 'The proteins that transmit the anandamide message to the brain receptors are located in the striatum, which accounts for the blissful feeling; the cerebellum, which is why I'm stumbling; and the hippocampus, hence the fact I can't remember the beginning of this sentence.'

'Come on, Harry. Time for home,' said Ailsa, admiring his shoulders as he struggled to put his T-shirt back on.

'Where have you been, Ailsa?' Harry asked as if he had only just remembered she was there.

'The midnight train down memory lane,' replied Ailsa.

IO

'Do you have any regrets?' I asked Mum. Her eyes had a dreamy, faraway look. Maybe she was tired from work. It was half-term but so far she'd spent most of the week at school. 'Are you listening?' She looked at me, struggling to focus. I followed her from the sitting room into the kitchen and back into the sitting room. En route she put a couple of dirty mugs in the dishwasher, shoved some clothes in the laundry basket and squawked with joy when she found the landline handset at the bottom.

'Why can't anyone put it back in the right place?' she asked, using a diversionary tactic that might have worked with Ben but not with me.

'You didn't answer my question,' I pointed out.

She opened a drawer and began rummaging through bits of paper.

'Of course I have regrets. Everyone does. But they're pretty trivial. Ha! Found it!' She slammed the drawer shut, causing Lucifer to leap off the sideboard. In her hand was a letter from Norfolk County Council.

'Like what?' I persisted. She thought for a moment and I knew she was trying to come up with the most uncontroversial example possible. Why could she never be honest with me? Was she worried that messing up might be inherited? Or contagious? Or that she might simply put an idea into my head that I'd never had before? Didn't she realize that secrets were almost always more corrosive than the truth?

'I wish I'd learned to play tennis,' she said finally. Brilliant. I couldn't have come up with something more boring even if I'd thought about it for twenty-four hours. She didn't see my eyes roll because she was too busy punching numbers into the phone. I don't know why I was angry with Mum when it was Dad who had betrayed her. I knew it was unfair. But I thought she should have trusted us with the truth and blamed her for lying to us over and over again about why we had to leave London when the fact was we had never asked Dad the same question. We'd felt sorry for him because Mum had dragged him away too and he'd allowed us to think that.

If I'm completely honest, and I still have self-loathing over this, I think somehow I held Mum responsible for the fact that Dad had done it, as though there was something lacking in her rather than something lacking in him. I should have felt empathy but instead I felt angry with her for being a victim. Later, the most useful conversation I had with the therapist was when I realized how my simultaneous discovery of Dad's betrayal and Jay's relationship problem meant the two became entwined in my head and that all my anger was most likely a mask for fear.

'Really? I don't think I've ever heard you talk about

your serve or even seen you watch Andy Murray play a match,' I said.

'It's crept up on me since we moved here. If I did something active and sociable it would help to meet people and keep fit.' She sounded really upbeat. She was good. I give her that. I persisted. The idea that she might genuinely be happy didn't occur to me. I thought it was all a front until the video of me appeared on the Internet and I made her really unhappy. Then I realized she wasn't faking it. Mum never said this, but at the point where she had managed to put everything behind her and start enjoying life again I blew it apart.

'I mean regret for something that you've done rather than what you haven't done,' I kept on, although of course if Rachel were right about Mum the opposite would hold true. 'And then having a crisis in a Joy Division "Love Will Tear Us Apart" kind of way.' She looked up from the phone, gave me one of her narrow-eyed looks and laughed.

'What are you doing listening to Joy Division?'

'Jay's grandfather knew their manager.'

I regretted mentioning Jay to Mum. I still felt the simple electric pleasure of saying his name but there was a bitter kick afterwards that felt close to unease.

'So what's going on with you and him?' She tried to frame it in a really casual way, with a knowing smile to underline the fact that she was cool about it. Over the past couple of weeks since her trip to London Mum had seemed more like her old self again, and that meant that she suddenly took way more interest in what I was up to at the precise moment when I could have done without the scrutiny. I had got used to operating under the radar.

'I told you, we're friends.'

'He seems like a nice uncomplicated boy.' I knew she didn't mean it because I'd overheard her telling Dad that it was incredible that such indiscreet parents could produce such a mysterious child.

'Marley's having an eighteenth-birthday party,' I said, trying to change the subject. 'When mocks are over.'

'Will you go with Jay?' she asked.

I nodded. 'And Becca and Marnie. They're going to come here to get ready.'

'Sounds fun.'

She was trying hard, but the sudden turnaround in her attitude irritated me even more than her previous disapproval because it was so obviously fake. She could sense my annoyance because she finally answered my question.

'The biggest regrets are always for the things that you haven't done,' Mum said finally, and I knew she wasn't talking about tennis. 'Not for the things you have done.'

'Like what?'

'Like not revising for your exams because love is tearing you apart,' she said. It was a tactic taken from the chapter in parenting manuals where they recommend dealing with serious subjects with humour. She would never understand.

'Why did we move here, Mum?' I was giving her one last chance to be straight.

'You prefer it here to London, don't you? I think we all do now.' Nice sidestep.

'Yes. But that wasn't what I asked.'

She put the phone to her ear again.

'I've told you a hundred times before, Romy.'

'It's just that Loveday was asking me the other day and I wasn't sure what to say.'

I knew this would get her attention.

'Why was she asking?'

'Maybe she thought I'd give her an honest answer.'

She gave me a piercing look that went straight to my stomach and for a moment I thought she was about to capitulate. But she pulled back.

'Because I got offered a job that I couldn't refuse. Because Granny had died and we needed to be closer to Grandpa. Because we wanted to get Luke out of London. Because we thought Ben would find it gentler in the countryside.' That was a new one. I hadn't heard her use Ben as an excuse before.

'Do you think if you say something often enough you end up believing it?' I asked, my tone more hostile than I had intended. 'Is that something you've learned from Dad? He's probably written a paper about it.'

She opened her mouth as if she was about to say something but instead her top lip did that thing where it tensed so much that her mouth turned into a cartoonish straight line.

'Hello, hello, is anyone there?' shouted a voice from the phone. Mum switched her attention to the call.

'At last a real person,' she said into the receiver. 'I want to make a formal complaint about a building that has been put up without permission from the council,' she said. 'I'd prefer to keep it anonymous if that's possible.' *Boring*, I thought to myself as I left the room.

If there had been a door to slam I would have slammed it. But that was the other problem with open-plan houses. They limited the possibility of self-expression. Funny that architects who are so keen to express themselves don't think of that.

I headed down into the basement. I knew Dad wasn't at home, because Ben had told me that he was taking him to a screening of *The Spy Who Loved Me* at the village hall. That was as good as it got for a Wednesday afternoon during half-term in Luckmore. At the last minute Grandpa had gone too. I had begun to notice that whenever Dad got angry with my grandfather he would always do something really nice with him the following day. The previous week he had shouted at him for using the chainsaw in the garden again. Then the next day he took him for a walk on Cromer pier and joked to Mum that it didn't once occur to him to push him over the edge. When Grandpa got back he said very loudly that it was really great to be home, and Dad got annoyed again so the following day he took him for lunch at the pub. Mum had teased that Dad was breaking one of his favourite rules and rewarding bad behaviour. 'Good one, Ailsa,'

Dad had laughed. I couldn't understand how they were getting on so well. Did Mum have no self-respect?

I hardly ever went into Dad's office even though it was opposite the TV room. It was never locked but the door was always closed and he didn't like anyone going in there in case we disturbed his work. He even vacuumed it himself so that no one muddled up the different piles of papers on the floor. Because it was full of boxes and had no windows apart from the panes in the single glass door it was dusty and, in the winter when you could hardly ever open the door into the garden, very claustrophobic.

The first thing I noticed was that at least one layer had disappeared from the huge wall of boxes that had previously surrounded his desk, so that you could now at least see across from one side of the room to the other. I did a rough calculation and reckoned that Mum must have unpacked about ten. I read this as a positive sign that she was putting down roots in Luckmore. Or at least putting down roots with Dad, because Norfolk had never really stopped being her home.

As far as I can remember, my thinking at that moment went something like this: Aunt Rachel thought Mum was an ostrich. I realized that if I didn't want to share the same fate I had to define myself in relation to Mum and make myself as different as possible. So if Mum's biggest failing was that she tried to avoid confrontation I would do the opposite. I didn't question Rachel's analysis, even though Mum was always the one taking action.

She just did it more quietly than most. Neither did I take on board Dad's theory that the criticisms we make of other people are more often than not a reflection of our own frailties. Instead I decided to be someone who always took action. I would deal with everything head on. And this was where I needed to start.

I closed the door behind me. The floor-to-ceiling bookshelf on the wall to my left was filled with books, journals and research papers. I couldn't tell whether they were organized thematically or alphabetically. I knew the answers to some of my questions were there. I just wasn't sure exactly where. Or even what the questions were.

The first few days after Jay's confession I had kept the curtains closed and ignored his attempts to communicate. I was frightened by what he had told me.

Eventually longing overcame fear and I messaged him: *Addiction is a disease not a character flaw.* He replied he missed me so much that his chest hurt.

I knew I should have been repelled, because that's what my parents told me later, but I wasn't. And really who were they to judge given everything that had been going on with them? I tried to conjure up disgust. I really did. It would have been way less complicated to cut Jay out of my life at this stage, especially when no one knew he was even in it. But the fact that he had lost an eighth of his life (his maths) to PornHub did nothing to make him less attractive in my eyes.

I wanted to help him. Dad always said empathy was a pre-frontal cortex issue, which meant it must be a good thing. He claimed it formed the basis for all moral behaviour. I guess I thought I could save him.

After we started messaging again I thought he might avoid me because he felt embarrassed or regretted confiding in me. The opposite was true. He sought me out at school at every opportunity and made sure that we caught the same bus home every evening. In Biology classes he hooked his leg around my ankle, and I sat there watching Mr Harvey's mouth moving without hearing anything, poised on the edge of something that lurched so swiftly between agony and ecstasy that it made me feel sick.

I thought Marnie and Becca would notice what was going on, but at the beginning of the week a scandal broke at school that eclipsed the fact that our threesome at break had become a foursome. Because at the end of break on Tuesday Stuart Snapchatted Marnie a naked selfie. Becca took a quick screenshot and enlarged the photo.

In PSHE we sat at the back of the classroom and instead of doing a spider diagram suggesting ways of promoting love, respect and care in relationships, we tried to work out if it was really Stuart's body or his head superimposed on someone else's. He had a big dick, Becca declared as authoritatively as you could when whispering. The received wisdom was that this was good. I wasn't so sure. I said I thought it looked lonely and forlorn, like it was the last penis left in the world, and Marnie and Becca laughed so much that Mr Harvey sent us out of the classroom.

Jay and I briefly debated whether we should stop doing the thing at the window, but he said that he thought it was progress to feel turned on by a real person and at least it took the edge off my desire. We talked about everything. He told me that for the first time he believed it was possible for him to change. He described the first and last time that he had tried to have what he called 'real, actual sex', a year ago. How the girl was a friend of Marley's and they had gone swimming naked in the sea after a party in Ibiza. He told me how they made out for an hour on the beach and he didn't feel anything. Eventually he told her that he had drunk too much. He tried to convince her that it wasn't her fault.

'I wanted to. I really tried. I tried to get her to do exactly what turned me on, but all I could think about was how much easier it would be if I could see her in a good scene,' he explained.

'What do you mean?' I asked.

'I'd rather watch her on screen than be with her in real life. She just wasn't like the girls online.'

'So what did you do?'

'Went home. Watched porn. Had a bash.'

'That's sick,' I said.

'You know that sound a computer makes when you turn it on, Romy?' I nodded. 'As soon as I hear that sound I think about it.'

'That's dopamine kicking in,' I said. 'Anticipation of pleasure. You need to create some different reward systems.'

'You're the only person who can help me, Romy. Will you help me get out of this?' he asked, blinking so fast that his fringe bounced up and down. Jay always did this when he was nervous.

'I can try,' I promised, trying not to show how elated I was that he had asked. 'Have you told anyone else?'

'I think Marley might realize. He looked at my Internet history once. My parents have no idea. They'd be horrified. They're all about tantric sex and women having multiple orgasms. Just on those grounds they'd be appalled.'

The anxiety in his face began to fade. We talked about what I had discovered about my dad. I told him that I had spent months feeling angry with the wrong parent. I said that I wanted to hate my dad, but every time I thought about what he had done to Mum it made me cry, which made me angry.

'Don't hate,' said Jay. 'It takes up too much energy.'

I managed a weak smile. I tried to explain how I felt that if Mum and Dad had lied to us all about this they could lie about everything.

'Parents lie for two reasons,' he said wisely. 'To protect their children or to protect themselves. There are good truths and bad truths and good lies and bad lies. Not telling you was a good lie in my opinion. Your mum was trying to protect you.'

I started to feel guilty again so I asked him if his dad had ever cheated on his mum and he said he thought he hadn't but only because it would be bad for business.

'What do you mean?' I asked, puzzled by this response.

'They made a best-selling sexual healing DVD for couples,' he said. 'It wouldn't look good.'

His tone was deadpan. He could have been talking about Wolf and Loveday doing something completely mundane like discussing how many piri-piri chicken shops there were in Norwich.

'Have you seen it?' I asked.

'Are you kidding?' he laughed. 'If you think watching porn has fucked me up then try watching your dad on screen giving your mother a vaginal massage. I'd need years of therapy.'

'I guess it shows that you have some judgement,' I said. I had a feeling that everything was in fast forward, as though I was on one of those really long escalators in Oxford Circus and someone had suddenly speeded it up. Everything was moving too fast for me to get a handle on it; everything was bigger than me and I understood nothing.

I looked round Dad's office. 'Where's your empirical evidence?' I could hear his voice ringing in my ears as I tried to make sense of the books on the back wall. 'Nothing can be proved or resolved unless you have evidence,' he would tell us when we were doing homework.

'Fantasy is for writers and English teachers. Facts are for scientists.' And I was a scientist.

I decided to start with a textbook. Less scientifically, I picked one out simply on the basis that it was the biggest. When I opened it up I realized it was a Neuroscience textbook for undergraduates doing the degree course that Dad used to run.

I leafed through the first few chapters, looking at the pictures, stopping to admire the photographs of feathery-tailed nerve cells. I remembered how Dad had laughed the first time he showed me a photographic image of a neuron because I was convinced it was a fairy holding hands with another fairy.

'They are magical in the way they're always looking for connections, and they never rest,' Dad had laughed. To me they were still mystical.

Later he showed me images from the new scanner at work. The brain was like a futuristic super-highway where the traffic never stopped, Dad explained. It was built on a cognitive grid system of neurons. One of the great discoveries in his lifetime was the fact that these neurons didn't stop firing until the day you died, he explained. Which meant there was always the possibility of change.

This reminded me why I was supposed to be here. I flicked through to the chapter on brain disorders and tried not to be tempted to stop at schizophrenia. Manic depression, Huntingdon's disease, multiple sclerosis and anorexia followed in quick succession. There was only one page on addiction. Dad is obsessive about people not touching his stuff so I was careful to put the book back exactly where it came from.

I headed towards Dad's desk and settled myself in the leather swivel chair that he had brought from his old office. On the wall in front of me, behind his computer, was a photo montage of all of us that Mum had put together when Ben was a toddler; in the middle was a photo of Ben's name spelled out with the small wooden trains that he collected. He stood behind, grubby-faced and proud. There were Luke and me in our red and blue primary-school uniforms on my first day at school, a newspaper cutting of Luke after his football team had won a competition and another of him dressed up in a magician's outfit. I had forgotten he was good at football and magic. Luke never did anything long enough for me to get a handle on it. In the bottom right-hand corner was a photo of Dad and me on the floor of our old sitting room in London, playing Operation. I was triumphantly holding a rib bone in the electric tweezers. Dad was beaming proudly at me. I noticed how our upper lips had the same slightly swollen quality and how our smile was identical.

We played this game all the time for a couple of years. It was always Dad and me. Never Dad and Luke. Or Mum and me. I remembered Dad complimenting me on my steady hand, telling me that I could become a surgeon. My Christmas present that year had been a plastic replica of the human body that you could take apart.

I remembered giving Mum the heart to show how much I loved her and Dad saying that we fell in love with our brain not our heart. Now I wondered how Dad felt working with the weight of family history upon him, and it occurred to me that Mum had probably hung this picture here for that very reason.

Above his desk was a poster with a quote that Mum had found in *The Winter's Tale*: 'I wish there were no age between ten and three-and-twenty, or that youth would sleep out the rest; for there is nothing in the between but getting wenches with child, wronging the ancientry, stealing, fighting.'

She was always providing him with titbits for his lectures. *Poor Mum*, I thought, feeling suddenly protective in a way I hadn't felt before. Wary of these feelings I swung round on Dad's chair using my legs and arms for momentum. Faster and faster I spun. I closed my eyes and felt the delirium of dizziness take over. I decided that I would focus my search on the place opposite where the chair stopped, which happened to be in front of his old leather briefcase. It was like playing Russian roulette.

I gently pulled open the briefcase, wondering if Mum had ever done the same and knowing that because she was an ostrich she probably hadn't. But at that moment I saw myself as an eagle. Loveday had urged me to find my animal spirit guide and I chose an eagle because, apart from the risk of being poisoned by human beings, it was never a victim. I wondered if Dad had some secret device so that he could tell if someone had been fiddling with his stuff in his briefcase. Like the alarm that went off if you went into Ben's bedroom. Although of course if Dad didn't want anyone to get into it he would have locked it.

In the first compartment was a book, *The Neuroscience of Risky Decision Making*. *Bit late for that*, I thought. Beside it was a bunch of research papers. I caught sight of one: 'DeltaFosB: a sustained molecular switch for addiction'. On top of it was a note in Dad's handwriting underlined several times. 'Nerve cells that fire together wire together,' it read. It was the sort of line that he liked to use to start a lecture. For a scientist he really liked words. *All very promising*, I thought. Because in my head I was justifying my nosiness by searching for anything that might help Jay.

At the bottom of the next compartment was a small wooden cigar box. As soon as I saw it I knew that this was what I had been looking for all along. Dad would blame my subconscious decision-making. And inside the box was a Nokia cardboard box and inside that was a cheap old-style mobile phone. It was like one of those Russian dolls. Some part of me was hoping that I wouldn't know how to work the phone or that it wasn't charged, but it flashed on instantly. There was no password. I held it in both hands for a moment, knowing this was the closest I would ever come to handling a hand grenade without a pin.

I remembered how in Year 7 we had done a class on proverbs. Each table had been given a subject to research. Mine was curiosity. These all came back to me now. *He who asks a question is a fool for a minute, he who does not remains a fool for ever. Better to ask a question than remain ignorant. A man should live if only to satisfy his own curiosity.*

Better to see if your dad is lying than never know, I thought to myself.

I quickly pressed the keys until I reached sent messages. The same number appeared over and over again. This should have been evidence enough. But it seemed cowardly not to look now that I had come this far. *Hypothesis, evidence, conclusion*, I thought to myself. Mum would have stopped herself at this point, which meant that I had to make myself look. I decided to look at the last sent message. *You make my cock so hard.* I dropped the phone as though it had given me an electric shock. Then I picked it up to check the in-box. I closed my eyes as I opened the message and half opened one eye so that I could only read one word at a time. *I luv luv luv it when you cum in my face.* I should have checked the dates but I didn't. By then I was in free fall.

I put the phone back in its box in the briefcase. I took down the photo frame from the wall, removed the back and, using a pair of scissors from the top drawer of his desk, I cut Dad out of the photo and put me back alone. I moved a picture of Mum down so that it looked as though I was smiling at her. After that I chopped up the picture of Dad until it looked like the shavings in the hamster cage and put it inside the cardboard box with the phone. I removed the SIM card and cut it in half.

Mum was right. There are some things you should never know.

I started spinning on the chair again. Round and round, eyes closed, until the words in the text messages started to fade. This time I didn't slow down when I began to feel sick. When my stomach heaved I forced the chair round even faster. I only stopped when I realized that Dad had come into the room.

'Hello, Romy.' His eyes darted to the briefcase. *You are so obvious*, I wanted to tell him. But fortunately he couldn't see the anger in my eyes because I felt so sick. I bent over his bin and retched and retched until there were tears pouring down my cheeks and my throat burned with acid.

'Are you all right, darling?' Dad asked, coming over to put his arm around me. 'What a silly thing to do. Even Ben wouldn't spin himself until he puked.' He laughed.

'Sorry,' I said, still crying. 'I'm so sorry.' I was. Not for looking and finding the phone but for what the discovery represented and the impact it would have on Mum. Because surely I would have to tell her about his communication with this woman? Secrets make you lonely. Thoughts, half formed, raced by before I could examine them. I stared down at the bin full of yellow bile.

'Were you looking for something?' he asked. I nodded.

'For an A-level Biology project on teenagers and addiction,' I said in a hoarse voice, appalled at my ability to think on my feet like Dad. He looked relieved but perhaps he was just pleased that I was interested in a subject so close to his heart. He went to the bookshelf and removed the same textbook that I had been looking at earlier.

'The main problem for teenagers is that you have Ferrari engines and crap brakes,' said Dad, smiling. I'd heard that one before. He stood beside me and began leafing through the book. 'Luke is a classic example of someone who can't control his impulses. There's a big imbalance between his thrill-seeking side and his ability to rationalize and make the right decisions. That makes teenagers more vulnerable to addiction. You're all about immediate gratification rather than long-term goals.'

Where were your brakes? I wanted to ask him. He stopped on a page with a couple of photographs. One showed an MRI scan of a normal brain. Beside it was a scan of a cocaine addict. There was more yellow in the centre of the addict's brain. Beneath there was an explanation about how drugs damaged the reward circuitry of the brain.

'The evidence would suggest it's the same for all addictions,' Dad explained. I stared at the page so that I didn't have to meet his gaze again until the photos started to go fuzzy.

He told me about an experiment carried out at the California Institute of Technology in the 1950s in which a rat had an electrode implanted in its brain. Each time it went to a particular corner of its box the brain was stimulated until soon it was spending all its time there waiting for the stimulation. I noticed how he always described experiments in the present tense and wondered if this was a measure of his own excitement or a way of keeping students engaged.

'Get this, Romy,' he said excitedly. 'This is the really interesting part. The researchers build a new box with a lever that the rat can control. Now it spends all its time pressing it over and over again. Won't eat or drink and only stops when it collapses with exhaustion.'

I tried to focus in case what he was saying could help Jay.

'They discover that the rat is working to stimulate the release of dopamine in the brain. Dopamine is the neurotransmitter that drives most addictions. Its release in the brain reinforces the behaviour that causes it. That's why it's so difficult to overcome addiction.'

I didn't say anything but I let him continue because it meant he was less likely to look down at his half-open briefcase.

'It stimulates feelings of pleasure and motivates behaviour. Addiction blunts the brain's response to dopamine so that you need more and more of the same thing to feel the same high. Sometimes addicts want a drug that they don't even like. Is this too complicated?'

I shook my head. 'I think I need to go and lie down for a while. I'm not feeling so good.'

'I'll pull out some research for you,' said Dad.

I got up and headed out of his office. I thought of the phone in the briefcase and wondered whether he would check to see if it had been disturbed. And what he might do. Just before I reached the door I stopped.

'Do you think people can change their behaviour?'

'What do you mean?'

'If you get addicted to something is it possible to stop?'

'Of course,' said Dad. 'The brain is plasticine, it's not fixed. And if you stop doing something addictive the brain can recover. But once the pathways have formed it's really difficult to get rid of them. They're incredibly efficient. Even after an alcoholic has stopped drinking for years, a trigger can ignite the pathway all over again.'

'Is it the same for all addictions?' I asked.

'It is,' he said. 'That's why it's more difficult for teen-agers to stop. The pathways run deeper and the pre-frontal cortex, which controls judgement, isn't fully formed. You ask good questions, Romy. You'd be a great researcher.'

Much later professionals – head shrinkers, as Dad called them – read a lot into this moment. Their neurotransmitters went wild with the desire to make connections, to find reasons to blame my parents for what happened, especially Dad. Adults always want a single reason for why things happen, when the truth is things happen for many reasons. They talked around the subject, trying to lay traps for me to fall into, but they never caught me out. I guess my pre-frontal cortex was a match for theirs. And besides, my plan to save Jay was already fully formed even before I found that phone. I knew exactly what I had to do.

Ailsa sat cross-legged in the sitting room of her parents' home, in front of a chest of drawers that she was half-way through clearing out. She pulled out the bottom drawer, berated the irrationality of the contents and tried to ignore the billows of dust from the carpet every time the wind blew through the open window. On the other side of the pane the marsh marigolds were start-ing to push up through the bogs to create a brilliant yellow carpet over the marshland. Later in the year the carpet would turn deep purple as the sea lavender emerged from the same muddy depths. When Romy used to ask her grandmother whether she got bored liv-ing in Salthouse, Georgia would wordlessly point to the landscape outside this window.

Ailsa returned to the drawer and pulled out a plastic bag stuffed with poker chips from at least ten different clubs, coins and notes from Europe before the euro and an envelope containing a one-line note from her mother to her father: 'Your drinking saddens and frightens me.' It was dated 28 June 1990. The month Ailsa sat her A levels. It was written in Georgia's neat sloping script, six weeks before the whale carcass was washed up on the beach. There was so much desperation in this short sentence. Yet somehow her mother had managed to maintain the ebb and flow of daily life and protect her children from the ugly currents that threatened to pull her under. Only now did Ailsa appreciate the courage this must have taken. She stuffed the note in the back pocket of her jeans.

Beneath the poker chips were bundles of catalogues from auctions that her father had attended forty years earlier. These she tossed straight into a black bin liner destined for the recycling centre before Adam came back into the room. Because although he had readily agreed to her suggestion to spend a day streamlining his belongings, now that he was back home he refused to throw anything away that reminded him of Georgia. He was filled with regret for the lost years, as he called the period when he was an alcoholic.

Harry said that people recovered from grief by calling up one memory at a time, reliving it and letting it go, so that new neural networks could be formed that allowed them to live without the one they loved. Going through her parents' belongings would ultimately be therapeutic.

Beside her, so close that Ailsa could reach out and touch her leg, sat Romy, listening to music and reading a research paper on teenagers and addiction for a Biology project. It struck Ailsa as slightly odd that Matt would have given such a big assignment the week before mock exams, but she knew better than to question Romy about schoolwork. Unlike Luke, she was entirely self-motivated.

'Do you want this?' Ailsa held out a large hexagonal paperweight with dead sea creatures inside that she had just found at the bottom of the drawer. There was a small starfish with arthritic-looking legs, a sea horse, a crab and a few decorative shells. Her parents had brought it home from a holiday in Mallorca in the 1960s. The holiday where Adam had fallen into a pool and broken his ribs.

Romy didn't respond. Ailsa looked across at her. Of course. She couldn't hear. A few years ago when Romy was going through her kitsch phase she might have welcomed the hideous offering. Now she would hate it. Ailsa put the paperweight in the bin liner. Seconds later she took it out again. She couldn't throw it away. Her mother had loved it. She would take it home and put it in Harry's office.

Romy was draped across the sofa where Adam and Georgia used to sit, one leg swinging gently across the arm. Her long blonde hair was in an elegant French plait and she was chewing a pink fluorescent pen. She had a new softer and more languid quality that Ailsa put down to the fact that she had finally grown into her awkward angles, although equally it could have something to do with the boy next door. It was difficult to tell. Romy was so difficult to read.

She was born inscrutable. They hadn't made her like this, Ailsa realized. Even when she had left her as an eight-month-old baby at the crèche at the school where Ailsa had just been promoted head of English, Romy had never showed any emotion, while Luke had clung to her so tightly that there were still little red imprints from his fingers on her hand when she got to the teachers' common room.

She opened another drawer, remembering Romy's first summer and how she had sat Buddha-like on a rug in a shady part of the garden, happily staring at leaves fluttering in the breeze for hours at a time. By then the pigment in her eyes had darkened so much that they were like bottomless wells. Luke was terrified that if she stared at him too long he could die. Ailsa tried to convince him that it was simply that Romy's pupils were indistinguishable from her irises, but Luke remained convinced of his sister's secret powers for at least a couple more years. Around this time, in that way that parents assign roles to their children, Harry and Ailsa had decreed that Romy was their uncomplicated and meditative child. And Romy had spent most of her life proving them right. Even more so when Ben, the human curve ball, came along.

Two vaguely unsettling thoughts occurred to Ailsa more or less simultaneously. The first was that they had defined Romy in relation to Luke and Ben rather than in relation to herself. And the second was that being uncomplicated and meditative was a euphemism for not knowing what was going on in someone's head, which was where Ailsa now found herself with Romy.

Feeling an overwhelming need for closeness with her daughter, she put out a hand and rested it on Romy's knee, expecting her to pull away when she thought Ailsa

wouldn't find it hurtful. For years Ailsa had taken physical closeness with her children for granted. She had
carried Ben around on her hip for so long that her shoulders were still uneven. Luke's hand had practically been
welded to her own for at least the first five years of his
life. Now proximity was something that had to be
achieved by stealth. To Ailsa's surprise, Romy took the
hand in her own. It was such a sweet, unexpected gesture that Ailsa didn't trust herself to speak.

'Are you all right, Mum?'

Ailsa nodded.

Romy didn't let go. Her tenderness was almost unbearable. 'I was imagining if you died and I had to go
through your things. It made me think how awful all this
must be for you.'

'Nothing is going to happen to me,' said Ailsa. She
used to say this to Luke all the time. He went through a
phase when he was about to start primary school where
he cried every time Ailsa left the house because he was
so worried she might never come home. 'Why doesn't
he worry about me dying?' Harry used to wonder.

'I'm not a child any more, Mum. You don't have to
protect me all the time. We can look after each other,'
said Romy. They hugged. Romy wouldn't let go.

At that moment there was a sense of possibility about
their relationship and optimism about the future. Ailsa
dared to allow herself to imagine Romy at medical
school, meeting someone who wasn't Jay Fairport, having a baby and a job that she loved. There was nothing

original in the happy endings that parents wrote for their children.

'You know if this relationship between you and Jay turns into something more serious and you decide in the passage of time that you want to have sex, we can talk about it,' said Ailsa mid-hug. 'Don't feel any pressure to do anything you don't want to do.'

'I know that, Mum,' said Romy gently. 'Don't worry about me. I'm good at looking after myself. Since when has anyone made me do something I don't want to do?'

She was making a joke against herself and Ailsa appreciated it.

'Mum. Really. Don't worry. All that's a way off. We're taking it very slowly.'

She disentangled herself from Ailsa and picked up the headphones, but there was nothing pointed in the gesture.

'You know you were born with your eyes wide open,' Ailsa suddenly said. She didn't want to lose her to her music quite yet.

'What made you think of that?

'I found a packet of photos that Granny took when you were a baby. It's a house full of memories,' said Ailsa, turning her attention back to the drawer. She pulled out a knife. It was the one her mother had used to scrape vomit off her father's trousers the day after the night before when he had drunk too much. She saw Romy looking at it and put it quickly in the bin liner before she could ask any questions.

'Aren't all babies born with their eyes open?' asked Romy.

'Most open them shortly after birth. You came down the birth canal with both beams switched on. It was extraordinary. You were like a meerkat. Even the midwife commented on it. She held you up and it was as though you were checking us all out.'

'You mean I actually saw your cervix? That's pretty gross. But also amazing. They showed us one in Biology. It looks like a sea anemone without the spines.'

'Dad was the first person who saw you after you were born. He confirmed it.'

'I wouldn't believe everything he says.' Now there was an edge to her tone. This was what happened when a daughter transferred her allegiance from her father to her first boyfriend, thought Ailsa. Harry was going to find this new stage difficult. It was easy to deliver a lecture on how falling in lust triggered one of the biggest neuro reprogramming events in the brain but it wasn't easy to apply the theory when it came to your own children. Ailsa searched for answers in Romy's inky eyes but saw only her own reflected back.

'I don't understand why they call it the birth canal either. It makes it sound wider than it is, as if the passage through it is smooth and calm like a boat going through the Panama Canal. Do you think it's part of a conspiracy to make women keep breeding? Childbirth looks pretty violent to me. They showed us a video in Year 10.'

Ailsa laughed. She pulled out a leather pouch from

the back of the drawer and dusted it down. It was Rachel's old cowboy and Indian kit. Inside there was a water bottle, a blade that you could rub to spark a fire and a peace pipe. She would give these to Ben.

Harry came into the sitting room to tell them that, despite the challenging conditions in the kitchen for a chef of his calibre, dinner was now ready. Ailsa laughed again. He kneeled down and hugged her from behind. Romy flinched and looked away.

'Remember, they're allergic to public displays of affection,' said Ailsa.

'What's this?' Harry asked, picking up the paperweight.

'I thought it might look good in your office,' said Ailsa hopefully.

'Whenever I look at the dead crab I will think of you,' he said, clasping it to his chest. Still Romy didn't smile.

Later Ailsa went over that mealtime many times because it turned out to be their final family supper together before the scandal broke. It was strange to reflect on, but at the time it was steeped in poignancy because, apart from her father, everyone around the table understood that this was their last meal in this house.

It was a low-key event. Adam expressed gratitude to them all for their help in preparing everything for his temporary stay at the sheltered accommodation Ailsa had found for him in Cromer, but even Ben understood the clear-out was a first step towards selling the house.

Harry, sensitive to the emotion of this unspoken milestone, prepared Georgia's garlic chicken recipe with dauphinois potatoes and peas. 'If they were good enough for the Count of Clermont-Tonnerre, they're good enough for us,' he joked to Ben, who was still young enough to appreciate obscure historical facts.

Everyone tried to be gentle with one another. Luke did a good version of a slouchy teenager but it required too much effort and his phone ran out of juice so instead he opted to entertain everyone with impersonations of various teachers at school. He did Mrs Arnold as Miley Cyrus in her 'Wrecking Ball' video with a panicked Matt Harvey trying to persuade her to put her clothes back on. Even her father laughed before retreating into nostalgia.

'Ailsa, do you remember how you and Rachel would burn the backs of your legs in the summer because you spent so much time on your tummies gazing into the creeks, waiting to catch shrimps and crabs?' he said, staring out of the kitchen window towards the sea as though he was actually watching them play.

'We kept them in saltwater aquariums in the house, didn't we, because we were worried the creeks would dry up,' said Ailsa. 'And we released them just before we went back to school.'

'They kept dying but I replaced them so you wouldn't get upset,' said Adam.

'Did you?' asked Ailsa. 'Even Rachel's one-legged crab?'

'It was your mother's idea but I was responsible for its execution,' explained Adam. 'I needed to impress her again after the incident with the salmon in America. Have you ever heard that story?'

'We have,' Luke quickly intervened.

'Wouldn't it have been better to tell Mum and Rachel the truth?' asked Romy.

'Why would we have wanted to upset them?' asked Adam, puzzled by the question.

'Wouldn't it have been better for them to know so that they didn't have illusions about how happy they deserved to be when they grew up? Wouldn't that have been a better life lesson?'

'The rest of life is a life lesson,' muttered Adam. 'God knows, I've had a few in my time.'

'What did you feed them?' asked Ben.

'Garlic chicken,' said Ailsa and Adam simultaneously. Everyone laughed.

'Did you find my passport, Ailsa?' Adam asked. 'Because I'll need it when I go on my trip.'

'I've got it in here, Dad,' said Ailsa, patting her handbag. When she got home the first thing she would do was hide the passport. She remembered the cowboys and Indians kit. 'Here, I thought you might like this, Ben.' He whooped with joy as he tipped it on the table. 'Now I'm a true Lakota,' he said.

Some time over pudding, Romy pulled out a scrunched-up newspaper article from the back pocket of her jeans. She tried to smooth out the wrinkles and ended up smearing black ink on the back of her hand.

'I found something in the paper today that might interest you, Dad,' she said.

'I thought you were meant to be helping Mum, not reading the paper,' Harry teased Romy in a mock-recriminatory tone, because of course he was delighted that she showed an interest in the news and flattered that she had thought of him as she read it.

'It's a science story,' said Romy.

'Geek alert,' teased Luke.

'It's about the discovery of a new part of the brain called the lateral frontal pole.'

'I think I read something about that in *Neuron*,' said Harry.

'What's *Neuron*?' asked Adam, who had drifted back into the conversation.

'It's some dodgy magazine,' said Luke. 'Read by people with a nerve-cell fetish. Kinky stuff. For the truly obsessed.'

'That's me,' admitted Harry.

'What's it about?' asked Ailsa.

'It's about how scientists have found the human conscience,' said Romy, looking straight at Harry. 'They say it's the size and consistency of a Brussel sprout.' She put out her hand and gently pressed a point just above Harry's left eyebrow. 'There's one here and one behind your eyebrow.'

'There are big hopes that it will help us study psychiatric disease,' said Harry, closing his eyes in contentment as Romy pressed the tip of her finger into the fleshy cleft above his eyebrow.

'So what does it do?' asked Luke.

'It makes you wonder if you've done something wrong and what choices you might have taken,' said Romy. 'How good the choices are that we don't take.'

'God, you think way too deeply about this stuff,' said Luke. 'You show me up in a shit light, Romy. Can't you go out and do something bad for a change?'

'What's conscience?' replied Ben.

'It's when you get that uncomfortable feeling that you've done something wrong,' said Ailsa. 'Like when you took down the fence to get into the Fairports' garden.'

'That was a good thing to do,' said Ben. 'It helped us to get to know them better, and I can reach the sweat lodge faster.'

'It's about the brain's connection to morality,' explained Harry, warming to the theme.

'Where does that leave religion?' mused Ailsa.

'Where does that leave Dad?' asked Romy.

'Is there something I'm missing here?' asked Luke. He was the only one to notice the hint of menace in Romy's tone.

'Probably with another idea for a chapter for his book,' said Ailsa.

'As the great H. L. Mencken once said, conscience is the inner voice that warns us someone may be looking. There's a good lesson for you all. Never do anything that you wouldn't want someone else to see you doing,' said Harry.

'Anything?' asked Luke, raising an eyebrow.

'I suspect it's not something that is well formed in the teenage brain,' said Harry. 'But who needs a lateral frontal pole when you've got Mum looking out for you?' he added, putting his arm around Ailsa.

'If Mum looks out for us, then who looks out for Mum?' asked Ben.

'Me,' said Romy, putting her arm protectively over Ailsa's other shoulder. 'I'll always take care of you, Mum.'

'That's such a lovely thing to say, Romy,' said Ailsa. 'Remember to save the newspaper piece. It might be a good one to bring up during interviews.'

School started again the following day with its familiar tension between surprise and routine. A few days later, Ailsa delivered an assembly on the amount of money that had been diverted from the sports fund to replace vandalized equipment and paint over graffiti. She even managed to raise a smile with a joke about how Banksy was unlikely to feel threatened by its quality. When she got back to her office she planned two more assemblies. One on the importance of timekeeping and the other on pupil behaviour in corridors. Then she wrote to a local company asking them to sponsor the newly formed girls' netball club and drafted a letter about a curriculum information evening for Year 11 parents.

Rachel emailed to say that shooting was about to begin on her zombie film and that she might be out of circulation for a while. *Were you ever really in circulation?* Ailsa teased. After a moment's thought she added a couple of kisses because she had given up on her sister weeks ago and it was easier to feel benevolent when you had zero expectations.

You always handled Dad better than me, Rachel emailed back. She asked when their father was moving into the flat in Cromer and offered to come up to help move him. She followed that up with a question about how Harry's book was going, which was Rachel's way of apologizing for her outburst when she was staying. Ailsa wrote back and said she was missing her.

During a prickly staff meeting after school Ailsa was informed that Stuart Tovey was responsible for the hijacked Facebook page. Matt Harvey explained exactly how he had done it, using lots of acronyms that Ailsa didn't understand. Stuart's technical expertise was terrifying. After much discussion with Mrs Arnold, it was decided he should be suspended from school for a week. Ailsa wanted to postpone the punishment until after exams were finished. Mrs Arnold wanted to implement it with immediate effect, which meant that Stuart would miss his mocks.

The parents of the boy who had been bullied were emailing every day, said Mrs Arnold. The school needed to show that it had reacted quickly and decisively to send a message out to other students that there was zero tolerance of cyber-bullying. He should be suspended with immediate effect. Ailsa overruled her. The best thing that could happen to Stuart would be to get the grades he needed to study Biochemistry at university. She proposed a new ruling on mobile phone use at school. Anyone caught using a phone outside break times would have it confiscated for twenty-four hours. There was unanimous agreement.

'That includes teachers,' she joked. Matt's phone rang and they all laughed, apart from Mrs Arnold.

Ailsa switched to the next point on the agenda. Without mentioning any names she informed staff that seven teachers had taken over three weeks to mark homework and that this would no longer be tolerated. Then she swiftly turned to a date and venue for the staff party.

Ailsa remained in her office for an hour after the staff meeting so that teachers could speak privately to her about anything that was bothering them. She checked her messages and saw one from Romy asking when she was coming home. Ailsa texted back to say it depended on how many teachers came to her with problems and how big the problems were. *The unknown unknowns*, Romy texted back, deliberately mimicking her. *Precisely*, Ailsa texted back, adding a smiley emoticon. She looked out of her window and saw two teachers waiting outside. The first was the head of Drama, who wanted to see whether Ailsa could secure a proper theatre in Norwich to perform the end-of-year play. It took Lucy Drummond at least twenty minutes to explain her idea.

'Brilliant idea,' Ailsa responded within seconds. She suggested a couple of companies in the city who might agree to sponsor programmes.

The second teacher, who marked books as he waited,

was Matt Harvey. He came into the room holding out his hand ready for Ailsa to shake and at the last minute opted for a less formal wave, which left Ailsa's arm floundering in mid-air.

'How's everything going?' Ailsa asked, trying to be as informal as possible while retaining professional distance. She could remember her first year as a teacher and knew how important it was that younger members of staff felt they could express their worries. She wanted to tell him how impressed she was, with not just his qualities as a teacher, but the way he ran Year 12. He was seen as someone approachable and fair without being a walkover. She had almost stopped being annoyed with him over Rachel, even suggesting to her sister that he should come over the next time she was in Norfolk.

'I've been doing a very interesting project with my Biology A-level students,' he said, pulling his chair towards her before she had even asked him to sit down. He cracked the knuckles on his left hand one by one. Ailsa winced. 'Sorry,' he said. Moments later the bone-crunching started up again.

She distracted herself from the noise by glancing at the final floor plan for the first ever careers fair to be held at the school in the last week of term. It was meant to be choreographed so that the twenty-six companies which Ailsa had personally persuaded to participate sat alphabetically in the assembly hall.

She suddenly noticed that Brewin Dolphin had been

located after Goldfinch Chambers and while no one else might notice this mistake it would bother her.

'It's an impressive achievement,' Matt said, 'getting all these companies to agree to come. You must be very persuasive.' He was tilting his chair like Luke at the breakfast table, and she had to quell the urge to shove the legs back to the ground.

'Thanks. It's about creating aspirations,' she said. 'And forging links with local employers. I'm hoping that some might agree to provide work experience and a few might even end up sponsoring students through university.'

He crunched the last knuckle on his right hand and Ailsa knew from previous experience in meetings that he would now stop.

'It's amazing how much you get done when you have three children and all the complications of family life to sort out.'

Ailsa frowned, wondering whether Rachel had said something to him. Honesty ranked higher than loyalty for her sister.

'They say that if you want something done you should give it to a busy person,' she said breezily. He was being kind but she wanted him to get to the point. 'I'm impressed with the dynamism that you've introduced into the Biology Department. Your reputation must have spread because we've got more students than ever before signing up for your A-level course. Romy speaks very highly of you. She's really taking her research project seriously.'

'That's what I wanted to talk to you about,' he said, sounding relieved that Ailsa had provided a conversational opening.

'Harry has given her some help. He pulled out a few papers for her on adolescence and addiction; I hope they're not distracting too much from her coursework.'

Matt looked puzzled and his chair finally came to a halt.

'Our project is related to the genetics component of the coursework. I've been doing some extension work on blood groups with students in the top set. It's got nothing to do with teenagers and addiction.'

'So why is Romy doing this project?' asked Ailsa.

'I've really got no idea. It's not work that I've set. Maybe she has a personal interest in the subject? I chose blood groups because they're a brilliant example of discontinuous variation, which is one of the topics on the A-level Biology syllabus. It's part of the genetics component. One of the companies coming to the career fair specializes in that area, and I thought they'd be impressed if the kids had some off-curriculum knowledge. Did Romy do the pinprick test on your finger?'

He picked up a pen from her desk and started twiddling it between his thumb and index finger so that it rotated like the arms of a windmill. Ailsa leaned over to remove it from his hand.

'I'd forgotten about it,' said Ailsa apologetically. 'It was a while ago.'

'Well, it takes a while to get the results back,' he said. 'And some of them took a while to get it all done. Sorry.'

'I wasn't questioning your efficiency,' said Ailsa. She put down the pen and he immediately picked it up again and began drawing a Venn diagram.

He outlined the three main blood groups, A, B and O. Blood types are inherited, he explained. A and B are dominant and O is recessive. Ailsa began to drift off as he muttered about genotypes and phenotypes, although she enjoyed the sound of all the unfamiliar words and his enthusiasm for the subject.

She knew from managerial courses that she had attended that it was important to hear people out. Listening was hugely undervalued in a culture where it was all about who shouted loudest. She wondered whether there was a part of the brain responsible for narcissism and whether social media encouraged it. She would ask Harry. She nodded as Matt explained how all the children had been given pin-prick kits to take home so that they could test different members of their family. These were sent off and the results had just come back. She was getting used to the way that he liked to paint the background of an issue, like a miniaturist. His tone, however, struck her as odd because it was somewhere between defensive and apologetic.

'So if the parents belong to blood groups A and AB it is impossible for their children to be O,' he said finally. 'I've checked and double-checked.'

'So how is this relevant?' asked Ailsa, wondering if she had missed something. 'I'm not sure that I completely understand your dilemma. Remember I'm not a scientist.'

'I have a family where the blood types don't add up.'

'Sorry, I don't understand.'

'The mother is AB, the father is A but one of the children is O.'

'So what does this mean?'

'The child's blood group should be A, B or AB. It's impossible for it to be O.'

'I'm not sure where this is going,' said Ailsa.

'There's a paternity issue.' He paused again. 'I now realize this was a pretty stupid idea. I was just trying to encourage the kids to see how scientific theory can be applied to everyday life. At least half the class have step-siblings or half-brothers and -sisters and a couple are adopted so the results have been fascinating in highlighting the whole issue of genetic inheritance. But I hadn't really thought through the consequences of the results. I want to make sure that I don't create a problem for anyone. Perhaps this is something that is already known to the family concerned.'

Ailsa stared at the pen revolving between his fingers. This was one of the things she liked about being a head teacher. The range of problems. The ability to make a difference in delicate situations. No two days were ever the same.

'There's a statistic of course,' he continued. 'Around 4 per cent of children are brought up by a father who is genetically unrelated to them. But there's biological truth and there's emotional truth, isn't there? Your father is the person who brings you up.'

In the seconds before she understood why he was telling her this Ailsa thought about everything she had to do. Put up a blind in Romy's room, buy cat food, make a list of the furniture her father could take to the sheltered accommodation in Cromer if he agreed to stay, book Luke's driving test.

'So who is the child?' Ailsa asked, because the conversation needed to be continued and Matt was clearly at a loss for words. But of course she knew already.

'Luke,' he said. 'But if Luke is O, one of his parents has to be O too. And since it's not you or Harry it would have to be another man. There could be a mistake. His blood sample could have been muddled up with someone else's . . .' He drifted off.

Ailsa sat completely still. Too many emotions were betrayed through gestures.

'You're right, there must be a mistake,' said Ailsa.

'I'll mark Luke down as AB, shall I?' he asked, nodding furiously, relieved that the problem had been resolved so swiftly.

'Yes, please,' said Ailsa, her voice taut. She wasn't good at accepting kindness. 'And if you could keep this to yourself I would obviously be very grateful. My sister doesn't need to know.'

'Absolutely,' he said, getting up. 'Absolutely.'

I 2

Things I have never done to impress a boy. Lesbian-kissed a girl. Sent a naked selfie. Worn a push-up bra. For the record, I have also never got so drunk that I was sick, or taken a legal high – or an illegal one for that matter. I say this because there has been a lot of speculation about my character, mostly by people who have never met me. I wasn't trying to reinvent myself. Nor was I an unhappy, insecure attention-seeker. I didn't see myself as a skank or a slut, although it seems a lot of other people do. I understand that people want to find reasons for what happened because they don't want to think it could happen to their own child. I get that. It's human nature.

'I'm so relieved Marnie's so sensible and talks to me about everything,' her mother told Mum a couple of months after the scandal, when she finally decided I wasn't a corrupting influence and allowed Marnie to come to my house again. 'Without communication there is nothing.' Sometimes Marnie's mum reminded me of Aunt Rachel. She said exactly what was on her mind at all times. Emotional honesty was her religion. But no one dared say what they really thought to her. Marnie rolled her eyes apologetically.

Afterwards I told Mum that Marnie most definitely hadn't told her mum that a) she had taken the morning-after pill after sleeping with Stuart Tovey, b) that he had dumped her when she thought she was pregnant, and c) she had given him a blow job to persuade him to go out with her again.

I read my therapist's notes. She left them on the desk when she went to close a blind and I took issue with the fact that I was 'a female victim of the ever-pervasive male porn industry that permeates contemporary culture', because if I was a victim then so was Jay. My real mistake was to believe in the possibility of change, which makes me nothing more reckless than an optimist. And optimism isn't a gender issue, it's a brain issue. Marnie and Becca agreed with me that the only issue open to gender analysis was perhaps the more female desire to save someone.

I'm not saying it wasn't a total mistake. A big error of judgement. A catastrophic series of events that will, as so many people said to me, probably hang over me like a dark cloud for the rest of my life (there were a lot of clichés flung around). But it was done with love and in good faith. And it was my idea. That was one of the things that everyone found hardest to accept. Especially Mum.

Anyway, a few days after I discovered the phone in Dad's office, I distracted myself by poring over the pages on addiction that he had photocopied from textbooks and a research paper that he had dug out, 'Is there a common molecular pathway for addiction?' Unfortunately I didn't get to the end of this one so I didn't read the paragraph about how moderation is impossible for addicts and their only hope of recovery is total abstinence.

One afternoon not long after school had started, when Mum was still at work, I sat with Dad at the kitchen table and he asked me to run through any questions that I had for him. He was anxious to help and patient with my queries. I don't know if this was because he had found the mutilated SIM card in his briefcase and was trying to forge some kind of messed-up alliance with me so that I wouldn't say anything to Mum. Or if it reminded him of the good old days when we used to play Operation together.

It gave me the opportunity to observe without him feeling my scrutiny. I stared into his dark eyes and decided they weren't the windows of the soul because his were empty. I considered how his eyes were also my eyes and whether this meant that I had no soul either.

I thought about asking him how he could have betrayed Mum like that. But instead I heard myself ask whether all addictions are the same. He started explaining how addiction studies show reduced cellular activity in the orbitofrontal cortex, a brain area responsible for judgement and control. He got very excited about research into cocaine addiction and overeating that showed the volume of that part of the brain actually shrank.

'Addiction causes anatomical changes to the brain. It hijacks the normal pleasure reward pathways by blunting the brain's response to dopamine.'

I wondered if he had applied this theory to himself. There were thousands of text messages on that phone.

'Do you think it's possible for someone to become addicted to watching Internet porn?' I asked. To his credit, he didn't look startled by the question.

'Actually the *American Diagnostic and Statistical Manual of Mental Disorders* has just added hypersexual disorder to its list, and that includes compulsive pornography use. But it will be addictive for some but not everyone. You have to take into account environmental stressors, personality, age of onset, genetic inheritance. If it blunts the response to normal sexual stimuli and affects someone's normal hierarchy of sexual needs then it's a problem and will affect pair bonding.' He had gone into lecture mode.

He started explaining how all addicts compulsively seek out their addiction despite the negative consequences, so they need higher and higher levels of stimulation to feel satisfied. 'If they can't consummate the addictive act, they suffer from withdrawal.'

He talked about the recent discovery of a protein over-expressed in the brain of all addicts from compulsive eaters to alcoholics, druggies and long-distance runners. And how teenage addicts produce higher quantities of it and this is what makes adolescents more vulnerable to addictions. 'Delta FosB, Romy. Doesn't it sound like a character from *Dr Who*?' He was so excited. He was never happier than when talking about his work. And I admit I longed for that time just three days earlier when I was just as happy discussing it with him.

More than anything, I wondered how it was possible to live alongside someone like Dad for so many years without ever really knowing him. I wondered whether he had been so immersed in researching adolescence that he had regressed and become a teenager again. Like that *Benjamin Button* film, where the Brad Pitt character gets younger and younger instead of older. I was still shocked by the language Dad had used in his texts to the woman. It sounds incredible but I had never heard him really swear. He recently took away Luke's mobile phone for a week when Mr Harvey overheard him call someone a wanker. His hypocrisy about everything disgusted me. When he touched me on the arm to check I was still listening, I shrank back. He looked hurt but didn't say anything.

'This will all really help with your application to medical school.' He smiled. *I hate you. I hate you. I hate you.* It wasn't original but there was conviction in my feelings. 'They love it when you can show off a personal interest in something esoteric.' Then I hated him even more for not noticing there was anything wrong with me.

'I've decided not to apply. Didn't Mum tell you?' I responded, knowing that this was the most hurtful thing I could say to him. The most hurtful thing I could *do* to him occurred to me later. I watched his face and took pleasure in the way it crumpled.

'Why? You seemed so certain. You've worked so hard to get this far.'

'Change of heart.' I shrugged.

'So what are you going to do instead?' His tone was almost pleading. He bowed his head and took a deep breath. I could see his bald patch, and what he'd done seemed even more pathetic.

'Take a year out. Go travelling. Maybe move to Ibiza with Jay for a while so I can work things out.' For a science student I was proving surprisingly imaginative.

'So things are serious between you two, are they?' he asked without losing his cool.

'Very. He's great. A good person.'

'What does he want to do with his life? Because I don't sense much drive there. I know we live in the age of gender equality but you don't want to end up carrying the weight of someone else's inadequacy. It never works.'

'He's really good at music,' I said defensively. 'And he's a really good person. He'd never do anything to hurt another human being. Especially someone he loves. He's honest and trustworthy. There's a lot to be said for that.'

'Another thing I should tell you about adolescent boys, Romy: they think about sex ninety times a day and almost every time it's with a different woman. They are literally drowning in testosterone.'

I almost laughed. At the peak of Jay's porn affliction,

as I preferred to call it, he estimated that he had seen more than 500 vaginas before he even got out of bed in the morning. Because the browsing part of the endeavour took longer and longer as he tried to find something new. Dad knew nothing. He was nothing.

'Romy, I understand you don't want to take advice from me, but one thing I've learned is that if the wind is blowing in your direction you should always take advantage. It's very competitive to get into medical school and they're looking for 100 per cent commitment.'

'And mine is running at about 60 per cent,' I told him.

'Don't let that boy get in the way of your future,' he warned.

Like the way you let that girl in the way of ours, I thought to myself bitterly.

Of course I had thought about telling Mum about my discovery. I had gone downstairs once since that afternoon to check that the phone was in its box, hoping that I had imagined the whole thing. I took it out, turned it over in my hand a couple of times but didn't switch it on. It would have taken less than a couple of minutes to bring it upstairs and hand it over to Mum. But I couldn't do it to her. It would break her heart. She had been through so much the previous year and had put so much effort into keeping our family together. I understood this now. I remembered overhearing her tell Rachel that staying married requires a lot more courage than getting divorced, and for the first time it made sense.

And if I'm completely honest, there was a more

selfish reason too. This phone and the messages it contained would surely end her marriage to Dad. They would get divorced, sell the house, and I wouldn't be able to live next door to Jay any more. We would probably end up in my grandparents' house on the coast, where there were more boats than cars.

What happened next was my idea. Jay didn't make me do it. I can't say that enough times. That same week we caught the bus back to Luckmore together. It must have been the end of February because there were daffodils poking through the hedges and it was no longer dark when we walked home.

Something Dad said had stuck in my mind. It was about how the reward system in the brain worked in the same way for healthy human functions, like reproduction and eating, as it did for unhealthy ones. Jay's brain needed to find a new way of getting the same high.

I thought of Loveday's explanation of the homeopathic principle of treating like with like. And the principle of vaccination, where you gave a tiny dose of disease to create immunity. I was his cure. It was a lightbulb moment.

'I have a plan.'

'That sounds good. I like your plans. Please elaborate.'

'It's more of an idea really.'

'I like your ideas. I love everything about you.'

'Even my forehead?'

'Especially your forehead.' He ran three fingers back and forth from one temple to the other and I closed my eyes in pleasure. He leaned towards me and kissed me on the lips. His tongue pressed against my mouth. It was the first time that he had ever kissed me in public and I could hear Stuart and Marley and other people from school whistling and shouting from the back of the bus. I didn't care. I wanted everyone to know that we were together because it somehow ironed out the kinks a little and I wanted to let a little light in on the darkness. Because to be honest I was getting worried about the pathways that might be forming in my own brain. *Neurons that fire together wire together.* I couldn't get Dad's favourite statement out of my head. Maybe I would never be able to have straightforward sex. Maybe I had caught his disease. Maybe I was going to turn into my dad. Everything whirred around my head so fast that I could almost hear it buzzing. I felt completely out of my depth. I pulled away from him.

This was the only time that I really considered telling Mum what was going on. I had texted her at school to see when she was coming home, but she said something had come up with one of the teachers. I thought about describing the situation as though it was someone else's problem. Marnie, for example. She was the obvious candidate. Her relationship dilemmas were legend in our family. This was exactly the sort of situation she might find herself in. For a moment I felt elated. Then I realized that Mum already knew that Marnie had the hots for Marley, and the trail would lead back to the Fairports when I needed it to lead away from them. I even considered calling up Aunt Rachel. Because she was a bit left of centre herself. Although, as I was learning, it wasn't telling someone the truth that was problematic but what they did with the information. That was the bit you couldn't control.

There was a big part of me that wished I had never found the phone. Because it had also begun to dawn on me that Rachel wasn't necessarily right about Mum being an ostrich. She was the one who had made all the decisions about moving here. It was more about Aunt Rachel being a rhinoceros, barging through life without considering who she might be trampling on. Sometimes discretion was the better part of valour. Although it sounds unbelievable in light of what happened later, I could see the value of caution.

'So what's the plan?' Jay whispered as the bus pulled up at our stop and we disentangled.

We started walking on the path beside the road and I told him about what I had discussed with Dad. Jay looked totally panicked. His face went shiny and he ran his hands through his fringe over and over again until it stood stiff as a meringue. 'You told your dad about me?' He stood stock-still for a moment and stared into my eyes without blinking, which made me blink even more. I put my hand on his arm. I could feel his arm muscles tense through his blazer.

'Of course not. I said I was doing research for a Biology project at school. Which it sort of is. Except you are the project.'

'If he knew, he wouldn't let me near you. He would

probably want to kill me. If you were my daughter, I would kill me. People would think I'm a total sick freak.'

'Don't worry,' I said. I put my arm through his to urge him to keep moving. 'You can totally trust me. I am the keeper of everyone's secrets.' He didn't say anything but he stopped running his hand through his hair. A thought occurred to me. 'Do you regret telling me?'

'Sometimes it's a relief. I feel like I've finally met someone who understands me. And I really appreciate that you don't think I'm a total wanker. Although of course that is literally what I am.'

Right use of literally, I thought.

'I feel a lot less lonely. But sometimes the fact that you know makes me feel more out of control, as though now I've got to think about what you're thinking as well as what I'm thinking. And then I freeze. I worry that I might not be able to stop. That I might let you down. When it was just me and the porn it was easier. I mean I felt shit afterwards but the two of us had this really good routine going.'

'The porn and me,' I corrected him, trying to inject a bit of humour into the situation. Because I recognized the truth of what he was saying. He had definitely been more subdued since he had told me. But mostly because I was realizing that I was facing a powerful rival in our relationship. His pair bonding, as Dad called it, was definitely well off-kilter.

'Sometimes sharing a secret makes it seem even bigger. More shameful,' he said.

'You need to create new healthy reward pathways in

your brain and close the old ones down,' I said breezily. 'Get your dopamine from other sources. It is possible. We need to rewrite your sexual brain map.'

'You make it sound so simple, Romy. Like building new roads.'

As we got closer to his house, instead of going home I suggested to him that we head to the sweat lodge in the woods. The timing was perfect. Mum was stuck at a meeting at school and Dad would be dealing with Ben. Wolf and Loveday would be doing downward dog. No one would disturb us there.

'To cleanse and purify?' Jay joked. 'I need some of that. Sounds a lot simpler and less painful than excavating new tracks in my brain.'

'Actually. Yes,' I said. He opened the gate into his front garden.

'This was where I saw you for the first time,' I told him, trying to make him less anxious. 'We were watching from the sitting-room window.'

'I know,' he said. 'We could see you hiding.'

'God, how embarrassing. What did you think?'

'Dad said we should put on a show so that you'd freak out about your new New Age neighbours. We refused but Mum and Dad did their worst.'

'You mean the bongos and the chanting?'

He nodded. 'I knew as soon as I saw you,' he said.

'What did you know?'

'That there was a connection. Marley caught me staring at you. That's why he thumped me on the arm.'

'What did he say?'

'That he was the oldest and had the right to first refusal.'

'That's like Luke getting the bedroom in the loft. Ridiculous,' I said, trying not to give away that I was flattered, because Marley Fairport was properly hot although I found him a bit obvious.

We closed the gate behind us and headed past the kitchen window deep into the back garden. I checked whether the slats had been removed from the fence, and they hadn't, which was good because it made it less likely that Ben was skulking around.

It was raining, silent rain, and the closer we got to the woods, the deeper my school shoes sank into the mud. Jay offered to give me a piggyback. I hitched up my skirt and jumped on his back, holding my shoes in one hand, and he cantered off with me clinging to his shoulders. My tights made me slippery as an eel and Jay had to keep hoiking me up so that I didn't slide to the ground.

'My lungs are on fire,' he panted as the mud got deeper. He said that he felt like a medic carrying the wounded through the Somme during the First World War, and we discussed whether the dead weighed more than the living.

'Maybe if it's a decomposed body and the bacteria have multiplied,' I suggested.

'I've never met anyone who thinks the way you think, Romy,' he laughed as we finally reached the sweat lodge. 'You are so original.'

It took a bit of time for him to untie the rope that had been threaded through the eyelets on the plastic door to keep it shut. I looked back to our house and wondered if Dad was in his office discovering that he had been outed. *Would he guess it was me?* Probably. Ben wouldn't understand what was going on. Luke avoided his office. It had bad karma for him because it was where he went when he and Dad had one of their man-to-man chats about his lack of a future.

Dad would feel sick. He wouldn't be able to breathe. Or stand up. I suddenly got worried that he might have a heart attack, like Granny. That someone else might discover the phone and put two and two together, and Mum would find out without ever having the opportunity to be reconciled with him and would have to carry the bitterness to her grave.

Jay bent down to crawl through the half-open door and I followed him inside. I watched as he sewed it up again. In the half-light I saw him go over to a table and pull out a box of matches from the drawer. He lit candles on a wooden shelf that ran around the edge of the sweat lodge and it slowly emerged from the shadows, allowing me to absorb each new detail as it appeared. Low wooden beds with animal skins on top; stools made from tree trunks circling the fire; antlers; beautiful old rocks in the hole in the centre. It was really lovely. Wolf was right about circular spaces being more inviting. It smelled of woods, childhood and freedom. I inhaled deeply.

'It's eucalyptus,' Jay explained. 'Sometimes they use

this resin from Guatemala called *copal* but it's difficult to source in Norfolk.'

Jay pulled back a plastic flap and took out a couple of bottles of Coca-Cola. 'That's not very spiritual,' I observed. 'Or organic.' He removed the tops using a pair of scissors, and I took a couple of gulps even though I hate fizzy drinks. Something else that marks me out as a weirdo, Luke always claimed.

'Dad hides them here. Mum doesn't like him drinking Coke. Even though she's fine with him smoking dope. Because she thinks it's more natural. Doesn't make sense, does it?'

'Nothing does with parents.'

I don't know why but I hadn't told Jay about finding the phone. Perhaps it was some residue of loyalty towards my dad. Or the fact that I didn't want Jay to think my family was a bunch of freaks. Although, given his own parents, that was unlikely. Most probably it was because I thought it might make him refuse to participate in my plan to save him. We lay down on the sheepskin rugs, limbs entwined, and kissed again, and my worries began to dissolve.

'So, Doctor. Give me your expert opinion,' said Jay, nuzzling the side of my neck with his mouth while his hand began to undo the buttons of my school shirt.

'I have a hypothesis. I have no evidence that it will work,' I said as he put his hand inside my bra and I curled towards him.

'Will it get written up in medical journals? Will you be able to roll it out as a global service? Will you give a TED Talk on the subject? Because I believe that you're capable of great things, Romy Field.'

'We don't have a control group,' I whispered. 'Although there are a lot of people out there in the same situation.'

'How do you know?'

'On reddit. I found this forum on the Net.' He didn't ask any questions. I couldn't work out whether knowing there were other people like him out there diminished or heightened the scale of his problem.

'I want you to want me sexually and no one else,' I said. 'You need to stop looking at what you find on the Internet and have as much interaction as possible with real girls,' I said, pulling away to do up the buttons of my shirt again.

'That's what I'm trying to do,' he said breathlessly, pulling me back towards him. 'I totally want interaction with you.'

'You need to release pheromones. You need to have real sex. You need to empty your head of all those other images.'

'How do I do that?' he asked. 'I can't wipe my memory.'

'We're going to make a film. With your phone. Then when we're not together you can look at us instead of all the porn.'

He looked at me, his eyes wide open, questioning and

yet not wanting to question because the idea was too irresistible to reject.

'God, Romy, are you sure?'

'I did lots of research. If we do this, it will gradually replace the images you have running in your head. It will create the necessary novelty, and the reward system in your brain will signal its approval. You'll strengthen the networks relating to me. We can have sex. And you will be cured.'

'More than anything I want a happy ending,' said Jay.

It all seemed so simple. We put the phone on the shelf and tried out a few angles.

I got him to stand up. I asked him to tell me what he wanted me to do to him and how he wanted me to do it. And then I did it. So you see Jay didn't force me to make the video. I didn't make it to impress him. I made it to save him. It was my idea. Our truth. It didn't belong to anyone else. No one else was ever meant to see it.

I3

'So what did you do last night, Romy?'

It was a throwaway question. Ailsa was looking for some uncontroversial diversion over breakfast. She had stayed up half the night surfing medical websites for information about blood groups that might prove Matt's theory wrong. When she found none she made an anonymous post on Mumsnet, asking for advice about her dilemma. Within a couple of hours she had thirty-eight contradictory responses, including four from women in an identical situation. *Oh what a tangled web we weave when first we practise to deceive*, one wrote back. *No one sums up a problem better than Shakespeare.* Common mistake. It was Walter Scott, but Ailsa didn't feel she was in a position to correct her. Two hours later, she deleted her post in a fit of nerve-jangling paranoia that someone might recognize her.

'Went to Marnie's. Watched *Gossip Girl*. Borrowed a dress for a party,' Romy said without missing a beat. Her mouth was full of muesli.

'Oh,' said Ailsa. 'That's nice of her. What party?'

Romy sidled around the kitchen, languid as the cat, bowl in one hand, trying to locate her Chemistry textbook beneath the piles of papers that had taken up permanent residence on the sideboard. Lucifer threaded himself in and out of her legs, doing figures of eight. Ailsa had given up years ago trying to get Romy to sit down for breakfast at the table, conceding that where she ate was less important than the fact that she ate at all.

'For Marley's birthday party. Remember. The theme is Professor Green meets *A Midsummer Night's Dream*.'

'Sounds very intellectual,' said Harry as he put the first chapters of his book in numerical order. 'Or is Professor Green a Cluedo reference?'

After six months in the countryside, Harry looked more youthful than he had for years. His hair was long and wild and his face wind-burned from all the time he spent outside. Exercise had given him a more angular outline. The tension of the previous year had finally dissipated. Ailsa cursed Matt for his overzealous research project just at the point when it looked as though their marriage was back on course and then berated herself for giving someone with so little experience such a free rein.

'That's Professor Plum,' Luke laughed. 'Professor Green is a rapper, Dad.'

It knocked Ailsa off course hearing Luke call Harry 'Dad'. She turned towards the window and closed her eyes for a moment. All she could see was Billy, with his lazy smile and sun-bleached hair. She touched her ear, remembering how he had introduced himself to her in assembly his first day at school by flicking her earlobe from the row behind and asking what Ailsa was doing at the end of the day. It had been as simple as that. Harry was right. Love at first sight is pure biology.

'Mum, are you listening? What do you think?' Romy pulled out a couple of diaphanous dresses from her school bag and held them up against herself.

Ailsa turned round. Marnie was at least half a foot shorter so she simply selected the longer dress. 'I prefer the teal colour,' she said with a quick smile. Even if her advice was ignored she was grateful to be consulted. 'It goes better with your eyes.'

'I'll wear the other one,' joked Luke, grabbing the dress from Romy and draping it across his torso with one hand while holding his arm above his head to take a selfie with the other. He jutted out his hip and stuck his chin in the air. *Just like Billy*, thought Ailsa, startled by the clarity of this thought. Luke laughed. Ailsa looked away. She had spent so many years searching for similarities between Harry and Luke, and now all she could see were their differences. Luke lifted the dress to his nose.

'Smells of roses. Like Marnie.'

'How do you know what Marnie smells like?' asked Romy suspiciously.

'She's been hanging out with us a bit, since you and Jay got together.'

'Marley?' asked Romy hopefully.

Luke shook his head. 'Stuart.'

'For real?' she said with disbelief. 'That's messed up.'

'I don't get it either, Romeo.'

They noticed their parents listening and stopped.

'So when is this great event?' Harry squinted from over the top of his book.

Romy ignored him.

'In two weeks,' said Luke. 'The night after mocks finish.'

The same night as the teachers' party, Ailsa noted. She was about to ask about parental supervision, surely an oxymoron where Wolf and Loveday were concerned, when Ben wandered into the kitchen still dressed in his pyjamas. Ailsa glanced at the clock. He was seriously behind schedule.

'Morning, Grub,' said Romy, ruffling his hair with her hand. Drops of milk dripped from her teaspoon into his thick curls.

'Why aren't you dressed for school?' Ailsa asked. She turned to Harry. 'You'll have to take him.'

'Because I'm not going,' said Ben. He crossed his arms defiantly.

'What's up?' asked Harry, putting down his papers and pulling him onto his knee. Ben resisted. He tried to summon up anger but Ailsa could tell that he was about to cry.

'Someone's taken my film off Wolf and Loveday's website,' he said, wobbly-voiced. 'It's disappeared. I've looked for it everywhere.'

'There was an anonymous complaint to the council,'

Harry explained. 'So Wolf and Loveday can't start their business at the moment. They've probably removed it temporarily. Until everything is sorted.'

'Don't worry, Grub. Nothing on the Internet ever really disappears,' said Romy.

'That's why you don't want to put some video of yourself pissed and upchucking on Facebook,' said Luke.

'Luke, I'll have to rewrite my job description. You're beginning to sound like a responsible adult,' said Harry, pretending he was about to pass out.

'I'll help you load the video on YouTube if you like,' offered Luke.

'It won't get the same traffic,' said Ben. 'Why would anyone complain about Wolf and Loveday when all they want to do is help people?'

'People aren't allowed to construct buildings and set up businesses without official permission,' explained Ailsa, annoyed with herself for not anticipating his reaction. Ben had spent hours filming Wolf building the circular roof frame. He had even helped to lay the wooden floor and wheel heavy barrows of mud from the centre where the fire pit would be. She hadn't taken on board his emotional attachment to the whole project. 'Especially if it involves something where someone could get hurt. People who offer expensive cures without any qualifications can be very dangerous.'

'How could anyone get hurt in my sweat lodge?' Ben asked. 'It's where people go to get better.'

'I don't know,' said Harry, stroking his head.

'There was an accident in a sweat lodge in America where three people died. The guy who ran it is in prison. You don't want Wolf to go to prison, do you?' Ailsa asked.

Harry's brow furrowed with disapproval. Ailsa met his gaze. 'You,' he mouthed. She nodded and he shook his head regretfully.

'I'd had over ten thousand hits,' said Ben. 'Rachel said it could be the start of my career as a film director.'

'It's an unpredictable industry,' said Romy, trying to comfort him. 'But that's a lot of hits for your first film. You should feel proud of yourself.'

Romy suggested he should revert to being a spy. Adam said that he could come and visit him the following week during his trial period at the flat in Cromer. Harry said he would try and find out who had complained and convince them they were wrong. He shot Ailsa a pointed look. Ben was inconsolable.

'Now my friends won't believe that I ever made a film. They'll think I'm a total loser,' said Ben with a deep sigh. 'Life is full of disappointments. I don't think I can take any more.'

'What else has gone wrong?' Ailsa asked, worried that she had missed other cues. Ben was finding it difficult to make friends at his new school and had taken to hiding food in his room again, always a sign that he was feeling anxious.

'Grandpa's moving out –'

'Only for a trial period,' interrupted Adam.

Ben continued: 'You won't let me join Facebook. And I thought when we moved out of London we'd move into a house like the Cluedo board.'

'What are you talking about?' asked Harry.

'I thought there'd be a billiard room, a conservatory and secret passages. There aren't even any doors in this house. I hate it here. I want to go home.'

Ailsa smiled. Ben's problems always seemed sweetly innocent beside those of his older siblings, their eccentricity injecting a distracting layer of humour into domestic life. She was forgetting that Ben might not see it this way.

'Why don't we go and talk to Wolf and see what's going on? I'll take you to school after that,' said Harry.

Ben gave a sad nod.

'Thanks,' said Ailsa. She hugged Harry for a little too long. He was so good at dealing with Ben.

'Come on, Romeo, let's go. Juliet's waiting for you by the front gate to go and catch the bus,' said Luke.

'Shut up, Luke,' said Romy happily, checking her face in the mirror.

'Don't forget your Biology project,' Ailsa reminded her.

'I've got it, thanks,' she said, patting her rucksack. 'All ready to hand in.'

'Hope I get a mention in the acknowledgements at least,' said Harry, almost bashfully.

'Not specifically,' said Romy, giving him a long hard look. 'Although you definitely inspired the conclusion.'

What's Romy up to? Ailsa wondered as she got in the car to drive to school. Why would she do so much work for a project that didn't exist? She was obviously interested in the subject of teenagers and addiction. According to Harry, her questions to him had demonstrated a real depth of understanding. But when Ailsa asked if he had actually seen anything Romy had written, the answer was no. And she wasn't doing it for her university application because Harry had told her last night that Romy was having doubts about studying medicine.

If Ailsa hadn't been so distracted by her discovery about Luke she might have taken this argument to its logical conclusion and realized that if Romy wasn't doing the research for herself then it was probably for someone else. She might have asked her what was going on and Romy might have told her. Could have, would have, should have. *Never live life in the conditional tense*, she used to tell her English students. It was too full of regret.

Instead Ailsa found herself behind the school bus at the crossroads at the top of the road thinking about Billy. She caught sight of herself in the mirror and massaged the faint line that was beginning to appear between her eyebrows. There were blue bags of exhaustion under her eyes. What would he think of her now? She stared out of the windscreen and thought how the tiny blurred spots of dead insects smeared on its surface looked a little like the red blood cells that Matt Harvey had found on Google Images yesterday evening as he tried to explain in the simplest terms the inheritance of blood type.

When she looked up she saw Romy waving her away through the rear window of the bus. It must have looked as though Ailsa was keeping tabs on her and Jay. Ailsa hung back to let the bus get ahead, remembering Matt's diagram showing the possible outcomes for a child whose parents had A and AB blood.

After his revelation about Luke, Matt had apologized for embarking on a project that could throw up potentially explosive results. He questioned his ability to be a teacher and wondered if he was really suited to the job. He explained that he hadn't thought through the repercussions of an anomaly. Except of course it wasn't an anomaly. Ailsa tried to reassure him by insisting that it was better it involved her rather than another family. Because this was the kind of issue that could get the board of governors really worked up.

Instead they could forget about it. It was probably a mix-up. Happened all the time. They both expressed relief at finding a satisfactory way out and exchanged a nervous smile. He tore up the piece of paper until it resembled confetti and threw the bits into Ailsa's wastepaper bin. She tried to disguise her anxiety. She didn't want him to feel bad. But, more selfishly, she understood that her calm was more likely to guarantee his silence.

'Would you rather I didn't come to your house with Rachel tomorrow night?' he had asked. Ailsa had totally forgotten that she had invited them over.

'It's fine,' said Ailsa. 'We're fine.'

She put the car into gear and edged towards the crossroads and stopped again. Her head was boiling over with memories of Billy, a man she had thought about for the past seventeen years only in the most impressionistic terms. She couldn't go into school and deliver an assembly on the importance of punctuality, especially now that she was going to be late. She opened the car window to get some air and switched off the engine. *Compose yourself*, she ordered the panicked woman in the mirror.

Ailsa liked to deal in facts. Facts were soothing. And the facts were these: Luke's father, Billy Weston, had joined the upper sixth of Ailsa's secondary school when he was seventeen, one term into the new school year. He arrived tanned from a summer spent in the Mediterranean. He had a surfboard, wore his hair long and grew his own marijuana from seed, and was impossibly exotic for Norfolk in the late 1980s.

He had already lived in New Orleans, Mexico City and Madrid because his father was a jazz musician and the family followed his work. By some miracle of fate, his parents had rented a house by the beach for six months, where they lived in happy chaos, their daily rhythms dictated by urges rather than routine. There were no mealtimes or bedtimes. Ailsa came and went as she pleased, which suited her because by this time Adam was drunk more than he was sober. Her mother encouraged her to escape, which meant that Rachel bore the brunt of this last dark period in their father's love affair with alcohol.

For six months Ailsa and Billy hadn't gone for more than a day without seeing each other. Then at the end of the summer, just before the new school year started, Billy told Ailsa that his family was moving to California. She went to his house the following week, after he didn't turn up at school, and found a letter from Billy with a forwarding address and a promise that he would write. The letter said he didn't believe in sad goodbyes. 'It's easier this way.' Ailsa didn't hear from him again until the day before her wedding six years later.

Of course she had suspected, especially in the early days. When she discovered she was pregnant she had consulted one of Harry's medical books and discovered sperm could survive in the Fallopian tubes for up to five days.

She had had sex with Billy the night before her wedding and sex with Harry the night after. Even thinking about it now, Ailsa felt nauseous. She had never told anyone – not her mother, who was waiting up for her when she arrived home at four o'clock in the morning, nor Rachel, who had questioned her about her bridal glow when she got up after just three hours' sleep the morning of her wedding.

When she discovered two months later that she was pregnant she knew the baby could be Billy's. But equally the baby could be Harry's. But as she now understood, suspicion was knowledge's more hedonistic cousin. Suspicion left things open-ended and allowed you to imagine multiple scenarios. The problem with knowing something was that it left no room for doubt. It required a reaction.

Ailsa pulled her phone out of her jacket pocket and did something that she had resisted doing for years: she googled Billy. Within seconds she knew that he was divorced and remarried with four children and living in San Francisco, where he worked as a cameraman for a local news station. There were a couple of family photos. Ailsa examined them. Even on the tiny screen she could see the resemblance between his youngest daughter and Luke. Something in the curl of the upper lip and the heavy eyelids. This was Luke's half-sister. She dropped the phone in shock on the seat beside her. If she wanted to she could get in touch with Billy right now. There was a phone number for him on the San Fran News website. A whole range of options had suddenly opened up.

Conflicting currents of thought buffeted against each other, like the sea when the tide was on the turn. She imagined telling Luke. He would surely want to meet his father, and Billy would be entitled to get to know his son. They would discover how alike they were and would hold Ailsa responsible for the lost years, even if neither of them ever articulated their resentment.

They would demand to know why she hadn't suggested DNA testing and what right she had to withhold her doubts from them. Back then parenting was all about nurture rather than nature. It seemed incredible now, but people had genuinely believed you could make your child a genius by playing it Mozart in the womb or cause irrevocable developmental damage by going out to work.

A new concern gained traction. Billy might not want to include Luke in his life, especially if he had just embarked on his second marriage. He might reject Luke. Another wave of anxiety broke over Ailsa's head. Luke would reassess his entire childhood in light of this new evidence. He would see a therapist, who would turn him against his parents. All three of them. He would take even less responsibility for his future. He would be given a perfect excuse to fail.

And what about Harry? They had betrayed each other. Harry was rational enough to balance this equation. He wasn't a jealous man. He knew about Billy, the sketchy details at least, that he was her first boyfriend and she had messed up her exams because of him, but not that she had seen him the night before her wedding. Her deception had lasted eighteen years; his six months. Maybe her betrayal had inadvertently led to his. Harry's relationship with Luke had come up at every session with the marriage guidance counsellor. It wasn't a reason for what he had done but Harry was right: it gave context.

The truth might make Harry feel less guilty about his inability to relate to Luke. But it might also make him feel worse. And hadn't he mentioned the other day how leaving London had been the making of his relationship with his eldest son?

Moreover Harry would want to know why when she had had the opportunity to tell the truth in the Italian restaurant all those years ago, she had chosen to lie.

'Did you see Billy again after he disappeared?' he had asked Ailsa in the middle of that meal. She was eating a mouthful of pasta arrabiata and somehow managed to keep chewing without losing eye contact.

'No. Why are you asking?' she asked, leaning forward so the zip dug into her pregnant stomach.

'Something your mum said.'

It was the biggest lie she had ever told. She told it to protect herself, Harry and the unborn baby. And because she didn't know for sure. A few weeks later, when the midwife placed Luke in her arms and she stroked the shock of dark hair and drew a line across the luscious perfect lips, she still wasn't sure. All babies looked like little old men, Harry observed, his voice choked with emotion as he decided Luke most resembled Adam.

What else could she have done? Were the choices that she didn't make any better than the one she had made? She remembered the newspaper piece about conscience that Romy had shown Harry and rubbed the soft dimple above her eyebrow. Her lateral frontal pole must be in overdrive.

Ailsa squirted water onto the windscreen and turned on the wipers at full speed to get rid of the dead insects. Her mind turned back to Matt, who had emerged as the improbable lynchpin of this unexpected drama. Could she count on him not to say anything? Ever? This defined the range of options that lay before her.

It seemed reckless to rely on someone she had known for less than six months. Yet if someone had asked for an objective appraisal she would have said that Matt was a trustworthy person who was discreet and unlikely to become loose-tongued when drunk. The likelihood was that he would never mention the issue again and would try to forget he ever knew.

Ailsa was reassured by the fact that he hadn't asked any of the obvious questions. Did Luke's father know he had a son? Did she ever see him? Did Harry know? Did Luke? She could see from the pained expression on his face last night that he understood what the truth could do, perhaps not its seismic quality, but certainly the fracturing of relationships that would have to be dismantled and recast. He wouldn't want that responsibility. And nor did she. She decided to live with the status quo for another couple of weeks.

Ailsa jumped as she realized there was someone knocking on the car window. She saw Loveday peering through the glass and swore under her breath then understood from the hurt expression on Loveday's face that she could lip-read. She fumbled with the electric window and realized that it wasn't working because the car engine was switched off. She turned on the ignition and lowered the window.

Loveday crouched down until she was eye level with Ailsa. 'We need to talk contraception,' she said dramatically.

'Contraception?'

For a split second, through the fog of paranoia and exhaustion, Ailsa thought that somehow Loveday had intuited her dilemma or read her post on Mumsnet. She must have noticed the panic in Ailsa's face.

'Not yours,' she teased. 'I don't want to become a grandmother before the age of fifty, do you? It's too ageing.' It slowly dawned on Ailsa that she was talking about Romy and Jay.

'I assume that you don't want Romy pumping her body full of hormones, and condoms are so unreliable. I've discovered a local person who fits the honey cap and was thinking that maybe we could all go together to get Romy fitted?

'Honey isn't as irritating to the vagina as spermicide and it immobilizes the sperm,' Loveday continued when Ailsa didn't say anything. *Some things never change*, thought Ailsa. *Having a son makes you liberal and having a daughter makes you conservative.*

'I really don't think they've reached that stage yet,'

said Ailsa. She paused for a moment. 'Do you and Wolf want to come round for a drink tonight?'

When she proposed to Rachel earlier in the week that Matt should join them for a drink the evening before their father began his week-long trial at Prince's Court, Ailsa wasn't acting entirely altruistically. It was a judgement call. Meeting Matt would take Adam's mind off the real reason for the get-together. The presence of an outsider would make them all behave better. And there would be enough people that any residual awkwardness between Ailsa and Matt over his relationship with her sister would be tempered.

The theory had been good. But this was before Matt had lobbed his hand grenade with his bloody blood group project. So Ailsa was glad Loveday and Wolf were coming to dilute the evening further. There were never any awkward silences when they were around and they owed them from New Year. Harry was mildly surprised by this softening of Ailsa's line on their next-door neighbours and promised to make quesadillas that they could all snack on around the coffee table in the sitting room. It would be more relaxed than sitting at the dinner table. Making food had become Harry's way of proving his loyalty to Ailsa. She offered to grate cheese. It was a subliminal acknowledgement of her guilt, she decided.

Loveday hadn't disappointed. Almost before she had sat down between Rachel and Matt on the sofa, she had launched into a diatribe about how many of the world's current ills could be explained by the uncoupling of male and female sexual energy. There was a fundamental imbalance that could explain anything from the culture of gang rape in India to the decapitation of Western hostages by ISIL.

'So what you're saying is that if these men had a way of expressing their yang energy through intercourse, this wouldn't happen?' Harry incredulously asked her from the armchair opposite. He was always blown away by Loveday's lack of empirical evidence and the way she totally rejected his. Her belief in instinct and self-expression was absolute. But he had stopped jumping out of his chair to adjust the lighting in the room every five minutes, which was good because Ailsa couldn't cope with anyone else's jangly nerves.

'Won't be much chance to rebalance my chakras in Prince's Court,' Adam observed. He didn't want anyone to forget the real reason for the get-together. He made a weak joke about the assisted bathing facility and how he didn't know the rules of bingo.

'Maybe you can teach everyone how to play poker,' Rachel suggested, putting her arm around him. 'Always good to bring something to the party other than a bottle of red wine.' There was no trace of recrimination in her tone.

Rachel sparkled. The changes to her script had gone down well. An idea she had generated about a zombie version of *Northanger Abbey* had created a buzz. She was creating a niche for herself. Less niche and more coffin,

Adam had joked. Everyone laughed longer and harder than the joke deserved.

'That's vampires, Grandpa,' Romy giggled before going back upstairs to finish her project. Romy had been appalled that her Biology teacher was coming to her house and had announced in advance that they couldn't really expect her to participate in any meaningful way.

Wolf and Loveday outlined the preparations for Marley's eighteenth-birthday party. There would be vegetarian curry, the trees would be alive with thousands of tiny lights, and Loveday would devise a unique cocktail to mark the occasion. They would be there the entire evening, Loveday reassured Ailsa several times in a way that made Ailsa feel as though she was being judged for being neurotic. Except then Loveday added reproachfully, 'I'm not such an irresponsible parent.'

When Matt had arrived, an hour ago, Ailsa had searched for his gaze across the room, exchanged a quick polite smile and, as soon as she had got over that hurdle, looked quickly away. Half a glass of wine later Ailsa glanced over at him again. He hadn't spoken much and looked stiff and uncomfortable in the suit he wore for parent evenings at school. Ailsa felt a stab of pity. It wasn't his fault that he had become embroiled in her mess.

She noticed he was examining the wedding photograph sitting on the chest of drawers beside the sofa and wished she had moved it. It had been taken just as Harry and Ailsa left the church at Salthouse, when the tension of the service had been replaced by euphoria that they were actually married. They looked like teenagers, thought Ailsa. She checked Matt again and realized that he was probably doing the calculations and wondering if Ailsa married Harry because she discovered she was pregnant.

Luke came in and accepted Harry's offer of a beer. Wolf asked how Luke's driving lessons were going, and Luke said Harry had combined them with a thorough survey of local pubs. Matt stood up abruptly and shook Luke's hand and muttered something about driving lessons being a good father–son bonding exercise. Mercifully Ben followed close behind. He threw his arms around Rachel and told her about his bad luck with the film of the sweat lodge.

'It has to be a place which brings people together rather than pushing them apart,' Wolf told him. 'I'm sure the person who objected to it will find it in her heart to reconsider when she realizes its power to transform lives.'

It was a pointed comment, but Ailsa's attention was consumed by Ben, who was handing over a small sports bag to his grandfather.

'What's this?' Adam asked, pulling him onto his knee.

'It's a survival kit for you in your shelter,' Ben explained. He opened the case and lined up the contents on the table. There was a box of matches, a water bottle from the cowboy and Indian kit and a list of phone numbers in code, in case Adam needed help. Ben pulled out his treasured Swiss army knife from his pocket and with a very serious expression handed it over to his grandfather. 'In case you need to find your way home alone. It's even got a toothpick.'

'That's very kind of you, Ben,' said Adam, his bottom lip trembling.

'I'll come and visit every weekend,' Ben promised.

'I'm six miles up the road,' Adam reassured him. 'Less, as the crow flies.'

'Why is it a crow?' asked Ben. 'Why not a pigeon? Do crows have a better sense of direction than other birds?'

'In the States we say "as the wolf runs",' said Wolf. This distracted Ben. Ailsa was grateful.

Her anxiety about Matt's discovery had displaced her feelings about taking her father to his new flat in Cromer the following day, but now these emotions spewed to the surface unchecked. Conversation continued around her. Ailsa tried to focus. Rachel said something about their father starting a new phase of his life as if he was Ben starting secondary school. Harry had a discussion with himself about how new experiences released dopamine in the brain and told his father-in-law that he might have a whole new lease of life. Ailsa, however, was blindsided by the conviction that this was another ending. Not a beginning.

She swallowed over and over again, and when she couldn't get hold of herself retreated into the kitchen and leaned against the cool wall beside the cooker, where no one could see her. The good thing about large groups of people was that it was easier to hide in the shadows for a while. She noticed the floor beneath her feet was slippery with olive oil, grabbed some kitchen roll and kneeled down to wipe it up. She imagined Matt in the room next door surreptitiously glancing from Harry to Luke, looking for their similarities or more likely spotting their differences. He would be wondering how Harry could not have questioned Luke's paternity when he looked so unlike every other member of the family. 'Like father, like son,' he might say in a well-meaning attempt to reinforce the bond between them. Ailsa had done a bit of that herself over the years.

This made Ailsa feel terrible. She and Harry had wreaked horrible destruction on their relationship. But the cruellest cut was other people knowing you had been betrayed when you didn't. Matt would treat Luke differently from her other children, more favourably perhaps, because he felt sorry for him. Or perhaps more cautiously. His attitude to Harry would be more restrained, in case he let something slip. Her thoughts ricocheted from Matt back to her father and then back to Matt like a game of pinball in her head. She was aware that someone was in the room beside her and knew even before she looked up that it would be him.

'Are you OK?' Matt asked. 'I just thought . . . There's a lot going on . . .' His voice trailed off. He stepped towards her and dropped down on his haunches until he was at her level. They were now invisible to the people on the sofas. Ailsa applied meticulous attention to the oil.

'Stop, Ailsa,' Matt said quietly. 'Please.' Her wiping became less vigorous. She noticed a small hole at the end of his trainers and then the pointy shape of his knee through his threadbare suit trousers.

'I'm fine,' she said finally. He stretched out his arm and covered her clenched fist with his hand until finally she dropped the ball of kitchen roll. But instead of releasing her hand his fingers slid between hers. He searched for her gaze and found it. *Look away*, she told herself.

'I didn't mean for this to happen,' said Matt eventually.

14

A few words about Wolf and Loveday. The standout characteristics at least, because you could write a whole book about them: they considered seven to be a magical number because the menstrual cycle occurs in four units of seven, as does the orbit of the moon around the earth. They sprinkled salt across their doorway to absorb negativity. They didn't really believe in sit-down toilets and worried about obstructed colons more than exam results. They even had a special machine in their bathroom imported from California for colonic irrigation.

Oh, and they lived by their conviction that men should ejaculate no more than twice a month to prevent chronic fatigue. Jay told me this was the best example of irony that he had ever come across. I tried to laugh with him but couldn't. Dad called them an anachronism. I wasn't sure what he meant but he said it fondly. Mum said they were kooky. Her tone was more disapproving.

I think in part she was envious because every Friday Wolf came home very publicly with a present for Loveday. Sometimes it was a bunch of flowers that he had picked from a hedgerow. Once it was an old Afghan coat that he had found in a second-hand shop in Norwich. In

December he arrived with a pot of translucent shells that he had picked up on the beach.

I thought of Dad's kindness to Mum over the past year and wondered whether Wolf was atoning too and whether all marriages were a series of atonements.

What I do know was that they professed to believe in personal freedom, trust and the essential goodness of humankind. Qualities which meant Marley's eighteenth-birthday party quickly became the hottest ticket in Luckmore. There would be no bouncers on the door frisking for alcohol, parents turning off the electricity when the music got too loud or rooms declared off limits.

The morning of the party I went to a hairdresser in Norwich with Marnie and Becca. I showed the stylist a picture of Jennifer Lawrence's pixie cut and came out one hour later feeling cold rather than cool. I hadn't realized how vulnerable the back of your neck could be. It didn't help that Marnie and Becca gave me sideways looks all the way back to the bus stop. 'So Audrey Hepburn,' Marnie kept repeating. We took a selfie and posted it on Instagram.

Ben cried when I got home because I didn't look like me any more. Luke glanced up from his phone for a nanosecond and said he'd already seen the picture that I'd posted. Mum said it looked great but I could hear the words getting caught on the lump in her throat. The last time I had such short hair I was a toddler, she explained.

Dad was speechless. He loved my long hair. Which is exactly why I had cut it off.

Marnie and Becca came back to my house to get ready. By this time the sun was going down. I opened the bedroom window so that we could hear when the music started. Wolf and Loveday had agreed the party could be held in the sweat lodge in the wood on condition everyone took off their shoes before they went inside. This was the sort of thing they obsessed about, Jay said. They would probably get angrier about dirty footprints on the new wooden floor than if he got a girl pregnant. Not that this was likely to happen soon, he quickly added. There was a note of caution in his voice that I hadn't heard before.

Only Ben was worried about the party venue. He'd come into my bedroom, ignoring the fact that Marnie was standing there in her most attention-seeking bra and knickers, and asked me to make sure that no one hurt his sweat lodge. His chubby hand squeezed my forearm tight. I was a little taken aback by his proprietorial tone but reasoned that he was still smarting from the disappearance of his film from Wolf and Loveday's website.

'Of course we'll take care of it, Grub,' I said. 'It's nice that it's being used though, isn't it?'

'I helped build it,' he told Marnie and Becca proudly. 'The stones in the centre represent our ancestors. They're special volcanic rocks. If we hurt them we hurt ourselves.'

Becca and Marnie laughed. They were used to Ben by now and his offbeat view of the world. We were in that pre-party mood where everyone laughed at everything even if it wasn't funny. If I had seen Dad before we left he would have said that our nucleus accumbens was releasing dopamine in anticipation of new stimuli.

'I'm being serious. Why does no one take me seriously?' Ben said.

He stropped out of the room. Usually I would have gone after him, but I was struggling to zip Marnie into a fluorescent pink glow-in-the-dark catsuit that she had bought that morning in Norwich.

I glanced over at Jay's bedroom. The curtains were pulled shut. I guessed he was out at the sweat lodge helping Marley fine-tune the playlist. They had spent days putting it together. Wolf believed atmosphere should define music and lectured them on the importance of spontaneity and living in the moment. They agreed with him and then ignored everything he had said. A strategy everyone should probably adopt with parents.

'What do you think?' Marnie asked. She spun on the spot to demonstrate how the cloudy pink silk wings that she had sewn to the shoulders of the catsuit blew in the breeze like tattered sails. She wore a ribbon around her forehead, silver filigree fairy ears and thin bangles on her arms which jingled every time she moved. On her arm was a quote from *A Midsummer Night's Dream*: 'And though she be little she is fierce.'

'Do I embody the spirit of Titania?'

'You look amazing,' I said, meaning every word.

'Good enough for Marley?' she asked.

'Don't you mean good enough for Stuart? I thought you were getting with him?' I asked. Becca looked surprised in that way that girls do when someone else from the group knows something they don't. 'Luke told me,' I quickly added because I hate there to be an atmosphere between friends.

'He's a means to an end,' said Marnie with a wicked smile.

'What do you mean?' I asked.

'So this is my thinking.' She sat down on my bed, cross-legged, looking serious. 'Stuart thinks I'm hot. He can't keep this kind of thing to himself, so he tells Marley, who sees me in a whole new light. Marley comes on to me. We drink a love potion and float off together to the Kingdom of the Fairies, for ever. Marley and Marnie. We are meant to be, like Bonnie and Clyde.'

'Remember the love potion made Titania fall in love with a donkey,' I warned.

'And Romy, you and I can do double dates with Marley and Jay,' said Marnie, too wrapped up in her fantasy to consider Becca's feelings. 'Oh my actual God!'

'I'll look forward to that,' said Becca flatly.

'Marley's attitude has changed already,' Marnie said dreamily.

'How exactly?' I asked.

'He's paying me more attention.'

Becca raised an eyebrow.

'He says hi every time he sees me at school. He asks

me for cigarettes and twice in the same day checked whether I was definitely coming to his party.' She paused for dramatic effect. 'He said I could stay over.'

'Only because Stuart is,' I pointed out, then when her smile briefly faded, I felt as though I had been cruel. Like kicking a puppy. 'What are you going to tell your mum?'

'That I'm staying at your place. She trusts your parents. Don't say anything. I'll be back in your bedroom by the time they get up.'

'You know, that's pretty fucked-up logic, Marnie,' said Becca. I was glad she had relieved me of the burden of pointing this out. 'Marley won't want to steal his best friend's girlfriend. He might think you're slutty and have sex with you once and then dump you. Girls who put it out always get hammered.' I think she could have been a little gentler but Becca was punishing Marnie for not telling her about Stuart.

'If it works you'll be congratulating me on the brilliance of my strategy,' said Marnie.

'Or going to your funeral if Stuart discovers,' said Becca.

'Are you still taking things very, very slowly?' Marnie turned to me with genuine curiosity as though I was one of those American kids who swear off sex before marriage. I nodded because what else could I tell her? In some ways I felt as if I was taking things very fast. But back then I often felt like that about my life. I felt very old and very young, sometimes all at the same time. One minute I would be guessing that Miss Scarlett killed

Professor Plum in the billiard room with the spanner, getting it wrong on purpose so Ben would win at Cluedo, the next I would get a message from Jay telling me he had watched the video (again) and that it was as hot as anything he had ever seen online. But the more he said it, the worse I felt because it underlined the fact that nothing had really changed between us.

There was one small but significant recalibration. Jay had taken to skyping me at night. He liked to watch me watching him as he watched the video of us. I had tried to explain to him that this reminded me of the Dr Seuss book where there was a bee watcher-watcher watching the bee watcher, and that at some point you had to stop being an observer and actually participate.

'Dad has an entire collection of first edition Dr Seuss books,' he said, hoping to change the subject.

'When you replace something in your life with technology you need to think about what it is that you are really replacing,' I advised him.

'What do you think I'm replacing?' he asked, interested in this new angle.

'Contact with real women,' I said. 'You need to connect physically with me. Not just visually. You need to use all your senses. Smell, touch.'

He kissed me and told me how much he adored it when I got scientific on him.

I got more direct. I said that we needed to try and be more like normal people, and he looked worried and said defensively that there was no such thing as normal.

I told him I understood that he was scared of trying in case it didn't work but that I was his best chance of being cured. 'I'm not ill,' he said. His tone had definitely got more defensive recently.

'Addiction is a disease of the brain,' I replied. 'If you don't stop this it might ruin your ability to ever properly love another human being.'

'But I love you, Romy,' he insisted. It was the first time anyone who wasn't family had told me that they loved me but although I wanted more than anything for it to feel right, it didn't. He didn't seem to get it. Later it occurred to me that he didn't want to get it. And later still that he couldn't get it. It was first love with complications, and that stays with you for ever.

I turned to Mum for comfort. I could only pose the most oblique questions. I wondered if there was a moment in her life when she felt she had finally become an adult and everything made sense. She said that everyone was just muddling through as best they could, and that as the years went by you just learned to do a better impersonation of being a grown-up. I wanted to warn her that Dad was doing a particularly poor job on this front but instead found myself giving her a hug and promising always to be there for her. The important thing, Mum said as I held her, was to try and avoid making any decisions that I might regret down the line. She said that she thought it was a mistake not to apply for medical school and that I should at least try and get some work experience before making such a dramatic decision. I couldn't face an argument about this so I retreated.

'It's good to take things slowly,' said Becca, sensing I was struggling. 'More romantic. He'll have more respect for you. Virginity is so retro chic, like vinyl and Polaroid cameras. In the long term less is definitely more with boys.'

I couldn't work out if she really meant what she was saying or was still working through some residue of resentment towards Marnie. If Marnie hadn't been there I might have told Becca about Jay. Not only was Becca completely trustworthy, she was also unshakeably unshockable. She would have told me to walk away. That Jay's problem was bigger than I was. She would almost certainly have told me to get rid of the video. It seems crazy now but the only thing I didn't worry about was other people seeing our film. I trusted Jay absolutely.

I pulled the dress I had borrowed from Marnie over my head and was freaked out by how short it was. It was made of a floaty material that would billow in the breeze. But it was too late to do anything about it. Becca crimped my hair. She drew three silver stars on my cheek while Marnie applied a cherry-black lipstick. I put on a pair of heavy black leather cowboy boots to balance the delicacy of the rest of the outfit.

'You look like someone from *Game of Thrones*,' said Becca. 'Forget taking it slowly. When Jay sees you like this, he'll throw you over his shoulder and take you straight up to his bedroom.'

'Really?' I asked, because despite what Mum thought I dressed for myself not other people.

'God, how am I going to pee?' Marnie shrieked. 'I hadn't thought that through either.' She had forgiven us. As I was soon to discover, that was one of Marnie's best qualities: her ability to forgive and forget so quickly. Although, as Mum said, perhaps if she forgave a little more slowly, she wouldn't forget so quickly and might learn more from her mistakes. Becca and I rashly promised that one of us would accompany her to the toilet at all times.

Ben came in to tell us excitedly that there were so many lights flashing in the Fairports' garden that the astronauts would be able to see the party from the International Space Station when they orbited over Norfolk later that night. Mum had already left for her teachers' party at school so I instructed Ben to tell Dad that we had gone. I guessed Dad was probably downstairs in his office. There was no way that I ever wanted to set foot in that room again.

Ben was right. The Fairports' garden glowed in the dark. Fairy lights had been threaded through the hedge adjacent to our garden and around the trunks of trees on the edge of the wood, so that it looked as though a million fireflies were watching over us as we headed towards the party. Lanterns hung from the branches of trees, some so high that Marnie claimed it gave her vertigo just to look up at them. The path was flanked by tall candles that stood erect like a guard of honour. We walked between them together, sisters in arms. No inkling of what lay ahead.

In the distance the sweat lodge pulsated with music, and the lights seemed to twinkle in time to the beat. Pink and green beams streamed through the roof into the night sky. I let Marnie and Becca drift ahead and stood still, craning my neck upwards. It was a clear night. The sky was shrouded with stars. I didn't see Jay approaching in the dark. He grabbed me from behind and pressed himself against me. Someone turned up the music. Daft Punk was playing.

'You look amazing. I love your hair,' he whispered in my ear. 'Whichever world you come from I want to come and live in it with you.' He kissed me on the nape of the neck and my entire body shivered.

Marnie and Becca had gone into a field, where a flock of matronly-looking sheep had been spray-painted in fluorescent colours. Marnie crouched beside a sleepy bright pink ewe that perfectly matched her outfit, while Becca took photos of her striking different poses and uploaded them on Instagram.

'What were you thinking about as you looked up at the sky?' Jay asked.

'Honestly?'

He tightened his grip around my shoulders and I stroked the muscles on his forearm, noticing for the first time how his arms were painted with strange black hieroglyphics.

'I was thinking about how the universe isn't infinitely old, it's fourteen billion years old, and that because the speed of light is constant you can only see objects that are less than fourteen billion light years away.'

'Is she for real?' Jay shouted across to Becca and Marnie. They all laughed and I joined in. Someone turned up the music and the fluorescent sheep started bleating.

'They're singing,' Marnie giggled, flapping her wings in time to the music. Jay and I swayed to the beat, bare arms entwined above our heads. It was the first time we had danced together and it felt completely instinctive. Marnie had a theory that if you danced well with some-one it was a sign of sexual compatibility. Becca had pointed out that Marnie danced best with the boyfriend who had turned out to be gay. I remembered that Dad couldn't dance at all and he was obviously sexually com-patible with the woman on the other end of the text messages. Maybe she couldn't dance either. Mum, on the other hand, was a great dancer. It was all so confusing.

'What do they mean?' I asked, tracing my finger across the lines on his arms. I wanted a night off from thinking about my mum and dad.

'One's a Navajo symbol of hope and redemption,' he said, nuzzling the side of my neck. 'The other is the *aum* sign.' He touched my head, his fingers running through my hair. 'I'm culturally promiscuous. Like my parents.'

Marley came over holding two murky green cocktails, one in each hand.

'It's a love potion concocted by Wolf and Loveday,' he announced. Marley never called his parents Mum and Dad. He looked as though he had been dipped in burnished gold, and as he got closer I realized that his entire body had been spray-painted. Even his lips and earlobes. His soft fuzz of chest hair was as stiff as candyfloss. He held two curly straws, the kind Ben loved, between his teeth. Marnie floated towards him. She stood provocatively right in front of him, so close that her breasts almost touched his T-shirt, and slowly slid the straws from the side of his mouth.

'Stuart surely is a lucky man,' Marley said. I sighed, imagining how long Becca and I would have to spend analysing this comment later. Did this prove he was interested in her? Or did it reinforce the idea that he viewed her as his friend's girlfriend, which put her off-limits to him? What was the significance of the use of the adverb *surely*? This would be analysed more closely than any passage in her English A-level syllabus.

Marley presented one drink to Becca, telling her how pleased he was that she could make it to his party and the other to me. He gave me a long hard look but said nothing, probably regretting that he had invited his younger brother's girlfriend. He was wearing a loose sleeveless T-shirt. Even his underarm hair had been spray-painted.

'Loving your wings, Marnie,' said Marley, trying but

failing to catch the edge of one of them between his fingers as Marnie danced sprite-like from his grasp.

'And I love your headdress,' she replied, jiggling from one foot to the other.

'Luke's grandfather got it at an auction years ago.'

'I've never seen it before,' I said, sipping the cocktail. It had a bitter taste. *Probably something healthy like kale*, I thought. Loveday put kale in everything. Even chocolate mousse and mashed potato.

'Do you know Luke?' he asked me, tilting his head to one side so that the headdress slid down his forehead. I realized that he didn't recognize me.

'It's me. Luke's sister. Romy,' I said, feeling embarrassed because contrary to what everyone said afterwards I really didn't like being the centre of attention. He did a double take.

'Wow,' he said, moving right in front of me. He took my hand and lifted my arm and led me away from Jay towards the light so that he could see me properly. His hand was enormous. The flames from the candles flickered in the breeze, throwing shadows across his face. 'You really look like you've come from the Kingdom of the Fairies.'

'I cut my hair off.' I looked down at the ground self-consciously and made circles in the dirt with the toe of my cowboy boot.

'Shall we go and get more cocktails?' Marnie asked him, linking her arm through his.

'Sure,' said Marley.

They walked back towards the house together.

'Smooth,' I said admiringly to Becca.

'Smooth,' she agreed.

'Dance?' asked Jay.

'Dance,' I agreed.

It was sweaty inside the sweat lodge, an observation that made Jay laugh. The music was too loud to speak unless your mouth was right next to someone's ear. Everyone was dancing in one glorious mass of swaying bodies and waving arms. There were a few outliers among the crew, throwing wild moves. I saw Marnie grinding against Stuart, one eye fixed on Marley, who was working the decks. The heat had made the feathers in the headdress wilt and the gold paint start to dissolve in patches so that he looked like a Friesian cow.

Luke was doing hip hop, which he had learned from the cool kids at school back in London. When he paused, Stuart offered him a plastic bottle. Luke shook his head. Stuart took a couple of tiny sips like a baby with its first bottle and put it back in his pocket. They did a complex version of a high five. Everyone was barefoot and I could feel the ground beneath my feet sticky with spilt drinks, sweat and mud. For a split second I thought of Ben worrying about the floor he had helped to lay, but what could I do?

Wolf and Loveday were the only couple dancing together in the old-fashioned way, Loveday's head resting on Wolf's shoulder. At one point it looked as though they were doing a waltz. No one seemed to notice or mind. Loveday was wearing a halterneck dress with a geometric pattern. She occasionally threw her head back in sheer exuberance. At least once or twice Wolf leaned over to plant a kiss just where her breasts cleaved. The music stopped for a moment. Loveday glided over towards us.

'We'll go in now so we stop cramping your style,' she shouted in my ear.

'I don't think anyone's style is being cramped,' I replied.

She brushed my cheek with her lips. 'You look fabulous, Romy. Really beautiful.'

'Thanks. So do you. It's a great party,' I said. 'So lovely with all the lights in the trees and the full moon in the background.'

'A party needs a full moon. That's why we chose this date. The solar yang and the lunar yin are in harmony, which means the atmosphere is supercharged but also balanced at the same time. Our vaguest desires can become realities. Did you know that people sleep less during a full moon?'

'It's because it's lighter, which means people produce less melatonin,' I explained. 'You need melatonin to get to sleep.'

She looked disappointed. 'Both our boys were conceived beneath a full moon.'

'That's too much information, Mum,' Jay interrupted. 'Romy really doesn't want to know how I came to be.'

He was right. His parents weren't like other people. But then neither were mine.

Things I learned about parties that night: they were subject to the same subtle changes in atmospheric conditions as the weather; there was hardly anything more fun than dancing with your girlfriends; and drink and drugs brought out the best and the worst in people. Some time halfway through, the party transmogrified, to use Luke's favourite word from World of Warcraft. Groups of people peeled away and subgroups formed and pulled apart again. 'Like nuclear fission,' I told Becca, explaining how new and different energy was generated when the nucleus of an atom splits, to release more neutrons.

'Just what I was thinking,' she teased.

We stuck around chatting outside the sweat lodge while I tried to locate my cowboy boots. There were unclaimed shoes everywhere. Stuart came up to us and asked if we wanted a couple of bumps of 2C-B and how it would kick off nicely where the E left off. At least that's what I think he said. He sounded like a Chemistry lesson. I wouldn't even take a swig of Coke from a can if Stuart offered it to me. So I said something about how I didn't want anything to get between the party and me. Becca told him he should stick to the Ritalin. Fortunately whatever he was taking had mellowed him out and he didn't react. I wondered where Marnie was but didn't want to ask in case she was with Marley.

I realized that I hadn't seen Jay in a while and told Becca that I was going to look for him in the house. I headed back up the path. Time had become elastic. It could have been anything between midnight and four in the morning. The only way I knew that we must have been there for hours was that the six-hour candles had burned down almost to the end of the wicks so you could only see people walking past from the calf down. I thought I spotted Marnie but when I called out her name no one responded.

I went into the house through the front door. It smelled sickly-sweet, grass mixed with patchouli oil and vegetable curry, I guessed. The sitting-room door was half open. Luke and a group of his friends were sitting around the table. He was cross-legged, expertly rolling a joint with one hand. They were totally licked and rambling on about how Google knew more about our lives than our parents did. 'And I mean every site you have ever visited, Luke,' joked a girl from his English class. Someone said that 90 per cent of the world's data had been created in the past two years. Luke asked for her empirical evidence. He sounded just like Dad. She said she'd read it on the Net. Where does it all go? someone else asked. It gets stored in the cloud, Luke explained.

'Have you noticed how they always give comfortable names to uncomfortable concepts?' he asked. '*Cloud* sounds so cute and fluffy but really it's a giant spy system.'

'It's all about the I not the T,' agreed the girl. I noticed that they were holding hands. I could have gone in and joined them. Luke was a good older brother like that. He never made me feel unwanted. 'Skins, please,' he said to the girl, pointing to a packet of Rizlas on the table.

In the kitchen another group was serving themselves vegetable curry and rice from two huge saucepans on the cooker. One of the girls waved and offered me a plate of food. In the other hand she whirled a ladle round and round like a baton, obliviously spraying sauce across the room. She was wearing a shimmery pair of disco trousers and a jean jacket with all the buttons done up. I recognized her as one of the girls that Luke had brought home earlier in the year, when Mum and Dad were going through their liberal parenting phase. Even though she had famously left her knickers under Luke's bed, I suddenly felt exposed in my short dress with spaghetti straps and wished that I had a jacket to throw over my shoulders.

'Have you seen Marley's brother, Jay?' I shouted to her through the gap in the door. She shook her head.

'Sorry, Romy.' She pronounced my name as though it had a hyphen between the two syllables, making the boys sitting at the table giggle.

'Row-me, Row-me,' they imitated her. 'Row, row, row your boat gently down the stream . . .' They fell about laughing.

There was no malice intended, but their teasing made me blush and intensified my sense of loneliness so I closed the door and went upstairs. The layout of the house was identical to ours and I wished for a moment that I was heading up to my own bedroom and could get into bed and go to sleep with Lucifer purring by my side.

By this time the party had spread throughout the house. There were clusters of people on the stairs. I dodged half-empty glasses, a pair of shoes and an abandoned mobile phone. A soaking ball of kitchen roll lay in the middle of a puddle of green cocktail that had spilt on one of the steps. The intention to clear up was sincere but the execution was poor. According to Marnie, Stuart had a stash of Es, which would explain the bottles of water everywhere. On the landing halfway between the ground and first floors I stopped outside the toilet, possessed by an urge to be on my own for a while.

I turned the handle a couple of times but it was locked. I could hear water running from a tap and the sound of someone being sick. 'I'm all right. I'm all right,' a voice slurred on the other side.

The door to Jay's bedroom was closed. I remembered New Year's Eve and the shock of Mum bursting through the door. Now that I knew what had been going on between her and Dad, her edginess made a whole lot more sense. I turned the handle like a burglar and slowly pushed it open.

The light was on and Jay's laptop was lying on the bed, the screen lit up. His guitar was under the duvet, its neck resting on the pillow as though it was asleep. I giggled and looked around in case he was playing a trick on me but he definitely wasn't in the room. I lay down on my side on his bed beside the guitar and pressed the mouse on his laptop. The screen lit up and split into two. On one side were the latest football scores. Norwich had lost against Manchester United 2–0. On the other a woman was giving a blow job to a man with a penis way bigger than the one in Stuart's selfie. The volume was turned down. The man's mouth hung open as he came all over the woman's face. I wondered if he was having a stroke. She tried to look up at him but there was so much sperm in her eyes that it looked as though she had a bad case of conjunctivitis. *Gross*, I thought, quickly closing down the web page. There were bundles of scrunched-up tissues under Jay's pillow.

'You total wanker,' I said out loud and laughed bitterly at the utter appropriateness of the insult.

I checked Jay's search history, knowing exactly what I would find. Today's list was so long I couldn't even reach the bottom of it. At least there was a certain consistency that made my decision easier. I understood that whatever he was trapped in was bigger than me. In that moment I knew it was over, even though it had never really begun. It was a stillborn relationship. I slammed shut the lid of the computer, hoping that I'd cracked the screen.

I went over to the window and scanned the garden for him, feeling sadder than I had ever felt before. I thought of my dad and I thought of Jay and wondered when everyone claimed it was the most natural thing in the world how sex could be so complicated. And how it brought everyone together and blew everyone apart. I understood why priests and Buddhist monks and Hindu sadhus were all celibate. I think this is when I started crying without being really sure who or what I was crying for. Dad, Mum or Jay. Crying always feels monumental, doesn't it?

Someone burst into the room.

'Sorry,' Marley said, checking the room for his brother. He closed the door behind him and leaned against it. He was wearing a pair of black jeans. His T-shirt was balled in his hand. 'I wanted to go in my own room but Luke's in there with a girl. Fucking awkward. Better than awkward fucking though.' He laughed at his own joke.

'Are you tired?' I asked, trying to compose myself. When in doubt, ask questions, Mum always advised. He shook his head and remained by the door. His upper lip had an ironic curl, which made it difficult to know if he was being sincere or cynical.

'I wanted some time out. To take stock. I want to remember everything about my party. Loveday always says you have better recall if you try and be consciously aware of the moment even if it's just for a minute.'

I nodded even though I didn't really understand.

'Now you'll be part of the memory.' His eyes narrowed. 'Are you all right, Romy?'

I quickly rubbed my swollen eyes with the edge of Marnie's dress, spreading mascara all over the skirt. Mum would know how to get rid of it. She had a cupboard full of different solutions for stains. Blood, cat pee, pollen.

Mum was reliable like that. I wondered if she had an antidote to a broken heart.

'It was meant to be waterproof,' I said to Marley. 'But it never is.'

'So was my gold leaf,' he said. He now resembled one of those trees whose bark peels off in sheets. He pulled at the edge of a wafer-thin layer of gold. It floated to the floor.

'Maybe it's the salt in sweat that dissolved it,' I suggested. 'Sodium chloride is really corrosive.' He laughed again and I tried to laugh back but somehow it made me start crying again. Laughter and tears are so close to each other. Like love and hate. And good and bad. I remembered Dad telling Mum that Johnny Cash's dogs were called Sin and Redemption. I felt overwhelmed.

Marley looked panicked. I opened my mouth to try and tell him that he could leave and that I would be fine on my own, but my chest was racked with sobs and instead I sounded like Mum and Dad's car when the engine wouldn't start. I got up from the bed and went over to the window with my back to him so that he couldn't see my face. He walked over and wrapped his arms around me. He felt both familiar and unfamiliar.

'You're the closest he's got to getting with someone,' he said gently as I kept crying. 'If it's any consolation.' I rested my head in the warm dip beneath his shoulder.

'You knew?' My voice was a whisper.

'Sort of. More suspected. You know what it's like.' He

stroked my hair a couple of times and his hand rested on the back of my neck.

'I don't really.' I looked up at him.

'We're all in it but Jay's the only person I know who can't get out of it.'

Marley had this odd way of speaking in a tone of utter certainty but with only the vaguest content. He held my face between his hands so that I was forced to look him straight in the eye.

'Don't think this has anything to do with you,' he said affectionately. 'You're perfect.'

I realized that I was still crying. He wiped away a tear with his thumb, like Mum might do with Ben, and hugged me to him again. We were standing in front of the window, swaying in time to the beat of the music from the sweat lodge. My only worry at that moment was that I might get gold leaf on Marnie's dress.

'I'll definitely remember this part of the party,' he said. I looked up at him. We took each other in. Then his lips were on mine and we kissed. It was pure pleasure.

'A kiss for what might have been,' he whispered.

A long and terrible scream came from the garden. It was followed shortly by a burst of hysterical crying, the sort where you panic someone has stopped breathing in between sobs. The pitch was higher than the music, which meant it was audible to everyone apart from a few stragglers still dancing in the sweat lodge. Marley and I disentangled. We opened the bedroom window and scanned the garden, trying to adjust to the darkness to work out where it was coming from. For a few seconds there was silence. Then the crying started up again: there were more tears and sobs but this time they were more nasal, muffled by phlegm.

'It's Marnie,' I whispered to Marley.

'How do you know?'

'I recognize the sound of her crying.'

'Does she cry a lot?' he said, sounding embarrassed in that way boys do when girls engage in extreme emotion. He put his arm around my shoulders.

'She just feels things deeply,' I whispered.

'Why are you whispering?'

'I don't know,' I said.

The sound wasn't coming from ground level. I adjusted my gaze up by twenty degrees and looked across at a platform built around a tree close to the back door. It wasn't a tree house, more a lookout post. I had never noticed it before, probably because it was hidden in the branches of a fir tree.

Marnie was leaning over a rickety railing, staring at Marley and me.

'You bitch, you total fucking bitch,' her voice wailed over and over again. It took a while to realize that she was addressing me.

'She's shouting at me,' I heard myself tell Marley in astonishment. 'Why is she shouting at me?' Marley tightened his grip on me protectively.

'I don't know. Because she's off her head on 2C-B,' he said. 'If she remembers, she's going to really regret this tomorrow morning. And the following morning. And next week and possibly next year.' I was surprised by the way he could think about the following day when I was unsure what might happen the following minute. I guessed that he was angry that Marnie was creating a negative vibe at his birthday party.

Marnie was either really drunk or really high. Or both. She was waving a bottle in one hand. Becca was with her, her arm around Marnie's shoulders, trying to pull her away from the edge of the platform. I felt guilty for Becca. She always ended up looking after people at parties. She was the one who magically rustled up clean T-shirts from nowhere when people were sick and made calls to parents suggesting it might be a good moment to come and collect their children.

Someone had turned down the music. It seemed like a sensible idea until I realized that it meant that the sideshow up the tree had suddenly turned into the main entertainment. By now small groups of people had gathered beneath the tree, heads craned, trying to work out what was going on.

'I need to go and help Becca,' I told Marley. There was the sound of glass breaking as Marnie dropped the bottle and it fell to the ground.

Someone yelped. 'That was my fucking head.' I recognized Luke's voice. He came into frame as he started climbing a ladder up the platform then temporarily disappeared before emerging through a hole at the top. He stood up and tested the planks then weaved his way precariously towards Marnie and Becca. He spoke but I couldn't hear what he was saying. Whatever it was it didn't have much impact.

'How could you do this to me, Romy? You knew I was in love with Marley.'

Marley looked mildly panicked.

'I thought she was with Stuart? Stuart definitely thought she was in love with him.'

Marnie leaned over the railing of the platform. I knew that she was sufficiently off her head to throw herself over the edge. She would see it as a tragic gesture in the best tradition of Shakespeare. *Romeo and Juliet* was her favourite English A-level text. Usually her grand gestures made me laugh.

I tried to shout back to her that nothing had happened. But behind us the bedroom door flew open and the metal handle slammed against the wall. A small piece of plaster fell to the ground. Jay stormed in. He looked wild. More *Game of Thrones* than *A Midsummer Night's Dream*. Someone had decorated his face with the same thick black paint that was on his arms and torso. There were three streaks across each cheek. Marley smiled at the make-up, his senses too dulled by alcohol and exhaustion to read his brother's mood accurately. Jay's blue eyes darted from Marley to me and back to Marley. I tried to warn Marley but I couldn't get the words to take shape.

Jay ran head down at his brother like a bull, his head slamming into Marley's stomach. Right by his spleen. *But you can live without your spleen*, I remembered thinking.

374

Kidneys were more vulnerable. They couldn't regenerate like the liver. They had always been the most difficult part to get out when I played Operation with Dad.

'What the fuck,' groaned Marley.

Even though Jay was shorter, the impact threw Marley hard against the bedroom wall. He instinctively leaned forward to protect his solar plexus as Jay hammered his fist into Marley's stomach. I heard Marley moan. It was an adult sound, more animal than human. He didn't hit Jay back.

Wolf and Loveday appeared at the door. Wolf was completely naked. *Don't stare at his penis ring*, I told myself as he rubbed his eyes. He was either half asleep or couldn't believe what he was seeing in front of him. Loveday ran in and shouted at them to stop. They ignored her. She tried to pull them apart, finally succeeding when she grabbed a handful of Jay's curls between her fingers.

Marley slumped back against the wall. There was a loud crash as the framed poster of Nikki Minaj fell on top of them all. Glass rained down. Loveday stood immobile and barefoot, covered in tiny shards as fine as snow.

The back of Jay's head took the impact but his thick black hair that I loved so much protected him. They were both lying on the floor, and I realized that Marley was holding Jay and that they were no longer fighting. Instead Jay was sobbing in Marley's arms, and Marley was hugging him and telling him that everything was going to be all right. Outside the window I could see that people's attention had switched from the drama in the tree to the bedroom. They could hear Jay crying, had put two and two together and assumed that it was because Marley and I had betrayed him. Marnie had planted the seed of the idea and it had taken hold like Japanese knotweed.

Only I knew that Jay was weeping for himself. Marley had an idea, but only I could know how truly alone he was. There was another scream from outside and then silence. We all went to the window, ignoring the glass on the floor, and saw Marnie lying at the foot of the tree. I stood with my hand over my mouth. I imagined Marnie in a wheelchair, unable to feed herself or go to the loo on her own, and how everyone would blame me. So you can see how I wasn't really thinking about where Jay's mobile phone might be.

15

Midway through the event in the school gym Ailsa realized with absolute clarity that she had always loathed staff parties. Almost simultaneously it dawned on her that now that she was in charge she could no longer duck out after dinner and would have to stay until the bitter end. Feeling trapped, she looked up at the strip lighting incubating them all from above and down at the paper plate wilting in her hand from the heat.

The yellow lighting highlighted every physical flaw: from nasal hair to pimples, broken veins and sagging skin. Everyone and everything had a liverish hue, and the vinegary smell of cheap wine added a few more notes to the thick soup of stale sweat that hung over the room.

Health and safety regulations meant she had to keep the fire doors that opened out on to the car park bolted shut. Ailsa would have overruled them and allowed people to smoke by the open doors if the deputy head hadn't been standing right in front of her. But she knew Mrs Arnold might use this against her at a later date to demonstrate Ailsa's ambiguous approach to discipline. She had to watch her back with Mrs Arnold in a way that she didn't with anyone else at Highfield. She was the only teacher Ailsa didn't call by her first name.

'So, in conclusion, I think we need a general review of disciplinary issues regarding the Internet,' said Mrs Arnold, who always spoke as though she were addressing an audience. *Why did she always wear those unflattering A-line skirts that ended the wrong side of her knee?* Ailsa wondered. Mrs Arnold was in her early thirties, a good decade younger than Ailsa, but in her drab grey shirt she could have passed for someone ten years older. 'Don't you? And the sooner the better in my opinion.'

'Absolutely,' said Ailsa, nodding so animatedly that a piece of baked potato fell from her plate onto the tip of Mrs Arnold's shoe. She was still bitter from being outranked by Ailsa on the timing of Stuart's punishment. She was the most ambitious teacher in the school by a long chalk. She hadn't said as much, but Highfield was definitely a stepping stone to a more prestigious job. The fact that Ailsa had been proved right when Stuart scored three top-level grades in his mock exams last week had only intensified her resentment.

Ailsa gulped down warm white wine from a plastic beaker, imagining the sulphates and chemicals reacting with each other to create the mother of all hangovers. *Slow down*, she told herself. She didn't have a high tolerance of alcohol and there was still a way to go until the evening was over.

'If you like, I can take charge of the review.'

Ailsa found herself fixated by the deep trench between Mrs Arnold's eyes. It ran horizontally, rather than vertically. Ailsa wondered what expression would create such a line. She unconsciously tried a few until she saw Mrs Arnold had noticed.

'That would be great. Thank you.'

Ailsa glanced around the room, looking for escape. She saw Phil Moore, the director of studies, animatedly talking to Ali Khan, head of Maths, who must have said something funny because Phil threw his head back and laughed so much that his big belly popped over the top of his belt. When she had started at Highfield, Ailsa had guessed that Phil, an activist closely associated with one of the more radical teaching unions, would be her biggest headache. But he was a conviction teacher and turned out to be the kind of person who liked resolving problems rather than breathing oxygen into them.

Behind them was another small group, mostly language teachers. They all resembled the language they taught, thought Ailsa, amused by this idea. The Spanish teacher was wearing a multicoloured flared skirt, white ruffle shirt and a flower, which might have been real, in her long dark hair. She was speaking to a couple of male French teachers, who stood out in sharp suits and thin ties, although they were accessorized with e-cigarettes rather than Gauloises. The German teachers were in chunky cardigans and sported retro facial hair that looked East German circa 1970. She continued this theme with the music staff, trying to match them to their instruments.

Despite the heat, the baked potato and quiche precariously balanced in the middle of her plate were lukewarm (the salad was already finished by the time she reached the front of the buffet queue). She could tell because the piece of Cheddar she had just bitten into had turned out to be a knob of butter.

'Oh God,' said Ailsa, spitting it into her hand as delicately as possible. Mrs Arnold pulled a look of disgust that revealed exactly how she had developed the horizontal furrow.

'I just made exactly the same mistake,' announced Matt, who had unexpectedly sprung up beside them, holding his own wilted plate of food. He was the only other person in the room besides Mrs Arnold who Ailsa wanted to avoid. 'It's interesting how some foods taste so good when you mix them with something else but so horrible on their own.'

'Butter tastes horrible on its own but baked potato isn't so bad,' said Ailsa. It wasn't the right response because it sounded as though she was looking for an argument when what she needed to do was to inject some distance into their interactions.

'I was thinking more of sugar and butter,' he said apologetically. 'Apparently the best-selling Krispy Kreme doughnuts are the ones that have exactly 50 per cent butter and 50 per cent sugar. It's a magic formula.'

Mrs Arnold was agitated at the way the conversation had been hijacked. 'Perhaps we can schedule in a meeting next week?' she intervened, deliberately ignoring Matt. 'How about early Monday morning?'

Matt made an awkward sidestep. 'Sorry. Have I interrupted something?'

'Not at all,' said Ailsa. 'We were finishing up, weren't we?'

'I'm not sure what the rules are on smoking e-cigarettes on school premises,' said Mrs Arnold as the French teachers came into her line of vision. 'Do you have a point of view, Ailsa?' She headed off towards them.

'Did you know her parents were Jehovah's Witnesses?' asked Matt. 'Her younger sister died because they refused to allow a blood transfusion because it's against the rules of their religion.'

'It relates to a passage in Leviticus,' said Ailsa.

There was a horrible screech of feedback from the pair of huge speakers that stood like bookends either side of the disco. Mercifully the lights dimmed, then less mercifully Village People started booming out of an ancient sound system.

'Apparently this is a ritual,' Matt shouted over the music. 'Begun by Phil the year he arrived. Which makes it more than twenty years old.'

At least half of the members of staff lined up in the gym and began turning themselves into human letters for the chorus of 'YMCA'. Phil stood in the middle at the front, so that people behind him could follow his moves. Shuffle sideways three steps, three taps with each toe, circle ... His performance was heart-stopping. Every ounce of energy was invested in his routine. For a big man he was good on his feet. His face was already baby pink. Ailsa was mesmerized by the rapidly expanding circles of sweat underneath the arms of his shirt as he threw himself around the dance floor. She found it all hilarious and for reasons that she was less able to fathom strangely touching. She might not love school parties but she loved the people at this school.

'Come on, you know you want to,' Phil yelled at Mrs Arnold, who so obviously didn't.

The deputy head retreated to the edge of the gym. Ailsa felt almost sorry for her. Her isolation might be self-inflicted but its origins were probably in some childhood trauma. Ailsa was now left standing beside Matt. She was relieved by the distraction on the dance floor because it meant that they didn't have to look at each other. Having spoken to Rachel earlier that day, she was reasonably confident that he hadn't mentioned anything to her sister. Unlike Ailsa, Rachel was utterly incapable of duplicity.

Over the past couple of days Ailsa's conviction that she was right not to say anything to Harry and Luke had strengthened. The moments when she was obsessively turning over the issue in her mind were now punctuated by longer periods of calm. New issues emerged: could she find a children's film course in Norwich for Ben during the Easter holidays? Should she tell her father that they were putting his house on the market so that he could get used to the idea or wait until a buyer had been found? Would she manage to find time to unpack the rest of the boxes sitting in Harry's office?

But Matt's presence filled her with doubts again. A new worry bored its way into her mind. Having dismissed the relationship between Rachel and him as something meaningless which would be over before it had even begun, she was now possessed by the idea that they might stay together for ever. What if it wasn't ephemeral and he became a permanent fixture in their family? Why hadn't this thought occurred to her before? And if she hadn't considered this possibility might there not be other eventualities that she had failed to explore?

Ailsa swallowed a couple of times. Her face felt unpleasantly hot. She could taste the wine in the back of her throat, acid as bile.

Sequences flashed through her mind like short films with inconclusive endings. Births, weddings and funerals. She imagined Matt at every major family event. There would always be this unwanted secret that they shared, and although he might never say anything, he would always know. He might subtly probe Rachel for clues about Luke's father. If he asked any questions about Ailsa's boyfriends before Harry, Billy's name would inevitably come up. He might google him, just as Ailsa had done. The idea that people had been deceived might eat away at him. Didn't they have a right to know the truth? Perhaps if she explained that her marriage had just survived one catastrophic event and that it might not be able to withstand another, he would understand. Ailsa remembered what he had told her about his own parents. He might even empathize.

Ailsa had a brief moment of calm followed by a new wave of anxiety as it occurred to her that Matt would feel even guiltier about keeping this secret from Rachel. She would have already told him her views on the absolute need for honesty in relationships and explained how she had learned this from the burden of keeping Adam's drinking a secret during their childhood.

Of course Matt would confide in her. They were at that stage when they wanted a total state of unity. They would share every detail of their lives. Ailsa could imagine Rachel wide-eyed, emphatically promising him never to breathe a word. But Rachel still hadn't forgiven Harry for his affair and Ailsa could easily imagine full disclosure during a moment of drunken vengefulness. Afterwards Rachel would argue that all secrets were corrosive. *Unworkable.* Ailsa used this word whenever she was trying to tell a member of staff that an idea wouldn't fly. Her current plan was unworkable unless Matt was out of Rachel's life.

'I was wondering if you still have many friends locally from having grown up around here?' he shouted over the music, so close she could feel his hot beer breath in her ear. 'Do you keep bumping into familiar faces?'

'No,' said Ailsa cautiously. 'We were brought up in a tiny village on the coast. It was quite an isolated existence. Just Rachel and me really. We were quite self-contained.'

Already it had begun. Was he fishing for information or was it an innocent question? She glanced at him. The expression on his face was good-natured, as if he wanted to underline his intent to get their relationship back onto familiar ground, but she could see the wariness in his eyes. Rachel obviously hadn't filled him in on the finer details of their childhood, because if she had he would know how they never brought friends home because there was no guarantee what state their father would be in.

'My father could be quite tricky.'

She had invited Billy back once, hoping the presence of a stranger, the son of a well-known jazz player no less, might restrain Adam. Instead the opposite had proved true. He drank even more and pretended that he was an expert on James Taylor. Ailsa stopped counting how many glasses of wine he had knocked back when he reached double digits. By dinner the skin on his cheeks sagged, his mouth hung open and the folds under his eyes had concertinaed until he resembled a blood-hound. Was it possible for someone's face to melt? she had wondered from across the table.

Adam told Billy that he used to play the clarinet and insisted Georgia should look for it even though they were in the middle of eating garlic chicken. Georgia found it in the chest of drawers in the hall. Adam removed it from the dusty case and tried to play, but in between the smoking and the drinking he didn't have enough puff, and when he blew into the clarinet, a mix-ture of dust and garlic spit flew out the other end onto Billy's plate and a blood vessel in Adam's eye burst. Billy had seen the comedy. She had felt only the shame. She hadn't thought about this for years. It was a couple of months after this that her father stopped drinking.

'Are you OK?'

Ailsa looked at her watch. It was almost eleven o'clock. She focused on her breathing, trying to remember what she had learned in classes when she was pregnant with Luke. But just thinking about Luke made her feel anxious again. Small beads of sweat slowly dripped down her forehead and beyond, towards the sides of her nose. She wiped her face with the sleeve of her jacket, which sent bits of potato flying onto the floor, and then took it off and tied it around her waist. *Breathe in through your nose and out through your mouth. Or is it the other way round?* Was that what was making her light-headed? She wasn't breathing out enough carbon dioxide. Romy would be able to explain this. On her out breath Ailsa tried to distract herself by imagining something wonderful like Romy dancing at Marley's party. She saw Romy's long blonde hair swaying in time to the music and remembered that she had cut it short that same morning. It struck her that there was a brutality in this action that Ailsa couldn't fully fathom and that somehow it was directed at Harry. Realizing this fuelled her angst all over again.

There was a lull in the music. Ailsa watched Phil as he leaned over to speak to the DJ, who was wearing a lab coat and red plastic glasses and she now recognized as the technician from one of the science departments. They exchanged thumbs-up signals. 'Night Fever' started playing so loudly that Ailsa could feel the vibrations through the floor of the gym. She felt something bony nudge her arm and looked down to see it was Matt's elbow.

'Are you sure you're OK?' he shouted again over the music. 'You don't look so good.'

'I think I need some air,' she shouted back.

As Matt held open the door at the back of the gym Ailsa glanced back. All eyes were on Phil as he swung his jacket around in the air and took off his tie to signal the beginning of his John Travolta routine, surrounded by an arc of applauding onlookers. When Matt followed her outside into the car park she didn't try to stop him.

Her colleagues had ignored the usual etiquette and cars were stationed in random huddles at untidy angles. One was even parked diagonally across the space usually reserved for Ailsa. Bizarrely this tiny demonstration of independent spirit made her feel slightly better about herself. She zigzagged through the narrow gullies between the cars away from the school buildings towards the grassy bank that marked the boundary between the school buildings and the football pitches. As long as she kept moving she would be all right.

'You know, I didn't marry Harry because I was pregnant,' she said when they had gone far enough to talk without shouting over the music. She kept walking, remembering a psychologist on a course once explaining how research showed that wherever possible you should tackle difficult issues with men and boys while doing something physical at the same time. 'I want you to know that. We were already getting married. We were completely in love.'

'You don't owe me any explanations, Ailsa. Really.' He

sounded out of breath. Ailsa slowed her pace until he had caught up with her.

'So I'm not quite as awful as you think I am. Although it did happen the night before our wedding, which obviously doesn't put me in a good light.'

'I don't think you're awful. Everyone messes up. You'd be inhuman if you didn't.'

They bumped elbows and pulled away from each other.

'But mostly they get away with it.'

'It's like that Bertolt Brecht quote; you know, the one about getting things wrong and dusting yourself down.'

'"Ever tried. Ever failed. No matter. Try again. Fail again. Fail better."'

'That's the one.'

'It was Beckett actually. Not Brecht.'

'I always learn something new in your presence,' said Matt, a hint of sarcasm in his tone. They had now crossed the car park and reached the grassy bank. She waited for him to suggest they turn back to the gym but instead he scrambled up the bank and down the other side. Ailsa followed, wincing as a stinging nettle licked the side of her calf as she sidestepped onto the grass beside him. He was still talking. 'I used to think that you enjoyed wrong-footing people, but then I realized that you're just anal. I've noticed how you do that thing where you line up your pens either parallel or horizontal to the edge of the desk.'

Anal. Interesting use of adjective, thought Ailsa fleetingly.

According to Rachel, a lot of men expected it these days. They were now both obscured from view by the bank. In front of them was a football pitch and on the far right a tall hawthorn hedge that ran parallel to the main road. Matt pointed towards the road and they continued walking, shielded from the night breeze by the bank.

'I assumed you were one of those awful people who make normal people like me feel like we can never quite live up to your very high standards. You know, Ailsa, it's so fucking good to discover that you are as flawed as the rest of us.'

'I'm not sure whether any part of that is a compliment,' she said, her feet already soaked from the longer grass. She tried to remember the last time a man had weighed up her character in this way. She was flattered by the attention and grateful to him for trying to make her feel better.

'All of it and none of it,' he joked. He was good company. She would give him that. He would have fitted well into their family.

'Full moon,' observed Ailsa, looking up at the sky and finding the North Star.

'Do you know why Polaris never moves?' He didn't wait for her to answer, no doubt relieved that she was no longer talking about Luke's conception. 'It's on a direct axis of the earth's rotation above the north celestial pole so all the other stars appear to travel around it. The distance changes slightly each year according to the equinox. At the moment the earth moves slightly closer to it each year, which is why it appears so big. From 2078 it will start to move away again.'

'I always learn something new in your company,' said Ailsa, imitating him.

'I deserved that,' he said.

Ailsa stared at the sky and thought of her mother. Georgia was the only one who had known that she was meeting Billy for a drink that night. 'I hope you know what you're doing,' Georgia had said when Ailsa arrived home in the early hours of the morning. Nothing more. The words reverberated in her head as if she were hearing them for the first time.

'I do,' said Ailsa.

'You do what?' asked Matt. She must have spoken out loud.

'He wasn't a total stranger either.'

'You're beginning to lose me.'

'Luke's father. He was my first boyfriend. It was big love.' She stretched out her arms to demonstrate and hit Matt's cheek with the back of her hand. 'Sorry. I'm really sorry,' Ailsa said.

'God,' he groaned, rubbing the side of his face. 'What did I do to deserve that?'

'He left without saying goodbye and I hadn't seen him for six years. He appeared the day before my wedding. We went out for a drink and he tried to persuade me to call off the whole thing and move to San Francisco with him. I needed to do it to see how I felt afterwards. To prove to myself I was making the right decision.'

'And how did you feel?'

'I stepped away from him on the beach and left him behind. He was the past and Harry was the present and the future.'

They both stopped.

'Aren't you cold?' he asked, noticing her bare arms and the jacket tied around her waist.

'I don't feel the cold. I'm completely cold-blooded, as you have discovered.'

'Don't be so hard on yourself. Lucky the person who strolls through life without having any shit thrown at them.'

'You are the only person in the world who knows this about me,' Ailsa said, 'and that is a burden for you and a burden for me.'

'Then the only option is to kill me,' said Matt, deadpan. 'My death is the price you have to pay for your peace of mind.' She couldn't see his face but she could tell he was smiling. 'I was wondering why you had lured me away from the party to an isolated corner on the outer boundary of the school grounds where a man's body could be hidden for years without anyone finding it. Except I can't see where you've concealed a weapon.'

'I wasn't luring you away from the party. You were leading *me*,' said Ailsa, pretending to be affronted. He stopped walking and turned to face her.

'You're good at keeping secrets,' he said.

He stood completely still. His arms hung awkwardly beside his hips, fingers flexed as if he was willing his hands to stay in that position. His eyes betrayed his intent. They narrowed and roamed slowly across her body, taking in the shape of her breasts, the swell of her hips beneath the jacket around her waist and the bare shoulder blade where the sleeve of her dress had slipped down one arm. No ambiguity there. Ailsa shifted from one foot to the other and his gaze slowly returned to her face. *This is all wonky*, she thought, recognizing the new note through the fug of alcohol. She turned around to walk away and felt his hand catch her own. She thought about Rachel. Then she thought about Luke. There was a hierarchy of needs in all families.

When he was certain that she wasn't going to pull away, he moved his fingers along her hand and traced exquisite circles on the inside of her wrist. Was this what she intended? It was too late for logic. She stood completely still. It would all be fine as long as she didn't turn around. She closed her eyes. Every cell of her body was alert to his touch and her head was finally empty of thoughts. God, it felt so good to be with someone else after years with the same man. And when he pressed himself against her she didn't flinch.

They didn't speak as they retraced their steps to the gym. But there were no words that could make good what had just happened. Ailsa knew that after a respectable amount of time (it turned out to be five months) Matt would quietly resign from Highfield. Eventually he would forgive himself just as she had.

They had come further than she remembered. The cool night breeze and physical activity meant that by the time they reached the car park, the effects of the alcohol had worn off.

Her car was the only one left in the car park and Matt's bike was chained to the railings in front of the school. She looked at her watch and was spooked to see that it was almost one in the morning. Where had all that time gone?

'They'll assume you called a cab,' said Matt. 'Rachel and I . . . it's probably run its course.' *Rachel and me.* She should do an assembly on the ten most common grammatical mistakes. She cried on the way home in the car without really knowing what she was crying for except that it had something to do with loss. For the father that Luke would never know. For Rachel, who would never understand what had gone wrong with her relationship with Matt. For Matt, because he would leave too. For her mother, whom she would never see again. For her father playing bingo with a room full of strangers in Cromer.

She climbed into bed and slid towards Harry. His bedside light was still on, and she carefully leaned over him to switch it off. He was wrapped in the duvet and she drew comfort from the solidity of the mound lying beside her.

'You're late,' he said, his voice muffled by all the goose feathers. Ailsa froze and anticipated his reprimand, like he gave Luke or Romy when they were late. He normally never waited up for her.

'It's like being the captain of a sinking ship. The head teacher can't leave until the last person has gone home,' Ailsa whispered, relieved that he couldn't see her red, puffy eyes. Her arm was uncomfortably arched over his body.

'Who was the last person?'

'Phil. Turns out he's an amazing dancer. Stuck in a 1980s time warp, but completely compelling all the same. You couldn't believe how such a big man could be so graceful. It almost made me cry.'

Harry laughed and slowly manoeuvred from his side onto his back as if it required a massive effort. He pulled back the duvet so that Ailsa could put her head on his shoulder and drew her towards him with an arm around her.

'You don't sound drunk. I love the way you always manage to keep a clear head when everyone around is losing theirs. Requires a lot of self-discipline.'

'Shall we talk about it tomorrow? I'm exhausted.'

'Sure.' He paused. 'So was it a good party?'

'Interesting.'

'Give me the headlines.'

'I discovered that Mrs Arnold probably wants my job. That Ali Khan's wife doesn't know that he smokes. That at least half of my staff could audition for *Strictly Come Dancing* and that warm wine from cartons is the devil's work.'

'Can I ask you something?'

'Shoot.' She sounded like someone from an American TV series. She never used words like that.

'Have you moved anything in my office?'

394

Ailsa groaned. Harry always blamed other people when he lost anything, but invariably it was his fault when papers went missing. She usually located them in the toilet. She drew comfort from the predictability of this scenario, as if order was being restored.

'I'll look tomorrow morning. I mean later this morning.' She now felt genuinely sleepy. 'Is it one of your chapters?'

'I haven't lost anything. It's just someone has been moving around some of my stuff. I wondered if you had taken anything out of the briefcase that sits under my desk? There's a wooden cigar box at the bottom. The lid is missing.'

'Not guilty. How did the party go next door?'

'It finished early. There was a drama. Apparently Marnie fell out of a tree and ended up going to hospital, so Wolf and Loveday sent everyone home.'

'Romy?'

'Asleep.'

'Luke?'

'I think he smuggled a girl in. Which means at least they kept the noise down.'

'So business as usual.'

'Business as usual.'

Ailsa switched off the light.

16

I had no idea what was going on when Mrs Arnold pulled me out of my Biology class later the next week and melodramatically informed Mr Harvey in front of everyone that the head teacher wanted to see me. It took me a moment to register that she was talking about Mum. *This better be good*, I thought, all eyes turned towards me in the back row as I packed up my bag.

It was almost the last lesson of the day and I was in the middle of a Biology past paper, labelling a diagram demonstrating the direction of blood flow in the human heart. Mr Harvey didn't believe in letting us off lightly after exams. At the beginning of the lesson he had taken me aside to warn that I had missed the grade I needed for medical school in my mocks by two points and suggested this test was the perfect opportunity to prove to him that I could raise my game. As I pushed my stool under the table I noticed Mrs Arnold exchange a knowing look with Mr Harvey and I understood, whatever it was, he was in on it too.

'Head teacher? Does she mean your mum?' Becca asked me in confusion. Becca had remained loyal since the party. She was one of the few people who didn't assume that I was a double-crossing scheming cow (polite condensed version of the chat online). I gave an embarrassed shrug and walked to the front of the classroom, head held high, everyone staring.

Jay looked down when I walked past him in the front row, pointedly turning his entire body away from me. He had moved next to Stuart at the beginning of the week in a very public demonstration of the new alliances formed since the party. We hadn't spoken since, and he hadn't responded to any of my messages. I understood why he didn't want to tell anyone the truth. Even from a distance I could feel his shame.

Stuart aggressively stuck out his tongue at me. I assumed he either blamed me for the humiliating end to his relationship with Marnie or was gloating because for the first time that year he had beaten me to the top of the class.

'Head down, Stuart,' shouted Mr Harvey.

'Maybe Romy could give some tips on that.' He smirked. Other students laughed, including some I wouldn't have expected to, like Ali Harn, a bespectacled nerd who was the only other person applying to medical school from my year, and Olivia Khan, the daughter of one of the teachers.

'Right. You're not having your phone back till the end of next week,' yelled Mr Harvey, who had confiscated Stuart's mobile earlier in the day after he caught him using it in class. Everyone was shocked into silence because Mr Harvey never lost it.

I wordlessly followed Mrs Arnold to Mum's office.

She was a parasite on other people's misery, and I didn't want to give her any pleasure by asking what was going on. She told me to wait on the bench outside.

'If you need to talk to me about anything. Absolutely anything, Romy, you know where to find me,' she said, putting her hand on my shoulder. She was big on using full stops to increase drama. She had what Mum called her lemon-sucking expression, both pained and bitter at the same time. I wanted to tell her that no sane person would ever come to her with a problem. 'You can speak to me in complete confidence.'

God, it must be bad, I thought as I pulled my Biology textbook out of my bag and began checking the diagram of the human heart to see whether I had answered the question correctly. 'Right atrium, left atrium, inferior vena cava, superior vena cava,' I whispered. All correct. The words soothed me. I noticed that Mum's blinds were drawn. This also seemed a bad omen.

My stomach cramped. What was going on? I needed the toilet but didn't want to walk past Mrs Arnold's window. I ran through the possibilities. My grandfather had suddenly been taken ill. Ben kept saying that old people gave up when they went into homes. Except as Mum kept explaining, it wasn't a care home. Grandpa had his own flat and friends his own age to keep him company. 'Dying is contagious,' Ben said, unconvinced by her argument. But if Grandpa were ill wouldn't Luke also be sitting here beside me? And surely Mum would have gone home? I remembered the phone and the mutilated

SIM card in Dad's briefcase and wondered if he had told Mum that someone had found it. But they wouldn't deal with this at school. Mum would sooner die than reveal Dad's dirty little secret to Mrs Arnold.

It had to be something related to what had happened at the party. Perhaps Loveday and Wolf had spoken to Mum about the fight or a snoopy parent had read someone's Facebook page and informed the school. It wouldn't be surprising. All anyone could talk about was how I had kissed my boyfriend's older brother, causing my best friend, who was in love with the same boy, to break her ankle falling out of a tree and Marley and Jay to have a fight, although Loveday was the only one who got hurt – her feet had been shredded by the glass.

Even Luke and Becca had raised an eyebrow when I told them my version of events the afternoon after the party. We were in Luke's bedroom. Me on the floor, Luke on his bed and Becca cross-legged on the desk by his window. The girl from the night before was still asleep in his bed. There was a trail of her clothes leading from the door to the bed. I felt a stab of jealousy at the ease of Luke's relationship with her. It was all I had wanted for myself. Instead I had ended up with something way beyond my amateur dealings with boys.

'So talk me through what happened one more time in case I missed something,' Luke instructed. He picked up a weight from the floor and did some bicep curls.

'I went into Jay's room and got really upset because

I realized that he wasn't in love with me and our relationship was over. Marley came in and found me crying. He tried to comfort me but we accidentally kissed each other.'

'How exactly do you accidentally kiss someone?' asked Becca sarcastically. 'Did you trip and suddenly find yourself with your mouth pressed against his? Because that happens to me a lot.'

'More his mouth pressed against mine,' I rambled. 'I can't really remember the details. We were both out of it.'

'You seemed very in control when you went to get the first-aid kit and bandaged Marnie's ankle and kept going on about tibulas and fibulas,' commented Luke. 'And when you called for the ambulance and described to them exactly how to get here.'

'Were you trying to make Marley feel sorry for you to get close to him because secretly you always fancied him, not Jay? Because that's what Marnie thinks,' asked Becca, trying a different approach.

'I was upset because I realized Jay wasn't in love with me.'

'I don't believe you, Romy,' Luke said, swapping the weight from one hand to the other as he shone his bedside light onto my face. 'You're saying exactly the same thing over and over again. I watched this film once about the Stasi in East Germany and it said that if people are telling the truth, there are subtle changes in their story. You're saying the same thing over and over again. You sound too rehearsed.'

Luke was like a sniffer dog when he got the scent of a lie. I put up my hand to shield my eyes from the light.

'Come on, Romeo. Tell me what happened. You know you want to.'

If I'd been alone with Luke, this was the moment when I would have capitulated. He was a surprisingly good listener and he would have good insights into Jay's problem. Because although he never talked about it, I was pretty sure Luke was not immune to the lure of PornHub. But Becca was there.

'I saw you and Jay dancing together at the party. You looked really happy,' said Becca. 'Actually I saw you kissing him too. I don't get why you suddenly thought he wasn't in love with you any more. I mean it's not like a tap that you can turn on and off.'

I had promised Jay that I would never betray his secret, and the best I could do was a partial truth, but with hindsight a total lie would probably have been better.

'Doesn't add up, does it?' Luke asked Becca.

'He was comforting me.'

'Come back to bed, Luke,' said a muffled voice from beneath the duvet. 'Please.'

Stuart swaggered down the corridor and stopped right beside me. I focused on the diagram of the heart until the words began to blur. I waited for him to say something and when he didn't I looked up. He put his middle finger slowly in and out of his mouth, laughing at my shocked expression, and turned to blow a kiss in the direction of Mum's office. Even then I didn't realize what was going on. Shortly afterwards Mum's assistant indicated that I should go in. Mum's face had that pinched grey look that I hadn't seen since we left London. Her lips had shrunk and her eyes were sunken.

'Come in, Romy,' she said formally, as if she was pretending I wasn't really her daughter.

'Everything is fine at home,' she said quickly as I followed her in. When I left the door open she went back to shut it, all the time asking me questions. What were we doing in the Biology class? Could I catch up another time? Did I realize how competitive it is to study medicine? None of it made much sense and I could tell she wasn't really listening to any of my answers.

'There's something you need to see, Romy,' said Mum suddenly. Her voice was all fragmented. The way she kept saying my name made me feel uncomfortable. It didn't sound like her speaking. It gradually dawned on me that she was in a state of shock.

'What are you talking about?' I asked.

Mum went over to her computer and tapped the keyboard.

'I'll sit on the sofa while you watch. I've seen it already.' She went over to the canary-yellow sofa beneath the window and sat with her arms crossed, staring at me. She was breathing out through her mouth and in through her nose like someone doing yoga in reverse.

'Is it something to help with my university application?' I asked as I sat down in her seat. She shook her head and pointed at her computer. In the centre of the screen on her desktop was a file called Romy. I pressed play and within a couple of seconds was watching the video that Jay and I had made together. I had only seen it once before on the tiny screen on his phone in the dim light of the sweat lodge, when we first filmed it.

Now it was blown up there were details that I hadn't noticed first time round. The slightly long preamble where the camera was focused on Jay's crotch as his dick rose in the air from his underpants and slapped against his stomach; the way I shuffled forward on my knees to meet it, mouth half open, eyes half shut, and the huge scab on my knee from slipping on the netball court. I couldn't believe that Mum had watched this when it was so obviously something private between Jay and myself. It was as though she had read my diary or intercepted my Instagram. I felt a brief moment of blind fury. Why did she always want to be so involved in my life? It was sick.

'How did you get this?' I asked angrily. 'You have no right to violate my private life like this.'

'Mr Harvey found it on Stuart's phone earlier today. We don't know how Stuart got it. Presumably someone else sent it to him. We're trying to trace back the trail.' Her voice got quieter and quieter. 'Your private life is very public.'

Afterwards Becca asked me how I felt at that moment. Pure terror is probably the only way to describe it. My entire body went cold until I couldn't feel anything. I couldn't move my fingers. My mouth was dry. Everything was completely numb. I remember thinking that I was paralysed. Just as I had got used to this idea I started to get so hot that within seconds I was soaked with sweat. My hands were bright red and the computer mouse slid through my fingers so I couldn't stop the film. My face was burning and my heart was beating so fast that when I looked down I could see it pulsing through my chest. I wondered if this was how my grandmother felt before she died and realized that living suddenly seemed a lot scarier than death. This was, I told Becca, the instant when I stopped being a child.

'Who is the boy?' Mum asked.

There was a loud thumping on the door of Mum's office. Dad burst through the door. For the first time in a while I was relieved to see him. He apologized to Mum for being late, came straight over to her desk, arms outstretched, and put them around me, one eye on the computer screen.

'Oh, my little girl, my little girl,' he said, as the film continued, 'what have you done?'

He pulled away from me and tried to shield my eyes from the screen with his hand like he used to when we were little and something inappropriate came on television. Except he was trying to protect me from myself. I knew what was coming next. I couldn't look at him. I put my fingers in my ears but I couldn't block it out completely.

'Oh, Mum,' I said. Mum looked up at Dad.

'How has this happened to us?' she asked.

'I love love love it when you come in my face,' I heard myself say in a breathless whisper on screen. The words resonated with Dad straight away because of course he was their inspiration.

'It was you, wasn't it?' His voice cracked.

I nodded without looking at him. At that moment I didn't think that I could ever look anyone in the eye again.

'Oh God,' said Dad, rocking backwards and forwards, holding me in his arms. I pulled away, desperate to get rid of the images on screen. 'It's all my fault.'

'Harry, we can't fall apart,' Mum said, her voice breaking. 'We need to be strong for Romy.'

Her face was so pale that it was as if all the blood had been drained away. I wiped my hand up and down my skirt to try to get rid of the perspiration and dragged the file to the trash folder to delete it.

'There's no point in doing that, darling. It's been uploaded everywhere,' said Mum gently. I could tell that she was trying to regain control of her emotions because she could see the fear in my eyes and wanted me to believe that she could sort everything out just as she had always sorted out all our problems. 'It's gone viral,' she said. 'Revenge websites, porn sites, Facebook . . .' The way she bravely struggled with all the unfamiliar terminology made her seem even more fragile. And it was this that made me really scared.

'What do you mean?' Dad asked.

Mum opened a notebook on her desk and pointed at a list written in shaky handwriting.

'Mr Harvey has been monitoring the situation. This is a list of where we know it has been shown. Matt has been in touch with them and some of them have got back to him. In the eyes of the law Romy is a child and they are distributing child pornography. Some have taken it down already. But some of the websites aren't registered here – one is in Latvia apparently, so they might not respond. And we'll never be able to know exactly where it has been sent. It's out there.' She pointed out of the window and I looked outside, wondering how it was possible that it had spread so far so quickly.

'Mr Harvey has watched the video?' I asked, appalled to think my Biology teacher, the man who couldn't get a condom on a banana in Sex Ed, had seen it. I thought about the boys in my class and realized they must have too, and possibly some of the girls. It was like wildfire. By now probably half the school had seen it. Mrs Arnold. Stuart Tovey. Marley Fairport. I couldn't believe that Jay had betrayed me in this way. And yet this kind of thing happened all the time. At my old school I had even been to an Internet talk on the dangers of sexting.

'The question is, how can we prove it is Jay?' asked Dad.

It took a minute for me to understand why they kept asking this question. Then it occurred to me that Jay's face wasn't visible.

Everything was so broken. I had lost Jay. I had lost Marnie. I had lost Dad. I had cried so much the past few days my eyes were already heavy-lidded, but still the tears came and once they had started they didn't stop. Mum and Dad put their arms around me and we all cried together.

'Did he force you to do this? Did he offer to buy you something or promise to be your boyfriend if you did this to him?' Dad sobbed. 'Was it his idea?' I knew he wanted the answers to be yes, in part because it would let him off the hook, but also because if I had been forced to do this then I was a victim and people would feel sorry for me. I knew right away that while most people would consider Jay to be a player, I would for ever be a slut. That was the way of the Internet. That was the way of the world.

The phone on Mum's desk rang.

'Don't get it,' Dad advised. 'Leave it.' Mum ignored him and picked up the handset. She turned her back and walked over to the window, where she had a terse conversation with the person on the other end of the line. She stared out of the window and I followed her sight line to the Biology classroom on the other side of the playground, where Mr Harvey was staring back at her.

'Who was that?' Dad asked.

'Chair of the board of governors asking if I wanted to take some time off until this is all sorted out. He said Mrs Arnold had called him and suggested that I might appreciate some family time.' Mum gave a hollow laugh.

'So what did you say?'

'I said that I thought I could manage the situation better from school.'

'And?'

'He said he was meeting the board of governors tonight to define their strategy. I told him that I would be there, and he said it would be better if I didn't come and that Mrs Arnold could keep me posted on what was discussed.'

I went to my locker to collect my schoolbooks. Mum offered to go with me but I refused so she sent for Becca. Becca said that the Biology class had disintegrated after I left and that Olivia Khan had explained about the video to her. She had even offered to show Becca a copy that she had downloaded onto her phone. Becca refused. I could tell that she felt let down. She had stuck her neck out for me over what had happened at the party and now there was this.

'I can't believe Jay has done this to me,' I said.

'If you had consulted me I would have told you it was a crap idea to make a sex tape,' she said flatly.

When I reached my locker I could see that someone had scrawled SLUT in big lipstick letters on the door. Marnie, I guessed. Then I remembered that she hadn't come to school that week. I started to feel afraid.

'Ignore it,' whispered Becca, conscious that everyone was watching us. She looked around nervously. I could feel that she wanted me to leave as quickly as possible. I was a liability.

'Attention whore,' a girl I didn't know whispered in my ear as I walked by.

'Fuck off,' Becca told her.

'Relax, just jokes,' the girl laughed.

I decided to go through the gym to meet Mum and Dad in the car park because it meant I didn't have to walk down the corridor past anyone else. On the way through I bumped into Mr Harvey coming the other way. I kept my eyes down, staring at my feet as I walked along the painted line that marked the boundary of the netball court.

'Romy,' he said, his voice echoing around the gym. I am a conformist person so I immediately stood stock-still. He fidgeted madly, putting his hands in and out of his pockets and fiddling with a biro, manically pressing the end in and out.

'Sometimes when the worst thing that could happen to you happens, it makes you a stronger person.'

'Thanks,' I said, my voice a low whisper. 'But what happens if it doesn't?'

I can't recall much of the journey home. I remember leaning my forehead against the window and enjoying the sensation of the cold glass and the blurry outline of the hedgerows as we sped down country lanes. My phone kept buzzing with messages. Mum said she would take care of them and I gladly handed it over to her because I knew they would be venomous.

Mum and Dad sat in the front of the car. They hardly spoke. At one point Dad turned towards Mum and I could see silent tears pouring down his cheeks. Over the past month since I had found his phone with the messages I had longed to hurt him so much that I made him cry, but this wasn't the way I had wanted it to happen. I wanted him to cry for what he'd done, not what I'd done.

'Please stop, Harry,' Mum pleaded. 'We need to work out what to do.'

'It's the loss of innocence in our relationship,' Dad kept saying. I realized he saw a causal effect between my discovery of his phone with the disgusting messages and the video. 'I can't bear it.'

17

Ailsa spent the next couple of days in Harry's office compulsively watching the video over and over again. She slowed it down, sped it up, and examined it frame by frame. She even played it in black and white. It was the scabby knee that got her every time: its childish innocence juxtaposed with the very adult scene taking place centre stage. She touched Romy's knee on screen and cried as she remembered the times she had stuck a plaster on similar injuries when Romy was little, feeling an overwhelming sense of impotence in the face of this current crisis.

Not that there wasn't a lot of activity. People called all the time. A friend from London phoned to say that she thought Ailsa should know her son had spotted it online. Rachel's ex-boyfriend Budgie did the same. She was touched by their kindness. Mrs Arnold phoned at least twice a day. She briefed Ailsa on a conversation with Marnie and Becca. Apparently (long emphasis on *apparently*), Romy and Jay had had a fight at the party. 'I know,' Ailsa lied. Her deputy warned Ailsa that Romy might be a suicide risk and it sounded like a rebuke. Then she said she had called an assembly to warn that any student caught with the film on their phone would face immediate expulsion. 'In future, please can you consult me before making a decision like this,' Ailsa had asked. Mrs Arnold said that the head of the board of governors had endorsed the idea.

Matt updated her on his efforts to track down where the video was being shown and who had agreed to take it down. Did he have her permission to use a credit card to access pay-to-view websites? he asked in an email. Yes, she emailed back. Among the long list of missed calls on her phone at least a dozen were from him.

Am I condemned to voicemail? he asked in a text.

Yes. It's better that way, Ailsa responded, and deleted the text.

Organizations that Ailsa never imagined she would be personally involved with swung into action: the Child Exploitation and Online Protection Agency, Internet Watch, Stop Bullying UK. Apparently it helped that they could prove that Romy was under eighteen. If not, websites weren't obliged to do anything. Matt explained that if sites showing the video were registered in the EU it was easier to get them to take it down than those registered in Vietnam. *Vietnam*, Harry had repeated over and over again, until Ailsa begged him to stop. The scale and speed of its spread was terrifying. It was like a sci-fi film where the main character was a virus, Rachel had said when Ailsa had called her to explain what had happened.

Ailsa walked towards the glass door that led into the garden and stared up at the vast expanse of sky overhead and for the first time in her life found it oppressive. The video was out there. It was in the earth's atmosphere. It was uncontainable. She went back to the computer, pressed play, and began a forensic sweep of the background. It was frustratingly sparse: just a few candles on a shelf and a pile of rubbish on a rough wooden floor. At this point Harry came into the basement to plead with her to stop and come upstairs to see Luke and Ben. But she couldn't. He tried a new tack.

'You need to go and see your father. He keeps calling to ask where you are.'

'Call Rach.'

'Why are you doing this? How is it going to help?' He leaned over her shoulder and angrily pressed the pause button before she could stop him.

'I'm looking for clues.'

'Clues to what?'

'I want to piece everything together. So that I can understand.' She spoke slowly, her tone deliberately calm so that he would leave her alone.

'You're punishing yourself. It's torture enough without watching it on a loop.'

'I deserve to be punished,' said Ailsa.

'Why?'

'For not protecting her. For not knowing what she was up to. For being distracted by other things. A few weeks ago . . . I think she tried to start a conversation . . .'

Harry kneeled down on one knee and kneaded Ailsa's hands with his fingers.

'Look at me, Ailsa. It's not your fault. How could you warn her about something you didn't know about? And if you think you'll develop immunity by watching it on a loop, I can tell you that's not the way that it works.'

Harry warned her that there was evidence to suggest moving images were stored in a different part of the brain from photographs and were more difficult to forget. He began a lengthy explanation of the structure of the hypothalamus and its role in visual memory, using horror films as an example of visual sequences that can stay with you for ever.

'I'm not interested in your science any more, Harry,' said Ailsa sharply, pulling her hands away from his. 'It doesn't help me feel anything differently and it won't resolve anything.' Then she felt bad because Harry was as broken as she was. It was just that their coping mechanisms were incompatible. She wanted to face it full on. He wanted to retreat into academia. There was little comfort in the familiarity of this dynamic.

Harry shook his head, unable to speak. They were both exhausted. For three nights they had hardly slept. Ben, always sensitive to changes in mood, had started climbing into bed with them in the early hours of the morning. He asked why Ailsa wasn't eating anything and anxiously reminded her that in the book *Fattypuffs and Thinifers* the Thinifers were always more miserable.

When they managed to drift off, there was always that lurch between sleep and wakefulness when they remembered what had happened. 'No one has died,' Harry had whispered to Ailsa over Ben's sleeping body, as they tried to console each other.

It felt like death, Ailsa had said. The shock, the sense of loss, the phone calls offering commiseration when there was none. It was the death of innocence. The Internet has added to our knowledge but taken away our innocence.

Hoping Harry would leave her alone, Ailsa explained that she was looking for evidence to prove that the boy was Jay. She showed him a sequence where the chewed end of a scrawny school tie fluttered past Romy's open mouth. Conclusive evidence it was another Highfield student, Ailsa insisted, although she remained convinced it hadn't been filmed on school grounds.

She would call the head of the board of governors to tell him. He would be pleased because it let the school off the hook. He was beginning to bypass Ailsa and rely too heavily on Mrs Arnold. 'How could websites post a film of children in school uniform?' she questioned Harry.

'They're not big on morality.' His irony irritated her because it was a defence mechanism. Harry pointed out that school uniform was a big theme in porn culture. And that this very detail might account for the terrifying speed at which the video had spread from Luckmore around the globe. The first journalists had called asking about a sex scandal at the school only minutes before Romy came into Ailsa's office.

'If she admits it's him, we can do something about it. He can be punished.'

'You really think that would help the situation?'

'It would take the spotlight off her. And it would send

a strong message to other boys who are tempted to post images of their girlfriends.'

'It won't get rid of it,' said Harry. 'It's out there.' He sounded defeated.

'Why should Romy's life be in tatters and he get away with it scot-free?' asked Ailsa, frightened by his lack of fight.

'I'm with you, I'm with you,' said Harry, trying to soothe her. 'I can't understand why he did this to her. I thought he was a pretty good kid. A bit flaky. But not vindictive.'

'That family . . . they're bad news,' said Ailsa. 'No moral compass. I tried to warn you . . .'

'You don't know for sure that it's him in the video.' Neither of them called Jay by his name any more.

'Who else could it be?'

'His brother?'

'Remember Stuart Tovey was behind the Facebook bullying. He has the technical expertise.'

'It doesn't look like him but maybe he was involved.'

There were so many unanswered questions. They had tried to talk to Romy but she didn't want to discuss anything and wouldn't confirm the boy's identity. She had spent the best part of two days upstairs in her bedroom, refusing to go to school, get dressed or come down for meals. She claimed to be studying, but when Ailsa had gone up earlier to collect the plate of lamb tagine that Harry had lovingly made, her Biology textbook was open on the same page and the food untouched. Romy had shut down.

Ben had gone up to see her as soon as he got home from school earlier that evening and had come back down to the kitchen to report that she was in the same position as when he had left her in the morning, lying on her side on the bed, hugging a pillow to her chest. He had opened the curtains when he said goodbye before school and they were closed when he came home so Romy must have got up at least once, he said hopefully. He wondered why she couldn't speak.

'What's happened?' he had asked Ailsa. 'Is Romy ill? Is she in trouble?'

'Someone at school has done something bad to her,' said Harry, fumbling for the right words.

'So why is she the one not going to school?'

'The bit at the end, where she turns to the camera and speaks . . . where you see for the first time that it really is Romy . . .' Ailsa's voice broke. She had frozen the screen on this frame. Harry put up his hand and fixed his gaze on the photographs on the wall. She noticed his hand was shaking. He found this part too disturbing. 'Do you think she's been watching porn? Apparently some girls do that nowadays, you know. Or do you think he told her to say that? It doesn't sound like Romy.'

The colour drained from Harry's face until he was almost grey. His reaction reminded her too much of the moment when he had first admitted to having an affair. Ailsa looked away and found herself staring at the same montage of photos in the frame on the wall behind the computer. In the bottom corner she noticed that Harry had been excised from one of her favourite photos of him and Romy, playing Operation in the sitting room of their old house in London. Ailsa frowned.

'Why would she do this, Harry?'

'Throughout history teenagers have always fucked up,' he said.

'Please. Not the line about Ferrari engines and crap brakes,' Ailsa said wearily. She needed more from him.

'Hear me out. What I'm trying to say is they used to be able to fuck up in private, and in time their mistakes were forgotten and everyone moved on. That's the big difference. Haven't you made mistakes and got away with them? Haven't we both?'

'We were worrying about the wrong child,' said Ailsa quietly. They both gazed at the computer screen in silence. 'I always thought it would be Luke who would do something like this. Not Romy.'

'Thanks for that vote of confidence,' said Luke, who had come into the office without them noticing and was now standing behind the swivel chair. He glanced at the frozen image of Romy's face turned towards the camera and quickly turned away.

'Do you understand what's happened, Luke?' Ailsa asked him, suddenly aware that she hadn't really taken him into account since the scandal broke. She felt a hot new stab of guilt as she realized they hadn't considered Luke's feelings or the fact that as the only remaining member of the family at Highfield he would be absorbing all the heat of other people's scrutiny.

'Of course I do,' he said angrily. 'It's a pretty hot subject. Which you would appreciate if you went in to work.'

'I'm not allowed to go in,' she said flatly.

'Says who?'

'The head of the board of governors.'

'Ignore him,' Luke said angrily. 'You need to fight this.'

'How is it? Being at school. Is it all right for you, Luke?' Harry asked. It was the right question. Harry was good at finding the right words.

'Well, thanks for asking, Dad, because actually it's shit listening to a bunch of wankers calling your sister a whore and offering you money for an introduction. It's pretty much out of control. I hope you've taken away her phone because some arsehole has posted her number at the end of the video and it's got thousands of hits. Probably a million by now.'

Ailsa and Harry were too appalled to speak.

'Have you seen it?' Harry asked finally, flicking the screen.

'Why the fuck would I want to watch my sister give some bell end a blow job?' Luke asked. 'That would be sick.' Ailsa was grateful for his uncomplicated honesty. 'You know, it could be worse, Mum,' said Luke.

'How exactly?' said Harry, impatient because this was Luke's stock response to any problem and one that Ben had adopted.

'It could have been something less vanilla . . .'

'How so?' asked Harry, looking at Luke to enlighten him.

'You know,' said Luke, shifting uncomfortably from one foot to another, staring at the floor. 'Other sexual acts.'

'For example?'

'Oral sex is pretty mainstream compared to most of what you see on the Internet.'

'Do you know who the boy is?' Ailsa asked, feeling completely out of her depth.

Luke shook his head in disbelief. 'Are you for real?'

He leaned towards the computer screen and contemptuously tapped the bottom right-hand corner with his index finger. 'Don't you recognize the location? Those stones in the background are the ones Ben says are his ancestors.'

Ailsa moved closer to the screen until her forehead was almost touching it.

'It's the Fairports' sweat lodge, isn't it?' said Ailsa. 'It's Jay.'

'No shit, Sherlock,' said Luke. 'Haven't you heard of revenge porn? Romy got it on with Marley at the party. Jay saw. It's all over those slut-shaming websites too. Get Mr Harvey to check them out too.'

Ailsa hammered on the front door of the Fairports' house with the flats of her hands. When no one came she curled her fingers into fists and began a rhythmic drumming that brought Romy to her bedroom window to see what was going on.

'What are you doing?' asked Harry, who had caught up with her. He tried to pull her away but she shook him off.

'We're going to have a little discussion with the Fairports,' Ailsa said firmly.

'Are you sure that's a good idea?'

'I'm going to nail him.' After days of deadlock it felt good to be taking action. *Know what you want to achieve* was Ailsa's advice to students when they were trying to resolve a conflict. *Always keep your eye on the bigger picture.* She applied the strategy now and knew that what she wanted was retribution.

'We need to talk,' said Ailsa as Loveday tentatively opened the door and peered through the gap. She was wearing her long purple kaftan with orange fringing around the neckline. No bra, noted Ailsa, turning her attention to Loveday's face. Loveday smiled but Ailsa could see no warmth in her eyes. She beckoned them in and closed the door without saying anything.

'Who is it?' Wolf shouted downstairs.

'Next door,' Loveday wearily shouted back. She sounded almost bored. Wolf emerged on the landing wearing a tie-dye sarong and a pair of socks. Ailsa glanced at the clock on the wall and saw it was almost nine o'clock. Where had the day gone? She realized that Loveday was in her nightdress and they must have been in bed together. Either having sperm-free sex or sleeping. Both possibilities enraged her. She held her arms stiffly by her side, clenching and unclenching her fists, her body aching as if she were coming down with flu.

'Sorry,' said Harry to Wolf as he stumbled downstairs rubbing his eyes.

Why is he apologizing to them after what their son has done to Romy? Then she realized he was apologizing for her, but the time for restraint was over.

'We'd like to talk to you for a moment,' said Harry when he realized that Ailsa couldn't speak. 'If it's inconvenient we could come round another time?'

'It's brave of you to come. Requires courage,' said Wolf gravely as he stepped forward to shake hands with Harry as if they had just agreed on some business deal. His Texan drawl was more in evidence late at night. They followed him into the sitting room.

'Please, make yourselves comfortable. Is there anything I can get you? A tea or a beer?'

'No, thanks,' said Ailsa.

She sat down on the sofa next to Harry, their knees touching. Wolf and Loveday were opposite them on the other sofa. A bowl of cherries sat on the table between them, and Ailsa was grateful for the screen it provided between her line of vision and Wolf's splayed legs.

'You are aware of what has happened,' Harry said.

'Marley told us. Something about a video. We haven't seen it of course.' Wolf was being disingenuous, Ailsa decided. Some people reacted in this vague manner as a way of trying to reassure Ailsa that it wasn't such a big deal. But this wasn't his strategy.

Loveday pushed the bowl of cherries towards them. Ailsa deliberately fixed her gaze on Wolf's face. He fiddled with his beard and said something about how it was a confusing time to be a teenager.

'All those contradictory messages for girls,' Loveday chirped. 'Twerking, Rihanna's S and M fetish, MILFs, thigh gaps . . .'

'Thigh gaps?' repeated Harry and Wolf in unison. If you weren't familiar with the term it sounded like something you might buy in a stationery shop, thought Ailsa.

'No one criticizes Paris Hilton's partner, do they? Or Robin Thicke for twerking with Miley Cyrus. Did you know that he's got a young daughter? He should know better. By criticizing these women instead of the men we are perpetuating female repression.'

'I'm afraid I've lost you,' said Harry apologetically.

'I'm talking about the way contemporary sex is all about male pleasure,' Loveday continued earnestly. 'Boys never come home from parties bragging about how many girls they have orally pleasured, do they?'

Ailsa caught Harry's eye. No matter how hard they tried, the Fairports always left them floundering around for a response.

'Wolf and I are at the vanguard of a new revolution. To bring men and women together sexually for the mutual benefit of both.' She put her arm towards Wolf and they held hands. 'Maybe we could help Romy to find her centre? I'm a trained sex therapist. This could be a wonderful opportunity for rebirth and renewal.'

'That's a very kind offer,' said Harry calmly. 'But we're not really here to discuss that.' He took Ailsa's hand and squeezed it. Ailsa took a deep breath. Her diaphragm was tight as a drum.

'The film of Romy is everywhere. Porn sites, social media sites. A lot of the kids at school have downloaded it onto their phones and sent it on to other friends at other schools in other parts of the country. We will never know who has it. We will never be able to get rid of it. There are comments on websites telling Romy to kill herself, threats to rape her on the way home from school. She has been called vile and terrible things.' Ailsa had forced herself to read all the comments that Matt had sent her way. Even though they had made her retch into the bin in Harry's office. She wanted every detail so that anything Romy might read, she had read first, and she could confront the situation head on. 'Even if this fades, she will never know who might have seen it. Every time she has a job interview she will worry that someone might do a background check on the Internet and find it.'

'Unfortunately in a world without privacy, it is the reactions of complete strangers that end up defining these situations,' said Wolf. 'It is terrible how one quick stroke on a keyboard can impact the rest of someone's life.'

'It will be impossible to know where it stops,' Ailsa continued. She paused for a moment until she was certain she had their full attention. 'But we know exactly where it started.' She waved her hand in the direction of the sweat lodge in the wood.

'The boy's face isn't visible,' said Loveday. Ailsa reeled.

Although she knew that it had been viewed by millions of people, every time she knew for sure that someone had seen it she felt sick all over again.

'I thought you hadn't watched the video?' Ailsa fired back.

'Marley has,' Wolf interjected a little too quickly.

'Not Jay?' asked Harry.

'Not as far we know,' said Loveday. 'It would be too painful for him to watch his ex-girlfriend with another boy, don't you think? He has been very hurt by Romy.'

'She wasn't his ex-girlfriend when the video was made,' said Ailsa. 'The date is recorded at the end. It was made at 21.57 on 28 February. That's three days before the party.'

In the silence that followed Ailsa caught Harry's eye. He looked simultaneously impressed and horrified by her meticulous grasp of detail.

'I don't see how this relates to us,' said Loveday with a shrug. She was stonewalling.

'You know as well as we do that the other person in the video is Jay,' said Harry impatiently. 'Your son has ruined our daughter's life.'

'We are aware there was a fight between Marley and Jay over Romy at the party,' said Ailsa. 'We know that he sent this film out to people as an act of selfish vengeance. His cynical motivation is crystal clear.'

'You don't have any proof,' said Wolf coolly. 'All this is conjecture.'

'The film was made in your sweat lodge,' said Ailsa. 'The stones are visible. The boy has removed his shoes.

He is wearing socks with a marijuana leaf insignia on the side like the ones you are wearing right now.'

Wolf glanced down at his feet and back up at Ailsa. He was frowning. She had got to him.

'And the earring in his left ear. It was a present from Romy,' said Ailsa.

'We intend to get the police involved,' warned Harry.

'I think you're overreacting,' said Wolf, now on the back foot. 'Teenagers do this kind of thing all the time. We need to work together to help them resolve this.' He gave a nervous laugh. 'Hormones and the Internet are a deadly combination.'

'Jay has committed a crime. Romy is seventeen. In the eyes of the law she is a minor and he has distributed child pornography. He could go on the sex offenders' list for five years. He will have a criminal record. We will press charges,' said Ailsa.

'You wouldn't do that, would you?' said Loveday.

'We have nothing to lose. Romy has lost everything already,' said Ailsa.

'If the police discover that he forced her to do this, the repercussions will be even greater,' said Harry. 'We will push for a sexual harassment charge as well.'

'Jay will of course be expelled from school,' said Ailsa. 'We have a zero-tolerance approach to this sort of bullying.' This wasn't true. As Mrs Arnold had pointed out with barely restrained glee at being vindicated, there was nothing in the rulebook about sexting, which now seemed a monumental oversight.

They both leaned back into the sofa. Harry put his hand on Ailsa's knee. There was a sense of relief. They could go home now and tell Romy that they knew it was Jay who had sent the video and that he would be punished. It was crucial that justice was seen to be done. It would take the spotlight off Romy and put it on him.

'Admit it. You hate us, don't you, Ailsa?' said Loveday, her jaw clenched so tight that it sounded as though she was hissing.

'I don't hate you, I hate what your child has done,' said Ailsa smoothly. 'And in my experience this kind of behaviour reflects the context in which a child has been brought up. You have a very loose and permissive approach to child-rearing where boundaries aren't properly defined, and Jay has been left too much to his own devices to work out what is appropriate behaviour. For all your therapy-speak you have no idea what he really gets up to. I'm sure he hasn't been helped by your line of work.'

'I strongly resent the inference of what you are saying,' said Wolf, abruptly standing up and using his index finger to emphasize each word. 'You understand nothing of our work.'

'You give complete strangers vaginal massages,' said Ailsa. 'I saw it on your website. What more is there to understand?'

'Believing in the power of vaginal orgasm doesn't make us pornographers,' said Wolf defensively. 'It makes us feminists.'

'God, you are such a stuck-up, patronizing, judgemental

cow,' Loveday interrupted. 'You've looked down on us right from the moment we moved in. You seem to be forgetting that it's your daughter's mouth around our son's penis, saying those disgusting words at the end . . .'

'He put those words into her mouth,' Ailsa shouted back at her. 'He wrote the script.'

'You can't be sure of that,' said Harry, appalled and bamboozled by the high-speed unravelling of this encounter.

'You are so fucking repressed, Ailsa,' yelled Loveday. 'No wonder Harry played away. You are so squeaky clean that you probably disapprove of all bodily secretions.'

'Compassion, Loveday, compassion,' shouted Wolf. 'Remember, we're all about compassion.'

'There can be no compassion when it comes to protecting our child,' shouted Loveday.

For a moment Ailsa wondered if Loveday had punched her in the stomach. She couldn't breathe. Her head and body felt liquid. How could Harry have betrayed her like this? To these awful people? Why would he have told Loveday? There must be something going on between them. Men and women only talked about sex together if they wanted to fuck each other. It was one of Rachel's pet theories.

'That is no way to speak to my wife,' said Harry, sounding like a character from a 1950s film.

'That was no way to speak to your student,' Loveday countered. 'Have you considered that Romy might have been inspired by you, Harry? Or perhaps neuroscientists will find there is a part of the brain responsible for sexting and Romy has inherited the gene. You're so good at expounding all your theories but not quite so efficient at putting them into practice.'

It took Ailsa a few seconds to pull together the different threads of this conversation. Harry looked completely panicked. Fight or flight. With Harry it was generally flight. She saw him head towards the door of the sitting room.

'How did you find out?' Ailsa asked as she pulled herself out of the sofa. Her body felt so heavy that every movement was an effort.

'Romy told Jay,' said Wolf, a hint of shame in his voice. 'Jay told us.'

'Romy doesn't know,' Ailsa countered. 'The children never knew about the problems in our relationship. We protected them from the truth. Unlike you, we don't believe that everything is up for discussion.'

'Some parents have no idea what their children get up to,' said Loveday, repeating Ailsa's words. 'Didn't you realize she found a phone with texts between Harry and his girlfriend?'

'Let's call the police, Harry,' said Ailsa coldly. She stood up and pulled out her mobile phone from her pocket.

'If you do that, we'll show the police the other images that your daughter sent to Jay,' said Loveday. 'Maybe we'll post them online. We'll tell them about her performance for Jay every night at her window. Did you know about that? About her pleasuring herself for Jay in front of her bedroom window? And we'll give them the context for all of this.'

'You've overstepped the mark now,' said Harry. They all stood facing each other. Harry and Wolf drew closer, chests puffed out like angry turkeys, until they were almost touching. There was a brief stand-off. Then Harry used his upper body to shrug off Wolf. Wolf lost his footing and stumbled backwards into the bookshelf. A couple of the painted Ukrainian eggs fell to the floor and shattered. Wolf righted himself and stepped towards Harry, oblivious to the broken glass underfoot, and tried to grab his shoulders.

'Slow down, cowboy!' shouted Wolf over the noise. He swatted Harry away with one hand while the other clung on to his sarong, which was threatening to unravel. Harry danced around him like a boxer, unable to decide where to land his first punch.

He pushed Wolf against the wall. Music burst out through the speakers; Wolf must have hit the switch for the music system.

'What service do you want? Police, fire or ambulance?'

Ailsa realized she had dialled 999.

A voice interrupted her thoughts as to what emergency service this situation called for. 'Stop it!' ordered a voice from the doorway. 'Stop right now.'

18

The worst has happened and I haven't died. That is how I felt in the days after the video went viral. I realized that shame is a chronic condition not a terminal illness. It was Jay's betrayal that hurt the most. That was all jagged edges. As I lay in bed and watched images flash by of a life gone past I saw myself as the survivor of a catastrophic event. I swear I could even remember being born and the exact sensation of my knee being stitched after I fell off my first bicycle.

Apparently this happens to people who survive extreme situations like drowning or heart attacks. People think it's a spiritual experience but it's got nothing to do with God. It's your brain playing tricks. According to Dad, you can actually trigger a near-death experience in the lab by stimulating the place where the temporal and the parietal lobes meet.

I thought about a lot of things that week. I remembered a game that Luke and I played all the time when we were small back in our house in London. We would push my bed into the middle of the bedroom and pretend it was a desert island where we had been washed up after our ship had sunk. The floor was the ocean and we'd lean over the edge of the bed to identify sea creatures in the mysterious shapes and marks on the carpet below.

I reminded Luke of this when he came in to see me after school on the first day, pointing out the coffee-stain sharks circling at the bottom of the bed. I could see from the way he shrank back that after a lifetime of trying I had finally managed to freak him out. I giggled, but Luke didn't smile or do that thing where he punched me in the shoulder and called me Romeo because I used to look like a boy. When he left I cried because he couldn't see beyond the video to the person I used to be. It was as if my shame was a stain that had spread over the whole family. Even Ben, who knew nothing, wasn't immune. People no longer invited him over to play, and he told me that the mums in the playground stopped talking if he went too close.

I must have spent almost a week holed up in my room. It felt safe there. Downstairs everything was noise. The doorbell and phone rang all the time. Later I learned that this was because Stuart Tovey had posted my home phone number on a copy of the video circulating on a slut-shaming site. The house was full of people whose voices I didn't recognize. After a couple of days I realized this was because all Mum's calls were on speakerphone so Dad could listen in. That was how I knew that Mum had removed my computer from my room following a warning from Mrs Arnold that I might be a suicide risk because of the hate messages. I resolved not to kill myself just to spite Mrs Arnold. The deputy head pastoral had finally justified her existence. It was also how I learned that the video had spread as far as Vietnam. Dad kept comparing it to a virus, but no virus I had studied could spread that quickly.

I learned a lot of things that week and one of them was that the reason most families fall apart after traumatic events is that people can only deal with their own grief. They can't deal with anyone else's. As long as I was on my own I was fine. What I couldn't handle were other people's reactions. Even when they didn't say anything you could see it in their eyes: Mum and Dad's pain, Luke's reproach, Ben's bewildered kindness, Aunt Rachel's tears.

Although it turned out these were as much for herself because Ben told me during one of his visits where he chatted and I listened that Mr Harvey had unexpectedly broken up with her. He asked if I wanted to play Cluedo and looked downcast when I said no because it required too much analysis. So I suggested he get down my old game of Operation from the shelf. We played the best of three. During the last match he lay flat on my bed, chewing his lip, and successfully removed the final rib.

'What exactly have you done wrong, Romy?'

I stroked his hair and he closed his eyes in pleasure, like Lucifer. He clung on to the rib in his hot little fist. Poor Ben. Until the Miseries started last year his life had been completely carefree.

'I trusted someone I shouldn't have trusted.'

'I don't believe what people are saying about you.'

'What are they saying, Grub?'

He was silent for a while.

'Bad stuff.'

'How so?' I was curious.

'That you're a ho.'

'What's a ho?'

'I don't know. But I can tell it's bad from the way they say it.' He threw his arms around my neck and clung on to me like a monkey.

'It's all right, Ben,' I said, my voice muffled by the force of his hug. He started crying and didn't stop until I offered to play another game of Operation.

Marnie stayed away. I'm still hurt by that. Initially I assumed she hated me because of what had happened with Marley, but when Becca came to visit she let slip that Marnie's mum didn't want her associating with someone like me. Apparently I was a bad influence. The gulf between how other people saw me and how I saw myself made me feel dizzy with anxiety because it was too big to bridge.

Becca brought me a present. It was a poster of a self-portrait by an artist called Frida Kahlo. It showed the artist's body lacerated with hundreds of self-inflicted tiny knife cuts after her husband had betrayed her by shagging another woman. *Why didn't she leave him?* I wondered. If someone treated you like that they weren't worth the pain. It was a strange choice of gift but I appreciated the gesture.

Becca was full of righteous anger on my behalf. She spoke about female exploitation and how the Internet was the last safe haven for women-haters like Jay. *Jay doesn't hate women*, I wanted to explain. But she wouldn't have believed me. Besides, she had already moved on to the hypocrisy of Stella Fay calling me a slut when she was the one who had had sex with seven boys in the year above. The hypocrisy lay in referring to girls as sluts and boys as players, I wanted to say. Because this was where there was no equality. I was beginning to realize that my opinion counted for nothing because everyone had already scripted their own version of events.

This was really brought home when I turned on the radio one day and tuned into a heated debate about teenage girls and oral sex. Apparently there was a blow-job epidemic in Britain. There were accounts of schools where teachers took turns to patrol toilets during breaks, parties where girls competed to see who could blow the most boys. The female presenter made it sound deadlier than Ebola. They interviewed a doctor who explained the link between oral sex and cancer.

As I listened I realized that the programme had been inspired by what had happened to me. At least I think it was me, because although they couldn't be specific they kept mentioning an oral-sex sexting scandal at a British secondary school. *Too much alliteration*, I told myself to quell my rising sense of panic at the sheer scale of it all. I had caused all of this. It was terrifying, as if I suddenly possessed superhuman powers.

I started getting up really early so that I could have a shower before anyone else in the house was awake. After that I went back to sleep for a while until Mum came up with breakfast on a tray. She cooked food that I used to eat when I was a child. Things like fish fingers with a bread roll or baked beans on toast. At first I thought it was to make me feel secure. Then I realized it was to reassure her that I was still her little girl. I got it. She sat on the end of the bed and watched in silence as I forced myself to eat a quarter-slice of toast. Jam, no butter. I appreciated her restraint but her eyes were full of unanswered questions and I couldn't wait for her to leave. We were separated by our dread.

I avoided food partly so that I could restrict trips to the toilet in case I bumped into someone, but mostly because I knew from Marnie, who described herself as a high-functioning anorexic, that not eating was the simplest way of re-establishing some control amidst the chaos. Most of the day I lay on my side under my duvet with the curtains closed, drifting in and out of sleep. I didn't get dressed. I didn't read.

I spent a lot of time considering what Jay had done to me. I wondered if he now understood that causing me pain was no cure for his own. This was a good lesson to learn early in life. It occurred to me that my future relationships might be damaged by what had happened. I would get the wrong kind of attention from the wrong kind of boys, and the nice ones would avoid me. Maybe I would turn into a voyeur? Ironically Jay and I had more in common than ever before: now we were both dys-functional. My gift to him turned out to be the agent of my own destruction.

I wondered if he thought before pressing send or if it was an impulsive action that he immediately regretted. Who did he send the clip to first? Was it to a group of people or a single friend? I guessed it was Stuart Tovey because Jay knew he would do something twisted with it. According to Becca, Jay's irresistibility factor among some of the girls at school had tipped off the scale. How did he seem? I had asked her. Like a deer caught in the headlights, she replied thoughtfully. He didn't seem to be exploiting his new-found popularity. And he walked away from the boys who wanted to high-five him.

I made lists in my head of all the people at school who would definitely have watched the video. I realized that for the rest of my life, every time I met someone new, I would wonder if they knew about it. I decided that I could no longer be a doctor because there would always be a risk that a patient would find out. I told Mum this so that she didn't have to worry about delivering the bad news to me.

Perhaps I could do research. I could work in a lab where my face was covered with a mask. I would inves-tigate where traumatic memories were stored in the brain in the hope that I would find a way to eradicate my own.

Dad didn't come up for days. I thought maybe he saw the scandal as Mum's territory, like one of those rites of passage such as the start of my period or the chat about birth control. When he finally knocked on the door yesterday and came in carrying a plate of pasta, I realized that I had read him all wrong. Blinking away tears, he tried to find the words to tell me that he knew I had found the phone in his office with the messages between him and the other woman. To begin with I thought that he was about to tell me off, then I realized that he was looking for forgiveness. He opened and shut his mouth as he presented his evidence but he couldn't bring himself to say the words I had appropriated from her so I filled in the gaps and he started crying again.

'I'm so sorry, Romy.'

'It's Mum you betrayed. Not me.'

'Did you make the video to get back at me? For revenge?'

He stood by the window, tears streaming down his cheeks. Somehow his self-pity made it easier to deal with him. For a moment I thought about lying. But I took pity.

'Don't be ridiculous. Apart from the ending, I'd planned it before I read the messages. It had nothing to do with you.'

'Why did you do it, Romy? Why would you risk everything for this?'

'You did. You lost your job. We had to move house. You almost lost Mum. And your pre-frontal cortex is fully formed.'

I turned on my side and faced the wall. There was a whole chapter in his book that could answer his questions. Our conversation was over. Shortly after that Aunt Rachel unexpectedly turned up at the house. *This must be bad*, I thought to myself as I heard Rachel explain to Mum that she was here to support her through this crisis.

Ben told me later that Rachel had offered to go to school to help Mr Harvey with his research and cried when he had turned her down. I understood that was more about being close to him than helping me. I didn't mind. After all, I wanted nothing more than to feel Marley Fairport's arms around me again, telling me that everything would be just fine. He was the only person who could have made things right for me. I could never tell anyone that.

This morning Rachel came into my room without knocking. She sat cross-legged on the floor with her head cocked at an empathetic angle and explained that she wanted to talk. Off the record, she emphasized. Just between her and me. She promised that she understood better than anyone else what had happened. She sounded sincere but I couldn't help wondering if she was doing research for something she was writing. I was certain, however, that even with her powers of imagination she couldn't possibly understand what it had done to me to know that my first big sexual experience had been seen by most people I had ever met and millions more that I hadn't.

I pretended to be asleep. She didn't give up. She said that she knew I had taken to my bed in order to rebuild myself. She used terminology that sounded as if it had been taken from the Lego website. She started banging on about Paris Hilton, Kim Kardashian and music videos simulating oral sex and how they might make you think you could become famous by making a sex tape. I couldn't work out if she was stupid or trying to provoke me into some kind of reaction. I've got more brain cells in my bum than Kim Kardashian has in her head.

'Give me some credit,' I said, my back still facing her. 'Actually give most teenage girls credit. This was never intended for worldwide release.' Her history of failed relationships might have heightened her empathy but it diminished the credibility of her advice. It was like that moment when I heard Mum and Dad had discovered that their marriage guidance counsellor was twice divorced.

'What's that noise?' Rachel asked, turning towards my bedroom window. I heard the sound of raised voices. Someone was shouting. Rachel stood up and opened the curtains. At first I thought it was Mum and Dad rowing. I knew that what had happened to me would open up all the old wounds in their relationship. They would probably get divorced and it would all be my fault.

'Holy shit,' muttered Rachel.

Another voice I didn't recognize joined in. Then lots of people were shrieking and shouting all at once, like an opera. I got out of bed and went over to open the window. I couldn't resist glancing over to Jay's bedroom. His curtains were shut tight. The noise was coming from one of the rooms downstairs at the Fairports' house. There were a few more dull thuds followed by silence.

I headed out of the room before Rachel could talk me out of it. By the time I reached the back door of the Fairports' house the row had started again. No one noticed me open the front door or my staccato breathing as I stood at the half-open door into the sitting room. Wolf was yelling at someone.

'Slow down, cowboy, slow down, cowboy,' he kept saying, over and over again in a tone that was meant to be appeasing but ended up the wrong side of patronizing.

It took a moment for me to realize that Dad was the cowboy. But then Wolf was an Indian. Sacred Warrior Coming Down was his Lakota name. Absurd, but not as absurd as Dad being referred to as a cowboy. Dad couldn't even change a spare tyre. He was more cowgirl than cowboy. Actually in our family Mum had always been the cowboy. I thought about the messages on the phone in the briefcase in Dad's office and the way he spent hours peeling the skins off tomatoes to make pasta sauce and got competitive over card games, even Snap. I tried to fit all the different pieces of him together and found that I couldn't. Maybe all of us were enigmas even to ourselves.

I jumped as I heard more thuds followed by music.

I felt someone's breath on my bare shoulder, and when I turned Jay was standing beside me, as close as you could be without actually touching.

'They're talking about us,' he whispered.

'Everyone is talking about us. Everyone.'

I don't know why we were whispering because no one could hear us above the commotion in the sitting room. I was about to ask him why he had done it but I was aware of Mum's voice. She sounded surprisingly calm as she threatened to call the police. It was an empty threat. *The fight will be over long before the police get here*, I thought to myself.

Through the gap in the door I saw Dad give Wolf a half-hearted shove as if he had been miscast as the baddie in a pantomime. People wearing reading glasses don't push people, I remember thinking as Dad's glasses wobbled on the end of his nose. It was the kind of niggling one-handed older-brother type shove that Luke might give me. But Dad caught Wolf off balance, and because he was wearing socks that slipped on the wooden floor he skidded into the bookshelf, which took the full impact of his weight. One by one the tiny hand-painted glass eggs fell to the floor and smashed.

Wolf crab-walked towards Dad, crunching the broken glass. He lunged and half-heartedly tried to hit him, but missed. Dad gave Wolf a shove. He fell back against the music system and Bob Dylan started playing.

Loveday followed in Wolf's wake. I noticed she was wearing a long purple dress and her hair was loose. She was screaming but over the noise of the music I could only catch odd words – *performance, pleasuring, context*. She shuffled in her bandaged feet towards Mum, who I now realized was standing in the corner by the door. I pushed my way into the room just in time to see Loveday raise her hand in front of Mum's face.

'Which service do you want?' a voice kept asking from Mum's phone.

'Stop it! Stop right now!' I ordered, insinuating myself between Mum and Loveday. I had never felt more part of my family than at that moment.

The voices fell silent but the music played on. I realized that Jay had followed me into the room and was standing behind me, slightly to one side, using me to protect him from Dad. I had never seen Dad look so angry. Even the tips of his ears were alert with tension. He was still wearing his reading glasses, but they were all steamed up so I couldn't see his eyes. At least if he tried to land a punch it would miss its target.

'You little shit,' said Dad, heading in our direction. 'If I discover that you forced her to do this, I will kill you.'

I glanced at Jay. His fringe manically bobbed up and down as he had an attack of nervous blinking. Wolf came over and put a protective arm around his shoulders. Jay shook him off and moved behind me.

'Did you ask her to do this?' Mum asked Jay. Her voice was ice-cold with menace. Jay's gaze flicked from Dad to Mum. His blue eyes were wild with fear.

'N-no,' he stammered.

'Did you threaten to stop going out with her if she

didn't make this video for you? Because I've done some research and I know that's the usual modus operandi in these situations, isn't it?' Mum continued.

Your pain doesn't help, I wanted to tell them; it just makes everything worse.

'Ailsa. Please. We need to protect the children from our anger,' said Loveday in a deliberately smooth tone that sounded as though she had dipped her vocal cords in honey. It was completely the wrong approach with Mum.

'How can you talk about protecting Romy after what your son has done to her?' asked Mum so coldly that even I shivered. I had forgotten how anger made her even more articulate. 'This isn't the kind of situation that you can remedy by lighting a couple of scented candles and dousing yourself in lavender oil.'

'It's all right, son,' Wolf said several times over, more to steady himself than Jay.

'Except it's not, is it?' interrupted Mum. 'It's not all right at all. It's worse than not right. What your sick son has done is illegal and he needs to face up to the full consequences of his actions.'

'You seem to be forgetting that your slut of a daughter created this problem by getting between my sons,' Loveday sneered.

'Stop, Mum,' said Jay. His voice was a husky whisper. 'Romy was trying to help me.'

'How does getting with your brother help?' Loveday spat out the words.

'I have some problems,' said Jay, clearing his throat. 'Big problems.'

'Don't say anything, Jay,' Loveday warned him.

That was when I realized that Loveday already knew. In my head everything went silent. Loveday and I shared a common idea: we both thought I could cure Jay. Our shared sense of purpose and her faith in me counted for nothing as I grappled with the fact that Loveday had permitted this to happen. She had used me to try and save her son from himself. I caught her eye. There was fear, desperation and anger all wrapped up in a single look, the Horsemen of the Apocalypse when it came to parents behaving irrationally. I realized that there was no love stronger than a parent's love for their child and that every adult in the room was united by similar emotions. Fear for their children, for themselves, for their unborn grandchildren. There was nothing they wouldn't do to protect their offspring. We are all animals.

'Romy made the video to help me,' said Jay, clearing his throat over and over again. 'It was a selfless act.'

'It was completely my idea,' I said. 'Jay didn't ask me to do it.'

My parents and Wolf and Loveday closed around us in an arc like a lymphocyte about to gobble up bacteria. Jay moved closer to me until our shoulders were touching. He did all the talking. Once he had found the right words he couldn't stop.

When he told them he thought he was addicted to Internet porn, Loveday used the hem of her purple dress to wipe her eyes and didn't stop crying until we left the house. Wolf stroked his beard and shook his head in disbelief. 'Sex is about freedom, not being a prisoner,' he said. 'Men need to preserve their yang energy. Have you learned nothing from your mother and I?'

I waited for Mum to correct his grammar but she didn't. Wolf took Jay's problems personally. I wished they could all stop relating everything back to themselves and consider the crisis in isolation.

Jay explained how I had come up with the idea to make the video after researching addiction. He described how I had wanted to create new neural pathways in the pleasure-seeking region of the brain. Dad stared at the floor, recognizing the truth of what I was saying. At one point I think we were all crying.

'She thought that I could replace the porn by watching the video of her and me instead.'

'How could you be so reckless, Romy?' Dad asked. I didn't point out the hypocrisy of this comment.

'I took a scientific approach.'

'We don't know exactly how pornography acts on the different neurotransmitter systems in the brain, Romy. It's a pretty new pathology. But even with drug addiction it's not that simple. Heroin acts on the opiate system, nicotine on the cholinergic system and cocaine on the noradrenergic and dopaminergic system. But I can tell you now, your plan wouldn't have worked. If you overstimulate dopamine release there is a homeostatic response. The dopamine reward system is down-regulated and you develop drug tolerance. This is probably what has happened to Jay. He would never have stuck with the one porn clip.'

'It was meant to be something beautiful,' I said.

Jay didn't look up. He looked as though he might die from shame. I almost felt sorry for him.

'What I don't understand,' said Mum, speaking to Jay for the first time, 'or at least the part I understand least, is why you sent the video to your friends after everything Romy had done to try and help you. She laid herself on the line for you.'

'It wasn't me,' said Jay simply.

'The video was sent from your phone. Mr Harvey has the proof,' said Mum.

'It might have been sent from my phone but not by me. I would never want to hurt Romy. I love her. She's the only person who has ever understood me or tried to help me. I lost my phone at the party. I found it on the floor in the sweat lodge the next day. Someone else must have sent it.'

'Who would have done that?' Mum asked. Her mistrust was obvious.

'I don't know,' said Jay hopelessly.

Marley came into the room. He glanced from Jay to his parents and tried to work out what was going on. He didn't look at me once. It was unbearable.

'There's something going on in the sweat lodge,' he said.

'What do you mean?' asked Wolf.

'It's all lit up.'

It wasn't a sixth sense, as some people said afterwards. It was a simple process of deduction.

'Ben!' I said. 'It was Ben.'

I knew I was right as soon as I saw the sweat lodge shimmering and glowing on the edge of the wood. It loomed larger than ever, unnaturally swollen, like the sun setting at the end of a long hot summer's day. Except it looked like the beginning of something rather than the end. It had never been more beautiful or enticing. We all left the house and ran towards it as if pulled by an invisible force.

'What's going on?' Loveday shouted across to Wolf, as she slammed the back door behind her. I could hear the panic in her voice.

'I don't know,' panted Wolf.

We must have looked like a ragtag army as we hurtled across the garden. The buttons on Dad's shirt had come off during his tussle with Wolf and now it billowed open to reveal his chest hair and the beginnings of a belly peering over the edge of his jeans. It still astonished me that any woman could find him attractive. But as I knew very well by now, the pre-frontal cortex doesn't engage at the start of a relationship. The thinking part comes later. At the beginning it's all about the reward, and desire doesn't make people discerning. It just makes them want to have sex.

Dad sprinted ahead, chin jutting out, arms pumping. Jay was at his shoulder, threatening but never quite managing to overtake, as though he was trying to beat him in a race. Wolf lost a bit of ground, disadvantaged by the fact he was barefoot and had to hold up his sarong with one hand, while Loveday's long purple dress restricted her movements even more, and she soon lagged way behind. Mum was beside me, utterly intent on the dome emerging from the wood. The closer we got the brighter it glowed. She didn't look over at me once, which was a relief after the unrelenting focus of the past week, because one of the worst things about this whole awful disaster was the way I had become the centre of all her concern.

We ran silently in formation for what seemed like ages. At this point I wasn't scared. I was just relieved to have escaped the interrogation in the sitting room and to be outside for the first time in a week. It felt so good to stretch my legs. As the lawn gave way to undergrowth, the terrain got more difficult. There were stinging nettles and hard crusts of mud underfoot, but Wolf didn't seem to notice and quickly caught up with us. *Interesting how adrenaline blocks pain*, I thought, realizing for the first time how terrified he was. I assumed he was worrying about the threat to their livelihood if something happened to the sweat lodge. They were already losing money because of the delay caused by Mum's complaint to the council. I wanted to tell him that Ben would never harm his stupid building and would never do anything to hurt anyone, but I was so out of breath from the running and dizzy from hardly having eaten for almost a week that I could hardly speak.

As we got closer, the sweat lodge became more and

more luminous. It occurred to me that maybe Ben had turned on the disco lights that we had used for Marley's party. I think it was at this point that Mum started screaming Ben's name over and over again: 'Ben, Ben, Ben . . .' Her voice cut through the still night air. I am still haunted by that sound. I remembered how the previous term in Biology Club Mr Harvey had run through examples of mother love in the animal kingdom: the distress of a whale at SeaWorld when her baby was taken away (even Stuart Tovey cried at that), the octopuses who starve rather than leave their babies unattended, ewes who run at dogs who get too close to their lambs. Mum understood that her youngest child was in danger long before the rest of us had grasped the situation.

19

By the time Ailsa and Romy reached the sweat lodge Harry was already on his hands and knees, pulling at the neat cross-stitch of ropes that held the door shut. He called Ben's name and shouted the same instructions over and over again: 'Wrap your top around your face. Try to crawl towards my voice. Take shallow breaths.' Ailsa waited for Ben's response but there was none.

Harry's face glistened with sweat. Every couple of seconds he stepped back for a moment and wiped his forehead. As Ailsa got closer she understood why. Heat radiated from the building. She touched its shiny surface with the palm of her hand and quickly withdrew it. It wasn't so much the heat, although that came as a shock, it was the realization of what was at stake.

'He must have lit the fire,' Harry explained breathlessly, echoing her thoughts. His face was distorted with tension. He began tugging at the rope again and continued shouting to Ben. Ailsa noticed his hands were trembling. 'I can't open the damned door. It's fastened tight from the inside.'

'He knows knots,' Ailsa said. Their exchange was economical; the priority was to free Ben as quickly as possible. Ailsa's eyes darted back and forth across the building, searching for another way in. At work she was valued for her ability to respond practically and decisively to any emergency. At least that was what the head of the board of governors had said to her this morning when he phoned to say that she had their full backing and could return to work immediately. But right now she couldn't chase any thought to its logical end.

She wished she had listened more attentively to Wolf's long-winded description of how he had constructed the sweat lodge. All she could recall was how it embodied the womb of Mother Earth and that at its peak the ambient temperature reached 39 degrees Celsius. Would a nine-year-old be able to survive such heat? She tried to calculate how long Ben might have been inside. Could she be certain that he was at home when they left for the Fairports? He might have slipped out of the house earlier. They had been in Harry's office in the basement for most of the afternoon. How long were they arguing in the Fairports' sitting room? It seemed like hours but it might have been minutes.

The sun had almost dropped out of sight. The arc of trees surrounding the sweat lodge cast long shadows and she squinted to try and adjust to the dusky light. Ailsa noted the multiple layers of plastic-coated canvas stretched across the surface. She searched for a seam where they overlapped, using her hands to feel her way. But when she finally found a join and tucked her fingers beneath the edge to lift the canvas, she knew instantly that it was too heavy and slippery to get any purchase. She imagined peeling back this layer and uncovering another one beneath and another beneath that. Like an artichoke.

Romy pulled at her shoulder. Ailsa didn't look at her in case she detected reproach in her face. If Ben didn't make it, she would have to look Romy in the eye and convince her that this wasn't her fault. She couldn't explain that everything had happened because of her. For a split second Ailsa wished it was Romy, not Ben, stuck in the sweat lodge. They could tell people that the wretched boy in the house next door had driven her to it. She closed her eyes and breathed in deeply, but instead of the usual earthy scent there was the acrid taste of burned plastic. What was she thinking? She loved Romy. She was a good daughter. After all that had happened that week, her mind was as treacherous as white water.

Poor Romy. It wasn't fair to condemn her for the gulf that had opened up between their aspirations and her fall from grace. She had been the repository of so many of their hopes. They had always expected more of her than they did of Luke and Ben.

'Mum, we need to find something sharp to cut the plastic,' Romy said.

Ailsa turned to Romy and saw she was savagely massaging her temples in the way that she did when she was stuck on Further Maths homework. Luke called it her hyperbolic function look. They nodded at each other and dropped to their hands and knees. Romy used her nails to comb through the grass and mud. She found a beer bottle left over from the party and smashed it on a flint. Ailsa pointed at the seam where she had tried to peel back the canvas and Romy used a piece of the glass to attempt to cut the plastic. It skidded and skated across the surface. She renewed her efforts. When she couldn't even inflict a superficial graze, she resorted to stabbing at the canvas.

'It's triple-layer woven PVC,' shouted Wolf, who had just reached them. 'Tougher than glass. Impossible to cut.'

He dropped down on his haunches beside Harry. The sarong was now knotted around him like a loincloth. Ailsa waited for him to take charge and redirect the rescue effort because as the architect of this building he would surely know exactly how to get inside. He would take responsibility. She was momentarily revived by the possibility of a resolution. There was a point in any drama with children where you dared to think everything was going to be all right. Where you could almost imagine looking back and laughing at your ridiculous panic. Surely this was it. Wolf was a practical man and would have a plan. Ailsa gave him a hopeful smile but Wolf offered nothing and instead fell in with Harry, tugging at the rope. He was devoid of ideas.

She tried not to panic when their combined efforts brought no reward. The door was fastened as tight as a corset. The idea that Ben was so close but so out of reach became unbearable. She called out his name again and hammered on the lodge with her fist but it only made a muffled thud like a heart beating. Ailsa didn't recognize her own voice. It struck her that the last time she had made a sound like this was when she had given birth to Ben. She finally surrendered to the overwhelming feeling of dread.

Did she make all this happen? Ailsa wondered as she

banged on the sweat lodge. Everything seemed connected, each new drama a reaction to something that had happened before. She hated the idea of destiny because if it existed Ben's death would undoubtedly be her punishment for the trail of events that she could trace back to the night before her wedding.

She wanted to tell Harry everything but now there was no time. She remembered the first time they had sex and woke up together the next morning entwined in his tent. She had described it as a *coup de foudre*. He had responded by describing how every decision, movement and emotion required the combined firepower of millions of neurotransmitters across entire areas of the brain. Everything acted in tandem. 'You have sex with your brain not your heart,' Harry said. 'It's matter over mind.' She had laughed. She had never met anyone who thought like Harry.

At that time he was a junior member of an international team doing research into how the brain makes decisions up to seven seconds before people make a conscious choice. Harry could predict what choice a volunteer would make before they were even aware they were making one. 'The idea that we have control over our lives is an illusion,' Harry said. 'Most decisions are made in our subconscious.' He described consciousness as a biochemical afterthought. 'Are you saying there is no such thing as free will?' she had asked. 'The concept that we have control over our life is an illusion,' Harry had replied.

She thought of the moment when Matt had slid his arm around her back to test whether she had the capacity to be as reckless as him and she responded by pressing herself against him. Perhaps her brain had decided to do that before she was even conscious of the impulse. Matt's discovery about Luke didn't constitute a real excuse for her betrayal. She found salvation in this concept. Not because it negated her responsibility but because it suggested that nothing was inevitable. There was no chain of events. If Ben died, it wouldn't be because Harry wasn't Luke's father.

She focused her efforts on rescuing Ben, turning her attention to the metal-framed eyelets through which the rope was threaded. Their edges were new and shiny and perhaps the friction caused by pulling the rope back and forth might cause it to fray. She bent down to examine the eyelets more closely and saw tiny funnels of smoke wafting through.

'I blocked off the chimney for Marley's party,' explained Wolf quickly when he saw that she had noticed. 'There's nowhere for the smoke to go. The heat isn't dangerous. It's the fumes.'

'Why didn't you say that before?' asked Ailsa.

'Carbon monoxide?' said Harry. Wolf nodded. Ailsa didn't want them to agree. She wanted them to argue over who had the best idea and come up with a radical plan. She took off her belt and used the buckle to try and prise apart the thick threads of the rope. Beside her,

Romy cupped her hands against her mouth and pressed them against the sweat lodge.

'Lie flat on the floor, Grub,' she ordered. Romy explained how carbon monoxide was lighter than oxygen. If he could hear her, Ben would do this for Romy. Ben would do anything for her.

Ailsa turned to the roof of the sweat lodge. She was surprised by its height. On top of the chimney she could see what looked like an upside-down metal bucket covering the flue. She stepped back a few paces and stumbled into Luke.

'What's going on?' Luke was puffy-eyed as if he had just woken up, oblivious to what had taken place. 'I can't find anyone at home.'

'Ben's stuck inside. He's fastened the door and lit the fire. The chimney is blocked.'

Ailsa pressed her hands down into his shoulders, uncertain whether she was trying to underline the sense of urgency or use him as ballast. Her fists were tight balls of tension and fear. Luke, taller than her, leaned down towards his mother and their foreheads touched momentarily.

'Don't worry, Mum,' Luke said. 'I promise I'll get him out.'

He called for Harry to boost him up onto the roof, a manoeuvre he managed in a single fluid movement. Once Luke had got his balance he tried to crawl up towards the chimney, but the combination of the sagging, slippery canvas and the steep angle meant that each time he slid back down. He stretched out his arms and legs to spread his weight and called down for someone to pass him a long stick. A branch was found. It was thick and heavy and took two people to lift it up to him, but once Luke laid it flat on the roof at least it reached the chimney pot.

He jousted at the chimney and managed to hit it several times but without dislodging the cover.

At some point soon after this Jay appeared with a bread knife. Ailsa hadn't been aware of his presence before and didn't know if this was his own initiative or whether someone had ordered him to fetch it. Harry snatched the knife from his hand and began sawing through sections of the rope. Each time he severed a new section, Wolf released it from the eyelets. Jay tried to help. They ordered him away. He wandered over to where Ailsa was shouting instructions to Luke, who couldn't see the chimney pot and was dependent on her to align the stick with his target.

Jay was at her side, waiting for her to give him instructions. Ailsa took in his wide shoulders and narrow torso. He was a man-child. She remembered how those shoulders had hung like two broken wings when he confessed the extent of his problem in front of them all. Four years. Six hours a day at its peak. Always searching. Never satisfied. At times his voice was almost inaudible, his embarrassment a stain that tainted them all. His remorse and shame were real. She had almost begun to feel sorry for him. Not wanting to let go of her anger quite yet she had focused on his flaky parents. How could Wolf and Loveday not have noticed? But hadn't she missed what was going on under her own nose? Her guilt was exhausting and without resolution.

Ailsa remembered herself at the same age, practically living with Billy, taking drugs, failing her exams. Her parents were too wrapped up in their own problems to notice what she and Rachel were up to. And it was a relief to be ignored. Back then you could mess up in private and move on. Memory has its purpose. But so does forgetting.

'One more try, Luke,' she shouted. He called down that he thought he had wedged the pointed end of the stick in between the chimney pot and the bucket and was going to try to lever it off.

'No, Luke! Don't!' Romy yelled. She had just noticed what Luke was trying to do. It was basic chemistry, but Luke had failed his GCSE and forgotten the effect of oxygen on a fire.

'Let him,' shouted Harry, who knew all about combustion experiments.

'Don't listen to Dad,' shouted Ailsa.

Harry turned to Ailsa. 'I love him like my own son, Ailsa,' he said, anticipating her thought before it had even fully formed.

Luke shoved the stick as hard as he could and the cover flipped off. The reaction was dramatic and immediate. Ailsa's recall of the exact sequence of events was hazy. There was an explosion and the hiss and lick of flames hitting the roof of the sweat lodge to consume the plastic sheeting. Luke disappeared through the gaping hole that appeared as if he had been gobbled up by the lodge. Ailsa felt as though she were sacrificing her children to assuage an angry Aztec god.

'I'm in,' shouted Harry, rolling up the canvas door until it was wide enough for Romy to crawl inside. Ailsa followed.

Inside it was dark in spite of the hole where the roof had been. Ailsa looked up and saw branches swaying in the gentle evening breeze. After its initial burst of furious anger the fire had lost its energy like a toddler after a tantrum. The stones glowed red but were no longer threatening. Ailsa picked her way across the floor. It was covered with debris: burned plastic, wooden joists from the roof, and smouldering sheepskin rugs that smelled of barbecued meat.

Romy had already reached Ben and was cradling him in her arms, picking out flakes of ash and burned plastic from his hair and his burning-red cheeks. His eyes flickered and he coughed and spluttered. Luke was lying on his side close to them. His breathing was shallow.

'What the fuck,' groaned Luke. He rolled slowly onto his back and sat up. His left arm flopped by his side like a broken wing. It took him a few seconds to realize that he couldn't move it. His shirt was torn and Ailsa could see a reddish bruise spreading over his shoulder. His clavicle stuck out at an awkward angle. Ailsa winced.

'You've broken your collarbone,' she said. 'Try to keep still.'

'How do you know?' Luke asked, his voice weak.

'Granny did the same once.'

'I did something bad. I needed to be reborn,' said Ben. He coughed again.

'Don't try to speak, Grub,' said Romy.

'Am I reborn good, Romy?' he asked more insistently.

'You nearly died so you must be reborn,' said Romy.

'It's all my fault,' whispered Ben. 'I didn't realize. I'm sorry. I wanted to make Sweat Lodge II.'

We all have darkness and light within us and are in control of neither, thought Ailsa as she gathered her children to her. She remembered the evening her mother tried to get her father to stop drinking by pouring every bottle of alcohol down the sink, even the cooking wine, and their tussle over a bottle of whisky that Adam refused to relinquish. Ailsa and Rachel had come into the room just as their father shoved Georgia to the kitchen floor. Ailsa could recall the exact noise of her mother's collarbone breaking as it hit the hard stone floor and the smell of the pool of whisky where she lay. She remembered the expression of horrified awe on Rachel's face when the ambulance man asked Ailsa what had happened and she explained that their mother had slipped over. He didn't believe her but she was adamant. It was the last time Adam drank until Georgia died. When Rachel asked Ailsa later that night why she had lied, she explained that she was protecting their future, without really understanding what exactly it was that she wanted to protect. Now finally she understood.

20

Mum has given me the last word. I appreciate that. I think after six months she's beginning to trust my judgement again. And she gets that after so much has been said about me it's important I find my own voice. To define myself in relation to what has happened, if you like. Because how other people see me has an impact on how I see myself. I am not the person that I was before all this happened. As the therapist has pointed out, I have to 'reconstruct and reinforce the foundations of self to deflect the glare of other people's judgement'. She likes analogies from the construction industry.

I told her that I think therapy reinforces the ego and that perhaps what everyone needs to do is see the world from other people's perspective a bit more. Get away from the L'Oreal 'because I'm worth it' point of view. She said my opinion was refreshing. But I knew she didn't agree. After all she was being paid to promote the ego. Mine specifically. And she had a Twitter account. I explained to her how self-disclosure activates the meso-limbic dopamine pathway in the brain, the same part that gets hijacked by addiction, but she just nodded and gave one of her Sphinx-like smiles.

I know lots of people were worried that I was a

suicide risk. Do you ever consider harming yourself? the therapist asked one month into my treatment. Are you asking if I have visions of suicidal ideation? I responded. She looked a little taken aback. Absolutely not, I lied. Truth be told, I did consider that option as the simplest way out of the mess that I had created, but I wasn't about to share this with her because she would turn it over in such relentless detail that she actually might provoke me to slit my wrists. She was like a dog with a bone if you threw her something like that. She had an overwhelming urge to make connections where there were none. That's the problem with the instinctive approach.

She was obsessed with the way I had appropriated the words from one of the messages sent by Dad's girlfriend to him, for example. If you mention Oedipus I will leave the room and never come back, I warned her. I might have some kooky sexual fantasies now and again but none of them involve my dad. I explained that it was my way of getting back at him. The only person I possibly wanted to have sex with back then was Jay. Then Marley. Especially Marley. Still Marley.

She brought up the subject of Dad's infidelity every couple of weeks. I tried to tell her that the thing with Jay had already started when I found out about Dad and the other woman. But this was an inconvenient truth that didn't fit with the narrative in her head. She didn't accuse me of confabulation but I knew that was what she was thinking. I acknowledged that sex and food are natural rewards for human beings and Dad had his needs. I regretted he hadn't been able to resist the itch, because it caused so much pain to Mum and was humiliating for them both. Moreover I thought that the text exchanges between Dad and that woman were pathological. No one wants to think about the mechanics of their parents having sex with each other, let alone other people, I said, adding that I hoped we could move on from this. Mum told me that she knew about the texts but not that Dad had kept them.

'Why would he do that?' I asked. 'Why would he give up his job, move house and leave London as a sign of his commitment to you but keep the messages?'

'Sometimes people find it difficult to let go of the past,' she said carefully. 'Relationships are complicated.'

The only lie I consciously told the therapist was about the self-harm issue. I admit I did find some online discussion groups on how to commit suicide but they were full of people who were way unhappier than me, including a lot of goths, and their empirical evidence was questionable. I mean, you can't ask someone who has killed themselves if their methodology is the best, can you? My heart wasn't in it. I couldn't do it to my family. Call it ego, but I just didn't feel they would be better off without me. I knew that as long as I was around, Mum and Dad couldn't split up. They had to stay together to mend me.

It was Ben who really put a brake on my plan. I absolutely couldn't abandon him. Ben blamed himself for what had happened more than anyone else. He had gone to the sweat lodge the morning after the party and cried when he saw the floor he had helped to build so scratched and stained. He had found Jay's phone on top of the secret Coca-Cola stash in the lining of the sweat lodge, where Jay had hidden it when he was dancing. The phone wasn't even locked. Ben watched the beginning of the video, and when he recognized the sweat lodge he uploaded it onto Wolf and Loveday's website because he thought it was a good way of promoting their healing retreats. There was a strange logic to his thinking. The rest is history, except of course there is no such thing as history on the Internet.

Mum wanted Ben to see the therapist. Dad and I talked her out of it. Ben hadn't even watched it to the end. What everyone needed to do was move on.

The week after the sweat lodge burned down Ben took all his electronic games and Mum's old iPod Touch into the garden and smashed them with a hammer. 'James Bond never leaves any trace of himself,' he told me afterwards. He had gone back to his world of espionage, which we all saw as a positive sign. Ben might truly be one of the few children in the world to grow up without a digital footprint.

Things between Luke and me are still a little awkward. I understand. He got a lot of shit from his friends, and that was stressful to deal with. He's left home now and gone to university to do English and Film Studies. When he comes home he no longer calls me Romeo and doesn't want to wrestle any more. Last time he came back he brought home a girlfriend, and I could tell from the way she looked at me that she knew. I had to accept that this would always define me.

Sometimes I think what has really been lost is my closeness with Luke. The distance seems unbridgeable.

Every generation thinks it is the first one to have sex. This is what Wolf said to break the silence that followed Jay's account of what had happened, the day the sweat lodge burned down. Sex began in 1963 and all that, Mum chipped in. Philip Larkin, she added when Wolf and Loveday looked baffled. She was always good at finding a quote to illustrate a point. Wolf tried to sum up his position. Their son, he said, putting one hand in Loveday's and the other on Jay's shoulder, was engaged in a classic rebellion against his parents' view of the world. Jay shook his head and said he had a problem that was way bigger than any of them and that he needed help. After all, his father had addiction issues too. He acknowledged that I had helped him reach this conclusion. No one was grateful for my input. Least of all Mum and Dad.

The week following the scandal Mum and Dad were grief-stricken. They talked about loss so much that at one point I wondered if I had died. But in Wolf and Loveday's sitting room that day I felt their anger for the first time. *Reckless. Naïve. Arrogant. Stupid.* These were some of the adjectives aimed at me specifically. I realized that it had been easier for them to see me as a victim

466

with Jay playing the role of aggressor than it was to see me as the protagonist of my downfall. I pointed out this contradiction to them.

I said that despite the chapter in Dad's book arguing that there is little gender difference when it comes to desire, they still bought into the idea that female sexuality was something that needed to be constrained. 'You didn't look like a woman celebrating her own sexuality,' said Mum when I tried to explain this. She said that our sexuality had been subverted by Internet porn and that far from liberating women it had subjugated female desire and made men focus only on their own pleasure. It had actually pushed men and women apart. For the first time she conceded that Wolf and Loveday's sex therapy might have a point. Dad said that it was an unprecedented social experiment on a massive scale and that he had some ideas for a couple of research projects.

I agreed with all this. I argued that women were given the impression that we were sexually empowered and presented with a world of unlimited sexual boundaries, but if we crossed them we got slated. I pointed out how even in novels women were punished for sexual subversion: Hester Prynne, Anna Karenina, Madame Bovary.

They both agreed with me. Finally we had reached consensus. But, as Mum said, understanding the complexity of the situation gave no clues to its resolution.

I took the decision to go back to school the week after the fire. Although the fact that Jay hadn't betrayed me made things more difficult for my parents, it definitely made things better for me and helped to rouse me from my slump.

I had to face the world again. Mum was against the idea. I think she wanted me to stay cocooned at home for ever to protect me. I reminded her of her own belief in the inviolability of routine and structure, and she gave a hollow laugh. After everything that had happened she didn't really trust her own laughter.

The school took a hard line on the online bullying, especially the slut-shaming element. In Mum's temporary absence Mrs Arnold had done me a big favour by declaring that anyone caught with the video on their phone or posting comments online would face immediate suspension. I stopped using all social media so I couldn't see what was being said. Becca joked that I was becoming Amish.

Jay and I took the decision to go into school together and to hang out with each other to present a united front. Mum couldn't understand this. Her urge was still to blame him for what had happened. She accused him of deviancy. I pointed out that the adults who were so quick to judge the situation needed to take some responsibility for wilfully ignoring the fact that a generation of sexually inexperienced teenagers was using the Internet as their main source of sex education, only for the adults to berate them when it all went wrong. It was difficult for Mum. No one wants their child to be the one who forces change because of a bad experience. It involves too much suffering. Parents are essentially conservative.

Dad still tries to argue that our brain defines who we are. But now I know Dad is only partly right. What really defines who I am is my digital profile. Because it won't surprise you to know the video didn't go away. It popped up over and over again like Whack-a-Mole. Every time it was taken down from one website it appeared on another. Mr Harvey made it his personal mission to keep it at bay and helped me with my application to medical school, even though by then he was no longer at Highfield.

When people ask me what I have learned from my experience I tell them that it is a lie that the truth sets you free. What really sets you free is other people not knowing your shit. No one tells you the value of privacy, because everyone is interested in knowing your business. Our data is a valuable commodity. But everyone needs a place to retreat to when the going gets rough.

I fired the therapist this week. She wanted to talk about early-attachment issues with my mother and whether the fact that she hadn't breastfed me might have triggered an oral fixation. I know that everyone has to earn a living and she was trying to do her job, but I was getting fed up with the way she kept trying to blame my parents for what had happened.

I told her that my genetic inheritance and early

environment undoubtedly had an effect on my brain development and contributed to my decision-making process on the day I decided to make the film for Jay. But that was the extent to which Mum and Dad were involved.

I said that Mum said the least but understood the most. The therapist looked interested, so I explained how Mum compared relationships to the reactivity series and said that some combinations were simply more destructive than others and I would learn when to look away.

I explained to the therapist about research that Dad had done showing how several seconds before we consciously make a decision in the brain the outcome can be predicted from its unconscious activity. And how my decision was down to the cumulative build-up of firing neurons which tipped the balance towards my fatally flawed choice.

It seemed to me that taking responsibility for what had happened was the only way I could move forward. Because one thing we all agreed on was the possibility of renewal.

Acknowledgements

I am very grateful to my editor Maxine Hitchcock for her impeccable editorial advice, and to the rest of the team at Penguin for their encouragement and ideas, especially Sarah Arratoon, Francesca Russell and Lydia Good. I would like to say a big thank you to Jonny Geller for his wise counsel and excellent observations and also to Kirsten Foster at Curtis Brown.

A number of people helped with research. I am very grateful to Professor Sarah-Jayne Blakemore at the Institute of Cognitive Neuroscience, University College London, Dr Bettina Hohnen, John Woods at London's Portman Clinic, Kelly Alleyne at CEOP, and the head teachers who gave up their time to speak to me.

Thanks to Helen Bairamian, Phil Robertson, Helen Townshend and Henry Tricks for reading the first draft and for being there at the difficult moments. Big debt of gratitude to Rachel and Eve Anthony, Alfie Hardman and Michelle Glover for all their comments.

To gain insight into the world of neuroscience I read the following excellent books: *We Are Our Brains: From the Womb to Alzheimer's* by Dick Swaab, *The Brain That*

Changes Itself by Norman Doidge and *Neuroscience: Exploring the Brain* by Mark F. Bear and Barry W. Connors.

As always, thanks to Ed and our children for simultaneously enduring and encouraging.

Points for Discussion

The Good Girl examines the urge to protect. How can we protect those we love? How much *should* we protect them?

Do you think that Ailsa is right to worry so much about her children, or could she trust them more? For all her multiple concerns is Ailsa essentially selfish?

When the identity of the girl in the video was revealed who did you feel most sympathy for, Romy or Ailsa?

If you could describe the central concern of *The Good Girl* with one word would it be *decisions* or *consequences*? Can you suggest another?

What were your first thoughts when you learned about Romy and Jay's video? Did you think there were particular victims, or certain characters to blame?

Is technology seen as a threat? Is Fiona Neill's aim to serve us a warning?

What does *The Good Girl* say about privacy? Does Fiona Neill suggest privacy has different rules and is understood differently at different ages? What is the difference between privacy for a family or a community?

Did you notice any similarities between Ailsa and Loveday?

How did you interpret Harry and Ailsa's relationship? Were they right to stay together? Can you ever truly forgive and forget? How much did her own parents' marriage impact on Ailsa's decision?

Do you think honesty is always the best policy or, for example, would it have damaged the family even more had Luke known that Harry was not his real father?

Is the power of attraction seen as unavoidably acted upon within the novel? Is sexual attraction portrayed differently for men and women?

Do you think that Ailsa would have forgiven Harry for his affair had it not been for her own discretion the night before their wedding?

What is the role of Ben in the story? Is his story a separate and self-contained one?

Were you surprised at Jay's confession? What did you think his secret might have been? What is the function of neuro-science in the book?

Is *The Good Girl* essentially about vengeance? Discuss through the actions of major and minor characters.